LISA JEWELL

WATCHING YOU

CENTURY

1 3 5 7 9 10 8 6 4 2

Century
20 Vauxhall Bridge Road
London SW1V 2SA

Century is part of the Penguin Random House group of companies
whose addresses can be found at global.penguinrandomhouse.com.

Penguin
Random House
UK

Copyright © Lisa Jewell 2018

Lisa Jewell has asserted her right to be identified as the author of this
Work in accordance with the Copyright, Designs and Patents Act 1988.

First published in Great Britain by Century in 2018

www.penguin.co.uk

A CIP catalogue record for this book is available from the British Library.

ISBN 9781780896434 (Hardback)
ISBN 9781780896441 (Trade Paperback)

Typeset in 12/16.5 pt Palatino LT Std by Jouve (UK), Milton Keynes
Printed and bound in Great Britain by Clays Ltd, St Ives PLC

Penguin Random House is committed to a sustainable future
for our business, our readers and our planet. This book is made
from Forest Stewardship Council® certified paper.

MIX
Paper from
responsible sources
FSC
www.fsc.org
FSC® C018179

To Selina and Jonny.
With love.

My Diary

20 September 1996

I don't know what to think. I don't know what to feel.
Is this normal? He's an adult. He's twice my age.
There's no way . . . No. There's no way. But OH GOD.

<u>I wish there was</u>.

Dear diary:

I think I'm in love with my English teacher.

Prologue

24 March

DC Rose Pelham kneels down; she can see something behind the kitchen door, just in front of the bin. For a minute she thinks it's a bloodstained twist of tissue, maybe, or an old bandage. Then she thinks perhaps it is a dead flower. But as she looks at it more closely she can see that it's a tassel. A red suede tassel. The sort that might once have been attached to a handbag, or to a boot.

It sits just on top of a small puddle of blood, strongly suggesting that it had fallen there in the aftermath of the murder. She photographs it in situ from many angles and then, with her gloved fingers, she plucks the tassel from the floor and drops it into an evidence bag which she seals.

She stands up and turns to survey the scene of the crime: a scruffy kitchen, old-fashioned pine units, a green Aga piled with pots and pans, a large wooden table piled with table mats and exercise books and newspapers and folded washing, a small extension to the rear with a cheap timber glazed roof, double doors to the garden, a study area with a laptop, a printer, a shredder, a table lamp.

It's an innocuous room; bland even. A kitchen like a million other kitchens all across the country. A kitchen for drinking coffee in, for doing homework and eating breakfast and reading newspapers in. Not a kitchen for dark secrets or crimes of passion. Not a kitchen for murdering someone in.

But there, on the floor, is a body, splayed face down inside a large, vaguely kidney-shaped pool of blood. The knife that had been used is in the kitchen sink, thoroughly washed down with a soapy sponge. The attack on the victim had been frenzied: at least twenty knife wounds to the neck, back and shoulders. But little in the way of blood has spread to other areas of the kitchen – no handprints, no smears, no spatters – leading Rose to the conclusion that the attack had been unexpected, fast and efficient and that the victim had had little chance to put up a fight.

Rose takes a marker pen from her jacket pocket and writes on the bag containing the red suede tassel.

Description: 'Red suede/suedette tassel.'

Location: 'In front of fridge, just inside door from hallway.'

Date and time of collection: 'Friday 24 March 2017, 11.48 p.m.'

It's probably nothing, she muses, just a thing fallen from a fancy handbag. But nothing was often everything in forensics.

Nothing could often be the answer to the whole bloody thing.

I

1

2 January

Joey Mullen laid the flowers against the gravestone and ran her fingertip across the words engraved into the pink-veined granite.

SARAH JANE MULLEN
1962–2016
BELOVED MOTHER OF JACK AND JOSEPHINE

'Happy new year, Mum,' she said. 'I'm sorry I didn't come to see you yesterday. Alfie and I had shocking hangovers. We went to a party over in Frenchay, at Candy's new flat. Remember Candy? Candy Boyd? She was in my year at school, she had all that long blond hair that she could sit on? You really liked her because she always said hello to you if she passed you on the street? Anyway, she's doing really well, she's a physio-therapist. Or . . . a *chiropractor*? Anyway, something like that. She cried when I told her you were dead. Everyone cries when I tell them. Everyone loved you so much, Mum. Everyone wished you were their mum. I was so lucky to have a mum like you. I wish I hadn't stayed away for so long now. If I'd known what was going to happen, I would never have gone away at all. And I'm sorry you never got to meet Alfie. He's ador-able. He's working at a wine bar in town at the moment, but he wants to be a painter-decorator. He's at his mum's now, actually, painting her kitchen. Or at least, he's supposed to be! She's probably made him sit down and watch TV with her, knowing her. And him. He's a bit of a procrastinator. Takes him a while to get going. But you'd love him, Mum. He's the cutest, sweetest, nicest guy and he's so in love with me and he treats me so well and I know how much of a worry I was to you when I was younger. I know what I put you through and I'm so, so sorry. But I wish you could see me now. I'm growing up, Mum. I'm finally growing up!'

She sighed.

'Anyway, I'd better go now. It'll be getting dark soon

and then I'll get really scared. I love you, Mum. I miss you. I wish you weren't dead. I wish I could go to your house and have a cup of tea with you, have a good gossip, have a bitch about Jack and Rebecca. I could tell you about the gold taps. Or maybe I could tell you about the gold taps now? No, I'll tell you about the gold taps next time. Give you something to look forward to.

'Sleep tight, Mum. I love you.'

Joey climbed the steep lane from Lower Melville to the parade of houses above. Even in the sodium gloom of a January afternoon, the houses of Melville Heights popped like a row of children's building blocks: red, yellow, turquoise, purple, lime, sage, fuchsia, red again. They sat atop a terraced embankment looking down on to the small streets of Lower Melville like guests at a private party that no one else was invited to.

Iconic was the word that people used to describe this row of twenty-seven Victorian villas: *the iconic painted houses of Melville Heights*. Joey had seen them from a distance for most of her life. They were the sign that they were less than twenty minutes from home on long car journeys of her childhood. They followed her to work; they guided her home again. She'd been to a party once, in the pink house, when she was a student.

Split crudely into flats and bedsits, smelling of damp and cooked mince, it hadn't felt bright pink on the inside. But the views from up there were breathtaking: the River Avon pausing to arc picturesquely on its mile-long journey to the city, the patchwork fields beyond, the bulge of the landscape on the horizon into a plump hill crowned with trees that blossomed every spring into puffballs of hopeful green.

She'd dreamed of living up here as a child, oscillated between which house would be hers: the lilac or the pink. And as she grew older, the sky blue or the sage. And now, at twenty-six, she found herself living in the cobalt-blue house. Number 14. Not a sign of a lifetime of hard work and rich rewards, but a fringe benefit of her older brother's lifetime of hard work and rich rewards.

Jack was ten years older than Joey and a consultant heart surgeon at Bristol General Hospital, one of the youngest in the county's history. Two years ago he'd married a woman called Rebecca. Rebecca was nice, but brittle and rather humourless. Joey had always thought her lovely brother would end up with a fun-loving, no-nonsense nurse or maybe a jolly children's doctor. But for some reason he'd chosen a strait-laced systems analyst from Staffordshire.

They'd bought their cobalt house ten months ago,

when Joey was still farting about in the Balearics hosting foam parties. She hadn't even realised it was one of the painted houses until Jack had taken her to see it when she moved back to Bristol three months ago.

'You bought a painted house,' she'd said, her hand against her heart. 'You bought a painted house and you didn't tell me.'

'You didn't ask,' he'd responded. 'And anyway, it wasn't my idea. It was Rebecca's. She virtually bribed the old lady who was living here to sell up. Said it was literally the only house in Bristol she wanted to live in.'

'It's beautiful,' she'd said, her eyes roaming over the tasteful interior of taupe and teal and copper and grey. 'The most beautiful house I've ever seen.'

'I'm glad you like it,' Jack had said, 'because Rebecca and I were wondering if you two would like to live here for a while. Just until you get yourselves sorted out.'

'Oh my God,' she'd said, her hands at her mouth. 'Are you serious? Are you sure?'

'Of course I'm sure,' he'd replied, taking her by the hand. 'Come and see the attic room. It's completely self-contained – perfect for a pair of *newlyweds*.' He'd nudged her and grinned at her.

Joey had grinned back. No one was more surprised

13

than she was that she had come back from Ibiza with a husband.

His name was Alfie Butter and he was very good-looking. Far too good-looking for her. Or at least, so she'd thought in the aqua haze of Ibizan nights. In the gunmetal gloom of a Bristol winter the blue, blue eyes were just blue, the Titian hair was just red, the golden tan was just sun-damage. Alfie was just a regular guy.

They'd married barefoot on the beach. Joey had worn a pink chiffon slip dress and carried a posy of pink and peridot Lantanas. Alfie had worn a white T-shirt and pink shorts, and white bougainvillea blossom in his hair. Their marriage had been witnessed by the managers of the hotel where they both worked. Afterwards they'd had dinner on a terrace with a few friends, taken a few pills, danced until the sun came up, spent the next day in bed and then and only then did they phone their families to tell them what they'd done.

She would have had a proper wedding if her mother had still been alive. But she was dead and Joey's dad was not really a wedding kind of a man, nor a flying-out-to-Ibiza kind of a man, and Joey's parents had themselves married secretly at Gretna Green when her mum was four months pregnant with Jack.

'Ah, well,' her father said, with a note of relief. 'I suppose it's a family tradition.'

'Hi,' she called out in the hallway, testing for the presence of her sister-in-law. Rebecca made a lot of noise about how delighted she was to be housing a pair of twenty-something lovebirds in her immaculate, brand-new guest suite – 'It's just so brilliant that we had the space for you! Really, it's just brilliant having you here. Totally brilliant' – but her demeanour told a different story. She hid from them. All the time. In fact, she was hiding from Joey right now, pretending to be arranging things in their huge walk-in pantry.

'Oh, hi!' she said, turning disingenuously at Joey's greeting, a jar of horseradish in her hand. 'I didn't hear you come in!'

Joey smiled brightly. She'd totally heard her coming in. There was a mug of freshly made tea still steaming on the kitchen table, a newspaper half read, a half-eaten packet of supermarket sushi. Joey pictured Rebecca Mullen twitching at the sound of Joey's key in the lock, looking for her escape, scurrying into the pantry and randomly picking up a jar of horseradish.

'Sorry, I did shout out hello.'

'It's fine. It's fine. I'm just . . .' She waved the jar of horseradish in a vague arc around the pantry.

'Nest-building?'

'Yes!' said Rebecca. 'Yes. I am. Nest-building. Exactly.'

Both their eyes fell to Rebecca's rounded stomach. Her first baby was due in four months. It was a girl baby who would, on or around 1 May, become Joey's niece. One of the reasons, Joey imagined, that Rebecca had agreed to let her and Alfie have their guest suite was that Joey was a trained nursery nurse. Not that she'd touched a baby since she was eighteen. But still, she had all the skills. She could, in theory, change a nappy in forty-eight seconds flat.

There was a stained-glass window halfway up the oak staircase that ran up the front of the house. Joey often stopped here to press her nose to the clear parts of the design, enjoying being able to see out with anyone seeing in. It was early afternoon, almost dusk at this time of the year; the trees on the hills on the other side of the river were bare and slightly awkward.

She watched a shiny black car turn from the main road in the village below and begin its ascent up the escarpment towards the terrace. The only cars that came up here were those of residents and visitors. She waited for a while longer to see who it might be. The car parked on the other side of the street and she watched a woman get out of the passenger side, a boyish, thirty-something woman with jaw-length, light brown hair wearing a hoodie and jeans. She stood by the back door while a young boy climbed out, about fourteen years old, the spitting image of her. Then a rather handsome older man got out of the driver's side, tall and leggy in a crumpled sky-blue polo shirt and dark jeans, short dark hair, white at the temples. He went to the boot of the car and pulled out two medium-sized suitcases, with a certain appealing effortlessness. He handed one to his son, passed a pile of coats and a carrier bag to his wife and then they crossed the road and let themselves into the yellow house.

Joey carried on up the stairs, the image of the attract-ive older man returning from his family Christmas break already fading from her consciousness.

RECORDED INTERVIEW

Date: 25/03/2017
Location: Trinity Road Police Station, Bristol BS2 0NW
Conducted by: Officers from Somerset & Avon Police

POLICE: This interview is being tape-recorded. I am Detective Inspector Rose Pelham and I'm based at Trinity Road Police Station. I work with the serious crime team. Could you please give us your full name?

JM: Josephine Louise Mullen.

POLICE: And your address?

JM: 14 Melville Heights, Bristol BS12 2GG.

POLICE: Thank you. And can you tell us about your relationship with Tom Fitzwilliam?

JM: He lives two doors down. He gave me a lift into work sometimes. We chatted if we bumped into each other on the street. He knew my brother and my sister-in-law.

POLICE: Thank you. And could you now tell us where you were last night between approximately 7 p.m. and 9 p.m.

JM: I was at the Bristol Harbour Hotel.

POLICE: And were you there alone?

JM: Mostly.

POLICE: Mostly? Who else was there with you?

JM: [Silence.]

POLICE: Ms Mullen? Please could you tell us who else was there? At the Bristol Harbour Hotel?

JM: But he was only there for a few minutes. Nothing happened. It was just . . .

POLICE: Ms Mullen. The name of this person. Please.

JM: It was . . . it was Tom Fitzwilliam.

2

Joey saw Tom Fitzwilliam again a few days later. This time it was in the village. He was coming out of the bookshop, wearing a suit and talking to someone on the phone. He said goodbye to the person on the phone, pressed his finger to the screen to end the call and slid the phone into his jacket pocket. She saw his face as he turned left out of the shop. It held the residue of a smile. His upturned mouth made a different shape of his face. It turned up more on one side then the other. An eyebrow followed suit. A hand went to his silver-tipped hair as the wind blew it asunder. The smile turned to a grimace and made another shape of his face again. His jaw hardened. His forehead bunched. A slow blink of his eyes. And then he was walking towards his black car parked across the street, a *blip blip* of the locking system, a flash of lights, long legs folded away into the driver's side. Gone.

But a shadow of him lingered on in her consciousness.

Alfie had been a crush. For months she'd watched him around the resort, made up stories about him based on tiny scraps of information she'd collected from people who'd interacted with him. No one knew where he was from. Someone thought he might have been a writer. Someone else said he was a vet. He'd had long hair then, dark red, tied back in a ponytail or sometimes a man-bun. He had a small red beard and a big fit body, a tattoo of a climbing rose all the way up his trunk, another of a pair of wings across his shoulders. He often had a guitar hanging from a strap around his chest. He rarely wore a top when he wasn't working. He had a smile for everyone, a swagger and a cheek.

In Joey's imagination, Alfie Butter was kind of otherworldly; she ascribed to him a sort of supernatural persona, and tried to imagine what they would talk about if their paths were ever to cross. Then one day he'd stopped her at the back of the resort next to the laundry and his blue, blue eyes had locked on to hers and he'd smiled and said, 'Joey, right?'

She'd said yes, she was Joey.

'Someone tells me you're a Bristol girl. Is that right?'

Yes, she'd said, yes, that was right.

'Whereabouts?'

'Frenchay?'

He'd punched the air. 'I knew it!' he'd said. 'I just knew it! You know when you get that feeling in your gut, and someone said you were from Bristol and I just thought *Frenchay girl*. Got to be. And I was right! I'm a Frenchay boy!'

Wow, she'd said, wow. It was a small, small world, she'd told him. Which school did you go to?

And Alfie had turned out to be neither supernatural nor otherworldly, a vet nor a poet, nor even very good at playing the guitar, but spectacularly good in bed and a very good hugger. He'd had her name tattooed on his ankle two weeks after their first encounter. He said he'd never felt like this about anyone, in his life, ever. He slung his heavy arm across her shoulder whenever they walked together. He pulled her on to his lap whenever she walked past him. He said he'd follow her to the ends of the earth. Then, when her mother died and she said she wanted to come home, he said he'd follow her back to Bristol. He'd proposed to her after she returned from her mother's funeral. They'd married two weeks after that.

But what do you do with an unattainable crush once it's yours to keep? What does it become? Should there perhaps be a word to describe it? Because that's the thing with getting what you want: all that yearning and dreaming and fantasising leaves a great big hole that can only be filled with more yearning and dreaming and fantasising. And maybe that's what lay at the root of Joey's sudden and unexpected obsession with Tom Fitzwilliam. Maybe he arrived at the precise moment that the hole in Joey's interior fantasy life needed filling.

And if it hadn't been him, maybe it would have been someone else instead.

3

Tom Fitzwilliam was fifty-one and he was, according to Jack, a *lovely, lovely man*.

Not that Joey had asked her brother for his opinion of their neighbour – it had been offered, spontaneously, apropos of an article in the local newspaper about an award that the local school had just won.

'Oh, look,' he said, the paper spread open in front of him on the kitchen table. 'That's our neighbour, lives two doors down.' He tapped a photo with his forefinger. 'Tom Fitzwilliam. Lovely, lovely man.'

Joey peered over Jack's shoulder, a half-washed saucepan in one hand, a washing-up sponge in the other. 'Oh,' she said, 'I've seen him, I think. Black car?'

'Yes, that's right. He's the headmaster of our local state school. A "superhead".' He made quotes in the air with his fingers. 'Brought in after a bad Ofsted. His school just won something and now everyone loves him.'

'That's nice,' said Joey. 'Do you know him, then?'

'Yeah. Kind of. He and his wife were very helpful when we were having the building works done. They used to send us texts during the day to let us know what was happening and calmed down some other not-so-nice neighbours who were getting their knickers in a knot about dust and noise. Nice people.'

Joey shrugged. Jack thought everyone was nice.

'So.' He closed the paper and folded it in half. 'How did the interview go?'

Joey slung the tea towel over the side of the sink. 'It was OK.'

She'd applied for a job at the Melville, the famous boutique hotel and bar in the village: front-of-house manager. The pleasant woman interviewing her could tell the moment she walked in that she was not fit for purpose and Joey had made no effort to convince her otherwise.

'Glorified receptionist,' she said now. 'Plus four night shifts a week. *No thank you.*'

She didn't look at Jack, didn't want to witness his

reaction to yet more evidence that his little sister was a total loser. She had quite wanted the job; the hotel was beautiful, the owner was nice and the pay was good. The problem was that she couldn't actually see herself in the job. The problem was . . . well, the problem was her. She was nearly twenty-seven. In three years' time she would be thirty. She was a married woman. But for some reason, she still felt like a child.

'Fair enough,' he said, turning the pages of the newspaper mechanically. 'I'm sure something will come up, eventually.'

'Bound to,' she said, her heart not reaching her words.

Then, 'Jack, are you OK about me and Alfie being here? Like, really?'

She watched her brother roll his eyes good-naturedly. 'Joey. For God's sake. How many times do I have to tell you? I love having you here. And Alfie too. It's a pleasure.'

'What about Rebecca, though? Are you sure she's not regretting it?'

'She's fine, Joey. We're both fine. It's all good.'

'Do you promise?'

'Yes, Joey. I promise.'

Joey got a job three days later. It was a terrible, terrible job, but it was a job. She was now a party coordinator at a notoriously rough soft play centre in the city called Whackadoo. The uniform was an acid-yellow polo shirt with red pull-on trousers. The pay was reasonable and the hours were fine. The manager was a big, butch woman with a crew cut called Dawn to whom Joey had taken an instant liking. It could all have been worse, of course it could. Anything could always be worse. But not much.

All employees of Whackadoo were required to spend their first week on the floor. 'Nobody gets to sit in an office here until they've cleaned the toilets halfway through a party for thirty eight-year-old boys,' Dawn had said, a grim twinkle in her eye.

'Can't be any worse than cleaning vomit and Jägerbombs off the bar after a fourteen-hour stag party,' Joey had replied.

'Probably not,' Dawn had conceded. 'Probably not. Can you start tomorrow?'

Joey stopped in the village on her way home from the interview and ordered herself a large gin and tonic in the cosy bar of the Melville Hotel. It was early for gin and tonic. The man sitting two tables away was still having breakfast. She told herself it was celebratory but in reality, she needed something to blunt the edges of her terror and self-loathing.

Whackadoo.

Windowless cavern of unthinkable noise and bad smells. Breeze-block hellhole of spilt drinks and tantrums, where a child shat in the ball pond at least once a day apparently. She shuddered and knocked back another glug of gin. The man eating his breakfast looked at her curiously. She blinked at him imperiously.

You could see the painted houses from down here, a bolt of running colour across the tops of the narrow Georgian windows. There was the cobalt blue of Jack and Rebecca's house, the canary yellow of Tom Fitzwilliam's. It was another world up there. *Rarefied.* And she, a half-formed woman working in a soft play centre: what on earth was she doing up there?

She looked down at her bitten nails, her scuffed boots, her old chinos. She thought about the elderly pants she was wearing, the decrepit bra. She knew she was two months past a timely trip to the hairdresser. She was drinking gin alone in a hotel bar on a Thursday at not even midday. And then she thought of herself only five months ago, tanned and lean, clutching her bouquet, the talcum sand between her toes, the sun shining down from a vivid blue sky, standing at Alfie's side; young, beautiful, in paradise, in love. 'You are the loveliest thing I have ever seen,' her boss had said, wiping a tear from her own cheek. 'So young, so perfect, so pure.'

She switched on her phone and scrolled through her gallery until she got to the wedding photos. For a few minutes she wallowed in the memories of the happiest day of her life, until she heard the bar door open and looked up.

It was him.

Tom Fitzwilliam.

The head teacher.

He pulled off his suit jacket and draped it across the back of a chair, resting a leather shoulder bag on the seat. Then, slowly, in a way that suggested either self-consciousness or a complete lack of self-consciousness, he sauntered to the bar. The barman appeared to know him. He made him a lime and soda, and told him he'd bring his food to the table when it was ready.

Joey watched him walking back to his table. He wore a blue shirt with a subtle check. The bottom buttons, she noticed, strained very gently against a slight softness and Joey felt a strange wave of pleasure, a sense of excitement about the unapologetic contours of his body, the suggestion of meals enjoyed and worries forgotten about over a bottle of decent wine. She found herself wanting to slide her fingers between those tensed buttons, to touch, just for a moment, the soft flesh beneath.

The thought shocked her, left her slightly winded. She turned her attention to her gin and tonic, aware that her glass was virtually empty, aware that it was time for her to leave. But she didn't want to move. She couldn't move. She was suddenly stultified by a terrible and unexpected longing. She turned slightly to catch a glimpse of his feet, his ankles, the rumpled cowl of grey cotton sock, the worn hide of black leather lace-up shoes, an inch of pale, bare flesh just there, between the sock and the hem of the trousers she'd been aware of him slowly tugging up before sitting down.

She was in the hard grip of a shocking physical attraction. She turned her eyes away from his feet and back to her empty glass and then to the wedding photos on her phone, which had only 2 per cent charge left and was about to die. But she couldn't, she simply couldn't sit here staring into an empty gin glass. Not now. Not in front of this man.

She was aware of him taking papers out of his shoulder bag, shuffling them around, pulling a pen from somewhere, holding it airily away from him in one hand, clicking and unclicking, clicking and unclicking, bringing it down to make a mark on the paper, putting it away from him again. *Click, click.* One foot bouncing slightly against the fulcrum of the other. She would leave when the waiter came with his food. That was what she'd do. When he was distracted.

The screen of her phone turned black, finally giving up its ghost. She slipped it into her handbag and stared at the floor until finally the barman disappeared at the sound of a buzzer somewhere behind him and re-appeared a moment later with some kind of sandwich on a wooden board arranged alongside a glossy hillock of herbs and curly leaves. She saw Tom move paper-work out of the way, smiling generously at the barman.

'Thank you,' she heard him say as she picked up her jacket and squeezed her way between her chair and the table, almost knocking it over in her keenness to leave without being noticed. 'That looks lovely,' he was saying as she crossed the bar, her heavy boots making a loud knocking sound against the dove-grey floor tiles, the strap of her shoulder bag refusing to sit prop-erly against her shoulder, her trailing jacket knocking over a small display of leaflets about the village farmers' market as she passed.

The barman called over, 'Don't worry. I'll pick them up.'

'Thank you,' she said.

She wrenched open the door and threw herself out on to the street, but not before, for just one flickering second, her eyes had met his and something terrible had passed between them, something that she could only describe as a mutual fascination.

4

26 January

Joey stared at Alfie sitting on the bed, cross-legged, the laptop open and balanced on his knees. His once flowing red locks were short now, growing back from the brutal number two he'd inflicted on himself when they got back to the UK that had made his head look suddenly slightly too small for his body. His lower face was covered in a mulch of four-day stubble. He was wearing a grey vest with deep-cut armholes that showed off most of his tattoos and a pair of elderly Gap underpants. He was huge. A solid brick wall of a man. Even sitting on a slightly fey bed he looked like a Celtic warrior. A Celtic warrior who'd forgotten to get dressed.

She scrutinised his hard, young man's body. And then she thought of Tom Fitzwilliam's soft, grown-up body and she wondered what would happen to Alfie's hard body as the years passed. Would he turn to fat or to sinew? Would he still be Alfie Butter, crap guitarist, brilliant hugger, hopeless painter and decorator, big-hearted romantic, attentive lover? Or would he be someone else? How could it be possible that she didn't know? That no one could tell her? That she would just have to trust in the universe to bring everything to some kind of satisfactory conclusion? How could it be?

Joey felt her brain swell and roil. She thought of her nasty Whackadoo uniform, the smell of fried nuggets and boys' toilets. She thought of Tom Fitzwilliam, the *click, click, click* of his ballpoint pen. She thought of the feeling that had enveloped her when he was in the bar, the feeling that had taken her the most part of the afternoon and evening to purge. She thought of her mother, the lack of her, the loss and she felt, suddenly, dreadfully, out of control.

'Are you OK?' said Alfie, looking at her curiously.

'Mhm.'

'You sure?'

'Yeah,' she said, making herself smile. 'Sure. Possibly having a tiny, baby, shit-job-missing-Ibiza crisis, but nothing worse than that.'

'Come here,' he said, big freckled arms spread apart, 'I'll hug it away for you.'

She acquiesced although part of her wanted to shout, *A hug is not always the right answer, you know.* But as she felt his arms around her, his warm breath against the crown of her head, she thought that it might not be an answer, but it was certainly better than yet another question.

She stopped at the corner shop on her way home the next day. It was the end of the first day of her new job and she felt rubbed raw by the rudeness of people, the loudness of children, the lack of sunlight, the sheer length of the day. She wanted to go home and shower and put on joggers and a hoodie and drink a cup of tea. But mainly she wanted wine. Lots of wine.

As she turned into the booze aisle of the shop she saw Tom Fitzwilliam's wife. What was her name again? Jack had told her but she couldn't remember. Something beginning with an 'N', she thought. She had her hand in the chilled drinks cabinet, about to pull out a bottle of cold mineral water. She was flushed, her hair sweaty and tied back, wearing shiny black leggings and a black fitted top that revealed a slightly sinewy, over-worked-out physique. On her wrist was a lipstick-pink fitness tracker. On her feet were bright white trainers.

She turned slightly as she became aware of Joey's eyes upon her. She smiled coolly, then took the bottle to the till at the other side of the shop. Joey could hear her from here, chatting to the cashier. She was well spoken with a slightly northern slant to some of her words. She told the cashier that she'd just started running again, a new year's resolution after a broken ankle the year before had put her out of action. It was wonderful, she said, to be pounding the tarmac again. She always felt out of sorts when she wasn't running regularly. Two miles a day cleared out the cobwebs, she said, got the cogs turning.

Joey peered around the corner of the cereal aisle to get a better look at the woman Tom Fitzwilliam had chosen to marry. She looked weightless, sprite-like. Everything about her was delicate, sinuous, as though she'd been drawn with sharpened pencils. Joey was small, but Tom's wife was doll-like, with hair as fine as gossamer and a button nose. She imagined those tiny hands grasping his soft waist. She wondered if he'd ever been unfaithful to her. She wondered how often they had sex. She imagined, suddenly, this tiny child's toy of a woman astride her big, handsome husband, her head tipped back.

She grabbed a bottle of something cheap with a screw-top lid and took it quickly to the till. As she walked back up the hill towards the painted houses she saw Tom's wife just ahead of her, a matchstick silhouette clutching a bottle of water, shoulders hunched against the bitter January wind.

And there, high above, in the pale backlight of a top-floor window in the Fitzwilliams' house, she saw a small beam of a light, the movement of a person, the fall of a heavy curtain, sudden darkness.

5

27 January

Freddie Fitzwilliam switched off his digital binoculars, let the curtain drop and wheeled his chair back across the bedroom floor, from the window to his computer. There was a shiny track in the carpet now recording the many journeys he'd made by office chair from one side of his room to the other. He was the captain of his own ship up here, in his attic room with its sweeping views across the village and the river valley and the landscape beyond. The digital binoculars had been a Christmas gift from his mum and dad. They had revolutionised his life. He could now clearly see Jenna Tripp's road from here. He could also see the

dimpled glass of Bess Ridley's bathroom which occasionally shimmered and radiated with the suggestion
of naked flesh behind. He could see Jenna and Bess
meeting up each morning outside Jenna's house in
their tacky Academy uniforms: short, short skirts and
bare legs even in the chill of January, linking arms,
sharing earbuds, gossip. He could even see what flavour Pringles they were eating.

Freddie didn't go to the Academy where his dad
was headmaster. He went to a private boys' school
across the other side of town that took him half an
hour to walk to every morning. He'd been in Melville
for one year and one month since he'd woken up one
morning in his old house in Mold and been told that
they were moving to Bristol and that they were moving
next week and that no, they weren't coming back. His
dad was a bigwig head teacher. The government sent
him all over the country to 'special measures' schools,
schools that were on the brink of being shut down
because they were so fucking terrible. This one had
been so fucking terrible that they'd had to sack the old
head and have him walked off the premises the same
day: something to do with embezzling school funds,
something really bad.

At first Freddie had hated it here. His school was
shit; it looked like a prison and it smelled worse. The

teachers were all really old and very British, not like his old school where they'd been mostly fresh-faced Europeans. He liked European teachers; he could impress them by talking to them in their mother tongues. They always loved that. He could get away with murder if he could compliment a teacher in fluent Spanish or whatever.

Freddie could speak six languages: French, Spanish, German, Italian, Mandarin and Welsh. The Welsh he'd picked up when they lived in Mold; the rest he'd taught himself. He could also speak in about twenty different accents to such an extent that locals couldn't tell he was putting it on. He was going to join MI5 when he left university. His parents had been telling him all his life that the government would love a clever little bastard like him, and he tended to agree with them. What else could he possibly do with all these brains, all these facts, the constant spin and bubble of his brilliant mind? It had to go somewhere. And, of course, the digital binoculars (and the Smartwatch spy camera and the spy glasses and the spy software built into his Samsung Galaxy) had played right into the whole Freddie's-going-to-be-a-spy narrative that he and his parents had been writing for nearly fifteen years.

And at first that was what he'd used them for.

In the absence of any friends or any real desire to

have friends, Freddie had spent the past year or so compiling a dossier called *The Melville Papers*, a kind of quasi-local paper about the local community. In it he reported on the comings and goings in Lower Melville as seen from his perch at the top of the house. He logged the visitors to the Melville Hotel – once he had seen Cate Blanchett going in; she was really, really small. He logged the dog walkers – *White-haired man with miniature schnauzer left home 8 p.m., returned 8.27 –* and the joggers – *two middle-aged women with big bottoms, left home 7.30, returned 8.45, bought expensive crisps from the deli.* He logged the occasional infraction of the law – a dog walker failing to collect their dog's poo, countless episodes of double parking or parking on the zigzag lines by the zebra crossing, at least three shoplifting episodes, one of which had ended with the shopkeeper chasing the man all the way to the other side of the village before almost having a heart attack.

But recently, Freddie had found his focus shifting from the humdrum and the day to day; there were after all only so many times he could make a note of the white-haired man walking his miniature schnauzer before it stopped being interesting. Nowadays, Freddie found most of his attention being taken up by logging girls. It was strange because Freddie had never liked girls, not ever. A dislike of girls had, in fact, been one of his defining characteristics. He had assumed that not liking girls was his default setting.

But apparently not.

Jenna and Bess were the two prettiest girls in the village by far. Jenna was tall and athletically built with fine dark hair and quite a big bust. Bess was small with what appeared to be naturally blond hair which she wore quite short with a fringe that hung in her eyes. They were older than Freddie, year eleven to his year ten. He spent most of his time logging them now; he knew what nights they did after-school clubs, what days they did PE, what their favourite Starbucks drinks were, how often they changed their earrings.

Yes, Jenna and Bess were by far his favourites. But there was someone new now. She'd moved into the blue house two doors down a few weeks ago and she was really pretty. He'd first seen her in the restaurant at the Melville down in the village when he was having dinner with his mum and dad. She'd been with a man. He was big and rough-looking with shaved red hair and tattoos that you could see through the fabric of his shirt. Freddie had heard her first, her Bristol accent, a loud laugh. He'd been intrigued, turned his head just a few degrees to check her out. She was necking wine in a floaty top. She had a really full mouth, big white teeth, white-blond hair in a messy bun, gold hoop earrings, small feet in blood-red suede boots with little tassels. And that was what he called her while he tried to find a way to discover her real name.

He called her Red Boots.

He was watching her now; he'd watched her get off the bus in the village, then lost her for a while before picking her up again trailing a few feet behind his mum up the hill. He zoomed in tighter and tighter until he was close enough to see that she looked terrible and now, as he uploaded the film on to his laptop he zoomed in further still and there, in one frame, he saw a yellow T-shirt worn underneath a big ugly coat. He went right in on it: there was the familiar yellow and red of the Whackadoo logo. He passed Whackadoo every morning on his way to school, a big yellow breeze-block building with a huge plastic toucan outside. It was for kids or something.

Christ, he thought, Red Boots is working at Whackadoo. What kind of crap job was that? He saved the film into the top-secret folder that no one in his house was even halfway clever enough to uncover. Then he went downstairs to ask his mum what he was having for supper.

6

3 February

Jenna Tripp kicked off her black trainers, unknotted her nylon tie, dropped her rucksack at the bottom of the stairs, pulled the hairband from her ponytail, rubbed at her aching scalp with her fingertips and called out for her mum.

'In here!'

She peered round the door into the living room. Her mum was perched on the edge of the leather sofa, the laptop on the coffee table in front of her, a notepad to one side of her, her phone on the other. Her pale gold hair was scraped back into a ponytail. She looked pretty with her hair off her face; you could see the fine angles of her bone structure, the shadowy dip below each cheekbone, the delicacy of her jawline. She'd been a model for a short while in her teens. There was a framed photo of her modelling a bikini on a windswept beach nailed to the wall outside Jenna's bedroom. Her arms were wrapped tight around her body (it had been November apparently) and she was smiling up into the sky above. She was pure joy to behold.

'Check out there, will you?' she said now, sucking her e-cigarette and releasing a thick trail of berry-scented vapour. 'Can you see a blue Lexus? One of those hatchbacks?'

Jenna sighed and pulled back one drawn curtain. She looked left and right around the small turning where their cottage was and then back at her mum. 'No blue Lexus,' she said.

'Are you sure?'

'Yes,' she replied. 'I'm sure. There's a blue Ford Focus, but that's the only blue car out there.'

'Oh, that's Mike's car. That's fine.'

She didn't ask her mum more about the blue Lexus. She knew what her mum thought about the blue Lexus. She let the curtain drop and went into the kitchen. She boiled the kettle and made herself a low-calorie hot chocolate into which she dropped a small handful of marshmallows (she'd recently learned that marshmallows were surprisingly low in calories) and then she took the hot chocolate, her school bag and her phone to her room. She stopped on the way to study the photo of her mum. Frances Tripp. Or Frankie Miller as she'd been known in her modelling and acting days. She'd changed back to Frances in her twenties when she'd married Jenna's dad and started campaigning for animal rights. He told her it would give her more gravitas. Jenna wished she'd known the girl in the photo, the carefree beauty with the wind in her hair and the sky reflected in her shining eyes. She reckoned she'd have liked her.

'By the way!' Her mother's girlish voice followed her up the stairs to the landing.

'Yes!'

'Did you change the bulb in your vanity mirror?'

Jenna paused before she replied, her shoulders falling. 'No,' she said, although it would have been easier in some ways to say yes.

'Right,' said her mum. 'Odd. Very odd.'

Jenna opened the door to her bedroom, slipped through and closed it behind her before she got pulled into any further conversation about the bulb in her vanity mirror. There was a Snapchat from Bess on her phone. It was a photo of her holding the local paper next to her face, pulling a kissy-face at a photo of

Mr Fitzwilliam on page eight. She'd scribbled a pink love heart around both of them. Jenna tutted. Seriously, what was wrong with the girl? Mr Fitzwilliam was so old.

'He has charisma,' Bess had said once. 'Plus he smells good.'

'How do you know how he smells?'

'I make a point of sniffing when I'm close. And he does this thing . . .'

'What *thing*?' Jenna had said.

'This thing with his pen. He *clicks* it.' Bess had mimed clicking a pen.

'He clicks it?'

'Yeah. It's hot.'

'You're on glue, mate, I swear.'

She replied to Bess's message now: *Meth head.*

Bess replied with a sequence of crystal emojis. Jenna smiled and put her phone on her bedside table to charge. Bess was the best friend in the world, the best friend she'd ever had. They were like sisters. Like *twins*. She'd known Bess for four years, ever since her mum and dad had split up and she'd drawn the short straw and moved to Lower Melville with her mum while her little brother Ethan had stayed with Dad in Weston-super-Mare. Not that there was anything wrong with Lower Melville. The cottage (or what Jenna's mum

46

referred to as a cottage, but was actually a tired post-war terrace with pebble-dashed walls) was in fact the house her mum had grown up in and while the cottage was as scruffy as it had always been, the village around it no longer was. Kids at her school thought she was posh because she lived here. They were so wrong.

'Jen!'

She closed her eyes at the sound of her mother's voice climbing up the stairs.

'Jenna!'

'Yes!'

'Check out the back, will you? Tell me if that man's still sitting in his window.'

She drew in her breath and held it hard inside her for as long as she could.

'Why?'

'You know why.'

She did know why, but sometimes she needed her mum to find the words to explain these obsessions, in the hope that it might wake her up to the nonsense of what she was saying.

She let her breath out, put down her hot chocolate and knelt on her bed. There was a man sitting in his window at the back of the terrace that faced the end of their garden. He was side on and absorbed in something on a

47

screen in front of him. She watched him lift a teacup to his lips, take a sip, put the cup back down, run his hand briefly round the back of his neck, and then start moving his fingers over a keyboard.

'No!' she shouted down to her mother. 'There's no one there. No man.'

There was a beat of silence, filled, Jenna assumed, not with feelings of relief, but of disappointment.

'Good,' her mother said a moment later. 'Good. Let me know if he comes back.'

'I will.'

'Thanks, darling.'

Jenna's phone pinged. Another Snapchat from Bess. The photo of Mr Fitzwilliam from the paper, his face covered over in Bess's lipstick kisses.

Jenna smiled and sent another message.

U R madder than my mum.

7

There was a photo of Tom Fitzwilliam on page eight of
the local paper. He was standing at the entrance to the
Academy, his arms folded across his stomach, a thin
blue tie blown slightly askew by the wind, looking at
the camera sternly with a half-buried smile. The head-
line said 'SUPERHEAD TACKLES GANGS'.

Joey did not read the accompanying article. She was
too intent on absorbing every last detail of the photograph: the lanyard around his neck on a yellow strap.
The dull gleam of the narrow gold band on his ring
finger. The way his waistband sat, no belt, slightly
slack, just above his hip bones. The jut of his chin. The
wide slope of his shoulders. The slight disarray of his

hair in the same breeze that had disordered his tie. And the way he stood in full and complete possession of his surroundings.

My school. My kids. My responsibility.

Tom Fitzwilliam.

SUPERHEAD.

She touched the outline of his stomach with one outstretched fingertip, caressing the image thoughtfully as she remembered the potent look they'd exchanged a week ago as she'd left the bar at the Melville. And then she jumped at the suggestion of a hand against her waist and a sudden bloom of warm breath on the side of her neck. It was Alfie, smelling of daytime sleep and stale T-shirt.

'Fuck, Alf, you made me jump!'

'Sorry, angel.'

His arm snaked around her body from behind and he buried his face in her shoulder and planted his mouth firmly against her skin. 'Mm,' he said, breathing her in. 'You smell fucking gorgeous.'

'I do not smell gorgeous. I smell of chips and boys' farts.'

'No,' he said, sliding his hand down the front of her terrible elasticated trousers and into the top of her knickers – the feel of his fingers against her so soon after her reverie staring at Tom's photograph almost winded her, 'you smell of your hormones.'

She covered his hand with hers and pushed it harder against herself. 'And what do my hormones smell like?'

'They smell like honey.' He encased her fully with his big dry hand and rocked with her from side to side, his words falling into the hot space between his lips and her skin. 'And summer rain. And birthday parties. And kittens' paws. And hot sand. And . . .' He paused and brought his other arm around her body, pulled her so close to him that they were virtually one being. 'You,' he finished. 'Just you.'

She turned then, spun inside his arms and kissed him hard. Then she dragged him up the two flights of stairs between the kitchen and their room, fast, desperate, the newspaper left open on the kitchen table below, Tom Fitzwilliam's eyes staring upwards at the ceiling.

'You know something?' Alfie said after, Joey's head tucked under his arm, their hands entwined together.

'No,' said Joey. 'Tell me.'

'You're probably going to think this is mad.'

She ran a fingertip down the tendrils of the climbing rose that covered his torso, following them to their tightly curled tips. 'Try me.'

He paused then and fell quiet for a very long time.

She saw a slight flush spread across his face and she turned to face him fully. 'What is it, Alf?'

'I know we've only been married a few months, and I know we've only known each other a short time, and I know we're both still quite young, but what do you think about the idea of starting to try for a baby?'

She felt a bubble of unhinged laughter rise from the pit of her stomach and she swallowed it down. 'Alf,' she said, taking his hand in her. 'God. I mean. Yes. Maybe one day. But we need to get ourselves sorted out. Get proper jobs. Find somewhere to live. I really don't think now's the time.'

Alfie looked perplexed. 'But, you said, remember, that night when we went down to Cala d'Hort with that really nice weed from that French guy, remember? And we were talking about the future? Yeah? And you said something like *I'd really like to be a young mum.'*

Joey blinked and shook her head. 'I wouldn't have said that.'

'But you did say that. I remember it, like *so* clearly because it was the last thing I'd thought you'd say because you're so, well, you *were*, you know, so . . .' He flailed around for a word for a moment. *'Unmaternal.'*

Joey flinched and Alfie stopped for a moment, licked his lips. 'No. No, not that. You're not that. But you're just, I don't know, you're just not like all the girls I knew from home, all those girls who grew up waiting for the first chance to get pregnant. You always seemed like you had more important things to do.'

'Ha!' The repressed laughter escaped like a clap of thunder. 'Me! Important things!'

He looked at her, his blue eyes clouded with confusion, and suddenly she felt horribly sorry for him. She brought her hand down on to his cheek and cupped the side of his face. 'No,' she said, 'no. I'm not really an *important things* kind of person. I'm still trying to work out what the important things even are.'

'Babies!' said Alfie triumphantly. 'Babies are important. And I am one hundred per cent ready to do this.' He wrapped her hand inside both of his. 'One hundred and *ten* per cent. Just totally *bring it on*. And you'd be an amazing mum. You really would.'

'And you say that based on . . . ?'

'On the . . . on *you*. Just based on you.'

'Alfie,' she said, 'I sometimes think . . . I worry that you think I'm something I'm not. I'm clueless, Alfie. Totally clueless. I'm not sure I could cope with the responsibility of raising an actual real-life person. Truly.' She looked at Alfie, reaching into his blue eyes, expecting to see disenchantment coming down like shop shutters. But his gaze was still bright, still hopeful.

'Well,' he said, 'I believe in you, Joey Mullen. I totally

believe in you and I think you and I could make the most beautiful baby you've ever seen and give it everything a child needs. Will you at least think about it?'

She cocked her head and regarded him. Beautiful Alfie, the love of her life.

'Yes,' she said, 'I'll think about it.'

8

8 February

Freddie checked the time: five fifty-three. He pushed his chair across the floor to the window and picked up his binoculars. It was early evening, dark already, but maybe he could get a couple of good shots of Jenna coming back from her Wednesday-afternoon netball club in her skirt and hoodie. She should be turning the corner of the high street any second now.

Freddie was not a voyeur. Voyeurism was a form of control, like mental abuse, like rape, like bullying. It was nothing to do with the physicality of the action, and all to do with the feeling of power it gave the perpetrator, the balancing out of delicate ids and egos. But

Freddie wasn't a pervert. He wasn't a bully. He wasn't a criminal. He watched girls in order to understand them. He was just trying to work it all out. It was just another project.

He focused his binoculars and trained them on to the village. He saw his mum hurtle past the Melville in her running gear, looking like a small boy with her hair scraped off her face and tucked inside a black baseball cap. He saw the man with white hair walking the miniature schnauzer. He saw two younger boys from the Academy, clutching skateboards, heading, he assumed, towards the playing fields by the river on the other side of the roundabout where there was a skate park. And there, there she was: Jenna Tripp, powder-pink sports bag slung over her shoulder, long, solid legs, white trainers, navy hoodie, earbuds, dark pony-tail and a huge clear plastic cup of some overpriced frappé from Starbucks in her right hand.

He got some more footage as she turned off the high street into her little side street and then he saw her stop and he panned out to see what she was looking at. There was a woman standing on the pavement outside Jenna's house. Freddie was pretty sure it was Jenna's mum. She was wearing a T-shirt with the words 'STOP FRACKING NOW' emblazoned across the front and held a 35-mm camera that she was using to photograph a car across the street. Jenna picked up her pace and approached the woman, who started to gesticulate agitatedly, pointing at the car and then, suddenly, chillingly, looking up and, very deliberately, pointing at him. Freddie snapped one more photo before diving off his chair and on to the floor. When he peered over his windowsill a moment later, Jenna and the woman were both gone. He plugged his binoculars into his computer and opened up the images. He went to the last photo he'd taken and zoomed in on the woman's face.

Her eyes were narrowed and locked completely on to him, her finger pointing at him and her mouth clearly forming the word *you*.

9

'Mum, what the hell are you doing?'

'What does it look like I'm doing?'

'Acting like a crazy person is what it looks like you're doing.'

'Did you not see him?'

'Who?'

'Up there, in the yellow house. He's taking pictures again.'

Jenna looked up at the painted houses above and found the yellow one. 'Where?'

'Up there in the top window. He's always at it.'

Jenna narrowed her eyes at the top window. She couldn't see anything. But then she hadn't expected to.

'Well,' she said, 'whoever it was has gone now.' She knew better than to try to disabuse her mother of her outlandish observations. She'd tried that approach for ages. It hadn't worked. 'Come on,' she said. 'Let's go in.'

Her mother narrowed her pretty blue eyes at her; then her gaze passed over Jenna's shoulder towards something behind. She said, 'Look at this. Look.'

Jenna sighed. The sweat from netball had dried on her skin in the cold evening air and she was shivering and desperate to get indoors.

Her mother crouched down next to her red Vauxhall Corsa and indicated a point just above the back-wheel arch. 'Look,' she said. 'That scratch. That was not there yesterday. And that's been done deliberately, you can tell. Someone's done that with a key. Look, you can see the teeth marks.'

Jenna leaned down and examined the scratch. Her mum's car was so old that she could remember being driven to her first day at nursery school in it. The scratch certainly looked newer than some of the other damage, but that meant nothing.

'Why?' said her mum. 'Why us? Why me? I don't understand.'

'Come on.' Jenna offered her mum her hand. 'Let's go in. I'm freezing.'

Her mum got to her feet. 'I think I need to call the

police again. For all the good that it'll do me. But honestly. It's getting ridiculous. And now your school seems to be involved too.'

Jenna pushed the latched door open and went indoors. 'What do you mean, my school?'

'Your head teacher. That *superhead*. It's him up there taking photos. I'm sure it is. And you know who else seems to be living up there now? That woman I told you about, the one who was on that tour with us in the Lake District? Remember? It's all connected. The whole thing is connected, Jen. And it's just getting bigger and bigger and bigger.'

Jenna dropped her PE bag in the hallway and hung her blazer off the banister. 'I'm going to run myself a bath, Mum,' she said. 'Do you want me to leave the water in for you?'

'Yes please, love. Thank you. Remember to rinse it out first though!' she called up after her. 'In case there's any broken glass!'

'Yup,' Jenna called back. 'Sure.'

10

11 February

Joey was sitting on the 218 bus on her way home from work on Saturday when she saw a tall man in a blue jumper and blue jeans leaving the big JD Sports holding a carrier bag and looking slightly lost. Her instinctive reaction, coming a split second before realising that the man was Tom Fitzwilliam, was attraction. Intense attraction. The sort of attraction that makes you burn at your core.

The bus came to a halt at the traffic lights and she watched him walking first in one direction and then in another. He appeared to be looking for something and then she saw his pace quicken to a gentle run and his arm extend from his body as though – it seemed momentarily possible – he was about to take to the sky, like Superman. As he pulled his arm higher above his head, his blue jumper pulled away slightly from his stomach and she glimpsed for a startling moment an inch of bare flesh, creamy pale with the smooth, supple give of freshly baked bread crust. His long legs took him swiftly to the kerb, to the taxi that had pulled over at his command (not request. No. Command). He swung in his big carrier bag and then himself. The taxi pulled away in front of Joey's bus and she watched it with some excitement from her seat near the front. By the time they'd loaded up with passengers at the next bus stop, Tom and his taxi were gone from view.

The house was empty when Joey got home. Alfie was at his mum's, in theory painting her kitchen, in actuality most likely watching sports on her leather sofa eating a home-cooked meal off a tray on his lap. Jack was at work and Rebecca was on a hen weekend in Gloucestershire. For a while Joey wandered from room to room, absorbing the sense of space. She still felt unable to spread herself around this house and usually went straight from the kitchen to her bedroom and from her bedroom to the front door without lingering or settling. When she did occasionally sit in the living room, it was as a guest, conscious of not outstaying her welcome. 'Make yourself at home,' her brother always insisted. But that was easy for him to say. They were siblings. Brother and sister. Extensions of one another. He would never feel her presence as a weight or an unease. But the same was clearly not the case for Rebecca. Joey was a stranger to her, someone to hide from and to avoid.

The rooms in her brother's house felt anonymous, no different in some ways to the rooms at the Melville Hotel in the village: all pale furnishings and soft golden objects with no obvious purpose. She could not imagine a baby coming into this house. She could not imagine the noise of it, the uncontrollability of it, the endless head space that it would occupy. Her thoughts returned, as they had a dozen times since Alfie's unexpected pronouncement of last week, to the concept of her own baby. *Wouldn't it be nice,* Alfie had said later that evening, *for our baby to be the same age as Jack and Rebecca's baby? They could grow up together. Be best mates forever.*

The clear implication being that they should make a baby *now*. Not soon. Not at some point. But *now*.

And Joey did not want a baby now.

Most definitely not now.

As she thought this she came upon a photo of her and Jack posed between their mother and father outside their grandmother's house in Exeter. She was about three years old, wearing a red sweatshirt and her hair in pigtails. Jack was an incredibly awkward thirteen-year-old with a heavy fringe that almost covered his eyes. He had his hand placed protectively on her shoulder. He'd loved her with a passion from the day she'd arrived. The ten-year age gap had never divided them. If anything the absence of sibling rivalry had brought them closer together. But it was her parents who drew her inspection now; if she was three in this photo then her mother would have been thirty-one. Thirty-one, married and a mother of a toddler and a teenager. Joey could see the bloom of youth still upon her mother's skin, the lustre of her chestnut hair. Young, she thought, my mother was so young. Only a few years older than I am now. She had not thought of her mother as a young person when she was a child and then her mother had died before Joey had had a chance to notice that she was now old.

On her way back up to her bedroom, she passed Rebecca's study door. Rebecca worked from home three or four days a week as a systems analyst. For hours at a time she wouldn't come out. Joey would hear the hushed tones of her voice through the door as she passed by on her way to her attic room, or the plasticky click of her fingertips against the keyboard. But more often there was silence. As though there was no one in there at all.

She peered down the stairwell to check no one had noiselessly returned home, before gently pushing open Rebecca's study door. She jumped and clutched her heart. A man, in the corner. But no, not a man, a life-size cardboard cut-out of her brother in Hawaiian swimming trunks. She remembered it from the photos of her brother's stag night. He and his mates had carried the cut-out all around Bristol, getting pretty girls to pose for photos with it along the way.

It was a small square room. Three walls were covered with built-in shelves and a fourth housed a deep bay window overlooking the street. There was a coffee machine and a kettle, a tray of mugs and cups, a small fridge, a small cream sofa. Everything to ensure that she need rarely leave the room. On her desk were three large monitors, two keyboards, neatly stacked paperwork, a photo of her and Jack on their wedding day. Joey picked it up and gazed at it. She could barely remember her brother's wedding. She'd arrived in the UK with a hangover and basically drunk her way through the next forty-eight hours until it was time for her to catch the Sunday evening flight home. She could not have told you what Rebecca had been wearing but, glancing now at the photo, it seemed it was a cream satin slip dress. She also saw that Rebecca had worn her hair down and combed to a shine and had small diamond drops from her earlobes. She had smiled, clearly at least once, and thankfully the photographer had been there to capture it. But Joey's overriding memory of the weekend was looking at her amazing brother's slightly mousey new wife and wondering why she wasn't smiling.

She put the photo down and let her hands wander indiscriminately over the objects on Rebecca's desk. A chartreuse paperweight. A tube of Cath Kidston hand cream. A very realistic plastic cactus in a green pot. A silver Links of London bracelet. A tiny photo of a Border collie being cuddled by a teenage girl who Joey assumed was Rebecca.

There was a window seat built into the bay, upholstered with grey ticking cushions. Joey sat down for a moment to take in the view across the valley. From here she could see over the tops of the trees opposite. She could see the chimneys of the houses in the village and the river and voluptuous hills beyond. And from the left-hand portion of the bay she could see directly into the right-hand portion of a mirror-image bay on Tom Fitzwilliam's house. She could see a suggestion of a table lamp, the blur of a mirror, the profile of a woman's face.

Nicola Fitzwilliam. Applying face cream. Her fingertips working into her porcelain skin.

11

Freddie heard the tantalising echo of high-heeled shoes against the paving stones outside and quickly pushed his chair across his bedroom floor to investigate. It was late afternoon on Saturday. The sky was growing dark, grey veins threading through the pale evening sky, a smudge of moon just visible on the other side of the river. It was her. Red Boots. And she was wearing her red boots. Red boots, skinny jeans, leather jacket, big scarf, blond hair all puffed up on top of her head, lipstick. She looked as pretty as he remembered her looking the first time he'd seen her at the Melville. He grabbed his camera and went back to the window.

Red Boots was already halfway down the hill. She turned left into the village at the bottom of the hill and he followed her with his lens across the road to the bus stop. He checked his bus app and saw that the next 218 was not due for eight minutes. She pulled out her phone and played with it for a while. Every now and then she would look upwards – directly, it seemed, towards the painted houses. He zoomed in on her and saw her bottom lip pinched between her teeth. What was she waiting for? What was looking at? Then suddenly, when the 218 was only two minutes away, she stood up abruptly and walked towards the village. A moment later he saw her walking across the other side of the road. The bus had been and gone and she had a bottle of something in a blue carrier bag which she took back up the hill.

She reached the blue house and bypassed it, coming to a stop outside his. What was she doing? Had she clocked him watching her? She couldn't have. He was brilliant at watching people without them realising. But then he thought of Jenna's mum last week, the pointing finger, the word *you*. Maybe he wasn't as stealthy as he thought he was. He pulled back into the shadows of his room waiting for her either to knock on his front door or to turn around and head back to her own house. But she did neither of these things. She stood there for exactly three minutes and eighteen seconds until there was the sound of footsteps up the hill and a man appeared, cast in the shadow of the street lights that had just been switched on. Freddie pushed open his window and put his ear to the gap.

'What are you up to, sexy?' asked the man. It was him. The husband.

'I don't really know,' Red Boots replied. 'I was going to get the bus into town and meet you somewhere but you didn't answer your phone. So I bought a bottle of wine and came home instead.'

'Sorry, baby,' said the guy. 'I ran out of juice and didn't have my charger with me.'

'Don't worry,' she replied. 'It was a pretty half-hearted attempt at going out; I'm not sure I really wanted to anyway. And now you're here so looks like it was too late anyway.'

'Yeah,' said the guy, 'I'm knackered. Guess what?'

'What?'

'I finished it.'

'Your mum's kitchen?'

'Yeah. All done. Just need to go back and do a second coat on the skirting. But apart from that, I'm done.'

'God, finally.'

'I'll show you pictures once I've got some charge in my phone. It looks really good.'

'So after all those weeks of farting about, it ended up taking you one day.'

'Yeah. I know. I just thought . . . after what we talked about the other day . . . it's about time I got serious about things.'

There was a short silence. Freddie couldn't see what they were doing. Then Red Boots said, 'Well, you're a very, very good husband, Alfie Butter. I'm very impressed.'

'And you're a very good wife, Joey Mullen, and I think we should go inside and drink that wine and do the things that good husbands and wives get to do on Saturday nights.'

'Netflix?'

'Possibly.'

'Come on then.'

Then Freddie heard the sound of a key in the lock of number 14 and the bang of the door behind them. He exhaled his held breath and thought two things; firstly that he now knew Red Boots's name. The second was that although he now had an explanation for her sitting at the bus stop for six minutes and then coming home again, he did *not* have an explanation for why she had stood outside his house for three minutes and eighteen seconds pretending that she wasn't.

RECORDED INTERVIEW

Date: 25/03/2017

Location: Trinity Road Police Station, Bristol BS2 0NW

Conducted by: Officers from Somerset & Avon Police

POLICE: Ms Mullen. Could you tell us what you were wearing last night?

JM: Yes. I was wearing a blue jersey dress from Primark.

POLICE: And what sort of shoes?

JM: Boots. Red suede boots.

POLICE: Did they have a tassel?

JM: Yes. I think so. Yes. They do have tassels.

POLICE: Thank you. And were you wearing these clothes when Tom Fitzwilliam met you at the hotel?

JM: Yes.

POLICE: So, can you give us the approximate timings of this liaison at the Bristol Harbour Hotel?

JM: Yes. I got there at about seven o'clock, just after, and checked in using my own card. Then Tom arrived about half an hour later.

POLICE: And what happened then?

JM: Nothing. We just talked.

POLICE: In a £180-a-night hotel room?

JM: Yes.

POLICE: And then what?

JM: Tom left.

POLICE: And this was at what time?

JM: I suppose it was about seven forty-five.

POLICE: And after Tom Fitzwilliam left?

JM: I stayed in the room.

POLICE: And why did you stay in the room?

JM: Because . . . I don't know. Just to get my head together. I stayed for another ten minutes or so and then I left. I got a taxi home.

POLICE: And then what did you do?

JM: Nothing. Just watched TV with my husband. Went to bed.

POLICE: So you didn't knock at Tom's door at eight fifteen?

JM: [Silence.]

POLICE: Well, did you or didn't you?

JM: No. I didn't. I nearly did. I thought about it. But I changed my mind. I went home.

POLICE: Thank you, Ms Mullen. That will do for now.

12

17 February

At the end of the week, after a particularly rough day at work, Joey's manager Dawn said, 'Let's go to the pub.'

Joey almost said no, she was skint and smelly and wanted to lie in the bath for two hours drinking Baileys and staring at the ceiling. But then she thought about Alfie and the way he kept looking at her as though he was wondering what she was thinking and remembered that he wasn't working at the bar tonight and she decided that drinks with someone she barely knew and who, as far as she knew, had no interest in having a baby with her would be preferable.

They took along a boy from the Whackadoo café

called Krstyan, who sat with his thumbs on his phone, taking rhythmic mouthfuls from a pint of lager and barely registering their existence. A few moments later Dawn's wife Sam arrived with a friend of hers from work and then that friend's friend joined them and chairs were procured from other tables and added to the small table where they'd started and soon there was quite a group of them, all pretty much strangers but all the better for it. Joey dealt with the strangeness of it by necking two vodka and tonics, and then a pint that someone bought for her without asking. The music in the background was loud and metal-based, the clientele mostly students and ageing rockers. The bar and the floorboards were painted lead black and a band was setting up in the back room where two lurchers sat with their heads on their paws looking as though they'd seen it all before and just wanted to go home.

'I'm going to order some food at the bar,' Dawn shouted over the music. 'Do you want anything?'

Joey shook her head. 'No thanks, I'm good.' She was enjoying the sensation of alcohol hitting the empty pit of her stomach, the soft swirl of it, the redistribution of her psyche into more manageable chunks. She didn't want to mop it up. Sam turned to Joey as Dawn made her way to the bar. She was a sweet-faced girl with pink-tipped hair and a pink stud in her nose who looked not much older than eighteen.

'How are you getting on in the seventh circle of hell?'

'Oh,' said Joey. 'Whackadoo?'

Sam blinked. 'Indeed.'

'It's pretty grim,' she said. 'But Dawn's a great boss. And sometimes it's even a bit fun. How long have you two been married?'

'Just over a year,' said Sam. 'And don't worry. I'm older than I look. I'm actually twenty-seven. In case you thought I was some kind of child bride. How about you? Are you married?'

'Yes,' she said, still finding the concept strangely unlikely. 'Yes, I am.'

'How long for?'

'Oh, just a few months, actually.'

'Oh, bless. Have you known each other long?'

'Ha! No. Also just a few months. It was a bit of a whirlwind.'

'Wow,' said Sam, 'I wish you luck!'

And it was as she said this that Joey cast her gaze around the bar and her eye caught upon the back of the head of a man standing at the bar. A tall, well-built man with short dark hair, silver at the temples, wearing a rumpled work shirt with the sleeves pushed up. He turned, his large hands forming a triangle around three pints of beer, his mouth turned up into a wry smile and Joey froze.

It was Tom Fitzwilliam.

He carried the three pint glasses towards the room at the back of the pub and he rested them on a table in front of two men with beards and waistcoats, the ones with the lurchers. He pulled a chair across and joined them, his long legs slung effortlessly in front of him. His hand reached down briefly to touch the head of the dog nearest him. The younger of the two men said something and Tom Fitzwilliam tipped back his head and laughed.

Joey's phone fizzed on the table in front of her and she pulled her gaze from Tom Fitzwilliam to her screen. It was a text from Alfie: *When you coming home?*

She started to compose a reply but could think of nothing to say so turned off her phone. When she glanced up again Tom Fitzwilliam was looking in her direction. Her heart pulsed hard for a second and her breath caught in her throat until she realised that he wasn't looking at her, he was looking towards the door of the pub where two more men with beards had just arrived. All three men in the other room got to their feet to greet the new arrivals and more pints were bought and chairs moved about and dogs petted and hands shaken.

Dawn brought drinks back from the bar – a vodka and tonic for Joey. 'It's a double,' she said with a wink. 'You look like someone who wants to get blotto.'

Joey grinned and said, 'You're very observant.'

She drank it in the space of three minutes, during which Tom Fitzwilliam's beardy friends had necked their own drinks and headed towards the stage where they started to pick up musical instruments and twang on guitar strings. The one in the beanie hat sat astride a squat stool behind the drum kit and rubbed a pair of drumsticks together. Tom Fitzwilliam's friends were the band. The band, according to the decal on the bass drum, was called Lupine. How on earth, Joey wondered, did Tom Fitzwilliam, government-feted superhead, middle-aged dad, consummate suit-wearer, know a hairy rock band called Lupine?

'Oh God,' said Sam. She tipped her head in the direction of the back room. 'Not this lot again.'

Joey looked at her curiously.

'They were on last week as well. Bloody racket.'

Dawn looked up from her chicken pie and groaned. 'Oh God, yeah. I remember them. Cats being tortured.'

'Donkeys being murdered,' agreed Sam.

'With chainsaws,' added Dawn.

'Do you know them?' Joey asked.

'The band?' said Dawn. 'God no. But apparently

two of them are teachers at the local comp. Geography teachers playing rock stars on their night off.' She laughed. 'Bit tragic really.'

Joey went to the ladies' toilet. Like everything else in the pub, it was painted matt black and smelled of stale beer and old mops. Through the thin wall she could hear the *rat-a-tat* of snare drums, an isolated *thwang* of bass guitar. She took in her reflection in the mirror. She looked terrible. She searched her handbag frantically for lipstick, for a hairbrush, for a stub of black eyeliner. She fixed herself, fluffed out the dry bleached ends of her ponytail, studied herself again. She would do. She would have to.

Tom Fitzwilliam turned the corner towards the toilet just as she turned it going the other way. The narrow space was immediately filled with him, with the solidity of his existence. Joey's first instinct was to squeeze herself small against the wall and give him space in which to pass. But his eyes were already on her and he was half smiling and he said, 'Oh. I know you. I think . . . do I?'

She could have said, *No, I think you are mistaken*, grabbed her coat from her chair, said goodbye to everyone and left. But she did not. She stood straight and she returned his half-smile and she said, 'I have a funny feeling we might be neighbours. I think I've seen you in the bar at the Melville.'

He folded his arms across his stomach and he made a show of appraising her and then he said; 'Yes. I think that's it. I remember you. You knocked over the leaflets.'

She smiled and her stomach roiled. He'd seen her. He'd noticed her. This big, important, handsome man. 'That sounds like me,' she said.

'And if I'm not mistaken,' he continued, 'I've seen you in Melville Heights. Coming out of Jack and Rebecca Mullen's place.'

'Yes!' she said. 'Jack's my brother.'

'Wow. I had no idea! Not that I know Jack all that well. I've only spoken to him a handful of times.'

'He's great, isn't he?' she said. She often did this subconsciously, pre-empted the Jack-love.

'He seems like a great guy, yes.' But the way his eyes searched hers told her that he was more interested in talking about her than her perfect brother. 'Are you here with friends?'

'Yes. Well, sort of. I'm here with my boss and her wife and some other randoms.' Joey paused. 'Who are you here with?'

'Ah, well, rather bizarrely I'm here with the band.' He gestured behind them with his head. 'I'm a teacher,' he said, 'over at the Melville Academy—'

Joey nodded, disingenuously, as though she had absolutely no idea who he was.

'—and a couple of the teachers are in the band and they asked me along. So here I am. Not where you'd normally find me on a Friday night. But it seemed churlish to say no just because I'm old and I'd rather be at home watching *Narcos*.'

They both turned then as two women walked into the corridor and they held themselves tight against the wall to make room for them to pass. Tom's hand pressed briefly against Joey's leg and she thought, *I knew this was going to happen.*

They turned to each other and smiled.

'Well,' said Joey. 'It was nice to—' at the exact same moment that Tom said, 'Are you going to watch the band?'

She paused to manage her response. There was intent there in those innocuous words. There was an invitation. An invitation she should ignore.

'My friend says they sound like donkeys being murdered with chainsaws.'

Tom laughed. 'Oh dear,' he said conspiratorially. 'I did have my suspicions.' He smiled. 'Well, unlike me, you're free to leave. But if you do stay, come and say hello after and I'll introduce you to the band.'

She smiled and nodded.

'I'm Tom, by the way.' He offered her his hand.

'Hi Tom. I'm J—' She stopped, for a split second. 'Josephine.'

'Josephine,' he said. 'What a beautiful name.'

Joey thought, *I knew you'd like it.* 'Thank you,' she said.

'Lovely talking to you,' he said.

Joey took her seat next to Sam and pretended to be listening to their conversation while keeping half an eye on the toilets. When Tom reappeared, he caught her eye and smiled. She pulled her phone from her bag and she replied to Alfie's text.

Watching a band in town with Dawn and some friends. Be home in a couple of hours.

13

Freddie's mother was knitting something. He had never seen her kitting before.

'What is it?'

'It's a blanket,' she said. 'For the lady in the blue house. The pregnant lady. She's having a girl in May.'

Freddie could see now that the design on a computer printout on the table in front of his mother involved ducklings and bunny rabbits.

'Why would you knit something for someone you barely know?'

'Because . . .' She pulled at the cream yarn and grimaced. 'I have no idea. Just because.'

His mum was always trying new things. It was part

of her psyche. If it wasn't growing vegetables it was t'ai chi and if it wasn't t'ai chi it was learning to play the piano. She said she had a low boredom threshold. She said it was because she was never in one place long enough to get a job and that she hadn't been put on this earth to be a housewife and needed a focus. She'd been running a lot lately, two or three hours a day, but clearly that was no longer enough to keep her mind in one place. So, now it was knitting. She would have made a special trip today to a special shop to buy everything she needed. She would have watched a tutorial on You-Tube. She would have made a project of it.

He stared at the top of her head, the high shine of her light brown hair, combed through with an expensive oil and something approaching anger every morning in the mirror in her bedroom. She spent an hour at that mirror every day. She fussed her skin with giant pads of cotton wool and lotions and potions that cost fifty pounds a vial. She blended colours on to her eyelids that were the same colour as her skin so you couldn't see they were there. She wanted to look 'natural', she said, casting subtle aspersions against women who preferred to look fake. She took pride in her tiny frame, dressed it in tiny clothes, often from children's clothes shops. Her appearance was extraordinarily important to her; her image was her obsession. But even Freddie could see she had no idea what she was doing.

She wore the wrong sorts of heels with the wrong sorts of jeans and then she would get chatting to a woman somewhere – the school gates, the martial arts' centre, the *wool shop* – and Freddie would see it; he'd see her carefully applied veneer start to crackle and peel, watch his mother's eyes roaming over the woman in question, over her shoes, her skin, her fingernails, forensically taking in every iota of her sartorial presentation. And then the wrong heels would be replaced by trendy trainers. The red nails with short unpolished nails. The neat padded gilet with a loose-fitting parka. But they'd be the wrong trendy trainers. His mother would still be all wrong. And then they'd move to a new town and a new set of rules would apply according to the type of area and his mother would have to start trying to fit in all over again.

Not that she ever did. His mum, like him, had no friends. It was as if they could tell, he thought, they could tell she wasn't ever going to be one of them. She was always going to be trying, never just being.

Freddie sighed. 'When's Dad back?'

'Any time, I suppose. Depends how soon he can politely get away.'

Freddie couldn't get his head round the idea of his

dad in the Weaver's Arms watching a rock band. It was too bizarre to process. His dad was just so . . . well, *boring*.

At ten o'clock he yawned and got to his feet.

'You off to bed, darling?' his mum said absent-mindedly, her thin hands still worrying at the knitting needles, the blanket still no more than a thin strip of cream wool.

'Yes. I am.' He looked at her for a moment. 'Are you all right?' he asked. 'Is everything OK?'

'Yes,' she said brightly. 'Of course!'

He wanted to say something else but he couldn't find the words. He wanted to ask if she was happy. If she and Dad were OK. If they were always going to stay married. If she was glad she'd married Dad. If she was glad she'd had Freddie. If the noises he sometimes heard from their room at night were anything to be worried about.

Instead he dropped a kiss on to the top of her head. Being able to drop kisses on to the top of his mum's head was one of the best things about his recent growth spurt, finally over five foot three at which height he'd feared he might stick, and now approaching five foot seven. He would never be as tall as his dad, but at least he was taller than his mum.

Through his bedroom window he watched the

good people of Lower Melville comporting themselves on a Friday night. The trendy Thai restaurant was heaving as was the trendy pizza place. He watched people going in and out of the bar at the Melville. He trained his binoculars on to the bathroom window of Bess's flat and saw nothing; then he moved on to Jenna's road where all was quiet and still. He was about to draw the curtain and go back to his desk when he saw the headlights of a car bulging over the top of Melville Heights. As the lights reached the crown of the escarpment the car stopped and Freddie watched as first his father and then Red Boots stepped out of a taxi.

At first, he thought he must be mistaken. Why on earth would his father be in a taxi with Red Boots? Then as he watched he saw Red Boots push her face into his father's back and his father turn and put his arms around her shoulders and Red Boots looked like she was trying to kiss his father and then his father was pulling back and she was pushing forward and it was a strange dance that they were performing until finally his father put his arms around her waist and walked her firmly to the front door of the blue house.

Freddie opened his window a crack to let some sound in and just about heard the words sorry, pub, few too many, no problem and sleep tight.

Then he saw his father stand, for a moment or even longer, on the street outside the blue house, his hands in the pockets of his coat, his eyes on Red Boots's front door, before turning slowly and heading back towards his house.

14

18 February

'What was going on last night?' Freddie asked his dad the next morning.

His dad grimaced at him. He was wearing his dressing gown and he smelled odd, that sugary-yeasty smell of middle-aged man pickled in clammy bedsheets.

'What?'

Freddie pulled a croissant from a packet on the counter. 'You and that woman.'

His dad stopped buttering his toast for a second, then continued. 'Oh. Josephine,' he said, through a pretty theatrical yawn that was fooling no one, least of all Freddie. 'She was at the same gig as me last night.

Turns out she lives two doors down.' He yawned loudly again. 'She was a bit the worse for wear so I got her home in a taxi.'

'Oh, Dad. You're such a thoroughly good guy, not just saving schools but now rescuing damsels in distress too!' Freddie couldn't help himself sometimes. His dad was just so fucking perfect. Or at least that was the overriding narrative. Amazing Tom Fitzwilliam. Isn't he handsome? Isn't he clever? Isn't he charming? Isn't he tall? Hasn't he got an enormously huge dick? Well, no one had ever actually said that, but he did. Freddie had seen it.

His mum subscribed to this narrative too. She looked amazed and grateful every time Dad walked in through the door at the end of the day, took his hand when they were out in public to show the world that he was hers. So in the absence of any peripheral checks and measures in the form of siblings, Freddie kind of felt it was his duty to keep his dad in his place, to remind him that he was not the be-all and the end-all. His dad took it in good grace. He did seem to like Freddie. But possibly that was because he didn't realise quite how deep the rivers of Freddie's antipathy sometimes ran.

His dad ignored Freddie's sarcasm and flicked the switch on the coffee filter. Soon the kitchen was dark with the smell of warm coffee. His dad stood with his hands in the pockets of his dressing gown and stared through the French windows towards the end of the garden. The hair on the back of his head was matted and flat where he'd slept on it.

'What's she like?'

'Who?'

'The damsel. The one you rescued from being raped in an illegal minicab?'

There was a prolonged silence and Freddie wasn't sure if his dad had heard him or not. But then he turned slowly and leaned against the counter. 'She's nice.'

'Nice?'

'Yes. Perfectly nice. I didn't really talk to her. We were watching the band. And then it became apparent that she was horribly drunk so I got us a taxi. She slept most of the way back.'

'She looked like she wanted you to kiss her.'

'What?'

'When you got out the cab. She looked like she was trying to kiss you on the mouth.'

His dad grimaced. 'Er, no. I sincerely doubt that.'

Freddie offered him a sardonic lift of his eyebrow and said no more. He knew what he'd seen. Yet another tragic woman succumbing to the inordinate charms of his father. Yet another woman allowing herself to be dazzled by the glittering illusion of a gold coin at the bottom of a well.

Nicola walked in damp-haired, scrubbed-faced, shower-fresh after her early-morning run. 'What do you sincerely doubt?' she asked.

'Nothing,' said his dad, sending Freddie a warning glance across the kitchen. His mum got really jealous sometimes. 'How was your run?'

'It was superb,' she said, pulling a mug off a shelf and pouring herself a coffee from the filter. 'It's beautiful out. We should do something.'

Freddie would have much preferred to do nothing at the weekend. The idea of doing *something*, with its undertones of brisk walks and silent art galleries and awkward lunches in smart restaurants, filled him with sick dread.

'I've got loads of homework,' he said. 'I need to stay at home today.'

His mum pulled a sad pouty face. 'Maybe you and I should do something?' She gripped his dad's arm and looked up at him hopefully. 'Pub lunch?'

His father patted her hand and smiled down at her. 'Yes,' he said. 'A pub lunch sounds just the ticket.'

Freddie saw pure joy bloom across his mum's face and then he thought of the taxi pulling up last night, of

Red Boots grabbing his father and the stern look on his face as he bundled her towards her front door. He thought of all the other times, the other women and girls who'd looked at his dad just a little too fondly or held his arm for a little too long. He thought of the smell of old beer coming off him this morning, the sour smell of secrets and lies.

He nodded just once towards his father, knowingly, and saw him flinch.

15

20 February

Jenna pulled the zip round her suitcase and hoisted it on to its feet. It weighed a ton: make-up brushes and hairbrushes and palettes of petrol-hued shadows and bottles of fixers and primers and toners. Barely any clothes really. Just make-up.

Year eleven were going on a four-night trip to Seville. The coach to the airport was due outside the Academy at 5.45 a.m. It was now just after five and the sky was still lit with night stars and the pearlescent sheen of the moon. Jenna peered into her mother's bedroom and caught the outline of her sleeping body and the whisper of her night-time breath. She would not wake her. Her mother was like a child – much easier to manage when she was sleeping. She tucked a packet of Nature Valley cereal bars into her rucksack, double checked inside the front pocket for the solid edges of her passport, took it out, double-checked that it was hers, slid it back in, smeared on some lip balm and silently left the house.

Bess stood on the corner with a battered metal suitcase at her feet, her hands tucked inside the sleeves of her blue Melville Academy hoodie, her bare legs glowing blue white in the early dawn. She yawned widely as Jenna approached.

'Morning,' said Jenna.

Bess groaned and lifted her case. It had no wheels and she had to carry it with both hands. It banged up against her shins as she walked. 'International travel sucks,' she said.

'We haven't even got on the coach yet.'

'Yeah. Exactly.'

'Would you rather be going to school today?'

'Yes,' said Bess. 'Actually. I really would.'

Jenna smiled wryly. She knew that Bess would be the one at the back of the coach waving at lorry drivers in a few minutes.

Outside school, the coach rumbled and the pavement filled slowly with sleep-glazed teenagers. Bess kicked her in the shin and said, 'Oh God. Look!'

When she turned she saw Mr Fitzwilliam striding towards them, a rucksack slung over his shoulder. He was wearing a dark hooded jacket and jeans.

'*Buenos días*, everyone,' he called. 'Señor Delgado's wife has gone into early labour and I'm the only other fluent Spanish speaker in the school so I've been dragged from my lovely warm cosy bed to accompany you all to Seville – you'll no doubt be *delighted* to hear.'

Jenna felt Bess's bony elbow between her ribs and slapped her away. She felt Bess's hot breath in her ear. 'Oh. My Fucking. *God*.'

Jenna sighed.

'Oh my fucking *God*,' Bess repeated. 'I'm going to die. I swear. I'm dying right now. Literally. I'm dead.'

'Shush,' said Jenna. 'He's only over there.'

'Don't care. Just . . . I just . . .'

'Please don't make a twat of yourself,' said Jenna. 'Promise me.'

Bess looked at her aghast. 'God, Jen – what do you take me for?'

Jenna turned towards the village, the soft glow of the street lights just visible from where they stood. She thought of her mother, folded warm within her duvet. She imagined her awaking and remembering that Jenna had gone. She pictured her rising from her warm bed and forgetting to eat breakfast in her compulsion to check the house for signs of *them*, the unknown, unwieldy gang who made it their lives' work to stalk, harass and torment her, who came into her home nightly to displace her ornaments, untwist her light-bulbs, drill small holes into her walls and scratch tiny hieroglyphics into her work surfaces. She would then retire to her computer to log all the nightly modifica-tions before signing in to one of the many chat rooms she frequented with other 'victims' of so-called gang-stalking to give credibility to each other's madness.

Jenna had not left her mother alone since she got properly ill, not for longer than the occasional sleep-over. Her dad had persuaded her to go on the trip; he'd paid for it and said he'd check in on her mum daily, that she must go and enjoy herself and not look back. Jenna strongly suspected that her dad would not check in on her every day; it was a ninety-minute round trip from his house in Weston-super-Mare where he ran a very busy ironmongery virtually single-handedly as well as looking after Jenna's little brother, Ethan. But now as she stowed her suitcase in the belly of the coach and took her seat next to Bess, it was far too late to worry about it all.

The coach pulled away and Melville faded to a tiny blurred point on the horizon and Jenna allowed herself a moment of excitement at the prospect of five days of sanity. Then she turned to share a smile with Bess and saw her staring dementedly at the back of Mr Fitzwilliam's head.

16

When Freddie awoke that Monday morning he could tell immediately that something was different. He'd heard the phone ringing late last night, heard cupboards being opened and closed, voices when there weren't normally voices.

'Daddy had to go to Spain,' said his mum, running water into the spout of the kettle. 'School trip. The Spanish teacher's wife went into early labour last night. She's only thirty weeks along – very scary.'

'Why him?' he said. 'Surely he's too *important* to go on school trips.'

'Daddy was the only other teacher at the school who can speak Spanish.'

'Dad can't speak *Spanish*,' he muttered incredulously.

'Well, he can speak enough to get by.'

Freddie grunted. This was exactly the sort of thing his dad loved. Spending quality time with his students. *Getting to know them.* He thrived on the intimacy. He would have jumped at this opportunity.

'When's he coming back?'

'Friday.'

He nodded but felt quietly anxious. Freddie didn't like changes in routine; he didn't like it when unscheduled things happened. He didn't like the way little holes opened up in the weft of his existence and let other, unexpected things in.

He walked the slow way to school so that he could pass by Whackadoo just as it opened its doors. He bought himself a bottle of mineral water and sat on a bench across the street to watch for Red Boots. Or Joey. Or Josephine. Or whatever the hell she was really called. He sat his phone on his lap, the video button just under his thumb and he waited. At eight fifty-five the 218 bus pulled up and the doors hissed open. There she was. He pressed the record button and filmed her as she half ran towards the play centre. Her blond hair was pulled back into a ponytail and she was frowning into her phone. She forced it into her rucksack as she approached the doors, pressed the bell and then stood with her hand in her pockets until a large woman with very short hair and lots of keys hanging from her belt came to let her in.

Freddie replayed the video and zoomed in on to Joey's face. She looked puffy and blotchy. She looked like she'd been crying. He wondered if it had something to do with Friday night, if it had something to do with his father.

17

'Hi, Mum!' Joey pulled a cloth from her coat pocket and used it to clear away the winter dust that had collected on her mother's gravestone. The flowers she'd left on the second day of the year were still there as well as another small posy; 50p-a-bunch daffodils from Asda that her dad would have brought.

Joey hadn't realised that her dad visited so frequently. Her dad was not one for grand gestures or shows of emotion. He'd maintained a cool detachment in the days and months after Mum had died. They'd been talking about splitting up for a year or so before the accident. Neither of them had been happy. But on the day of the accident they'd been in a good place.

They'd been up to see Jack and Rebecca's house renovations. Afterwards Jack had taken them for lunch at the Melville. They'd had wine; Mum and Dad had shared a sticky toffee pudding. It had been a good day. Jack had said he thought maybe they wouldn't split up after all. And then later that day Mum had been halfway to the shops at the bottom of the road to buy a lottery ticket when a ninety-year-old man called Roger Davies mounted the kerb in his Ford Fiesta and pinned her to a letter box. She'd died ten days later.

Dad didn't talk about it much. Jack had tried to set him up with a grief therapist. He'd gone to one appointment and never returned. He'd cleared Mum's stuff out within a week of her death, rearranged things over the hollows so you'd never know it had been there. And, to the absolute horror of both Joey and Jack, he already had a girlfriend. Her name was Sue and Jack was convinced that she had been in the picture long before their mother's death. The day their father had told them about Sue had been one of the worst that she could remember and neither she nor Jack had seen their father since.

But here, with these cheap but carefully placed daffodils, was proof that he hadn't moved on entirely. Joey tried to picture her father here. She tried to imagine what he did, if he talked to her, how long he stayed. She wondered if he cried. She hoped that he did.

'So. Lots has happened since I last saw you. I've got a job. It's a bit of a classic Joey job. As in, you know, *crap*. But at least I'm earning some money. Alfie's still at the bar in town but he's trying to get some more work as a painter and decorator. So, we're kind of getting there. But . . .' She paused and looked briefly over her shoulder, as though someone she knew might be hanging around in a cemetery on a Monday afternoon. 'I've done something really bad. Like, really, really, really bad. Worse than anything I've done before and I know I've done a lot of bad things. I'm not even sure I can tell you what it was because you'll disown me. Actually, I'm not going to tell you, because even thinking about it makes me want to throw up.' She sighed and looked down at her fingernails, pulled at a loose tag of skin. 'I really thought that I was growing up at last, Mum. I really thought that getting married and moving back to Bristol was going to be the start of the big new grown-up me. But if anything, I'm regressing. Because that's the problem, isn't it, that's what I'm starting to realise. I'm still me, Mum, wherever I go in the world, I'm still just me. Joey the fuck-up. Joey the pain. And I wish you were here because I know that was always enough for you. And I'm not sure it's enough for anyone else.

'Anyway.' She pulled herself to standing. 'I'm sorry

to come here and just be all *me me me*. Nothing new there though, I suppose. I love you, Mum. I love you so much. I'll come again soon and hopefully by then I'll have sorted out my life. Bye, Mum. Sleep tight.'

Joey turned at the sound of Alfie bursting into the bedroom.

'I've got a painting job!'

'Huh?'

'Just now. Like, literally! The woman two doors down. She saw me in my overalls and she asked if I was a decorator and I said yes and she said can you decorate my living room and my kitchen.'

'What woman two doors down?'

'Here.' He felt in the pockets of his overall and pulled out a card. ' "Nicola Fitzwilliam",' he read. 'She lives there.' He pointed. 'In the yellow house.'

The very sound of the word *Fitzwilliam* on Alfie's tongue made her shiver.

'Did you go in?'

'No. We just chatted on the street.'

'And literally, she just literally asked you to paint her house? Just like that?'

'Yeah! It was so cool! I'm going over later to cost the job for her.'

'You're going to her house?'

'Yeah! Gonna jump in the shower and head over. Wanna come with?'

All the blood in Joey's body rushed to her head. She pictured Tom's face when he saw her standing in his hallway. For a moment she found it hard to breathe properly. 'No.'

He looked at her curiously. 'You OK? I thought you'd be really happy.'

She cupped her hand over her temple. 'Sorry. I'm just a bit headachy. Long day. Kids. You know.' She wanted to jump to her feet, to throw herself at big, handsome Alfie and hug him and tell him she was proud and delighted. But fear kept her anchored to the spot. She glanced at him and said, 'I am really happy, Alf. I really am. It's brilliant.'

This seemed to satisfy him and he beamed at her. 'I'm getting there at last,' he said. 'Finally getting there. Before too long we'll have a place of our own. And then . . .' His smile faded and he didn't finish the sentence. She knew exactly what he'd been about to say.

She watched him peeling off his clothes, leaving them snaking across the floorboards in his wake. She let her eyes linger on his buttocks for a brief moment before he disappeared into the en suite. Such remarkable buttocks. Why would a woman with access to such a pair of buttocks ever wish to place their hands upon any other? Why would a woman married to the nicest man in Bristol want to waste even a moment thinking about Tom Fitzwilliam? What was the matter with her?

Shouldn't the memory of the look of utter dismay on Tom Fitzwilliam's face as he pulled her hands away from his body outside the Weaver's Arms have been enough to kill off her fixation?

Shouldn't the thought of him struggling to find the words to express his shock and displeasure – *Christ, God, no! I mean, no! You're gorgeous! You're really gorgeous! But you're married! I'm married. And I would never. I would just never. God!* – have stopped her in her tracks?

Technically speaking, Joey had assaulted him. If he'd wanted to report her to the police, he would have been completely within his rights.

But there'd been a moment, when her hand had first gone between his legs: his whole body had lurched towards hers; he'd tipped his head back at the feel of her fingers going to the back of his neck, he'd groaned and for a short moment his lips had met hers. That had happened. As drunk as she'd been, as pumped full of adrenaline and hormones and lust, she knew that had definitely happened. And it was that, that single, gossamer-thin element of time, that stopped her from wanting to kill herself out of pure humiliation.

She heard the shower start running, the shower

door open and then close. She looked at Alfie's clothes on the floor: the paint-splattered overalls, the ripped T-shirt, the old boxers, the small rumpled socks. In the corner of the mirror she could just make out the blurred pinkness of Alfie's naked body in the shower.

Her gut ached with guilt and self-hatred.

'You sure you don't want to come with me?' he asked a moment later, towel-drying his hair. 'Keep me company?'

He was feeling shy, Joey realised, self-conscious about going into a posh lady's house on his own to discuss business.

'I'm not your mum, Alfie,' she said, somewhat harshly. 'You don't need me to hold your hand.'

She winced when she saw the flash of hurt pass across his face. 'Yeah,' he said, rallying. 'Fair enough.' He pulled on clean jeans and a button-down shirt. Then he rifled around the shelves beside the bed looking for a notepad. Joey found him a pencil while he tied his shoelaces. She tucked it into the top pocket of his shirt and she straightened his collar. 'You look very nice,' she said. 'Don't undersell yourself. Remember: this is Melville Heights. People expect to pay through the nose for things. So if you quote anything less than through the nose she'll definitely go for it.'

He checked his phone for the photos he'd taken of

his mum's kitchen and the ones of her neighbour's home office that he was currently working on. 'I should get a better camera,' he said. 'These look shit.'

'They look fine,' Joey said. 'They show what a good job you can do and that's all that matters.'

She waited a moment after he left the room and then went to the landing where she watched through the window as he walked towards the Fitzwilliams' house. Tom's car was parked outside. He must be at home. She felt a wave of nausea rising through her at the thought of Tom and Alfie coming face-to-face.

And then she jumped away from the window as she saw down below, in the undergrowth across the road, a pair of eyes. She approached the window again. Yes, there was someone down there. Crouched down and staring at the front door of Tom's house. It was a woman, hard to make out her age in the dark. Blondish hair. Small build. Joey saw her take a mobile phone from her bag and take pictures with it.

'Jack!' she called over the banister. 'Jack! Are you there?'

Her brother appeared in the hallway a floor down. He had a mouth full of food and frowned at her. 'What?' he mumbled though his dinner.

'Look outside. Quickly. Across the street. Look – behind the red car.'

He frowned again, opened the front door and then looked back at her.

'Just look!' she said. 'There's someone there! Crouching!'

He sighed and disappeared through the front door. Joey watched from the landing window. At the sound of his footsteps the woman in the undergrowth started slightly and hid herself further behind the red car. Joey knocked on the glass. The woman looked up and for a moment their eyes met. She was in her forties, Joey could see now, and pretty in the way of a fading film star. Joey recognised her from somewhere; she had definitely seen her before.

'There's nothing there,' her brother called up the stairs.

She heard the front door close again and then she saw the small blonde woman run.

'She's gone,' she said, walking down the stairs towards Jack. 'She ran away when she heard you.'

She sat herself on the bottom step and cupped her face in her hands. She looked up at Jack. 'She was a blonde woman,' she said. 'Middle-aged. She was watching Alfie. Taking pictures of Tom Fitzwilliam's house.'

Jack yawned and sat down next to her. 'Ah, yeah. I think I know the one you mean. She lives in the village. She's a bit odd. I've seen her down there, staring at people, making notes in a book, tiny little marks. Mental health issues, I'd say.'

'I wonder what she's doing up here then,' Joey said. 'I wonder what she wants with Tom Fitzwilliam.'

'Ah,' said Jack, getting to his feet and stretching his body. '*Everyone* wants a bit of Tom Fitzwilliam.'

She looked up at him, wide-eyed. 'What does that mean?'

'Nothing much. Just, he's one of those guys, isn't he? *Women want him. Men want to be him.*' He said this in the style of an American voiceover.

'Do you want to be him?' she asked.

'No,' said Jack. 'Not really. But I can see why he might send some more, you know, *vulnerable* people a bit over the edge. He's very charismatic. Very attractive. And he has this charm about him. Dashing, almost. As if he could save you from yourself.'

He walked backwards away from her, towards the kitchen door. 'Going to finish my dinner,' he said. 'Fancy joining me?'

'I'm OK,' she said. 'I'm going to head upstairs.'

'Sure?'

She nodded and smiled and sat on the step for a moment longer while her brother's words echoed in her head.

Vulnerable people.

She thought of the woman in the undergrowth. Then she thought of her own pathetic infatuation and it occurred to her that maybe they were not so different after all.

RECORDED INTERVIEW

Date: 25/03/2017
Location: Trinity Road Police Station, Bristol BS2 0NW
Conducted by: Officers from Somerset & Avon Police

POLICE: Your full name please, for the recording.

DP: Dawn Michelle Pettifer.

POLICE: Thank you. And your full address.

DP: 21 Bath Place, Bristol BS11.

POLICE: Thank you. And can you tell me what you told our officer earlier today.

DP: Yes. But can I first say that I think Joey Mullen is an incredible human being. I'm massively fond of her. She works really hard and she's great with the kids, and yeah. Just an awesome person.

POLICE: Thank you, Ms Pettifer.

DP: It's just – and maybe it's nothing, you know, completely a red herring, but a couple of weeks ago I went out for a beer with Joey after work and she told me she was obsessed with Tom Fitzwilliam. She said . . . her obsession was driving her insane.

POLICE: She used that word? Insane?

DP: Yes. She did. She said that her obsession was killing her.

POLICE: Great. Thank you. And yesterday? At work? How did Joey seem?

DP: Edgy.

POLICE: Edgy?

DP: Yes. Edgy. Not herself. When she left I was worried about her.

POLICE: And why were you worried about her?

DP: I don't know. She looked scared. She looked . . . agitated.

POLICE: In your opinion, Ms Pettifer, did Joey Mullen's demeanour on Friday evening seem 'agitated' enough for her to be capable of an act of gruesome violence?

DP: Well, you know, anyone can be capable of anything, can't they, under the right circumstances. You read about it all the time. So yeah, maybe she was.

18

20 February

The hotel in Seville was a shithole. Jenna had known not to expect much for £330 a head for the whole trip, but seriously – five of them had been squashed into a room meant for three, with two camp beds stuck in the corner so there was no room even to walk around the room and they'd had to put their suitcases on the balcony. The bathroom was minging. The bed sheets had rips in them and smelled like they'd been boil-washed in old dishwater. Bess had even found a rolled-up panty liner tucked into the U-bend behind the toilet.

'I wanna go home,' she said now, her small body curled around a pillow. 'I wanna go where I have like a *floor with a carpet*, and a *nice comfortable bed*, and a lovely big bathroom with no stains and no used panty liners. You know . . .' She sat up straight. 'I bet if we showed Mr Fitzwilliam our room he'd get un upgrade for us. I bet he would.'

There was a knock at the door then and Lottie opened it up to a load of lads all peering over each other to get a look into the girls' room. They were the alpha girls in year eleven, Jenna knew that much. She, Bess, Lottie, Tiana and Ruby. They weren't like a clique or anything, just five girls who all got along and who were all quite good-looking.

'God, your room sucks,' said one of the lads.

'I know, right!' said Bess. 'What's yours like?'

'Ours is cool. We've got, like, a sitting area.'

'Yeah, it's a suite.'

'Oh my God!' Bess turned to each girl in turn, her mouth hanging ajar. 'They've got a fucking suite! That's it.' She jumped to her feet. 'I'm going to tell Mr Fitzwilliam.' She looked at Jenna. 'Come with?'

Jenna nodded. She put her trainers back on and followed Bess down the dingy corridor towards the rooms at the end where the teachers were staying.

Mr Fitzwilliam opened the door to his room looking as crisp and fresh as he had at five thirty that morning. 'Ladies,' he said, 'what can I do for you?'

'It's our room, sir,' said Bess. 'It's really bad. I'm not sure we can stay in it, I'm not gonna lie.'

She had her fists at her mouth and was talking in a voice about 20 per cent higher than her usual pitch.

Mr Fitzwilliam moved his balance from one foot to the other, folded his arms across his waist and looked down at Bess. 'What's wrong with it?'

'It's got, like, two extra beds in it. Really rubbish camp beds. And there's five of us and we're all squashed in and there's nowhere to put our suitcases. They're on the balcony, sir.'

Mr Fitzwilliam nodded. To Jenna's surprise he appeared to be taking her concerns seriously.

'And Connor Mates just told us that they've got a suite. With, like, seating and stuff. And it's not fair, sir. I mean, we all paid the same, didn't we?'

He let his arms drop to his sides and he said, 'OK, then, let's have a look at this room. Lead the way.'

Bess threw Jenna a triumphant look. Jenna shrugged.

The other girls all sat up straight when they saw Mr Fitzwilliam at the door. 'Well, ladies,' he said, after scanning the room with his eyes for a moment, 'I have to agree. This is clearly unacceptable. Leave it with me, I'm going to talk to reception, see what we can sort out for you. I will be right back.' He smiled and touched his temple with his fingers, in a kind of military salute.

After he'd gone all five girls looked at each other in a kind of shocked silence before bursting into embarrassed laughter.

'Oh my God,' said Lottie. 'He's so cool.'

'I know, right,' agreed Tiana. 'If that had been, like, any other teacher they'd have just told us to quit whining.'

'Yeah, right?' said Lottie.

'You can all fuck off,' said Bess. 'He's mine.'

'Ew,' said Ruby, 'but he's really old.'

'He's not old,' Bess replied. 'He's mature. Like wine. Like cheese. I love him. I actually love him.'

Jenna nodded. 'She actually does,' she said.

Half an hour later she and Bess had a room of their own. It was a large suite with a big double bed, a sofa, a view over the park opposite and two sinks in the bathroom. The management had also sent up a bowl of fruit by way of apology. They sat now, cross-legged on the sofa, eating bloomy Spanish grapes as though they were chocolate truffles and laughing at their good fortune.

'Cheers,' said Bess, knocking her complimentary plastic bottle of water against Jenna's. 'To Mr Fitzwilliam. A god amongst men.'

They had half an hour in their rooms before they were to meet up in the lobby to head out for what Mr Phipp had described as 'a sandwich and some culture'. The itinerary that Jenna had remembered to slip into her rucksack that morning said they were going to the Plaza de España where they would be perusing food stalls and ordering and paying for their own lunches from vendors in Spanish, before having a wander round and looking at some bridges. The weather was nice; not like Spain in the summer, when Jenna had been to Spain before, but way better than Bristol where it had been five degrees and raining yesterday.

She pulled her make-up bags out of her suitcase and arranged them on the side of her sink in the en suite. She looked tired and grey in the tile-framed mirror.

'What do you reckon his wife's like?' Bess called from the bedroom.

Jenna rolled her eyes. 'Oh, you know, she's probably really fit and hot and young.'

'Yeah,' said Bess. 'Yeah. I bet she is.'

'With really huge breasts. And they're probably having sex like *all the time*,' she continued, applying an extra layer of mascara. 'Like porn stars.'

'Oh God, Jen. Stop it.'

She paused to examine her refreshed visage, before pulling a tube of plumping lip gloss from her case and applying it. 'I'm only joking,' she said. 'I've seen his wife. She's not all that.'

Bess appeared in the reflection in the mirror. 'Is she young?'

'Yeah. Youngish. Younger than him. Always wearing running gear and a baseball cap.'

'Hm,' Bess replied, 'sounds like every middle-aged woman in Melville.'

Jenna's phone popped. She glanced at it. A text message from her mum.

Did you move the recycling bin this morning? It's facing the wrong way!!

She closed her eyes. She had not touched the recycling bin this morning. It was pitch black when she left the house, she hadn't even *seen* the recycling bin.

Yes, she typed back, *I did move it.*

Why?

There was a cat stuck behind it.

What cat???

Christ, now even the local cats were in on it.

I don't know. Just a black one. Stop worrying about it.

Did you see that weird mark in the butter? It looked like a swastika. Look.

Jenna's shoulders dropped. A second later her phone popped again. There was a photo of the butter. In the top of the butter was the mark she'd left there last night with a knife when she'd buttered a crumpet. It looked nothing like a swastika.

I had a crumpet last night. That was me.

Good, her mum replied. Then: *Remind me when you're coming home again?*

Friday afternoon.

And remind me where you are?

I'm in Seville.

That's nice. I love you.

I love you too mum.

She switched off her phone and stared at its dead screen for a moment. Then there was a knock at the door and Bess went to open it and there was Mr Fitzwilliam, wolfish and fresh in a navy hoodie and chinos.

'Are we happy, ladies?' he said, taking in the room quickly with his eyes.

'Oh yes,' said Bess. 'Thank you so much, Mr Fitzwilliam. We are, like, so so grateful. And you are totally the best.'

He smiled down at her. 'Well, that's very nice of you to say, Bess. But I was just doing what needed to be done. And I'm very pleased with the outcome. I will see you both in the lobby in . . .' He looked at his wrist, at an old-fashioned steel-faced watch with a red and yellow striped canvas strap. 'Six and a half minutes!'

'See you, Mr Fitzwilliam!' said Bess, closing the door behind him, then collapsing against it with her hands to her mouth and saying, 'Oh my God, he knows my name. Mr Fitzwilliam knows my name.'

'He knows everyone's name, Bess.'

'Yeah, I know – but he *said* it!'

But Jenna wasn't really engaged with her friend because something was playing on her mind. Something to do with Mr Fitzwilliam's watch. The watch with the yellow and red strap. Because she'd seen it before, somewhere else, when she was young.

And then it came to her: the Lake District.

When she was ten.

When Ethan was six.

When her mum was sane and her parents were together. And they'd stayed at a beautiful B & B with four-poster beds and the owner had had six basset hounds who all trundled together around the grounds. It was thirty degrees. One of the hottest days of the year. They'd been on a sightseeing coach trip and had stopped for ice creams at the side of a lake when a woman had appeared from nowhere, screaming. She'd been wearing a vest top and linen shorts, bright pink flip flops.

You, she'd been shouting. *You!*

Then a man had appeared from somewhere behind them, a tall, commanding man. He was part of their tour group, with a younger wife and a small son. He'd approached the screaming woman and he'd put his hands against her bare arms and she'd screamed *You! You! How could you!* And the man had talked to her softly and sternly and then he'd walked her firmly away from the staring hordes. And he was wearing that watch. She'd noticed it because it matched his striped shirt. And it *was* him. Mr Fitzwilliam *was* the man that her mum kept saying he was.

They'd never found out why the woman was screaming at him. They never worked out what had happened next. It had just remained as a kind of pale stain on their holiday, a tiny, unsettling sentence without a full stop. Remember that man, they would say for days and weeks afterwards. And the woman screaming at him? Hitting him? Remember? I wonder what that was all about . . .

And for so long Jenna had assumed that her mum's belief that her new head teacher was the man by the lake was simply part of her mum's madness. Her mum was always seeing people she was convinced she'd seen before. Sometimes they'd be taller and she'd say they were wearing lifts in their shoes, or blonder and she'd say they'd dyed their hair, or younger and she'd say they'd had a facelift. They didn't have to much resemble the person she was convinced they were. There was no rhyme or reason to her delusion.

But this time her mum was right.

They had seen Tom Fitzwilliam before.

He'd been the man by the lake, the man the woman was shouting at.

Jenna felt a shiver of unease run down her spine.

19

Freddie was sitting at the top of the stairs. The doorbell had just rung and he'd heard a man's voice he didn't recognise. He pitched backwards when he saw who it was. For a moment his heart began to race. It was the big guy with the red hair and the tattoos: Red Boots's husband. What on earth was he doing here? Had he somehow discovered that Freddie had been secretly filming his wife?

But as he listened he could hear that the big guy was being friendly. There was laughter. His mother said, 'Come in, come in. Can I get you a cup of tea?' And the big guy said, 'No, thank you, I'm fine.' He was wearing nice shoes which he spent an inordinate amount of time wiping back and forth across their tatty doormat, like a tradesman. Freddie tiptoed to the next landing and listened to their voices coming from the kitchen. He caught the gist of the conversation. The big guy was going to be decorating their living rooms and the kitchen. 'Just normal colours,' he heard his mother say. 'Off-whites probably.'

'Any wallpapering?'

'Oh no. No. I don't think so. I like plain walls.'

Freddie went back to his room and waited till he heard the front door opening and closing, his mother saying, 'Thank you so much! We'll be in touch!' before coming downstairs and saying, 'What was he doing here?'

'I saw him when I was coming back from my run,' his mother said. 'He was in paint-spattered overalls and I just thought, well, we seem to have a decorator on our doorstep and I'd been thinking about finding one because this house . . .' She looked around it despairingly. 'Well, you know, it's not exactly to our taste, is it?'

Freddie quite liked this house. It had dark blue walls and bits of mahogany panelling, strips of dark floral wallpaper here and there. It was scruffy but it had a bit of character, unlike most of the houses they'd lived in over the years.

'I don't want my room doing,' he said. 'I like my room.'

'Yes, well, we can't agree to anything until I've had a quote back from him. And obviously I'll have to speak to your father.'

Freddie sat down on the settle in the hallway. 'What was he like?'

'Who? The painter?'

'Don't you even know his name?'

'I didn't ask! Hold on . . .' She pulled a card from the console table. 'Here. Alfie Butter. Ha! What a funny name!' She put the card back on the console. 'He was very nice. But young. You know? Not much upstairs.'

She glanced at him then as if she'd just remembered something important. 'Are you hungry?' she said. 'What would you like?'

'What is there?'

It was a trick question. She wouldn't have been shopping. She only shopped when Dad was home. Dad was her first priority from the moment she woke up to the moment she went to bed.

'Gosh. Not much. There's pasta? Or some nice bread. I could do you eggs on toast?'

Eggs on toast was his dad's favourite dinner. He nodded. There was no point holding out for anything better.

After tea, which he ate on his own while his mum had a shower and got changed, he went back to his room. He'd taken the long route home from school today, past St Mildred's, the private girls' school three roads down, to check out Romola Brook, the new girl everyone at his school was talking about.

He'd got some shots of her chatting with a guy from their sixth form. He'd gone in really close, got her pulling her hair from her face, touching her lips every now and then with her fingertips, her eyes staring at the pavement. Then he'd followed her home. She lived in a tiny modern house in a new-build mews just outside the city. It had a Buddha out front and a longhaired chihuahua waiting for her in the front window. He'd photographed her letting herself in and bending down to greet the tiny dog.

Now he loaded the photos and the film footage on to his PC and started to edit them. He pressed save to secure the changes he'd made to the photos and then he went to his security log, as he did every evening, to make sure that nothing had been compromised. His heartbeat staccatoed for a second.

There had been five invalid login attempts.

Breathlessly, he clicked on Quick Access to see if files had been opened and then sat back heavily against the back of his chair, all the air leaving his lungs in one bolt.

JT1.jpg. JT2.jpg. JT3.jpg. JT&BR1.jpg. JT&BR2.jpg. JT4.jpg.

These were his early photos of Jenna Tripp and Bess Ridley. He hadn't looked at them in ages. He had not opened these files. Someone else had. And Freddie had no idea who it was.

20

Bess and Jenna laughed together as they tried to keep their footing on the cobbled streets in the stupid heeled boots they'd both packed for the trip. They'd bought them in Primark, the week before, especially for Seville. The itinerary had specifically stated that footwear should be 'comfortable and practical'. They had paid no heed.

They were heading for dinner in the old town. The night was moon-bright and balmy and the group were in high spirits, loud, shouting over each other, laughing too hard, just about staying the right side of out of control. In the restaurant they were split up over four huge tables in a private room at the back. Each table was assigned a teacher. Jenna felt Bess's boot connect with her shin when Mr Fitzwilliam came and sat down with them.

'Well,' he said, 'lucky group B. Looks like you're stuck with me.'

Huge menus with laminated pages were passed around. Mr Fitzwilliam handed one to Jenna with a smile. 'Well, I don't know about you lot,' he said, 'but I am starving.'

'Didn't you have something nice at lunch, sir?' said a boy called Ollie.

'I did, thank you, Ollie. I had some excellent *albóndigas*. Can anyone tell me what *albóndigas* are?'

'Meatballs!' someone shouted across the table.

'Yes. Exactly. I had meatballs. And if I recall rightly, Thomas here,' he patted Thomas' shoulder, 'had a delicious-looking *bocadillo de tortilla*. Anyone know what that is?'

'A crisp sandwich!'

'No,' he replied. 'Not crisps. That's a different sort of tortilla. Anyone else?'

'Omelette sandwich?' suggested Jenna.

'Yes. An omelette sandwich. Does anyone know what goes into a Spanish omelette?'

Hands went up.

'Eggs!' said someone.

'Potatoes!' said someone else.

Jenna saw Bess staring across at Mr Fitzwilliam meaningfully. Then she looked around and saw that nearly everyone was staring at Mr Fitzwilliam meaningfully, hoping to be noticed, to be singled out for praise. They were all frantically trying to impress him, boys and girls, first by getting the answers to his questions right and then, when the conversation shifted, by trying to make him laugh. Which he did, frequently and with genuine pleasure.

She looked at him, trying to see what Bess saw. She could tell that he must once have been quite handsome. And he did have a nice smile. But to her he was still just an old man. There was an area on the top of his head where his scalp glowed white. His hands were gnarly. And he had old man teeth: that nameless shade of putty.

Mr Fitzwilliam turned and caught her gaze and she inhaled sharply as she saw something pass across his face. She couldn't pinpoint it or give it words. Words weren't her strong point. She used an online thesaurus a lot at home to find the right words when she was doing her homework. But it was something primal and wrong.

She lowered her gaze and felt her cheeks flush. He'd seen her curiosity and it had meant something to him. He'd reacted to it. She felt trapped somehow, complicit in something strange and unsavoury.

And then the word came to her, the elusive word

she'd been chasing through her thoughts. The look that Mr Fitzwilliam had given. It had been *predatory.*

Bedtime was 11 p.m. Lights out was eleven thirty. It was eleven twenty and the teachers would be coming round any minute to make sure everyone was tucked up in bed. But Bess was still not back from hanging out in Lottie, Ruby and Tiana's room a floor above. Jenna had come back to their room early to do her skincare routine in peace. She sent Bess a WhatsApp message. *WTF are you?? You're gonna get a warning????*

She stared at the sent message for a while, waiting and waiting for the two blue ticks to appear. But they didn't. The time turned from eleven twenty to eleven twenty-five. She sent another message. But still it went unread. Then she went to the door of their room and peered up and down the corridor. She could see Miss Mangan with her head round the door of Kat and Mia's room, telling them to turn off their phones. 'I'm going to stand here until I see them going off, girls. I've got all night. I'm not going anywhere.'

There were two more rooms to check on this corridor before Miss Mangan got to theirs. She sent a message to Lottie. *Tell Bess to GTF down here now. Miss Mangan's like 2 minutes away!*

The message immediately showed as read and a

reply arrived a second later. *She's not here. She left like 20 minutes ago!*

She went back to the door and glanced up and down the corridor again. Miss Mangan was one door down. And then she saw Bess coming in the other direction. She was with Mr Fitzwilliam. Something deep inside Jenna clenched up hard.

As they neared, Mr Fitzwilliam looked at Jenna, a smile buried beneath a faux-stern façade. 'Jenna. I am returning your roommate. Found hiding underneath a bed in one of the boys' rooms. I am not going to make a record of it because it is the first night and we're all a bit over-excited. But seriously, the rules are there for a reason, Bess. They're not there to stop you having fun. They're there to protect you. What might have happened if you'd had to find your own way back to your room in the middle of the night? Along these dark corridors? Who knows who you might have bumped into? Huh?'

'I'm really sorry, Mr Fitzwilliam,' said Bess, her head bowed.

He looked at Jenna, fresh-faced and scrubbed, her hair tied back, teeth brushed ready for bed. 'Keep an eye on her,' he said gently. 'I can tell you're a sensible girl.'

Jenna nodded briskly.

'I don't want to have to be making any terrible phone calls to anyone's parents. OK?'

Both girls nodded. And there followed a strange moment, brief but loaded. The two girls, one still in her party clothes, her hair awry and her heeled boots clutched in her hand, the other in pyjamas and ready for bed, and there, stationed between them, a tall, broad-shouldered man who was neither their father nor their friend. In the background of the vignette lurked the double bed spread with the ephemera of teenage girls: a red bra hooked over the bedpost, a crumpled, lipstick-stained tissue on the bedside table. The room held the sugary smell of the Superdrug beauty aisle, the medicinal tang of Clearasil. The scene seemed like a portrait, captured in minute detail with tiny touches of a tiny brush, before suddenly vaporising into nothing as Mr Fitzwilliam straightened and smiled and said, 'Well, goodnight, ladies. Get straight into bed. And I'll see you both for breakfast at eight thirty sharp.'

Bess dashed in and they closed the door behind him. But when Jenna put her eye to the spy hole in the door, she saw him there, just outside their room, his hands in his pockets, his gaze on hers.

21

21 February

Rebecca was home when Joey got back from work on Tuesday evening. She was in the living room, a laptop on the table in front of her, her ears plugged with buds. Joey stood for a moment just at the door and took in the scene. She rarely saw Rebecca in the house. When she was home she was almost always locked away in her office on the first floor.

Where had she come from, this woman? Where once there had been the nebulous, thrilling concept of the person her brother might one day end up with, there was now Rebecca. She didn't quite seem to fit the bill. It felt somehow as though she'd wandered into the wrong room at an audition and been given a part in the wrong play. Not that her brother appeared to have noticed. For him it could have been no other way. But Joey felt cheated out of another outcome, another sister-in-law, a cool girl who liked a drink and a club and the occasional lost weekend. Or someone mater- nal and cuddly who might have plugged the hole in her life left by her mother. Joey had been invited to her hen night. Rebecca and a couple of friends had spent a day at the Thermae Spa in Bath and then had dinner at a posh hotel. She'd passed. Not worth leaving Ibiza for. But maybe she should have made the effort. Maybe they'd have bonded over some foie gras and things wouldn't feel so awkward between them now.

'Hi,' she said loudly.

Rebecca didn't hear her.

'Hi!' she said again.

This time Rebecca turned. 'Oh,' she said, pulling out an earbud. 'Hi.'

'You're home early.'

'Yes. I had a hospital appointment, so I came straight back.'

'Oh,' she said. 'Everything OK?'

'Yes. Just a routine check-up. They took some bloods.' She showed Joey the bloom of a dark bruise beneath a small plaster on her inside arm. 'But it's all good.'

'Good,' said Joey. 'That's good. How many weeks left now?'

'Twelve. Ish.'

'Wow,' she said, in the absence of any more meaningful response.

There followed a short silence. Joey could see Rebecca's fingers playing with the earbud she'd removed upon Joey's entrance. She saw her gaze return to the screen of her laptop.

'Can I get you a cup of tea?' she said.

'No.' Rebecca shook her head apologetically. 'Thank you.'

'You sure?'

'I'm sure,' she replied, the earbud now held halfway to her ear. 'Thank you.'

Joey was about to leave the room, but turned suddenly towards Rebecca. 'I was just wondering,' she said, 'how did you decide? That you wanted to have a baby?'

Rebecca let the earbud fall again and blinked at Joey.

'I'm asking,' she continued, 'because Alfie wants us to have a baby.'

'Oh!' Rebecca put a hand to her collarbone. 'That's . . .'

'Well, it's great. Of course it's totally great. I love Alfie so much and I want to make him happy and I'm going to be twenty-seven this year so it's not as if I'm too young or anything. And imagine how cute our babies would be? But I just . . . I don't think I'm cut out for it. I'm not mother material, you know. When I see women with kids it's like looking at people from another tribe, you know? I just think, *I'm not like you.* And if I feel like that now, then I'm scared that maybe I'll always feel like that, and then what?'

'Well, have you told Alfie?'

'No. I mean, how could I tell the man I just married that I'm not sure I want to have his baby?'

'For what it's worth, Joey, I'm not a baby person either.' She put her hand to her stomach and looked down, then up at Joey. 'I never wanted kids. I still don't want kids.'

'But—' Joey started.

'Jack wanted a baby. I want Jack to be happy. So.' She smiled sadly and rubbed her stomach.

'You'll love it when it comes,' said Joey, slightly desperately.

'Ha! And if I said to you, have a baby with Alfie, you'll love it when it comes, what would you say?'

'I'd say . . .' She paused. 'Fair point,' she said.

'Do you think you'll still be living here', said Rebecca, 'when the baby comes?'

'I don't know,' she replied. 'Do you want me to still be here?'

There was a brief silence. Joey thought for a moment that Rebecca was trying to find a way to ask her to move out. But then she lowered her eyes to her bump and said, 'Yes. I think that Jack . . . and I . . . I think we're really going to need you.'

22

Jenna sent her mum a text that morning. *When was it that we went to the Lake District?*

A moment later a reply came. *Summer holidays, about five years ago. You were ten. Why?*

Nothing. Just couldn't remember.

Did you water the cactus by the back path? It's not rained and they're damp?

No. And it has rained. The day before yesterday. Remember?

They feel damper than they should. They feel freshly watered.

Why would someone water our cacti?

Exactly! I know! It's so crazy! These people! What will they think of next!

'Who are you texting?' said Bess.

'Mum.'

'Ah,' Bess said, nodding with gentle understanding. 'She OK?'

'Freaking out about someone watering the cactus.'

Bess shrugged and sighed. 'Your poor mum,' she said.

Bess was the only person apart from Dad and Ethan who knew the truth about Jenna's mum. Being Bess she had no idea what to say or do about it. But that was fine. At least Jenna could be open with her without fear of judgement or consequence.

She opened up Chrome on her phone and typed in *Lake District 2011 Tom Fitzwilliam*. All that came up was article after article about Mr Fitzwilliam's illustrious career: the schools he'd been parachuted into, the changes he'd wrought, the miracles he'd delivered. There were numerous photos of him outside numerous school gates looking masterful and imposing. But there was nothing related to him being in the Lake District five and a half years earlier.

'Aah!' said Bess, leaning over and peering at the screen of Jenna's phone. 'Is the old Mr Fitzwilliam magic starting to rub off on you too by any chance?'

Jenna pulled her phone away from Bess's gaze. 'Fuck off,' she said, appalled. 'No! I just remembered something about him. He was on a coach trip with me once, when I was small. And something happened. And I was just wondering about it. That's all.'

'Yeah, right.' Bess stroked her chin sceptically. 'Right.'

'Christ, Bess. I do not fancy Mr Fitzwilliam, all right? I think Mr Fitzwilliam is fucking gross.'

'Hmmmm.'

'And what was going on last night with you, anyway? What were you doing in the lads' room?'

'I wasn't in the lads' room,' Bess replied with a superior tilt of her chin.

'What?'

'Well, I mean, I was in the lads' room to start with and Mr Fitzwilliam did find me hiding under the bed but then we just sort of chatted for a while.'

Jenna sat up straight and stared at her friend incredulously. 'Chatted for a while?'

'Yeah. Just like on a sofa, on the landing.'

'I don't understand. What were you doing chatting on a sofa on the landing?'

'I dunno. He started asking me about how I was enjoying my first time out of the country and then we walked past this sofa and we both just sort of sat down. And chatted.'

'What were you chatting about?'

'Just stuff. All the countries he's been to, countries he

thought I'd enjoy. He told me about his gap year and going inter-railing with his mates – we should totally do that by the way – and I don't know, just things like that.'

'How long were you chatting for? On the landing?'

'Ten minutes or so. And then he was like, *Oh shit, look at the time, we need to get you back to your room before Miss Mangan finds you out of your room.*'

'But why didn't you tell me last night?'

Bess shrugged. 'You didn't ask. You were all just like *I'm going to sleep now* and huffy.'

'I was not huffy.'

'Yeah you were.'

'I so wasn't! I was just tired. Been up since bloody five in the morning.' Jenna glanced at her friend. 'Don't you think it's a bit strange?' she said. 'Him doing that?'

'Doing what? Talking to me? Why's that strange?'

'I dunno. He's, like, fifty; you're fifteen. It was bed-time. He should have just brought you straight back. It's fucking weird.'

'Are you a bit jealous by any chance, Jenna Tripp?'

'Fuck off!' Jenna picked up a cushion and shoved it at Bess. Bess laughed and bashed it back towards her. Then there was the terrible sound of a smartphone hitting a tiled floor and they both stiffened and looked at each other before peering over the edge of the bed.

Jenna leaned down to pick up her phone and held it to the light to check for damage. 'Bollocks,' she said, '*bollocks.*' There was a chip in the corner of the screen. She fingered the chip gently. She'd only had the phone a few weeks.

Bess looked at her and said, 'I'm sorry.'

Then Jenna thought of tiny Bess sitting on sofa on a landing with Mr Fitzwilliam chatting about his childhood holidays and she felt a terrible stab of concern. Her beautiful, hopeless, vulnerable friend.

'That's OK,' she said, pulling Bess towards her for a hug, smelling the familiar tang of her scalp through her soft blond hair. 'It's only a phone.'

That night after dinner Jenna made sure she stayed close to Bess. Lottie, Ruby and Tiana came to their room and they mucked around on Snapchat and made prank calls to the boys and laughed like they might die of it until 11.15 p.m. when the other three dutifully made their way back to their bedroom on the floor above. Jenna could hear Miss Mangan coming down the corridor, the clicks and whispers of her visits to other rooms. She changed into her pyjamas and brushed her teeth, removed her make-up and squeezed a spot. As Bess slipped into the bathroom after her she heard a gentle rap at the door. She pulled it open expecting to see the pinched, anxious face of Miss Mangan. Instead she was confronted with the looming presence of Mr Fitzwilliam.

She folded her arms across her chest, aware of the fact that she was braless under her vest top. 'Oh.'

'Good evening, Jenna. Just thought I'd better check in on Bess. I didn't find her hiding under any beds on the boys' floor so I'm just making sure she's with you?'

'She is,' she replied. 'She's in the bathroom.'

Mr Fitzwilliam looked at the bathroom door and then back at Jenna. 'Are you sure?'

'Yes. Totally. She's getting ready for bed. She's been in here all night with me.'

'Bess!'

Jenna jumped slightly at the sound of Mr Fitzwilliam calling over her shoulder.

'Hm?' came a muffled reply.

Mr Fitzwilliam smiled down at Jenna as though he had been somehow vindicated. 'Good,' he said. 'That's very good.' And then he was gone, the door clicking shut behind him just as Bess emerged from the bathroom, her toothbrush clenched between her teeth and a towel wrapped around her body. 'Washat Mishter Fitshwillum?' she asked through her toothbrush, her eyes wide.

'Yeah. Checking up on you. He's gone now.'

Bess pouted and went back in the bathroom to spit out her toothpaste and returned a moment later, smiling. 'See,' she said. 'Isn't he just the sweetest, loveliest man in the world. Isn't he, like, *everything*?'

23

22 February

Since Monday night Freddie had stopped absorbing information properly. His mind roiled and cycled constantly with theories about his hacker to the point where he'd been told off by Mrs Johnson in Latin for doing the wrong exercise when the right exercise was clearly written on the whiteboard. Freddie did not like being wrong and he certainly did not like being publicly trounced for being wrong and he carried the small humiliation around with him for the rest of the day along with the gnawing mystery of the hacker, so that by the time the bell went at the end of triple science on Wednesday afternoon he was ready to hit something.

But then he thought of Romola Brook and her sparkling eyes and he thought: I would like to see her; it would make me feel better. So he turned left towards St Mildred's and he loitered on the other side of the street for a few moments waiting to see her emerge. There was no smarmy sixth-former hanging around her this time; she was alone, staring at her phone, oblivious to the boy across the road watching her with thirsty eyes.

'Mum,' he heard her say into her phone as she crossed at the zebra, 'I'm going to be a bit late. I have to go to Ryman's to get some folders. Can you give me the money? When I get back? Or put it in my account. OK then, see you in about half an hour.'

He picked up his pace to follow her towards the high street. He watched her put earbuds in her ears and select something on her phone to listen to. She stopped for a moment outside Forever 21 and eyed a suede skirt and vest top in the window. He pictured her in it. The cinnamon of the suede would set off her chestnut hair perfectly, he thought, and suddenly he found himself mired in a fantasy scenario in which he entered Forever 21 and bought the suede skirt for Romola Brook and passed it to her on the street with some kind of suave commentary about her hair and her eyes and in this weird fantasy scenario he saw her smile at him and say, *Wow, thank you, I love it.*

She'd stopped looking in the window of Forever 21 and was now heading towards Ryman's. Her hair was thick and cut blunt at the ends. Some of it was tied back and the rest was left down and it swung side to side as she walked. She had thin legs, almost too thin, slightly string-like, and her gait was rather odd, as though she had a stone in one of her shoes, but this only added to her appeal, made her less perfect, less out of his reach.

Freddie was about to take out his phone and get some shots of her stringy legs but then she stopped for a moment, just before turning into Ryman's. Her body stiffened and stilled like a forest animal sensing it is being followed. Freddie turned away briefly and when he turned back Romola had gone into the stationery shop. He crossed the road and watched from the other side of the street. Something strange was happening to him. He'd done this a hundred times: watched people, followed them about, photographed them. But he'd never felt nervous before, never worried about being caught. But something about having his private computer files hacked into had made him feel vulnerable and foolish. Someone had seen the unique mechanics of his own personal world, the world where he was the boss, and he didn't like the way it made him feel. It made him feel as though he was doing something wrong, as though he himself was in some way wrong.

Freddie did not like feeling wrong. Freddie was never wrong.

He felt a simmering of something deep inside him. He pictured himself walking into Ryman's and deliberately pushing himself up against Romola Brook, wordlessly pressing her into the filing display; he imagined the sweet sugar of her shocked breath against his cheek, the slight tremor in her skinny legs. He wanted to do it; he wanted to do it really badly. It would purge the voice of the Latin teacher in his head; the thought of someone somewhere, a stranger or maybe even someone he knew, leafing through his files and photos, not understanding what they were, shaking their head in condemnation.

Instead he waited for her to leave and he got a full-frontal shot of her face. When he got home he locked his bedroom door, drew the curtains, photoshopped Romola's head on to the body of a naked woman, blew it up to full screen on his laptop and pulled down his trousers. He stared at the image, his hand upon himself, and then he saw something in the eyes of the disembodied head, something that took his breath away. He saw a human being looking at him. He saw a skinny girl in a new town and a new school. A girl who loved a stupid tiny dog and wanted things from Forever 21 that she couldn't afford. A girl who went into Ryman's for folders oblivious to the strange boy loitering outside.

He pulled his trousers back up and shut down the image, feeling the shockwaves of something new and extraordinary ricochet around his head.

24

24 February

Tom Fitzwilliam was back. Joey had heard a scooter zipping up the hill, looked from the top-floor window and seen a Deliveroo driver pulling off his helmet and reaching for the zip-up bag from the back of his moped. She'd watched as he'd taken the bag to the Fitzwilliams' house and then seen Tom appear in a soft grey jumper and jeans, take the delivery from the driver, hand him a tip and close the door again.

Her heart raced and she felt a terrible blend of sickness and excitement. All week she'd felt it like a lump in her gut, the thought of seeing him again. The lump had grown bigger and bigger as the week had gone on.

On Wednesday she'd passed his wife in the village. Joey had stared at her as she passed as though she were someone from a dream become real. The wife had seen her staring but not reacted, just mustered a small smile and carried on her way. Tom hadn't told her about what had happened at the Weaver's Arms, it was clear. But still the lump was there, the hard knot of horror and anxiety.

His car had remained in the same parking space all week and eventually Joey had come to the conclusion that he must be away somewhere, on business.

And now he was home, just two doors away from her.

She wanted to escape, not to be here. She texted Alfie: *Where are you?*

Just got to work.

Can you bunk off?

No can do. Short-staffed.

Can I come and sit at the bar?

Sure thing babe.

She threw on a black off-the-shoulder jumper and some huge gold hoop earrings, put on some red lipstick and her red suede boots and walked to the bus stop, her heart hammering under her ribs. As she sat waiting for the bus she gazed up at the painted houses. She saw the mottled kaleidoscopic glow of the stained-glass window in her brother's house and two doors down she saw the muted gold glow of lights shining in Tom's house. At the top of Tom's house, a figure moved across the window. She caught the glint of something in the figure's hand. For a moment she thought it might be Tom but as the figure came closer to the glass she saw it was someone much smaller, either the wife or the son. Her breath caught. And then she heard a voice coming from behind her, a woman's voice, saying, 'I see you. *I see you up there!'*

Joey jumped and turned. Behind her was a small woman, fine-boned and pretty, early forties or so. Joey turned back to the window and saw the figure at the top of Tom's house slowly extend their middle finger and leave it there for a moment before walking away from the window again.

'Did you see him?' the woman said, sidling up towards Joey. 'Up there?'

Joey nodded. There was something alarming about the woman, a dark intensity in her eyes, her body language. She was not a person to engage with in the dark.

'He's always up there,' said the woman. 'Always taking photos and staring through his binoculars. He's just a child, you know, a teenager. He's working for his father.'

Joey nodded again, politely, not wanting to add any

fuel to this woman's conviction that she was up for a conversation.

'Do you know his father?' the woman said. 'The head teacher?'

'No,' she said. 'Not really.'

'He brought you home in a taxi last week though?'

'What?'

'I saw you, last Friday night. He brought you home and took you to your front door.'

Suddenly it hit her. This was the woman; the woman hiding in the trees the other night.

'He's been having me followed,' the woman continued. 'He's been getting his son to photograph me. And my daughter.' The woman put a thin hand to her throat and sighed. 'He's the main one. There are at least a dozen of them. But he's the main one. The first one. It's because of what we saw. Me and my family. Years ago. We saw a woman attack him and he tried to brush it off, tried to say she was just mad. But you know the saying: no smoke without fire. Why would a woman just randomly attack someone in the middle of the Lake District if they hadn't done anything wrong? Hm?'

Joey peered desperately up the road, praying silently for the bus to appear and rescue her from this unsettling encounter.

'Everyone thinks he's some kind of god. It makes

me sick. If people knew, if people knew what he was really like, him and that son of his.'

The figure in the window of the yellow house had gone now and the strange woman began to back away. 'Just don't get involved. Keep away from him. Or you'll end up like me – tortured. Completely tortured.'

25

'Mum?' Jenna had heard the front door click.

'Yes!'

Jenna came halfway down the stairs and peered into the hallway. 'Mum, where've you been?'

'That boy is up there again. In his window. And he gave me the finger.'

'I don't blame him, Mum. He's probably sick of you staring up there all the time.'

Jenna had been home for two hours and already she was aching nostalgically for the big sunny suite in Seville, the late-night dinners in noisy restaurants, the thrilling conveyor-belt toaster in the breakfast hall, the freedom from being constantly told that she was being watched and played with and persecuted.

'She was there too. At the bus stop. The woman Tom Fitzwilliam brought home in a taxi last week. I talked to her. She claims not to know anything about him. But I think she was lying.'

'Oh God, Mum, tell me you haven't been talking to strangers about all this. Please tell me you haven't.' This was a new development. Another step down the road to insanity.

'Well, I wouldn't call her a stranger. She's a local. Locals talk to each other.'

'And what did she say? This local woman?'

Her mum shrugged. 'Not much. And then her bus came.'

'Oh God.' Jenna sat heavily on the stairs and pulled her hair from her face. 'Mum. You've got to stop going out and doing all this stuff. You're becoming as bad as these people you claim are stalking you. Just suppose, just suppose for one minute that you're wrong; that Mr Fitzwilliam is not a bad man, that his son is not taking photos of you, that all of this is in your head – how do you think they're feeling? Knowing you're out there, creeping about, talking to their neighbours. You'll be making them feel as bad as they're making you feel. Doesn't that seem wrong to you?'

Her mum rolled her eyes. 'When are you going to wake up, Jenna? Wake up and see the truth? I know it makes no sense. But it's true and it's happening. Every minute of every day. And I'm not alone. It's happening to hundreds of people. Three that I know of just in the Bristol area. All being stalked. All being followed and persecuted. It's a terrible, terrible scourge, Jenna, but no one wants to talk about it. And men like Tom Fitzwilliam get to swan about in their big shiny cars without a care in the world with everyone thinking the sun shines out of their bloody backsides.'

Jenna inhaled slowly. She thought of Bess sitting on the landing with their head teacher in the middle of the night, the inappropriate, slightly loaded visits to their room, the red and yellow watch strap. 'Tell me again, Mum,' she said, 'about the Lake District. Tell me again what actually happened.'

Her mum sat a few stairs below Jenna and held her daughter's socked toes in her hand, massaging them absent-mindedly. 'Well, it was our third day, boiling hot, thirty-two degrees or something crazy, too hot for walking or cycling. So we booked ourselves into an air-conditioned coach tour of the Lakes. And there was a family on the tour. Him' – she gestured broadly in the direction of Melville Heights – 'and his wife and boy. And I'd noticed them because I thought he seemed a bit high and mighty, you know? As if being on a coach tour was somehow beneath him. And I noticed that the wife and the boy seemed sort of in awe of him, as though he was all that mattered in the world. Every time we got off the coach they would wait for him to lead the way. I just felt, I don't know, that there was something *off* with them. And then the first stop after lunch – it was Buttermere, I think – he was just getting back on the coach and this woman appeared from nowhere. A dark-haired woman, about fifty or so. She was wearing a black vest and gold chains and she was quite attractive, quite stylish, but her face was distorted with rage and she kind of threw herself at him, threw him up against the side of the coach and was shouting in his face: *You fucking bastard, look at you! Just look at you! How can you live with yourself? How can you live with yourself?* And she kept saying something about *viva*. Do you remember? *Viva*, this, *viva* that. I can't really remember. I just remember her thumping his chest over and over again with her fists. And then another coach went by and blocked our view and by the time the coach was gone, she was gone too and he was straightening himself up and looking really humiliated. He was trying to act like nothing had happened. When we got back on the coach I passed him and I said, *Everything OK?* And he looked at me as though a human being had never spoken to him before and he nodded, like this' – she nodded abruptly – 'and the look he gave me.' She shuddered. 'It cut through me like a knife. And that was that. That was the moment. The moment that changed everything. I saw him and he saw me, and for whatever reason he decided to start all this; he decided to make me his victim.'

'He was on our trip. He came to Seville,' Jenna said, knowing even as she said it that it was the wrong thing to say.

'Tom Fitzwilliam?'

'Yes. The Spanish teacher couldn't come because his wife went into early labour. So Mr Fitzwilliam came instead.'

Her mum stopped massaging Jenna's toes and stared up at her. 'Was he staying at your hotel?'

'Yes.'

'And' – her mother dropped her foot and placed her hand to her chest – 'he was there, with you, all week?'

'Uh-huh.'

'God.' Her mother cast her gaze to the floor as though she might find the correct response down there. She looked up again. 'Are you OK?'

'Of course I'm OK. He's just a man.'

'And did he . . . did he say anything about me? About us? About the Lakes?'

'Of course he didn't! Mum! I will grant you that he is the same man from the Lake District, you're right about that. He was there, on the coach trip, something strange happened, we have no idea what it was, and it had nothing to do with us, and now he lives over the road from us and it's all just a coincidence. That's all it is.'

Her mum shook her head. 'No,' she said. 'It absolutely is *not* a coincidence. And the fact that you can't see it when it's so incredibly clear scares me, Jenna. Promise me you'll stay away from him. Please.'

Jenna sighed and got to her feet. 'I'm going to unpack,' she said.

'Stay away from him,' her mother called after her, 'or I'm taking you out of that school.'

26

They ate pizzas in front of the TV. Dad was back in his usual spot next to Mum on the sofa, Freddie once again relegated to the armchair. He saw his mum turn her head a couple of degrees every now and then, almost as if she was checking that Dad was still there.

There was a charge in the room, as though everyone was nursing a secret too big to be entirely contained. Freddie stole a glance at his dad. When was it going to come? When was he going to take him aside and quietly inform him that *he* was the one who'd logged into Freddie's secret account and seen his photos and that he knew exactly what he'd been doing and what he intended to do about it?

'Good week?' his dad asked him in a way that could have been loaded with hidden meaning (*Has your week been unfavourably affected by the fact that I hacked into your files and discovered your reams of schoolgirl photos?*) or nothing more than a casual enquiry after his week.

'Not bad,' Freddie replied. 'Pretty boring. How was Spain?'

'Well, thank you for asking.' His dad gave him one of his dry smiles and a cocked eyebrow. 'It was superb. Wonderful children, wonderful staff, lots of learning, lots of fun. Unforgettable, I think it wouldn't be stretching things too far to say.'

Freddie's mum threw his dad a look. 'How's the baby?'

'The bab—? Oh, the baby? Doing very well apparently. They're still in the special care unit. But it seems that they're out of the woods.'

'Is it a boy or a girl?'

'It's a girl, I believe. But please do not ask me her name or how much she weighs because I have absolutely no idea.'

His dad smiled and squeezed Mum's knee. The gesture felt like an odd afterthought and for a moment Freddie felt that neither he nor his mother quite believed in the existence of this premature baby. For a moment the already charged air filled with small particles of yet another substance, a kind of nervous scepticism.

For over a year, since their arrival in Melville, things had stayed on an even keel. For over a year there had been no week-long silences, no strange noises from his parents' room, no feeling that something was happening within their marriage that he was not privy to but that might tear a hole through his very existence. Melville had been a good move; things had been good in Melville.

After dinner he went back to his room. For a while he flicked through the photos of Romola Brook on his computer screen. He noticed things about her and collected them in the drawers of his mind like mementoes. The strand of her hair nearest her face that was two tones lighter than the rest. Her huge feet, surprisingly endearing. The odd earrings: a gold stud in her left ear, a diamond in the right. The streak of old black varnish on a bitten thumbnail. Something scribbled on the back of her hand that he couldn't read even when he zoomed in to the nth degree.

In the photo of her leaning down to greet her tiny dog in her hallway, he zoomed in on her hand cupping the dog's chin, her nose held close to dog's snout, the tenderness of the moment. He zoomed in even closer to the background, trying to get a sense of her home, of how she lived, of who she might conceivably be.

And then, before he could ask himself what the hell he thought he was doing, he opened a browser, went on to the Forever 21 website and ordered the cinnamon suede skirt.

RECORDED INTERVIEW

Date: 25/03/2017
Location: Trinity Road Police Station, Bristol BS2 0NW
Conducted by: Officers from Somerset & Avon Police

POLICE: So, Ms Mullen. Moving on. We have spoken to your employer, a Miss Dawn Pettifer?

JM: Yes?

POLICE: She came here of her own volition this morning, to tell us that she recalls a recent conversation with you where you apparently told her that your obsession with Tom Fitzwilliam was driving you 'insane'. Is that correct?

JM: No. No, that's not true.

POLICE: So, Miss Pettifer was lying?

JM: No, not lying, exactly. I may have said I had a crush on him. I may have said I was preoccupied with him. But I never said I was insane.

POLICE: She claims you were 'agitated' when you left work last night.

JM: Well, yes, I probably was. I was about to meet a married man in a hotel room. I was nervous as hell.

167

POLICE: OK. Moving on. We wanted to talk to you about this object. For the sake of our records, we are referring to item number 4501. A red suede tassel. Do you recognise this tassel, Ms Mullen?

JM: Well, yes, sort of. I mean, it looks like the tassels on my boots. And one fell off.

POLICE: It fell off? When exactly?

JM: God. I don't know. It was just there. And then it wasn't. Could have been any time.

POLICE: Well, this was found, Ms Mullen, at the scene of the crime, very close to the victim's body. Do you have a possible explanation for this?

JM: No. I mean, definitely not. It can't be from my boot in that case. Because I wasn't there. So it must be from someone else's boot.

POLICE: Well, we've searched the victim's house very thoroughly looking for items that this tassel might have dropped from, and there is absolutely nothing even vaguely similar. So, can you explain this being there, Ms Mullen, at the blood-soaked scene of a heinous crime?

JM: No! Of course I can't. It's just . . . well, it's crazy. I mean, someone must have put it there.

POLICE: You think so? Like who, for example?

JM: Well, I don't know. I don't know who would put it there. But it wasn't me.

II

27

7 March

Joey thought she would be safe down in the village in the middle of the day. She'd thought Tom Fitzwilliam would be at school. But there he was, striding towards her in a dark suit and leather shoes, his bag slung diagonally across his chest. If she moved now he wouldn't see her. But she couldn't move. She felt the blood rush from her heart to her neck and then to her face and for a moment her breath came fast and hard enough to make her dizzy.

She was outside the dry cleaner's. She could go into the dry cleaner's. But she had nothing to drop off and nothing to collect and the shop was empty and the man who worked in the dry cleaner's was standing there looking bored. As she mulled this over she realised it was too late. Tom had seen her.

She watched his face switch from blank unawareness to uncomfortable awareness in the space of a split second. She tried to do things with her own features to make the situation better, but failed, utterly. And then something extraordinary happened: Tom Fitzwilliam smiled.

'Josephine!' he said, reminding Joey of her pathetic drunken attempts at sophistication. 'How are you?'

It was said with the emphasis on the *you*, which suggested genuine interest in her well-being, not on the *are*, which would have suggested concern or sympathy: *How* are *you after the last time I saw you when you grabbed my groin outside a pub and I had to take you home shit-faced in a taxi?*

'Oh, hi,' she replied, managing to sound vaguely breezy. 'I'm good, thank you. I'm good. And I'm . . . God. I am so sorry.'

He had a hand up before she'd even got to the second syllable of the word. 'Please,' he said. 'We've all been there.'

'Well, I don't suppose you have.'

'We've all been there,' he repeated with a gentle smile.

'Well, anyway, thank you so much for getting me home. I would have thanked you before, but I felt too embarrassed. I've actually considered leaving the country.'

He laughed. 'Oh no, please don't do that! You only just got back.'

He remembered some of their conversation then. She smiled.

'And it looks like you'll have to stay in the country for at least a couple of weeks as your husband is about to start decorating our house, I believe?'

'Oh, yes. He is. Next week, I think?'

'So I've been told. My wife's project.'

'But your house?' She gave him a humorous don't-patronise-your-wife look.

He gave her a you-got-me look and said, 'Yes. My house. Well, my rented house. My actual house is in Kent. But we don't get to live there.'

'Because of your career?'

'Yes, because of my career.'

The conversation paused for a moment and Joey gazed at the pavement, waiting for Tom to tell her that he was on his way, in a hurry, *better get on*. Instead he said, 'You know, I really enjoyed spending time with you at the gig. I don't often have the chance to get to know my neighbours. We should do something again?

Maybe you and your husband could come over for a meal one night? And your brother and his wife?'

'Yes, yes, that would be lovely.' She nodded, slightly too hard. 'Maybe once Alfie's finished decorating.'

'Yes!' he replied, apparently delighted. 'Yes. Like a small housewarming. I'll talk to Nicola. See what she thinks. She's not much of a cook but . . .'

She gave him another warning look. 'You can cook though, right?'

He winced, caught out again. 'No. I'm not much of a cook either. Sorry,' he continued. 'I'm a bit of a muppet. Child of the seventies, still think radio alarm clocks are kind of amazing. Must try harder.'

Joey smiled. 'Well,' she said, 'I guess I'll see you around.'

'Yes,' he said, returning her smile. 'I'd like that.'

'And again,' she said, 'about the night at the pub. I am so sorry.'

He put his hands into his trouser pockets and rocked back lightly on his heels. He appraised her, sensitively. 'Please do not apologise. You cannot begin to imagine how flattered I was. You cannot begin to imagine how much . . .' He smiled regretfully. 'Well. You just don't need to apologise. Take care, Josephine, and see you soon, I hope.'

'Yes,' she said. 'See you soon.'

She stood for a moment after he went. The lump of anxiety she'd been carrying around inside her had dissolved, turned into something warm and golden. Tom Fitzwilliam was flattered that she'd practically sexually assaulted him. Tom Fitzwilliam had enjoyed the time he'd spent with her. Tom Fitzwilliam liked her and wanted to get to know her better. She turned and caught the eye of the man behind the desk in the dry cleaner's. He looked startled to have been caught staring at her.

She waved at him and he waved back, slowly, dazedly, delightedly.

28

8 March

Jenna was having lunch the following day when she saw Miss Farooqi approaching her across the classroom.

'Jenna,' she said, 'when you're done, Mr Fitzwilliam would like to see you in his office.'

As Miss Farooqi swept back through the classroom to the door there was a moment of weighted silence followed by a zoo-like cacophony of noises. Bess threw her a look, a mixture of awe and horror. 'Oh my God,' she whispered.

Jenna finished her Weight Watchers chocolate bar, disposed of the wrapper and the rest of her packed lunch in a bin and slowly made her way down the corridor towards the suite of rooms where Mr Fitzwilliam, his two deputies and their secretary worked.

It smelled different down here, away from the gravy tang of the dining hall and the pungent traces of unwashed PE kits. Down here it smelled of fresh flowers and dry paper. She peered round the door into Miss Farooqi's office. She was peeling the film off a pre-prepared salad. 'You can go straight in,' she said, sliding the packaging off a plastic fork. 'He's waiting for you.'

Jenna nodded and turned the corner to the end office. Here was Mr Fitzwilliam's perch: twice the width of the other offices, looking directly over the front entrance and the car park, long plate-glass windows the full width of the back wall. Mr Fitzwilliam sat not at his desk in the centre of the room, but at a small table to the left around which were clustered four squashy, dark red chairs. There was a heathery lambswool jumper over the back of his chair and his hair looked all messed up and staticky as though he had just that minute pulled it off.

'Jenna,' he said pleasantly, 'so sorry to drag you away from your lunch break. I won't keep you long, I promise. Here – take a seat.' He pulled one of the squashy red chairs away from the table and she sat down.

'How are you today?' He said this in that fly-buzzy, mindless way that adults sometimes did when they talked to children. Not looking for real answers. Just saying words.

'Good,' she said. Then she cleared her throat.

'Nothing to be nervous about,' he said, leaning towards her marginally and ramping up his eye contact. 'Just a . . . well. Something that's playing on my mind a bit. And I wanted to run it by you. Before I take things any further.'

Jenna's heart rate doubled.

'You live in the village, don't you? Just by the hotel?'

She nodded.

'With your mum?'

She nodded again.

Mr Fitzwilliam sighed and steepled his fingers. He looked down and then up at Jenna and she felt a shiver go across the full surface of her skin. She saw it there, in his steady gaze, a hint of something as cold and dazzling as sunbeams ricocheting off ice. Her eyes fell to the red and yellow canvas strap of his watch.

'And your brother lives with your dad? Down by the coast?'

'Yes.' She tried to raise her eyes to meet his but felt them being dragged downwards by her discomfort.

She stared at her fingernails in her lap, at the pale salmon polish she'd painted on them two nights ago.

She heard Mr Fitzwilliam draw in his breath and felt him lean a little closer towards her. 'My wife seems to think that your mother is stalking us.'

She stole a glance at him and saw the beginnings of a wry smile. 'Oh,' she said. 'Right.'

'Now, it could be that my wife is mad. She has been known to be a little eccentric. But generally speaking she does not make things up. So I thought, possibly misguidedly, that I might just run it by you, see if you had any insight? Any background?'

'What did she say?' she asked, quietly. 'Your wife?'

'She said . . .' He paused, allowing the enormity of what he was about to say a moment to coalesce. 'That she has seen your mum outside our house taking photos and that your mother often follows her around the village. And once ran a few feet behind her while she was out jogging. While wearing her slippers. It's all a bit . . .' He paused again. 'Unsettling.'

Jenna hooked her hands into the sleeves of her jumper and then unhooked them again. She had no idea how to react.

'Is there anything going on at home, Jenna? Anything that it might be helpful for us to know about? Anything that might be impeding your learning?'

She shook her head. She did not want to be taken to live with her father. She did not want to go to a new school. She wanted to stay here until she'd done her GCSEs. She had only two terms left. She needed everything to stay on an even keel until then.

'She just . . .' she began. 'She thinks she knows you. That's all. I'm sure she hasn't been following you about on purpose. Just, you know, trying to work out if you're who she thinks you are.'

The sound of excitable girls' screams rose from behind the school like distant ghouls. Mr Fitzwilliam narrowed his eyes at Jenna and then readjusted his sitting position, his hand clasped to his tie. 'Right,' he said, 'well, that might make sense. Any idea where she thinks she knows us from?'

She shrugged. 'A holiday, I think.'

'Oh,' he said. 'Any idea whereabouts?'

She shrugged again. 'Don't really know,' she said. 'It was a few years back.'

'And does she often recognise people? When you're out?'

'Not really,' she said. 'No.'

'Because' – Mr Fitzwilliam adjusted his seating position yet again so that he was bent at the middle, his face not much more than a foot from hers – 'interesting fact, but thinking you recognise people a lot can sometimes be a symptom of some mental health issues. Schizophrenia, for example?'

Jenna nodded. She could smell something sweet on his breath, something sugary and malty. 'I don't think she's got that,' she said.

He pulled away and smiled. Jenna allowed herself a deep breath.

'No.' He pushed his tie back into place. 'No. I don't suppose she has. But could it be something else? Maybe? Because most people if they thought they recognised someone from a holiday would probably say something? Not' – he expelled a hunk of wry laughter – 'follow them about?'

'I don't really know what to say,' said Jenna.

He sighed. 'Well, maybe you could have a word with your mum when you get home? Tell her to come and have a chat, next time she sees me, or my wife? Say hello. Maybe we can work out where we know each other from? Yes?' He smiled warmly. His laser-beam eyes turned soft.

'Yes.' Jenna nodded eagerly, sensing the end of the conversation.

'Good. And remember, you have good friends here. Not just me and the staff, but your peers – Bess, for example. People who really care about you. So never feel like you can't talk about things. Because you totally can. OK?'

'OK.' She nodded again and began to rise from the squashy chair.

She felt the touch of Mr Fitzwilliam's hand against her sleeve and something rushed through her, sluice-like, ice cold but red hot both at the same time. She pulled her arm away and covered the spot with her own hand.

'Thank you,' she said. 'Bye.'

'Goodbye, Jenna. Stay in touch.'

Bess ran to catch up with her at the end of school. For a moment Jenna was tempted to cold shoulder her but she knew that would be pointless. Bess didn't have the neural pathways to intuit things like cold shoulders.

'So,' she said, falling into step with her as they neared the gates. 'What the hell? Tell?'

'Nothing,' she replied. 'It was nothing.'

'It can't have been nothing,' she said. 'No one gets called into the head teacher's office in the middle of lunchtime for nothing. So?'

'Urgh.' Jenna capitulated. 'His wife told him she'd seen my mum following them about. He was just asking me about it, that's all.'

'Oh.' Bess inhaled sharply and fell a step behind her before quickly catching up again.

'You told him, didn't you?' said Jenna, stopping and turning to face her friend. 'I could tell he knew something. You told him about my mum.'

'No! I didn't. I swear! He just . . . he asked me if I knew what your mum looked like. That was all.'

'Was this when you were chatting on a hotel landing in the middle of the night?'

Bess nodded, nervously. 'But it wasn't anything like what you're thinking! He just said, *What does Jenna's mum look like,* and I told him and he nodded and that was that.'

'But didn't you want to know why he was asking? I mean . . . it couldn't just have been that. Like, no context, nothing. He must have asked something ese.'

Bess shrugged. 'He asked if she was all right. He asked if you were all right. I said . . .'

Jenna inhaled.

'I said your mum had some issues but that it wasn't my place to talk to him about them and that if he wanted to know about them he should talk to you.' She tipped her chin up stubbornly. 'So—'

'Fucking hell, Bess. *Fuck!*'

'What? It was nothing! I didn't say anything! I swear.'

'You said enough though, didn't you? Enough to have him asking questions. Enough for him to get other people involved. And now everything's going to get completely fucked up!'

'God, Jen, it's already fucked up! I don't see how it could get any worse! You know everyone in the village is starting to talk about your mum? My mum said when we were in Seville your mum was out on the high street all the time, talking to people, being really weird. Maybe it's a *good* thing if Mr Fitzwilliam wants to help. Maybe you should let him.'

29

The cinnamon suede skirt had arrived on Monday.

'What's this, love?' his mum had asked, handing him the package distractedly. 'Forever 21. Isn't that girls' clothes?'

'It's a thing,' he'd said, taking the parcel from her. 'Costume. For a project.'

'I could have ordered that for you,' she'd said. 'No reason for you to be paying for school things out of your own money.'

'I know. But you weren't here and I needed it.'

She'd turned to locate her handbag, pulled out her purse. 'Here,' she'd said, fingering a twenty. 'How much was it?'

He hadn't wanted her to pay for it. He'd wanted it to come from him. 'Just cheap,' he'd said, 'four pounds. Something like that. Don't worry about it.'

'No,' she'd said, moving her fingers to the coin section. 'No. I insist. Here.' She'd handed him two two-pound coins.

He'd taken them. 'Thanks, Mum.'

In his room he'd unwrapped the package. The skirt had looked disappointingly cheap in the crinkly plastic bag but once he'd pulled it out and refolded it and wrapped it in some silver tissue he'd found in the Christmas bag under the stairs it looked fine.

He took it to school on Wednesday in his rucksack, folded inside a manila envelope. Attached to the package was a note saying, 'From an admirer.' Each time he reached into the rucksack he felt the contours of the thing like a whispered secret in his ear. He left school urgently at 4 p.m., whistled down the corridors and bolted through the front door, eyes straight ahead. He walked unnaturally fast towards town, casting his gaze over his shoulder every now and then, checking for the flash of royal-blue blazer. By the time he reached Romola's house he was breathless and sweating. He heard the high-pitched yap of the chihuahua as he approached the front door. He pushed the package swiftly through the letterbox, not waiting to see if anyone was home.

He passed Romola on her way home a few moments later. Her hair was in two complicated-looking plaits that were woven into her scalp. He saw her eyes pass over the badge on his blazer before resting once again on the pavement beneath her huge feet. She didn't look at him. Didn't notice him. She passed by in a wash of odd sadness and gut-gnawing beauty. Freddie felt his head spin and for a moment he forgot how to walk. After a few steps he stopped and turned. He saw Romola from behind, watched her strange gait, her plaits, her glory, walking out of view.

He overheard a conversation between his mum and dad the next morning. They were in the kitchen. From outside he could hear drawers sliding and banging, cutlery jangling, plates from the dishwasher being stacked one on top of the other, the low rumble of BBC news in the background.

'I spoke to the girl yesterday,' he heard his father say. 'The daughter.'

'Oh yes.'

'Told her what you said.'

Freddie heard the plate-stacking come to a sudden halt, then his mother's voice. 'Yes?'

'She says that apparently her mum thinks she knows us. That they met us on holiday a few years back.'

'Oh.' He heard a cupboard door open and then bang shut. 'And did they?'

Silence again.

'She didn't seem to know. She was vague. Had no idea even where this holiday might have been.'

'Well, it's not like there's a lot to choose from. It's not as if we've even really been on holiday the last few years. Apart from the Lakes that time and a few nights at your mum's. And I certainly don't recognise her.'

Freddie drew in his breath. He hated thinking about the holiday in the Lake District. It had been the worst, worst, worst time. His dad hated holidays and had made it clear from the outset that he didn't want to be there and resented them both for persuading him to go. He'd been grumpy all week, which had made Mum even more subservient and desperate to please him and they'd both walked on eggshells constantly and it had been hot, so, so hot. The steaming B & B with the sealed-up windows, Freddie's mattress on the floor at the foot of his parents' bed, like a baby, even though he was nine years old, and his mum shushing him every time he opened his mouth to complain about something. And then there'd been that day when they went on a coach. And that woman had come over and hit Dad. Really hit him, hard. Her face had been contorted and spit had spun from her lips as she shouted. Freddie had never before seen a person so angry, so black and red with rage.

Then the woman had said swear words that wouldn't rattle Freddie now but had shocked him at the time, the sound of each word cutting into him like a knife. She'd been shouting at his dad: *How can you live with yourself,* she kept saying, *how can you live with yourself?*

His dad had taken the woman by the arms, quite roughly, and moved her like a sack of rocks to a spot across the street. Freddie had watched as they gesticulated silently at each other, their words swallowed up by passing cars. Then thirty seconds later his dad had stalked back across the street and hustled him and his mum back on to the coach. 'Get on!' he'd hissed in Freddie's ear, his hand tight round Freddie's arm. 'Just *get on.'*

And everyone had been standing and staring, and Freddie had felt his face burn hot.

When they got back on the coach Freddie peered through the window to the spot across the street where the woman had been standing with Dad. She was still there, encircled now in the arms of another woman, a younger woman, similar in appearance. The younger woman looked up at the coach and caught Freddie's gaze. Inside that gaze he saw pure, distilled hatred. He looked away and buried his face in his mother's shoulder.

When he looked back again, both the women were gone.

Neither of his parents would talk about it afterwards. *Just a loony,* they said. *Thought Dad was someone else. Mistaken identity. Just forget about it. There are some very strange people in this world.*

But the rest of the holiday was even worse after that. His mum stopped being subservient and was instead brittle and silent. His parents barely spoke a word to each other until it was time to come home. And then all they talked about was road directions. It was at least a week or two until things felt normal again.

'Anyway,' he heard his dad continue, 'I said we're here to help. I still suspect mental health issues. It's one thing to think you recognise someone. It's another to hide in the undergrowth taking photos.'

Freddie nodded to himself. Of course. They were talking about the weird woman across the way. The one who watched him when he was watching her. The one he'd given the finger to. Jenna Tripp's mum. Was it possible, he pondered, that they'd met them on holiday? Had they been at the B & B? Had they been there that day? Had they seen what had happened? Did they know the truth?

A blurred figure appeared the other side of the stained-glass panes of the front door, followed by a polite thrum of the doorbell. Freddie opened it. It was him, the big guy with the tattoos, Joey's husband. He was wearing paint-splattered overalls and huge brown boots. He peered down at Freddie and said, 'Morning, mate,' before wiping his feet at least ten times on the mat. 'How are you doing?'

'Good,' said Freddie, closing the door behind him.

'Glad to hear it,' he said. 'Your mum about?'

Freddie pointed in the direction of the kitchen.

He watched the big man head down the hallway, knock gently on the kitchen door, push it open and say, 'Morning Mrs Fitzwilliam, Mr Fitzwilliam,' and then he heard his mum say, 'Please, Alfie, I keep telling you, call me Nicola. Cup of tea?'

The door closed behind him and Freddie stood alone. He grasped the banister for a moment. There was crazy stuff swirling about his consciousness, disconnected things randomly hurtling towards each other: the strange woman in the village and the angry woman in the Lake District; Red Boots and his dad; his dad and his photos; his photos and Romola; his mum and the big man in the kitchen come to paint their walls for no particular reason because wouldn't they be gone from here soon anyway? Wasn't that how their lives worked? The moment Freddie found a reason to want to stay somewhere his dad breezed in and told him it was time to move on.

He rested his forehead against the cool wood of the banister and kicked his foot hard against the skirting board. He wanted . . . he didn't know what he wanted. His giant brain was not helping him now. His ridiculous IQ was not showing up on a white steed to navigate him through this maze of weirdness. He just wanted to touch Romola's hair. That was it. He wanted to touch her hair and make her smile.

30

9 March

Jenna saw Mr Fitzwilliam at his usual post the next morning, standing sentry at the school gates, greeting each student by name, throwing out hail-fellow-well-met greetings as though they were dog treats. She noticed how the children loved them, lapped them up. She could see why he was so lauded, why they called him the Superhead. He clearly knew how to run a school, knew what to feed it, how to nourish it, when to slap the back of its hand and when to pat its head. He had the aura of humorous capability and effortless control that children liked in an adult.

But still.

That didn't mean she had to like him too.

He shouldn't have touched her arm like that in his office. It was unprofessional. A bit like talking to fifteen-year-old girls on hotel landings in the middle of the night. And he shouldn't have approached her directly about her mother. She was sure there were other paths he should have taken, protocols he should have followed.

Jenna could see the shadow of a white T-shirt beneath his thin blue shirt. She didn't like the idea of it, of Mr Fitzwilliam in a white T-shirt. It was sort of gross.

She passed him with pursed lips and a hard, awkward grind to her stride.

'Good morning, Miss Tripp,' he said.

'Morning, sir,' she said without making eye contact. But even without looking at him she could tell he was smiling down at her. She could sense his hands in his trouser pockets, the subtle rut of his hips, a twinkle in his eye. Was it in fact mildly inappropriate for him to call her Miss Tripp?

She strode towards the front doors and marched up to the lockers. Bess was already there. She'd left without her this morning; Jenna had seen her halfway up the road out of the village. She'd written a text saying, *Wait up bitch*, but deleted it. Then she'd watched Bess run to catch up with Lottie and Tiana and she'd felt a stab of sickening sadness in her guts. Now that she was face-to-face with Bess she didn't know what to say.

'Sorry I didn't wait for you,' Bess said, nibbling on a fingernail. 'Just felt a bit weird after yesterday.'

Jenna ached to say, *Me too,* and draw the line and make things good. But she couldn't do it. The words were too deeply buried under piles of other stuff for her to quite reach them.

'Whatever,' she said instead. She unlocked her locker and started to fold her coat into it. She wanted Bess to say something, but she didn't. She just locked her locker and took her books and turned away. Jenna watched her walk down the corridor, tears aching against the back of her throat.

Bess didn't eat her lunch in the classroom that day and she wasn't waiting for Jenna to walk home together at the end of the day either. Instead Jenna walked home alone, listening to a Sam Smith channel on Spotify. As she passed Caffè Nero on the other side of the main road she spotted Bess's creamy blond head, tipped back with laughter, surrounded by the heads of Tiana and Lottie and Ruby. Jenna turned the volume right up and walked faster.

As she walked she became aware of someone behind her, matching her pace. She turned and saw a boy wearing a black blazer from one of the posh schools across town. She recognised him, vaguely; he was familiar. As her eye caught his he picked up his pace and stood alongside her.

'You're Jenna Tripp?' said the boy.

He was odd-looking; around the same height as her, a pinched face, too much very straight hair growing downwards from his crown like a spillage, a slight air of dark superiority.

She suddenly realised that it was Mr Fitzwilliam's son. She pulled out her earbuds and nodded.

'Freddie Fitzwilliam,' said the boy, holding out his hand for her to shake. 'My father is the head at your school.'

She stared at him, not sure how to respond.

'And I live just over there.' He pointed towards Melville Heights, a stripe of dark colour in the distance. 'Near you.' He paused and took a deep breath. 'Can I ask you something?'

'I don't know,' she said. 'It depends.'

'It's about the Lake District.'

She stopped walking and turned to him. 'What about it?'

'Is that where your mum recognises my dad from?'

'What?'

'I overheard my dad telling my mum that the

reason your mum keeps following him is that she remembers him from a holiday. And we've only been on one holiday. And that was the Lake District. Was it that? Were you there?'

Jenna shrugged. 'Don't know,' she said. 'Can't remember. Why does it matter?'

The boy called Freddie stared intently at a spot on her shoulder, stepped from one foot to the other and back again. He put a delicate hand to the side of his face and made a strange noise. He looked as though he was about to say something and then he suddenly brought his gaze from her shoulder to her face and said, 'It doesn't. Really. Forget I said anything. And don't tell my dad.'

She shook her head slightly.

'Promise.'

'Yes,' she said. 'Yes. Whatever.' She wanted this boy gone; she wanted this encounter to end.

He looked once more from her shoulder to her face and then back again before picking up his pace and darting ahead of her. She stood in place watching him until his outline was a smudge in the distance and then she carried on home.

Her mum was at the computer when she got back. She was on one of her chat rooms, one of the many places on the internet where she could go to have her craziness validated.

Gang-stalking.

Jenna had googled it the first time her mother had triumphantly lifted her head from her laptop, eyes blazing and said, *It's real! It's happening to thousands of people all over the world! I'm being gang-stalked!* It belonged to the same school of delusion-based psychiatric disorders as Morgellons and alien abductions. Her mother genuinely believed that she was being persecuted by a huge network of strangers, and that Mr Fitzwilliam was the puppet master. She believed that strangers came into their home while they slept and rearranged things and stole things and damaged things, just to mess with their heads. Her mother believed that her persecutors saw it as a kind of perverse hobby, a huge, boundless real-life game that ate into their own time and finances. She believed that she was being persecuted for her many political protests as a young person. She believed that Mr Fitzwilliam was not a head teacher but a powerful man with connections to the government who was being sent into schools and communities to manage the gang-stalking from the inside.

'Look,' said her mother, resting her e-cigarette on the table next to her and turning the screen of her computer to face Jenna. 'Look what's happening. Just across the border in Mold. There's a woman, same age as me, same political history as me. Mr Fitzwilliam was the head at her local school before he came to Melville and it happened to her too. It started from the minute he arrived, she says. Scratches on her car. Chips in her kitchen surfaces. Light bulbs loosened. Bits of broken glass in the bath. And she says she was in the Lake District too.'

Jenna stopped unzipping her rucksack and stared at her mother. 'What? When *we* were there?'

'No.' Her mother returned her gaze to the screen, picked up her e-cigarette and inhaled deeply. 'No. When she was a child, I think. But still.'

Jenna rolled her eyes and pulled her homework books out of her bag. She knew that Mr Fitzwilliam had been the head at a school in Wales before he'd been brought into Melville Academy. That much was probably true, but the rest of it . . .

She went into the kitchen and made herself a low-calorie hot chocolate with a sprinkle of miniature marshmallows. She took her homework and the hot chocolate up to her room and arranged herself cross-legged on her bed.

'Is he there?' she heard her mother call up the stairs.

Jenna didn't even need to peer from her window to

verify that the innocuous bespectacled man who sat at his computer every evening in the house behind theirs would be there, because he always was.

'No,' she called down. 'Can't see him.'

She pulled out her phone, desperate to text Bess or Facetime her, desperate to tell her about her freaky encounter with Mr Fitzwilliam's son on the way home from school. She opened WhatsApp and held her finger over the video call button. But then she put the phone down again. Bess was probably still in Caffè Nero with their friends. Instead she opened up her laptop and typed *Tom Fitzwilliam Mold* into her browser.

The school in Mold had brought him in in January 2014. He'd turned it from a school in special measures to an outstanding school within two years and left for his new role in Melville at the end of the winter term in 2016. Before Mold he'd been in Tower Hamlets. Before Tower Hamlets he'd been in Manchester. And before Manchester, back in the year 2001, the year Jenna had been born, he'd been promoted to deputy head of a school in Burton upon Trent where he'd taught since he was twenty-eight.

Mr Fitzwilliam was squeaky clean. His reputation was unblemished. Everywhere he went he brought nothing but light and harmony. Happy children and sunshine. But the woman in the Lake District didn't like Mr Fitzwilliam, Jenna's mad mum didn't like Mr Fitzwilliam and now, for no particular reason, Jenna herself did not like Mr Fitzwilliam.

Was the woman in the Lake District also mad, perhaps? And in that case, was she, Jenna, perhaps mad too? She thought back to her encounter with Freddie Fitzwilliam and her curiosity began to bloom. What had he wanted to say to her? And might it have shed some light on the strange things she'd been thinking and feeling?

She closed her laptop and picked up her phone again. She checked Snapchat to see what Bess was up to but she hadn't posted. She felt a terrible hollowness open up inside her, a sense that she was all alone, that she had in fact always been all alone, that the corners of her life were folding in and folding in and that there was nothing she could do about it.

31

Freddie caught his breath at the top of the escarpment before straightening and continuing to his front door. He had not meant to approach Jenna Tripp like that. He hadn't even been expecting to see her. He did sometimes see her on the walk home, but she was usually with Bess or some other girls. It took him by surprise to see her walking alone. It had seemed preordained in some way, so soon after the question of the Lake District had raised its ugly head again. He thought, as he followed behind Jenna Tripp, that it must mean something, her being there, alone, right then. He'd thought it must be destiny. He'd thought a lot of strange and entirely fatuous things (how could someone as clever as him be thinking about destiny, for goodness' sake?) when she'd turned suddenly and clamped her eyes on his and he'd had to wing it, horribly, with panic blowing and building inside him at the realisation that he was much closer to her than he'd thought he was, oppressively close, and that the only way to make it seem better than it was, was to make it look as though he was deliberately catching up with her to start up a conversation.

Once he'd started the conversation he'd felt a terrible awareness growing and boiling inside him, from the pit of his gut upwards, that not only was he having a weird conversation with a stranger but that the stranger was a teenage girl and that it was, in fact, quite possibly the first time he'd had a conversation with a teenage girl since becoming a teenager himself. And Jenna Tripp, now he was here, standing right next to her, was even prettier than she looked from a distance and her lips were very full and soft and her breasts made a shape in the fabric of her blazer that was both innocuous and awe-inspiring. He found that he could look neither at her face, because he wanted to touch her mouth, or away from her face, because then there were breasts, so had chosen instead a neutral corner where her shoulder met the wall of the shop behind her and fixed his gaze there.

And then he'd realised that he was mad to be having this conversation with her, that she would tell his dad and that his dad would then know he'd overheard their conversation, and that anyway, he didn't really know what it was he was trying to uncover, that he shouldn't have approached her before properly formulating a line of enquiry. The whole thing had been shambolic and embarrassing and humiliating and that was why he'd needed to stop for a moment before he could face the normality of walking through his front door.

Instead, though, he was confronted by a stepladder and paint-spattered dust sheets flung up the stairs and the smell of wet paint and the entirely abnormal sound of his mum laughing in the kitchen.

He followed the sound and came upon his mother leaning up against the kitchen counter, her hands wrapped around a mug of tea and Alfie the painter sitting across from her at the kitchen table in his overalls, huge long legs crossed at the knee, fingertips tapping the sides of another mug, halfway through a story that was clearly the funniest thing his mum had ever heard.

'Good evening, my friend,' said Alfie the painter.

'Afternoon,' Freddie replied with a satisfying spritz of pedantry.

'Hello, darling.' His mum turned briefly and hit him with a smile the likes of which he had not known she was capable of producing. 'Alfie's telling me stories about being a groundskeeper at a dreadful-sounding holiday resort in Ibiza! You wouldn't believe the things they get up to on these all-inclusive holidays!'

Alfie threw Freddie a look of what could only be described as awkward regret. Freddie suspected that he had not meant his stories to elicit such amusement but that now they were he'd decided to go with the flow.

'Anyway,' said Alfie, giving the mug one last ripple of his big, paint-stained fingernails and lowering his gigantic foot to the floor. 'I had better get back to it. I've got one more coat to do on the skirting boards before I go. Thanks for the tea, Nicola.'

Freddie stared at him. He tried to work him out, ferret out some dark intention, some element of shade or wrongness. But there was none to be found. He was as he appeared. A large, harmless man of small ambition and mediocre intellect. But something about him had caused his mother to postpone her afternoon run, to drink tea in the kitchen, to laugh, really properly to laugh, to glow, even.

Freddie added this to the growing conundrum of his entire existence and went to his bedroom.

* * *

Freddie had completely abandoned *The Melville Papers*. He no longer logged anything that he saw from his bedroom window, not even Jenna Tripp and Bess Ridley in their PE kits. The comings and goings of Lower Melville were of no interest whatsoever to him any more. The truth was that all of Freddie's time these days was taken up in pursuit of Romola Brook. Or not so much in pursuit of, but in paying homage to. Appreciating. Adoring. Studying. Learning about. He'd started a new log. It was called *The Romola Papers*.

He followed her home most nights now, if she happened to leave school at the same time as him. Last night she'd gone home via Tesco Metro where she'd picked up a packet of custard creams and some dog food. He'd added this fact to his log. Just in case he ever wanted to buy her biscuits. Tonight she hadn't been there. He'd waited for ten minutes until the school caretaker had come and locked the gates and then he'd given up. But that was OK because he could still find her on the internet.

He placed his camomile tea on his desk, removed his tie and clicked his way on to a conversation that Romola was having on Instagram with someone called LouisaMeyrickJones. It was pretty boring. To do with a teacher who'd been unfair during lunch break and how so and so had been in tears and then so and so joined in and there was lots of talk about how maybe they should report the unfairness and so on and so forth and Freddie was about to switch screens and find something else to do for a while when someone else popped up and said something about the spring ball.

He read on.

It was a joint event with Freddie's school, just over a fortnight away.

A few weeks ago, he would barely have noticed the reference. But now he saw it as the portal to something extraordinary.

'Mum!' he called down the stairs. 'Are we doing anything on the twenty-fourth of March? It's a Friday?'

He waited a moment for his mother to reply. 'I don't think so,' she replied. 'Why?'

'There's a party I want to go to. A type of ball. At my school. Can I go?'

'Of course you can, darling! How lovely!'

'The tickets are really expensive,' he called down. 'Twenty-five pounds. Am I still allowed to go?'

'Yes.' His mother's face appeared at the bottom of the staircase. 'Absolutely. I think it's great that you want to go. We'll have to get you a tux! How handsome you'll look! Just imagine it!'

32

10 March

Joey ignored the insistent beeping of the car horn, at first. Either it was someone hooting at her from a white van in which case she had no interest in looking up and having to deal with some moron and his mate with their tongues hanging out. Or it was someone hooting at someone else entirely and then she'd look like a sad loser who'd been secretly hoping it was two morons in a white van.

But then she heard a male voice calling out 'Josephine!' and she turned to see Tom Fitzwilliam leaning from the passenger window of his car and signalling for her to approach. 'Can I give you a lift? I'm heading into town.'

He pulled his car into a space alongside her and she looked at him, then up towards the city. She'd been on her way to the bus stop.

'Er, yes. Thank you. If you're sure?'

'Of course I'm sure! Jump in.'

She slid in next to him and reached for the seat belt. 'This is very kind of you,' she said.

'Not at all. I see you at the bus stop a lot but I'm usually heading the wrong way for you.' He turned to her and smiled and Joey thought: *I am in a car with Tom Fitzwilliam. I am in Tom Fitzwilliam's car. Here I am. I am here. It is happening. Right now.* She clicked her seat belt into place and returned his smile. 'Well, thank you,' she said. And then, 'Where are you off to? Not going into school today?'

'No,' he said, peering into his wing mirror ready to pull back into the morning traffic. 'Today I have a big meeting at the town hall with the LEA. I'd love to tell you all about it, but then I'd have to kill you.'

He smiled again and there was something wicked in it, something that made her feel like maybe he actually would.

'So, you're still at the soft play centre?' he said, eyeing the logo on her polo shirt.

'Unfortunately, yes,' she said. 'Although it is growing on me. Nice people.'

'People are everything,' he said. 'That's one thing I've learned. If you're with the right people then you're generally in the right place.'

'Unless it's a prison.' She laughed. And then immediately hated herself for the sound of her laughter, so harsh and fake.

'No,' he said. 'Even if it's a prison. Seriously! Or at least, if you are in prison because you've done a bad thing and not because of a terrible miscarriage of justice.'

She ran her hands down the leather sides of her seat. How many times had she stared into the passenger side of Tom's car when it was parked outside her house, imagining herself sitting right here? And now it was actually happening and Joey's head could barely process anything. She pulled herself straight and shook her head slightly.

'So, you're not still planning on leaving the country, then?' he asked with a small smile.

'No.' She shook her head. 'No. I'm over that.'

'Good,' he said, 'that's good.'

The traffic out of Melville was heavy and there was a chance, without the expediency of bus lanes, that she might arrive late to work. She did not care. She breathed in the smell of Tom Fitzwilliam's car: worn leather and showered man. She stared at his hands where they gripped the steering wheel. Such good hands. She could not look at them without imagining them on her face, inside her clothes, pulling at her. She felt her need for him bubbling up inside her, so fast and so red hot that she was convinced he must be able to tell what she was thinking.

As they approached the turning to the Academy she watched the sea of grey blazers pouring from all directions. It was incredible, she thought, that the mild-mannered man sitting next to her was responsible for each and every one of these half-formed people every single day.

'What about you?' she asked. 'Do you think you'll stay in Melville for much longer?'

'Well, we've only been here a year,' he said. 'I'd like to see through two years minimum. That's when you know that all the huge changes you made when you arrived have rooted themselves. It's like snagging, you know. You want to be around just to tidy up all the bits you missed when you were doing the big job.'

'Have you ever failed?' she asked.

He glanced at her quickly before returning his gaze to the windscreen. 'Failed?'

'Yes. At one of your schools? Have you ever been brought in to fix a school you couldn't fix?'

He smiled. 'No,' he said, 'or at least, *not yet.*'

'What would you do? If you couldn't fix it?'

'I don't know. I've genuinely never thought about it.'

They fell silent for a moment. The traffic barely moved, and Tom pointed over Joey's shoulder. 'Oh, look,' he said, 'there's the bus you would have been on if I hadn't picked you up.' They watched its wide rear-end pass them by in a wreath of grey fumes. 'Sorry,' he said. 'You'd have been there earlier if I'd left you.'

'I forgive you,' she said.

He turned and smiled. 'Good,' he said. 'Good.'

'So,' she said a moment later. 'How long have you and Nicola been together?

'Oh,' he said, 'God. I'm not sure. Twenty years, I guess. Something like that.'

'And is your son – is he yours? Or both of yours?'

He laughed. 'You're very full of blunt questions.'

'Sorry. It's just Nicola looks so young to be his mum. I thought maybe she was a second wife?'

'No. Very much a first wife.'

Joey nodded, running some vague arithmetic through her head. If Nicola was the age she looked – roughly the same age as Jack and Rebecca, then she and Tom must have got together when she was . . . No. She must be older than she looked.

'Where did you meet?'

'We met, as unromantic as it sounds, on a bus in

Burton-on-Trent. She came up to me and told me that I'd been a teacher at her school.'

'She was a schoolgirl?'

Tom laughed. 'No! Not then. She was nineteen, twenty, something like that. She remembered me, but I didn't remember her. I didn't actually teach her. She was in a lower set.'

'Well, phew, thank goodness for that because that would have been a bit cringey.'

'Would it? Why?'

She shrugged. 'I don't know. Teachers. Students. It's all a bit murky, isn't it?'

He turned to her and for a moment she thought he was going to shout at her, tell her she was wrong. But then his face softened and he smiled and said, 'I suppose it *could* be. But in this case, it was murk free, I promise.'

Joey smiled tightly and changed the subject. 'So, does your son go to your school? To the Academy?'

'No. No. Most definitely not. Not, *of course*, that there's anything wrong with my school. Clearly my school is brilliant! But it's easier, when you move around a lot, to go private, otherwise you're farting about with catchment areas and waiting lists and criteria. Private you just show up with your chequebook and your child's last report card and you're away.'

'Jack tells me your son's a genius?'

'Yes. He is a bit. Very high IQ. Brilliant at languages and technology. Regional chess champion a couple of times. And he's already done three GCSEs and he's only in year ten. So yes. Very bright. But he's a funny little guy.'

'Is he?'

'Yeah. He is a bit. I *think* he's just starting to notice girls as well. Which should be interesting. Not sure his basic skill set really extends to charming the ladies. But we'll see, I suppose.'

Tom looked at her. His eyes, she noticed for the very first time, were, like her own, green. Only 3 per cent of the population of the world has green eyes. Her mother had always told her that in an effort to make her feel special. Jack's eyes were blue. Blue was very common, apparently. Her mother had been aware of how inferior she felt to her brilliant brother and was always keen to give Joey a little boost where she could.

'You've got green eyes,' she found herself saying.

'Have I?' he said.

'Yes!' She laughed. 'Surely you know what colour your eyes are?'

'Not really,' he said. 'I think I thought they were a kind of murky blue. I've never really thought about it.'

Joey narrowed her eyes at him. Was he being disingenuous?

'Well, they're green. Officially. And I should know because mine are green too.'

He turned briefly to look. 'Yes,' he said. 'So they are. You have very beautiful eyes. If that's an OK thing to say?'

'It depends on the context,' she replied.

'And is this the right context to tell you that you have beautiful eyes?'

'I don't know,' she said. 'I think so.'

'Phew,' he said. 'That's a relief.'

They'd arrived in the city now. The early morning streets of Bristol thronged with people heading to work. An awkward silence descended.

'You know,' said Tom, peering at the traffic stretching towards the next junction, 'it would probably be quicker for you to walk from here.'

'Yes,' Joey agreed quickly. 'Yes. It probably would be.'

'Next time the lights go red, you can jump out.'

'Yes. OK.'

She unclipped her seat belt. A sensor began to ping. She waited for Tom to slow the car to standing and then she said, 'Thank you for the lift,' and he said, 'You are most welcome,' and she searched his face for something, some other meaning, some sense that he didn't want her to go, that he was fighting a terrible urge to pull her back, to grab her, to push his mouth on to her mouth and make the cars behind hoot their horns with frustration at being kept waiting. She searched for a full five seconds until Tom looked ahead and then back at her and said, 'Quick, they're changing to green again.'

She got out of the car and dashed to the pavement. The lights changed, and she watched Tom's car pull slowly forwards and away from her.

She shivered – a nauseating combination of embarrassment and lust – then turned and headed to work.

RECORDED INTERVIEW

Date: 25/03/2017

Location: Trinity Road Police Station, Bristol BS2 0NW

Conducted by: Officers from Somerset & Avon Police

POLICE: How long would you say your infatuation with Mr Fitzwilliam has been growing?

JM: I wouldn't call it an infatuation. Just a mutual attraction.

POLICE: Well, in that case, how long would you say it has been since you discovered your mutual attraction?

JM: I really don't know. I suppose since the first time I saw him.

POLICE: Which was?

JM: Early this year? January?

POLICE: And this mutual attraction – how did it manifest itself?

JM: I don't know what you mean?

POLICE: I mean, were there clandestine meetings? Lingering looks?

JM: There were looks, I suppose. I don't know if they were lingering.

POLICE: For the purpose of the recording I am showing Ms Mullen a series of photographs. Numbers 2866 to 2872. Could you describe these photographs to me, if you would?

JM: They're photographs of me.

POLICE: And what are you doing in these photographs?

JM: I'm looking at Tom Fitzwilliam's house.

POLICE: And can you tell me where these photographs were taken?

JM: They were taken on the path around the back of the houses.

POLICE: So you are familiar with the back exits to the houses on Melville Heights?

JM: Yes. Yes I am.

POLICE: And these, Ms Mullen – for the sake of the recording, I am showing Ms Mullen another set of photographs, these numbered 2873 to 2877 – could you describe these photographs, please?

JM: They're photos of Tom Fitzwilliam's house.

POLICE: Or, more specifically, of the *inside* of Tom Fitzwilliam's house?

JM: Yes. It looks like it.

POLICE: These are photographs we took off your phone just now, Ms Mullen. Could you explain what photographs of the interior of Mr Fitzwilliam's house were doing on your phone?

JM: Yes. I can totally explain it. My husband did a decorating job for them. I said I'd take some pictures for him, so he could show them to other clients.

POLICE: And this one, in particular. Could you describe this photograph, for the recording?

JM: Yes. It's a photograph of the conservatory thing at the back of Tom's house.

POLICE: Clearly showing, I think you'll agree, a broken window.

JM: What?

POLICE: I am showing Ms Mullen a detail on photograph number 2876. Could you describe what you are looking at?

JM: It's one of the windows. Next to the back door. It's tied together with string.

POLICE: Thank you, Ms Mullen.

JM: But I didn't even notice it. I didn't even know—

POLICE: Thank you, Ms Mullen. That will do for now.

33

10 March

'Mum!'

Jenna peered behind her mum's bedroom door. She wasn't there. She went to her own room and knelt on her bed so that she could look down into the back garden. Before she'd started using e-cigarettes, her mum had spent hours out in the garden, smoking. Her smoking table was still there: the sad chair by the sad table, the sad ashtray full of damp, mulchy old butts. Now she rarely went out there. It was a slight improvement, but not much.

There was no sign of her mum in the garden so Jenna pulled her trainers back on and then her hoodie, and headed out into the early evening gloom towards the bus stop outside the Melville. This was her mum's favourite vantage point for watching Tom Fitzwilliam and his family. Her mother was not there. She crossed the road and went to the bottom of the escarpment, peering up the road to check that her mother wasn't hiding in the undergrowth near his house again, and as she stood there, her hands knitted together, unsure what to do, she became aware of a brilliant blue light ricocheting off windows and cars. She followed the source of the light to a silently approaching police car. The car slowed as it made its way down the high street and then pulled up opposite Jenna, right next to the Melville. Two policemen exited the car, adjusted their uniforms, one said something into a walkie-talkie and then they entered the hotel.

Jenna felt her heart contract and then thump. She crossed back towards the hotel and peered through the window into the bar. There she saw exactly what she had expected to see. Her mother sitting at a table by the bar being spoken to by one police officer while on the other side of the bar a worried-looking couple and the manager talked to the other police officer.

'Fuck,' she said, under her breath. 'Fuck.'

She pulled in her breath and walked into the bar.

'Ah!' she heard her mother say. 'Here's my daughter.

She'll tell you. She'll tell you everything. Jen. Come over here.'

The bar fell silent; all eyes were on her and her mother.

'What's going on?' she asked the police officer.

'Could you confirm your name? And your relationship to Mrs Tripp?'

'I'm Jenna Tripp. I'm her daughter.'

'And how old are you, Jenna?'

'I'm fifteen. Nearly sixteen.'

The police officer turned to the bar manager and said, 'Is this OK? She's under age.'

The manager nodded and the police officer said, 'I'm PC Drax and we've been asked to come and talk to your mother about some alleged threatening remarks made to some other patrons. Apparently she was refusing to leave.'

Her mum tutted and rolled her eyes. 'They were not threatening remarks, officer. For God's sake. We were having a conversation!'

Jenna turned to look at the couple sitting across the room who could barely make eye contact with her. She had no idea who they were.

'That's the thing,' her mother continued. 'No one will talk about this stuff. No one will admit that it's happening. We sit in our little cotton-wool cocoons pretending that the world is all soft and safe and lovely because we can't face the truth. They're all in it. Him up there' – she pointed towards Melville Heights – 'half the village, probably. And this isn't just about me. I'm not that stupid as to think that I'm the only one who gets all this . . . all this shit. It's happening on a global level. And there are other people like him' – she pointed upwards again – 'powerful people. All over the world. And if we don't talk about it, it will keep on happening. And I heard these nice people just now, while I was standing outside, I heard them talking about him and saying what a great job he's doing and all I said was *you don't know the half of it*, but nobody wants to hear it, nobody wants to bloody hear it.'

Her mother kept talking and Jenna stared at her and thought, *This has suddenly become something much bigger than me.*

'Is there anyone you can call?' PC Drax asked her. 'An adult?'

Jenna looked at her phone clutched inside her hand and thought that she should phone her dad. Then she thought that if Dad came he'd make her go back and stay with him. And if she went to stay with him then she would end up living with him and she didn't want to live with him because her life was here. And then she thought of Bess, who had once again not waited for her this morning or after school this evening, and she looked at her mother who was very close to as far as she could go in life without some serious help from the outside world, and she wondered if the life she had here was worth as much as she'd always thought it was.

'My dad lives in Weston-super-Mare,' she said. 'I could call him?'

'Yes,' said the police officer, 'maybe you could.'

She typed in her dad's number and watched the couple across the way talking to the other PC. They were shaking their heads and saying, 'No, no, it's fine.'

'And you know,' her mother was saying, 'in actual fact it should have been *me* calling the police. To report an assault. This gentleman' – she pointed at the manager – 'was really quite physical with me.'

The manager rolled his eyes. 'I barely touched her,' he said. 'Literally, just put my hand on her elbow trying to encourage her to leave. But she refused.'

Her father's phone rang and rang and rang. Jenna pressed end call and looked at PC Drax. 'No reply,' she said, a whisper of relief in her tone.

'Where do you live?'

'Just around the corner. Literally one minute away.'

'Do you think you could get your mum to come home with you? Now? There's no charges to be brought here. I think it's best if we can just end this nice and quietly. What do you think?'

'Yes,' Jenna said brightly. 'Yes. I can get her home. Mum?' She went to her mum's side and touched her shoulder.

Her mother clasped her hand over hers. 'My daughter knows what I've been through. She can tell you. She can tell you everything. Maybe then someone will listen.'

'Mum, we're going home now.' Jenna gently pulled her mum to her feet and started to lead her towards the door.

'I've written to the chief superintendent *three times* in the last six months. I've written to my councillor and my MP. Nobody wants to know. I get *fobbed off* with these meaningless stock replies. Maybe now, maybe someone will actually listen. And you two!' Her mother turned suddenly as they neared the front door and pointed at the embarrassed-looking couple. 'I'm sorry I had to approach you both so heavy-handedly. I can see that wasn't ideal. But as long as decent people like you keep believing what you're told about people like him, nothing will ever change.'

'Come on, Mum.' Jenna kept her moving. The police officer held open the door and finally her mum was out of the hotel bar, on the pavement. People stopped and watched. Traffic slowed as it passed.

The two police officers escorted Jenna and her mum back to their house and stayed for half an hour, asking Jenna lots of questions, the answers to which she knew would be going straight to social services. No, she said, her mother had never approached strangers before as far as she was aware. Most of the time, she said, her mother sat at her computer. Most of the time she said her mother was perfectly normal. And, well, yes, maybe she had noticed a slight increase in her mother's paranoia over the past week or so. Her mother had always been up and down, yes, possibly she had a slightly bipolar aspect, but no, it had never caused any problems for her, no. Life was fine. Her mum was fine. On the whole, yes, it was all good.

Her phone rang about two minutes after the police finally left.

'Jen, love, it's Dad. Is everything OK? I'm really sorry I missed your call; I was in my t'ai chi class.'

Jenna let a moment of silence fall as she wondered, briefly, if now was the time finally to offload her fucked-up life on to someone else. But then she sighed, and made herself smile and said, 'Everything's fine, Dad. Honestly. I just wondered if I was going to see you over the Easter holidays. That's all.'

34

Freddie scooted on his office chair from the window to his bedroom door.

'Dad!' he called down the stairs. 'Dad! That woman! Jenna's mum! She just got arrested!'

His father's voice rose up the staircase. 'What on earth are you talking about?'

'That woman! The stalker woman! Mrs Tripp or whatever. She just got taken out of the Melville by two uniformed policemen.'

He heard his father slowly taking the stairs and his face appeared between the banisters. 'Are you sure?'

'I am entirely sure. She was talking to two people

outside, and I could tell she was getting agitated and I could see they were trying to get away from her and then she followed them into the bar. Ten, fifteen minutes later there were blue lights and the cops got out and then the daughter turned up and five minutes later the daughter and the mum were being escorted off the premises.'

'Into a car?'

'No,' said Freddie, mentally downgrading the excitement factor. 'No. I think they walked them home.'

'God,' said Dad. 'That's not good.'

'Why don't you go down there? To the bar?' Freddie suggested. 'Ask what happened? You're all pally-pally with them in there, aren't you?'

'Well, yes,' said Dad. 'I guess I could. I suppose so.' He narrowed his eyes at Freddie. 'Want to come with? I can get you a Coke and a bowl of scratchings?'

Freddie nodded. In one way he didn't want to go anywhere at all. It was warm in here. It was dark and cold out there. But he never went anywhere on his own with his dad. Normally his dad wouldn't even be here now. Normally he'd still be at school. Often he didn't get home till gone ten o'clock but he'd been home early tonight because he'd been at a meeting at the LEA all day. He'd appeared while Freddie was eating his supper, full of bonhomie and joy, ruffled his hair, called him his *fine boy*, made them both Nutella on toast for afters, exclaimed about the smartness of the newly painted hallway, poured himself a generous glass of red wine, put his arm around Mum and just been generally jolly and like the sort of dad you wished got home from work at six o'clock every night.

And now he was offering Freddie Coke and scratchings and a chance to find out first-hand what on earth was going on with Jenna and her mum. He grabbed his shoes from where he'd thrown them and pulled them on.

Freddie loved the Melville. They came here sometimes for Sunday lunch. Once they'd brought Grandma here for afternoon tea in the little lounge area behind the reception desk. They'd been given tiny cakes with gems and rose petals and fluffed-up cream fillings. They'd had a teapot each with an antique strainer and a bowl of sugar lumps. The fire had been lit and there'd been low-level jazzy stuff playing in the background and Freddie had thought that somehow he'd jumped straight into a really nice dream.

His dad held the door to the bar open and suddenly there was the flutter and excitement of grown-ups discoursing, the dense smell of beer and scented candles, the theatre of muted wall lights and towering vases of tropical flowers.

His dad went straight to the bar and ordered Freddie a Coke and himself a pint of something local and spumy.

'Saw some blue lights here earlier,' his dad said to the very young man tending the bar. 'Hope there hasn't been any trouble?'

The boy – he didn't look much older than Freddie – said, 'Not really. Just a woman. With some issues. She was giving that couple over there a hard time. We asked her to leave. She wouldn't.' He shrugged, flipped the beer tap upwards and let the last few drops hit the frothy head.

'God,' said Dad. 'And you had to call the police?'

'She just refused to go. It was creating a disturbance. Rob tried to ask her nicely. Made her even madder. You know.'

'And a bowl of scratchings please,' his dad asked, pulling out his wallet.

The boy nodded and put the beer and the Coke on the bar top.

'And what was she shouting about, this woman?'

'I dunno. It was all this weird stuff about *powerful people* and being controlled. You know. She was telling them that they shouldn't believe things they read in the papers, conspiracy theories, all that. Just, you know, like, *mad stuff.'*

'Probably unkind to use the word mad, you know, Luke,' his dad chastised gently, being Saint Tom Fitzwilliam, as usual. 'Shall we say, maybe, troubled?'

As he said this, the male half of the couple from the other side of the bar approached Freddie's dad and said, 'Mr Fitzwilliam. I'm Ralph Gross. Our son Felix is at your school, in year eight. That's my wife, Emma.'

Emma raised a polite hand and then lowered it back on to the stem of a large glass of wine.

'I just wanted to say how happy we are with what you've done at the school this last year. We'd been so close to moving away from the area. We'd even made an offer on a place in Wells. But since you came Felix has been so happy at school, and doing so well. And I'm sorry, but that woman, the one they just took away, the things she was saying about you were just nuts. Really.'

'What things was she saying?'

'Oh, just nonsense, really. That you were controlling her and had been sent to undermine the whole town, blah blah blah. Ridiculous. I just wanted you to know. In case you hear things via Chinese whispers. No one will pay any attention. You've got nothing to worry about. Everyone in the area knows you're brilliant.'

'Well, thank you so much,' said Freddie's dad. 'I really appreciate your reassurance. I know Felix and he's a great boy. I'm glad you didn't have to move him away.'

The man shook Dad's hand and went back to his wife, who was smiling really creepily at Dad and had that look in her eyes that women always seemed to have when they were around him.

Freddie grimaced and followed his dad to a table in the corner by the door. They toasted each other and crunched on scratchings and Freddie thought, *Well, this is nice, but kind of strange,* and they chatted for a while about how Freddie was getting on at school and the spring ball he wanted to go to, and his dad attempted some light teasing about girls which Freddie managed to brush off quite suavely with a practised 'I'm not ready for girls yet' even though it appeared currently no longer to be the case. And as this conversation meandered along it occurred to Freddie that his dad might be building up to asking him about the photos on his hard drive and he sat straight and bolstered himself, ready with some bullshit nonsense about school projects and the study of psychological disorders – like maybe, *voyeurism* – but the question never came and soon they were talking about days gone by, remembering old places they'd lived in and strange people they'd known and his dad was being so loose-limbed and genial, so focused on him and their conversation that Freddie found himself asking, 'Dad, did you ever find out what was going on with that angry woman in the Lake District?'

His father suddenly tightened up. 'What angry woman?'

'Remember? That woman who came up to you when we were on that day trip and started hitting you?'

He rolled his eyes. 'Oh. God. Her. God, yes, I remember her. I don't know. It was all so . . . *odd*. Wasn't it?'

'And you know, when you took her across the street, when you were talking to her. I always wondered what she was saying to you? And what you were saying to her?'

'Christ. I don't know. Probably just telling her she was being inappropriate, that she was upsetting my wife and my child. Calming her down, I suppose.'

'It was horrible,' Freddie said softly. 'That day. It was scary. And it was horrible.'

'Was it?' asked his dad.

'Yes. I'll never forget it. And now this woman, Jenna's mum, she hates you too.'

'Ah, well, I think there is a difference between Mrs Tripp and the lady in the Lakes. The lady by the lake thought I was someone else; it was a case of mistaken identity. Jenna's mum . . . well, she's clearly got some kind of psychological disorder.'

Freddie nodded, agreeing with the distinction, but still uncertain about one thing. 'Do they know each other, do you think?' he asked.

'Who? Jenna's mum and the lady at the lake?'

'Yes. Because . . .' Freddie paused, selecting his words carefully. 'I heard you and Mum talking. Saying that Jenna's mum remembers you from that holiday.'

'You heard us? When?'

'The other morning. In the kitchen.'

His dad sighed. 'Well, you weren't supposed to hear that, but I don't suppose it matters as Jenna's mum was not on holiday with us and her thinking she was is just part of her disorder. Poor soul.'

'Will Jenna be put into care?'

His dad sucked in his breath. 'God. I really hope not. But it's possible, I suppose. If her mum ends up being sectioned. If her dad can't take her. But hopefully it won't come to that. Hopefully I can make sure it doesn't.'

Freddie nodded sagely.

His dad, the superhero.

35

Joey had seen it all. It had just begun to kick off as she got off the bus that night on the other side of the street. She'd stood and watched it unfold: the shouting woman, the blue lights, the police escort.

She hadn't been the only one watching. There'd been a little bank of spectators. Nothing exciting ever happened in Melville – crazy people being escorted out of bars was the sort of thing that happened in the city, not here in this cosseted backwater – so when it did it couldn't be ignored.

When she returned the house was in full darkness and it was quiet enough to hear the sound of the tap dripping into the kitchen sink, the gurgle and buzz of the refrigerator. She wondered if she was alone. She went to Rebecca's study at the top of the landing and knocked quietly on her door.

'Yes.'

'Ah,' she said, pushing open the door, 'you *are* at home.' She saw the screen on one of Rebecca's monitors switch quickly from some kind of image to a sheet of data.

'Yes.' Rebecca stared at her. 'Hi.'

She looked chalky white in the glow of her computer screens. Her eyes were fixed wide, as though she'd been staring without blinking for hours. The window was slightly open and the room was cold, yet Rebecca sat in a thin blouse and bare feet.

'God, it's freezing in here! Aren't you cold?'

Joey walked to the window to shut it, her eyes quickly searching the dark reflections of Tom Fitzwilliam's bedroom window for a glimpse of his wife. But the room was empty, the lights were off. She peered down into the village. Between two passing cars she saw what looked suspiciously like Tom Fitzwilliam and his son entering the bar entrance at the Melville.

Her heart quickened and, almost breathlessly, she said to Rebecca, 'Fancy going down to the Melville for an early supper? On me?'

* * *

They walked into the bar half an hour later. Joey had showered, brushed her teeth and put on tight jeans and earrings with small diamanté drops that she knew would glitter in candlelight. At first she didn't see Tom. She thought with a heavy heart that she must have missed him. But as she stood at the bar she turned slightly and saw him tucked away in the corner with his son at a tiny table for two. He looked up just as she looked at him and she saw it, immediately, bright and unmistakeable: a look of excitement.

She returned his diamond smile and mouthed a *hi*.

She and Rebecca took a table slightly out of sight of Tom's table; it was the only one free on a Friday night.

'Thank you,' Rebecca said, touching her Virgin Mary to the side of Joey's Bloody Mary, 'this was a good idea. Sometimes I really do need to be reminded about the big world out there, I become so . . .' She trailed off suddenly and her gaze left Joey's face and drifted to someone approaching behind. Joey could feel him before she saw him. Her heart lifted and her blood ran quicker. She looked up and smiled.

'Hi, Tom,' she said. 'I would have come over but I didn't want to disturb you and your boy having special quality time.'

'Bless you,' he said, leaning in to kiss her cheek,

which, because it was Tom Fitzwilliam, felt like an appallingly erotic and complicated manoeuvre that could go wrong in so many unthinkable ways that she could barely breathe. She rose slightly from her seat to meet him halfway and the kiss passed without incident and Joey managed to pull herself together sufficiently to say, 'You know my sister-in-law, Rebecca, I suppose?'

'Yes!' Tom replied brightly. 'Yes, I do. Lovely to see you again. It's been ages. I've barely seen you since you moved in.'

'No,' Rebecca replied drily. 'I keep myself to myself.'

'And I see you and Jack have been busy.' He nodded towards Rebecca's stomach and there was a moment of slightly painful silence prompting Tom to say, 'Oh, God. Tell me it is a baby. It *is* a baby? Yes?'

Joey waited for Rebecca to reassure Tom that, yes, of course it was a baby, but she didn't, she merely stared at him with her mouth slightly agape leaving Joey to say, 'Yes. It's a baby. My niece. Due in approximately two months.'

'Lovely,' said Tom. 'Congratulations. How's Jack?'

'Jack's fine,' Rebecca replied. 'Thank you.' A crisp afterthought.

'Good,' said Tom, throwing Joey a sideways look so loaded with intimacy that it made her feel light-headed.

He turned back to his table where his son was staring intently at his smartphone, casting his eye across the room every couple of seconds, 'I should get back to Freddie. In fact, I should get him home. No doubt he's got a ton of homework to do. Lovely to see you, Rebecca. And lovely to see you again, Josephine.'

'*Josephine?*' Rebecca hissed at her as Tom sauntered back to his table. 'Why does he call you Josephine?'

She shrugged. 'I must have told him that's what I was called. That night when he had to bring me home. And now it's sort of stuck.'

'Why would you tell him your name was Josephine?'

'Because it is.'

'But no one calls you that.'

'Oh, God. I don't know. Maybe I was trying to impress him or something. Maybe I thought it made me sound better than I am.'

Rebecca blinked at her. 'Why would you want to do that?'

'Because . . .' Joey pushed her celery stick around the edges of her glass. 'I don't know. You wouldn't understand.'

'I might. Try me.'

'Well, imagine,' she said, 'just imagine spending your whole entire life in the shadow of a guy like Jack.

Imagine cocking everything up, literally everything you do, and every time you look up from your own mess for even a minute there's Jack, right there, doing literally everything right. And not just that, but being so fucking lovely about it. And I'm just, you know, stupid, chaotic *Joey*. And then I find myself talking to *another* incredible properly grown-up human being who does everything right and solves everybody's problems and maybe I just wanted him to think that I was a smart, together Josephine. Not a stupid Joey. You know?'

'I get that,' said Rebecca. 'I do. I feel that way too, sometimes.'

'About Jack?'

'Yes. About Jack. About people I work with. Most people really.' She shrugged. 'You know, when I first met you I was terrified of you. I still am.'

'What!'

'Yes. Jack always talked about you like you were some kind of cowgirl, out there in Ibiza, wrangling the rowdy stags, up all night, unstoppable, fearless. And then I met you and you were just so young and so cool, you give off this vibe like you could, you know, ride wild horses, shoot tin cans off walls. You seem so spontaneous, so free. While Jack is, yes, very successful but also so very measured and careful. Everything planned and thought through. No room for surprises. And I'm the same, so I guess in a way I find that side of you inspiring. But also scary.'

'Well,' said Joey, 'please do not feel scared of me for another moment. I can assure you that I cannot ride wild horses and I have zero spontaneity and I am absolutely just a sad, sad loser.'

'Stop it, Joey. Please. Just stop it. Because the thing is, the longer you tell yourself you're a loser, the more likely it is that that's what people will see you as. And you're not. You're superb. And you know . . .' She plucked at the cuffs of her thin blouse. 'I knew someone very like you, once upon a time. She was amazing and vital and beautiful and cool and she never believed in herself and she thought everyone was better than her and that everyone else knew what they were doing apart from her and then, one day when she was fourteen years old . . .' She paused, her gaze fixed upon her hands. Then she looked up at Joey and continued: 'She killed herself.'

Joey gulped and stared at Rebecca. 'Oh my God,' she said, 'who was it?'

Rebecca pulled her cuffs down over the heels of her hands. She looked up at Joey again and said, 'She was my baby sister.'

RECORDED INTERVIEW

Date: 25/03/2017
Location: Trinity Road Police Station, Bristol BS2 0NW
Conducted by: Officers from Somerset & Avon Police

POLICE: Please could you give your full name, for the recording.

AB: Alfie James Butter.

POLICE: And your address?

AB: Fourteen Melville Heights.

POLICE: Thank you. Just a couple of very simple questions for you, Mr Butter.

AB: Please call me Alfie.

POLICE: Certainly. Of course, Alfie. Where were you on Friday night, 24 March?

AB: I was at my mum's until about seven o'clock. And then I headed home.

POLICE: And where does your mum live?

AB: She lives in Frenchay.

POLICE: Thank you. And how did you get home?

AB: I got the bus. I haven't got a car right now. I'm saving for a van. For my painting job.

POLICE: So you got the number . . . ?

AB: The 218, from the city.

POLICE: And you got back to Melville at?

AB: At about seven forty I suppose.

POLICE: And can you talk us through what happened after you got back to the village?

AB: Yeah. Sure. I stopped in at the corner shop and bought a couple of bottles of beer. I'd just texted Joey . . .

POLICE: That's Ms Mullen?

AB: Yeah, that's right. And she'd said she was staying in town shopping and wouldn't be back for a while. And I needed a drink. You know. Friday night and all that. Then I walked up the hill to the house.

POLICE: And did you see anyone as you walked up the hill?

AB: No. I didn't see anyone.

POLICE: And you live with Ms Mullen's older brother and his wife. Is that correct?

AB Yes. That's spot on.

POLICE: And were either of them at home when you returned?

AB: No idea. I didn't see either of them. It's not my place so I try to just keep my head down as much as I can. Don't want to get in their way. So I wasn't going to go seeking them out. You know? So, yeah, I just took my beers and went straight up to our room to wait for Joey.

POLICE: And what time did Joey get home? From the shops?

AB: It must have been, I dunno, about eight fifteen. Eight thirty?

POLICE: Can you be more specific?

AB: Yeah. No. I dunno. Roughly that.

POLICE: And did she come straight up? As far as you're aware?

AB: I had music playing so I wouldn't have heard the front door going. But, yeah. I reckon she'd come straight up. She was still in her coat and her hands were cold. And her cheeks. Like she'd just come in from outside. Why?

POLICE: And how did she appear to you? Did she appear anxious? Or breathless in any way?

AB: No. She seemed . . . well, a bit, I don't know – she said she'd had a stressful day. That the shops were rammed. She was tired. All that. So she wasn't exactly jumping with joy or anything. But she was all right.

POLICE: All right?

AB: Yeah, she was fine.

POLICE: And what did she do, when she came upstairs?

AB: I don't really know. We chatted for a bit. And then she took a shower.

POLICE: And what did she buy? At the shops? Did she tell you?

AB: A new bra. Apparently.

POLICE: Did she show you the bra?

AB: Yes. She was wearing it. What's the deal here? You don't think Joey had anything to do with this? Do you?

POLICE: Thank you, Alfie. That's it for now.

36

10 March

It was an hour since the police had left and Jenna lay in her fleece pyjamas in a foetal ball on her bed. She held her phone in her cupped hands and stared at the screen. Bess was out with Ruby and someone called Jed. Jenna had no idea who Jed was but he seemed to like sticking his tongue out any time someone pointed a camera at him. They had started off at a KFC in town and now appeared to be in someone's bedroom. It wasn't Bess's bedroom. Jenna knew Bess's bedroom almost as well as she knew her own. Snap Maps said she was at 24 Hawthorne Drive, a road in Lissenden, the next village along.

Her gut clenched at the thought of the parallel world in which she had gone to KFC after school with Bess and Ruby and Jed and was now sitting cross-legged in someone's bedroom larking about in that carefree Friday-night way. Jed, despite his constantly protruding tongue, appeared to be quite good-looking. Maybe Jenna could have flirted with him. Maybe Jed would have ended up, in this parallel existence, being her first love, the boy she lost her virginity to. But she would never know, because she was here, curled up in bed, her stomach still churning in the aftermath of the hideous episode in the Melville, the humiliation of walking out with the policemen while the locals stood across the street gawping at them, the stress of lying to the PCs, to her father, to everyone.

She clicked on Snap Maps again and saw that Bess was still at number 24 Hawthorne Drive. It was ten forty-five. Bess's mum liked her home by eleven at the weekends. She'd have to leave soon if she was going to make it.

She could hear her own mum downstairs, puttering about. In the old days, before she was ill, her mum always liked to be in bed by ten with a herbal tea and a good book, but now she was regularly downstairs until midnight, 1 a.m., 2 a.m., chatting online with people in the US, checking and rechecking things, taking photos, making endless notes. She could hear her going through the kitchen cupboards now, making a mental inventory of everything so that in the morning she'd know if anyone had been in in the night to rearrange their cutlery drawer.

Jenna rolled over on to her other side and looked at her phone again. Bess had left Jed's house. She was moving quite fast so she must be in a taxi, or her mum might have gone to collect her – which was unlikely as their block of flats had first come, first served off-street parking and her mum refused to move her car for anything other than emergencies. She watched the little icon heading towards Lower Melville. She pictured Bess in the back seat, feeling awkward and not knowing whether she should talk to the driver or not. She'd be staring resolutely at her phone right now and Jenna thought about messaging her but her thumb slid away from the screen again.

At ten fifty-five the little icon stopped on the high street and Jenna waited for it to show her best friend safely tucked up at home. She waited and waited but still the icon showed her on the high street, opposite the Melville. The time turned to five past eleven and Jenna uncurled herself and sat on the edge of her bed. Why wasn't Bess at home? She refreshed the app to see if maybe it had frozen, but still the icon showed Bess where the taxi driver had dropped her. Suddenly Jenna pictured the doors of the taxi being locked, the windows steamed up, her little friend pinned on the back seat under some big sweaty man, frantically trying to get the attention of a passer-by. She jumped off the bed, ran down the stairs, pulled on her mum's coat and old gardening shoes and dashed from the house.

As she got to the end of her road she could see that there was no taxi with steamed-up windows parked across the street. She narrowed her eyes, searching for the pale blond dome of her friend's head and when her eyes finally found it she stopped and caught her breath so hard it hurt. Because there, standing together in the doorway of the local pharmacy, deep in conversation, were Bess and Mr Fitzwilliam.

37

Freddie's dad had left the house at gone eleven, walked down the escarpment to Lower Melville and come back fifteen minutes later with what looked like a box of cornflakes. But his father didn't eat cereal. His mother didn't eat breakfast. The only person in the house who might have had the slightest interest in cornflakes was him, Freddie. But even then, his interest in cornflakes was minimal and certainly not strong enough to precipitate a middle-of-the-night dash into the village. The whole evening had been unsettling. The incident with Jenna's mum and the police, and then his dad taking him out and being really nice and allowing him to open up about the thing in the Lake District, and then Red Boots walking in with her mate and her dad being all flirty and weird with her. And there'd been a strange moment, just as he and his dad left a moment later, when he turned briefly to look at Red Boots and caught the eye of her pregnant friend and something in her gaze had sliced through him like a laser.

He got out of bed and crept to his door. He could hear his mum and dad murmuring together in their bedroom across the landing. He heard the murmuring climb up the dial towards lively debate and then head rather quickly towards hushed shouting.

His stomach clenched. He stood for a few more minutes listening to the shouting buck and reel. He could make out the odd word and the occasional phrase: '. . . that girl. Nothing to do with me. Never, ever, ever. How could I have known?' But he could not string enough of them together to form a coherent thread. For a moment his parents fell silent and a blade of fear cut through him. He tensed his body and squeezed his eyes closed and waited and waited for it to come: the terrible slap of flesh against flesh, the muffled moans of pain, the thud of bodies being flung about. Nausea swept through him. How could a night that had started with a glass of ice-cold Coke at the

Melville with his dad be ending like this? It couldn't. It just couldn't.

But the silence continued and after a moment he opened his eyes again, unclenched his fists, let his breath out slow and steady. He heard the toilet in his parents' en-suite shower room being flushed, the click of the light switch, the innocuous squeak of bed-springs. He moved away from his bedroom door and back towards his window.

The village was closing down for the night: the last stragglers were leaving the Melville, the Thai restaurant was already locked up and switched off, the pavements virtually empty. And down there, out of sight, were Jenna Tripp and her mad mum. He wondered what they were both thinking tonight. He wondered how Jenna was feeling. He held his hand to the cold glass of his window until it left a ghostly, foggy imprint; then he drew his curtains again and climbed into bed.

38

11 March

'You never told me that Rebecca had a sister who killed herself.'

Jack glanced up from the pile of letters he'd just put on the kitchen table. He was in a T-shirt and pyjama bottoms, his dark hair awry and slightly pungent. He did not look like a man who had spent seven hours the day before performing open heart surgery. He looked like he'd been in the pub all night and had a kebab on the way home.

'What?'

She reached for a box of Weetabix. 'Rebecca. Last

night she told me she had a sister who killed herself when she was fourteen. Why didn't you tell me?'

'God,' he said, 'I don't know. Probably because you weren't here when I was at the finding-out-all-about-Rebecca stage of things.'

'But she's my sister-in-law. I *live* with her. It would have explained so much. It would have made me . . .' Joey paused. She'd been about to say, *It would have made me like her.* 'Understand her better,' she finished.

'Sorry,' he said. 'It didn't occur to me. And besides, maybe I thought it was none of my business. You know, she's very private.'

'Yes. I do know that. But still. It's such a huge thing not to know about someone.'

'Well,' Jack said, 'now you know.'

'Why . . . ?' Joey paused again. She didn't want to sound as though she was being ghoulish. 'Why did she do it? Rebecca said she didn't really know.'

Jack sighed. 'No one knew. She didn't leave a note and everyone blamed everyone else and the whole thing was a horrible mess. I think for a while they all thought it had been something to do with a teacher at her school. That there'd been some kind of inappropriate relationship. But it turned out that there was nothing to it. Just a schoolgirl crush. It turned out that she killed herself for nothing.' He sighed. 'Her dad ended up turning to drink, and her mother died a few years ago having never come to terms with it. It completely destroyed them.'

'I just can't imagine,' Joey began. 'I mean, God. If you'd done that when you were fourteen. If I'd lost you. And then Mum. I would just . . . I would never have been happy again. Fuck.' She felt a tear start to form in her left eye and blinked it back.

'Are you crying?'

'Not really,' she replied.

He peered at her closely. 'Oh, God,' he said. 'Triple bypass *and* crying women. It's all too much. Come here.' He opened up his arms to Joey and she stepped inside his embrace. He smelled of bed and unwashed hair. He smelled of home.

'You'll never die, will you?' she sniffed into his T-shirt.

'I'm going to try really hard not to.'

'Good.' She nodded. 'That's good. Because I don't think I'd be able to live without you.'

Alfie was lying across the bed, naked, in a post-coital tangle of sheets. She'd waited up for him to get back from his bar job until 1 a.m. the night before, then pounced on him. He'd been surprised and pleased and had then ruined it by suggesting towards the end, breathlessly and lovingly, that he not use a condom.

'Fuck!' she'd said, her eyes wide in the dark of their room. 'No! We haven't decided about that yet! We haven't decided! You can't just randomly suggest it in the middle of sex!'

'No,' he'd said gently. 'No. You're right. I'm sorry. I just thought. You seemed so . . .'

'What, into having sex with you?

'Well, yes.'

'And why would that mean that I suddenly want to have a baby?'

'It doesn't. Not at all. It was just . . . I'm sorry, OK? Can we forget it?'

They'd managed somehow to get back to the point where they'd left off and finish in a reasonable state of harmony. But as Alfie faded into a deep sleep, Joey un-pinned his arm from around her torso, moved to her own side of the bed and then lay awake for an hour, trawling her psyche for the real underlying reasons why she didn't want to have a baby with Alfie. Which inevitably redirected her thoughts to Tom Fitzwilliam. Her mind began replaying and replaying the journey into work that morning in Tom's car, the intimacy of it, the way it had felt when he told her she had beautiful eyes, and then she'd moved on to the feeling of his hand against her arm in the Melville when he kissed her hello. She'd finally fallen asleep at about two thirty and when she awoke six hours later she found she'd been dreaming of Tom Fitzwilliam.

'Morning, lover,' she said now, climbing on to the bed and sitting cross-legged.

'Morning.' Alfie rolled over and wrapped his arms around her knees.

She dropped a kiss on to the crown of his head. 'Fancy dim sum in town later with Jack and Rebecca?'

'What's that?' he said. 'Dumplings?'

'Yes,' she said. 'Dumplings. In little baskets. And noodles and things.'

'Sounds fucking awesome,' he said, nuzzling his face into her thigh. 'Dumplings. Awesome.'

39

13 March

Jenna sat outside Mr Fitzwilliam's office. It was nine o'clock on Monday morning and this time she knew exactly why she'd been asked to come and see him. She pressed down the fabric of her pleated skirt and fiddled with the clasp of the fluffy pompom that hung from her school bag. She was missing physics. She hated physics. But she kind of wanted to be in physics today because it was one of the only classes she shared with Bess this term.

She heard Mr Fitzwilliam finish a mumbled phone call, and then clear his throat before opening the door of his office and gesturing her through. 'Good morning, Miss Tripp,' he said.

She wanted to say, *Please don't call me that. Just call me Jenna!* But she didn't. She smiled instead and said, 'Morning.'

'And how are you today?'

She shrugged and said, 'Good.'

He led them to the same set of comfy chairs where they'd sat the week before.

'Good,' he said, pulling out a chair for her and then pulling one out for himself. 'Good. Right, well, I suppose you know why you're here?'

'My mum,' she mumbled.

'Yes. Your mum. Although actually, really, mainly *you*, in fact. Because as much as I care about your mum, as a teacher at your school, *your* welfare is my primary concern. And really, I want to know how you are?'

'I'm good,' she said.

'Yes,' he replied. 'I know you're good, in that way that all children these days are *good*. And I know that's just shorthand for *I am a swirling whirlpool of insecurities and dark thoughts that I have zero interest in talking to* you *about, buddy.'*

Jenna shuddered inside at the word *buddy*. Who even said things like that?

'But clearly there are things at home that you are having to deal with and I know it's just you, that your father and your brother live twenty miles away. And after what happened on Friday night I'm getting a much clearer picture of how things are for you. Listen . . .' He did that thing again, where he leaned right forward, so his face was just a few inches from her, and engaged her in such heavy-duty eye contact that it made her want to close her eyes. 'I get that you're months away from your GCSEs and that this is where your friends are and that you're scared that if the social services get involved you might have to move. I totally understand that. But you need to know that you have options. Lots of options.'

She blinked at him. She had no idea what he was talking about.

'You wouldn't have to go and live with your dad. I'd make sure of that. I'd make sure that you could stay in the area and stay at the Academy until the end of your exams. Or longer.'

She wanted to say, *How?* but she kind of didn't want to know. If she asked him he'd tell her and then she couldn't help feeling she'd be dragged into something weird that she didn't want to be involved with.

'Does your dad know?' he asked. 'Does he know how unwell your mum is?'

'Kind of,' she said, staring into her lap. 'Sort of. Most of it. I mean, that's why they split up.'

'Because of your mum's illness?'

'Yes. Well. It didn't seem like an illness then. It just seemed like she was, you know, a bit paranoid. A bit scatty. It just seemed like they weren't getting on.'

'And this was how long ago?'

She shrugged. 'About four years ago, I suppose.'

'And since then, things have got worse?'

She wanted to shake her head and say, *No, not really.* But instead she found herself nodding, and then, to her absolute horror, she found a tear rolling first down one cheek and then the other.

'Oh, Jenna.' Mr Fitzwilliam leaned over to a small table behind him and grabbed a box of tissues. 'Oh dear. Here,' he said, pulling one out with a flourish and handing it to her. 'Here.'

She scrumpled it up between her hands and pressed it to her face. She breathed in hard to try to keep the tears at bay but she could feel them building tsunami-like at the base of her gullet, her whole head throbbed with them and then suddenly they were out and she was sobbing and she couldn't stop it and she pressed the heels of her hands hard into her eye sockets but it made no difference, they kept coming.

Mr Fitzwilliam didn't say anything. He just sat, his

hands held together and hanging between his knees, and he watched her cry. Once the tidal wave of tears had subsided slightly, she chanced a look up at him. She was surprised to notice that his eyes were green.

'Sorry.' She sniffed. 'I'm really sorry.'

'No,' he said. 'Please don't be sorry. Please just cry for as long as you need to cry.'

'I'm done now,' she said.

'Are you sure?' he said. 'Because I'm free for another . . .' He looked at the watch with the red and yellow strap. 'Forty-eight minutes. So, you can keep crying for quite some time if you'd like.'

She found herself smiling. 'No,' she said. 'I'm good. Honestly.'

He passed her a waste-paper bin for her to drop her used tissue into and then he passed her the box of tissues again so she could take a fresh one.

'So,' he said. 'Your mum's got worse, has she?'

She nodded. She could hardly deny it now. 'Yeah, she has a bit. Since you arrived,' she said.

'And this is because, as you said before, she thinks she remembers me from a holiday some years ago?'

She nodded and sniffed, rolling the new tissue around between her hands. 'Yes.'

'And why do you think she thinks she remembers me?'

She sniffed again. 'Because it's true. We did meet you on holiday. I remember it too. I remember your watch.' She nodded towards his wrist. His other hand went to it and touched it briefly.

'You remember my watch?'

'Mm-hm. It matched your shirt. That's why I noticed it.'

He looked at her askance. 'Gosh,' he said, 'you've got a good memory. And where was it that our paths crossed? Exactly?'

'On a coach trip. In the Lakes.'

She looked straight into his eyes watching for his reaction and when it came he looked so horribly trapped that she had to look away again immediately. But within a split second the soft expression was back in place and he said, 'Ah, yes. *That* coach trip. I assume you remember the episode with the lady.'

She nodded.

'You know, I never worked out what that was about,' he said, twisting himself back into his seat. 'Very odd. And for some reason, if I'm understanding you correctly, whatever it was that happened that day, your mother saw it and decided it had something to do with her?'

She nodded again.

'And now she thinks . . . ? That I'm somehow *stalking* her?'

'Kind of.'

'And that I'm in charge of lots of other people who are also stalking her?'

'It's called gang-stalking,' she said abruptly. She couldn't bear the drip-feed of information and just wanted to get it out there now in one chunk. 'It's a psychotic delusional disorder. There are, like, thousands of people across the world who think it's happening to them. They call themselves targeted individuals. TIs. And they all chat to each other on the internet all the time and the more they chat the more they believe it's real and that's what's really made things worse. Not my mum's illness, but her talking to loads of other mad people about it.'

'So, really, if it hadn't been me she'd fixated on, it might have been someone else?'

'I guess.'

He nodded and narrowed his eyes at her. Then he sighed. He looked vaguely relieved. 'You can't carry on like this on your own, Jenna, you know that, don't you?'

'It's fine,' she said. 'Seriously. It's totally fine. I don't need anything. I know how to handle it.'

'What did the police say?'

'Nothing,' she said. 'They just asked a load of questions and went.'

He nodded and held the knuckles of one hand briefly to his mouth while he formed his next comment.

'Well, listen: for now, Jenna, at the very least, please, please will you tell your dad about what happened on Friday? Please?'

'But there's no reason for him to know. He's got enough on his plate. He's running a shop and looking after my brother.'

Mr Fitzwilliam sighed. 'You know, Jenna, I could just call him in. It would probably be the right thing to do. I can see that you're a very capable young woman. And I can see that you are very keen to cope with this situation by yourself. But I want to know that someone else is looking out for you. And that person should be your father. Will you promise me, Jenna, that you'll call him?'

She nodded.

'Today?'

She nodded again. 'Yeah,' she said. 'I guess.'

'Good.' He smiled. 'And meanwhile, remember: I'm here. Whatever you need. Whenever you need it. OK?'

He threw her a look. It was supposed to be cosy and reassuring but it just looked creepy to her. She tugged her rucksack on to her lap and got quickly to her feet.

And then, just as she was about to leave, once there

was enough physical distance between them for her to feel able to breathe and think again, she turned and said, 'Sir, why were you talking to B—?'

He grasped his tie. 'I'm sorry?'

'Nothing,' she said, losing her nerve. 'Nothing.'

40

Freddie didn't have any friends at school. He walked to school alone. Even if his journey coincided with a boy or two from his form there would be no acknowledgement of his presence, no nod of the head or casual *All right Fred?* He ate lunch alone in his form room. Twice a week he went to lunchtime chess club sessions, but there was no bonhomie there, no banter or potential for friendship. And once a week he went to coding club after school. Not because he wanted to but because his dad had said he had to do at least one after-school club or he'd cut off his access to the internet. Coding was all right. There was a guy there called Max who always made an effort, said hello, asked how he was, partnered up with him when they were told to do things in pairs. Freddie wouldn't call him a friend but he was as close as it came.

But Max was of no use to him right now because Max was five feet tall, about six stone, had long hair and wore squashy shoes, and it was obvious just from looking at him that he had precisely zero interest in girls, let alone any useful insight into them.

Posters for the spring ball had gone up around school and tickets were on sale. Romola had mentioned it in a chat on Instagram the night before; some girl had posted a photo of herself posing in a changing room in a skin-tight dress with the caption #springball17 #sayyestothedress #doesmybumlookbiginthis.

After a slew of girls piling in to say *ohmygod, no of course your bum does not look big, are you mad? like, you're so perfect, ohmygod,* Romola left a comment saying *that is a really very nice dress indeed.*

Freddie had zoomed in on the photo, looking for some clue as to where it might be from, and found half a logo painted on to the inside of the cubicle that looked like the letters URBN arranged into a square. He'd googled URBN and found that it was the Urban Outfitters' logo and he'd gone straight onto their website to find the dress and ordered it, even though it was sixty pounds.

'You going to the spring ball?' he asked Max now.

Max peered at him through the curtains of his hair. 'What?'

'The spring ball? Next week. You know, the one with St Mildred's?'

Max grimaced. 'No,' he said. 'Why would I?'

Freddie shrugged. 'I didn't say you would. I just asked if you were.'

'Are you?'

'I don't know,' he said casually. 'I'm thinking about it.'

'Christ,' said Max. 'Think I'd rather die.'

'Thought you'd say that.'

'What's your motivation?'

'A girl,' he said. 'I want to take a girl.'

'What, like a particular girl, or just some random girl?'

'Yes, a particular girl.'

Max looked at him curiously and said, 'Hmm.'

'Hmm what?'

'Nothing,' said Max. 'Nothing.'

'No. Seriously. Tell me what you're hmming at?'

'Nothing. Really. Just, you know, guys like us' – he pointed at himself and then at Freddie – 'we don't get to take girls to dances. It's against the laws of nature. Of natural selection.'

'What the fuck?'

'Unless she's a moose? Is the girl you want to take to the dance a moose?'

'No. She's entirely gorgeous.'

'Well then, my friend, forget it.'

Freddie blinked slowly. He felt a terrible dark swirl of fury building inside him. He wanted suddenly to hurt Max. Not just lash out at him with a swinging fist, but somehow to *dissect* him. Pull him into tiny bits, slowly, agonisingly.

'I am not', he said through gritted teeth, 'a guy like you.'

Max shrugged and turned back to his laptop. 'If you say so,' he muttered.

Freddie turned to his computer and tried to concentrate on the task they'd been given but his head was too full of hatred of Max. He stared at his pathetic face in profile: his downy skin and droopy baby cheeks, the lank hair that hung in his eyes.

'I bet', Freddie hissed in his ear, 'that you sleep in your mum's bed and wake up every morning with a tiny little hard-on.'

Max threw him a look of disgust. 'Christ, you're sick.'

The hands on the clock on the wall of the IT room turned from 4.59 to 5 p.m. Freddie pulled his blazer from the back of his chair and stalked from the room. He snatched his stuff from his locker and left the school building, letting the doors slam closed in someone else's face.

He walked to Romola's house even though he knew she was probably already tucked up inside. He stood at the entrance to the little mews, pretending to be texting someone. A man appeared by his side. The man paused briefly to look at his own phone before sliding it into his jacket pocket and continuing past Freddie into the mews. Freddie watched with interest as he pulled a set of keys from his pocket and approached Romola's house. The little dog started to yap behind the front door. The man opened the door, herded the dog gently back into the hallway with the edge of his foot and then closed the door behind him again.

Romola's dad.

The thought that he'd seen Romola's dad gave him a rush of something to his chest, a kind of dopamine, winning feeling, as though he'd just cleared a level on a computer game. Now he'd seen her dog *and* her dad. He glanced up at the first-floor windows: tiny squares covered over with smart, slatted wooden shutters. Up there was Romola's room. He wanted to see inside

Romola's room. He wanted to sit on her bed and watch her getting ready for the spring ball.

At the thought of the spring ball the memory of Max's comment about *guys like us* reappeared and made his head fill with rage again. He kicked his foot against the wall where he was standing and muttered under his breath. How could he be a guy like Max? There was just no way, literally no way. He was way better than Max. He was way better than most of the guys at his school.

He was about to turn and head home when he heard the unmistakeable sound of multiple teenage girls behind him; that ambiguous noise which sat exactly halfway between mirth and terror. He looked up and then quickly down at his phone again. He turned away from the mews so that he was facing the other way and leaned, as casually as he could, against the wall he'd just kicked. It was Romola and two girls who both looked like total fucking bitches.

One of them had a paper packet of McDonald's chips in her hand, the other a paper cup full of Starbucks shit. Romola had just a bottle of water. They passed him in a swathe of body spray and horrible honking laughter. All three eyed his Poleash Hall blazer warily, looked him up and down to see if they knew him and then turned their gazes quickly away when they realised they didn't. He watched surreptitiously as all three walked up the mews to Romola's house. Even from here and based on under one minute of observation, Freddie could tell Romola wasn't comfortable, that she'd somehow been coerced into after-school jollies with these girls, somehow allowed them to invite themselves back to her house. She was the new girl. She would, he knew from vast experience, take what she could get in the early days.

He heard the dog yapping again as Romola unlocked the front door, he heard the honking girls start to squawk and squeak with excitement about the tiny dog – 'Ohmygod, ohmygod, he's sooo cute!' – then the door banged shut behind them and it was quiet again.

He looked at the time. It was five thirty-five. He was hungry. He headed home.

His mum was sitting in the kitchen watching a game show on the telly. She didn't turn when he walked in.

'Hi, Mum,' he said.

'Hi, love,' she replied, still without turning.

'You OK?'

'Yup. I'm fine.'

He put down his school bag and stood between his mum and the TV.

Her face was pale. She looked wan and run down.

Ever since they'd moved to Melville, and especially since her broken ankle had healed and she'd been able to start running again, he'd been used to seeing his mum with a vital glow, cheeks flushed with colour, eyes bright with life.

'You not going running today?'

She looked at him distractedly for a moment, and then managed a smile. 'No,' she said. 'Not today.' As she said this her hand moved vaguely towards her throat and then away again. It was a tiny, throwaway gesture, but Freddie had seen it before and he knew what it meant. His eyes searched for and found the tinge of reddish-blue bruising above the collar of her shirt.

His stomach churning with nausea, he climbed the stairs to his bedroom.

41

14 March

Jenna could see him trundling down the hill from Melville Heights the next morning, his weird oil-slick hair curtaining his eyes, that look of pained disdain visible even from here. She waited by the bus stop in case he was going to get the bus, but he didn't, he carried on out of the village, towards the city where his posh school must be. She followed behind him for a moment, practising her opening line over and over in her head, and then she increased her pace to catch up with him.

'Freddie,' she said.

He turned sharply at the sound of his name and then looked at her in utter shock. 'Oh. Right. Hi.'

'I was just thinking', she said, 'about what you were saying the other day. About that time in the Lake District. And I *was* there. Me and my mum and dad and my kid brother. I remember it.'

Freddie stopped walking and turned to face her. 'Oh yes?'

'I remember you all on the coach and I remember the woman coming out of nowhere and screaming at your dad.'

He nodded encouragingly but seemed to be having trouble forming a verbal response.

'So,' she said, 'you said you wanted to talk about it? What was it you wanted to know exactly?'

'It was . . .' She saw a red veil creep up his face from his neck. 'It was . . . Do you know what happened?'

'No,' she said. 'No. I thought you might know? I mean, who was that woman?'

Freddie shrugged. He rubbed his chin with his fingers and seemed to be trying to look thoughtful, but just looked a little odd. 'I don't know. My father always maintained that she'd mistaken him for someone else. But I always had this . . . this feeling that there was something more to it. Something he didn't want me to know.'

'Like what?'

He shrugged. 'I think I never really believed that he didn't know her. It didn't ring true.'

Jenna nodded.

'How well do you remember it?' he asked.

'I remember it really well,' she said. 'It's just one of those things; when you're a kid, and you see adults being really angry, really aggressive, it sticks in your mind.'

'Yes,' he said. 'Exactly.'

There followed a brief silence. Jenna felt that there was more to this conversation, something Freddie was holding back, but she wasn't sure how to dig it out of him. They'd almost reached the turning for Jenna's school.

'Do you remember her saying *viva*?' she asked in a rush.

Freddie stopped. 'Yes,' he replied. 'Actually, I do.'

'Can you remember her exact words?'

Freddie touched his chin again. 'Something about how viva was her life, viva was her everything.'

'What do you think viva was? Could it have been a person?'

Freddie shrugged. 'I always assumed it was.'

Jenna saw a familiar figure appearing at the bottom of the road. It was Bess. She was on her own. She turned to Freddie, an unplanned question suddenly burning at the tip of her tongue. 'Do you like your dad?'

'What?'

'Your dad? Do you get on with him? Is he an OK dad?

'He's all right.'

'Is he nice to you?'

'Yes,' he said. 'He's pretty nice to me. Much nicer than I am to him.'

'You're not nice to him?'

'No. Not really. He's kind of a dick. Well, not a dick, but, you know, everyone thinks he's so amazing. And I live with him and I see him all the time and I know he's not that amazing and sometimes he's really hard to live with and moody and he can be really—' He stopped and she saw his gaze fall hard to the ground. 'He can just be difficult. But basically, he's fine.'

'Do you think your dad would ... would he ever ... ?' She stopped. She wanted to ask him about Mr Fitzwilliam, about his taste for young girls. She wanted to know if her best friend was in danger of being manipulated or not. But she couldn't. Of course she couldn't. This was his son.

'Nothing,' she said, stopping at the crossroads. 'Look, I'm going to wait for my friend to catch me up so you should go ahead. I'll see you around, OK?'

Freddie looked flummoxed for a moment, as though there was something else he wanted to say. Then he nodded and said, 'Yeah. Cool. I'll see you around.'

She watched him loping off towards the city and sighed. She'd hoped that Freddie Fitzwilliam might have offered up a nugget of insight into his dad, something that might make sense of her strange dislike of him, of her mother's bizarre obsession with him, of the oddness she felt about him and Bess. But she was none the wiser.

She took a deep breath, turned on the spot and waited for Bess to catch up.

'Hey,' she said as Bess came alongside. 'You OK?'

'Yeah. I'm good,' Bess said. 'Who was that you were talking to?' She jutted her chin towards the road into the city.

'Just some boy,' Jenna replied, 'from a private school.'

'Why were you talking to him?'

She shrugged. 'Just was.'

They stood at the pedestrian crossing, waiting for the red man to turn green. 'You around at lunchtime?' Jenna asked awkwardly as the light changed and they started across the road.

'Yeah,' said Bess. 'I guess so.'

'Want to have lunch?'

'Sure,' said Bess.

Mr Fitzwilliam was stationed at the door. He eyed

them walking in together and said, 'Miss Ridley! Miss Tripp! Good morning!'

'Morning, sir,' said Bess, her comportment shifting immediately from awkward and monosyllabic to gushing and cute.

Jenna threw him a tight smile and passed him as quickly as she could without running.

She found Bess in the home room at lunchtime. She was sitting alone, doing her Spanish homework. She looked up when Jenna walked in and gave her an uncertain smile. 'Hi.'

'Hi,' said Jenna. She glanced down at Bess's homework. 'Shit,' she said, 'Didn't you do that?'

'No. Forgot.'

'But there's, like, loads. You'll never get it all done.'

'I know,' Bess said. 'I'm going to pretend my printer broke down halfway through printing it out.'

'Isn't that what you said last time?'

Bess looked up at her uncertainly. 'That was physics, wasn't it?'

'No,' said Jenna. 'It was Spanish. Definitely.'

'Shit,' said Bess. 'Well, what shall I say then?'

Jenna contained a smile. After almost a week of not talking, they'd slipped back into their traditional roles in under a minute.

'I dunno. Maybe you could just hand it in and when he asks where the rest is you could just act all surprised and say you *thought* it didn't seem like that much, maybe the rest of it got muddled up with some other papers. Something like that. Or' – she smiled – 'you could just let me help and do it all?'

Bess smiled back. 'Yes. Option two. Please.'

Jenna laughed and sat down next to Bess.

'You not eating?' she asked Bess, unzipping her lunch bag and taking out a chicken and pasta salad. She glanced at the nutritional information. Six hundred and eighty-two calories. God, she thought, how could salad have so many calories in it?

'No,' said Bess. 'I'm trying to skip lunch this week.'

'Why?'

'Because I'm getting fat.'

Jenna grimaced. 'Don't be so fucking stupid.'

'I am,' said Bess, leaning back to show her the waistband of her school skirt. 'Look. Fatty McFatfat.'

Jenna rolled her eyes. 'That's just water retention, you dick. You're not fat. Here.' She unzipped her bag again and pulled out a spoon. 'Share this salad with me. It's way too fattening for me to eat it all.'

Bess sighed and smiled and took the spoon from Jenna. 'OK then,' she said, digging it straight into the pasta and wolfing it down.

For half an hour they shared the pasta and worked through Bess's Spanish homework. Then, as the clock ran down towards the end of lunchtime, Jenna took a deep breath and said, 'Saw you were over in Lissenden on Friday night.'

Bess looked up at her. 'Yeah,' she said. 'We were at Ruby's cousin's place.'

'Jed?' said Jenna.

'Yes,' said Bess. 'Jed. You been stalkin' me?'

'No, just saw it on Snapchat. Was it good?'

'Yeah. It was fun.'

'Is he fit?'

'Yeah. He's fit. But he's really annoying? Thinks he's such a clown. You know, you just want to say: *Be yourself. Stop being like this professional buffoon. Then maybe some girls might like you.* 'Cos you're properly fit.'

Jenna smiled. She didn't care too much about Jed and she was running out of time to ask the question she really wanted to ask. 'I saw you get a taxi back. On Snap Maps.'

'Oh my God, you have so been stalking me!'

She shook her head. 'When you didn't get out of the taxi I came to find you. I thought you were being, like, raped on the back seat or something.'

'No way.'

'And when I came out, I saw you over the way.

Talking to Mr Fitzwilliam.' She paused and watched her friend's reaction. 'What was that all about?'

'Oh God, yeah, that! I got out the taxi and he was just sort of there. Said he was on his way to the all-night shop.'

'Oh, right. And what were you talking about?'

'Just – stuff. You know.'

'No,' said Jenna. 'Tell me.'

Bess laughed. 'There's nothing to tell!' she said. 'Just, you know, where've you been, how're you doing sort of thing.'

'Were you talking about my mum?'

'No.'

'Do you swear?'

'I totally swear. We just chatted, like about boring stuff.'

'Didn't it feel sort of *weird* though?' she asked.

'No,' said Bess. 'Why should it feel weird?'

'Because he's our head teacher. And he's a man. And he's old. And it was the middle of the night. Didn't it feel awkward?'

Bess shook her head. 'No,' she said, a smile spreading across her face. 'No, it didn't feel awkward. It felt really nice.'

Jenna frowned. 'What's going on with you and him, Bess?' she hissed.

'Going on?'

'Yes. Is he, you know, trying to *groom* you or something?'

The minute she said it she knew it was the wrong line to take. Bess turned and stared at her. 'Oh my God, Jen,' she said. 'Are you serious?'

'I just don't get it,' she said. 'I don't get what you see in him. I don't get why you like him. I think he's really dodgy.'

'He so is not dodgy. God. He's the total opposite of dodgy. He's kind and caring and nice. I swear. He's just the nicest, nicest man in the whole world. Please, Jen,' she said, holding her hands in hers, 'please don't turn into your mum.'

Jenna pulled her hands from Bess's and then pushed back her chair so hard and so fast that it nearly fell over. She stalked from the room, slamming the door shut behind her.

42

A day that started with a conversation with one of the most lusted-after schoolgirls in Melville was always going to be unsettling. A day that started with a highly personal conversation about his relationship with his father, even more so. But it was Jenna's closing comments that stayed with Freddie as he walked towards the city. *Do you think your dad would . . . would he ever . . . ?*

Ever what?

What had she been alluding to?

What did she think his dad might be capable of? More interestingly, what did *he* think his dad might be capable of?

He could air a theory or two but that's all they were: flimsy hypotheses based on nothing more than hazy childhood memories, no facts to back anything up, just a sense that something bad had been following them about as a family ever since he could remember.

He recalled vividly how, as he'd stood and watched the mad woman hit his father by the lake that day, he'd experienced a strong, almost dizzying sensation that he was about to discover something remarkable about his father, about his family, the kernel of something that would explain everything. But it hadn't come.

He'd always thought it was he and he alone who suspected there was something off about his dad. But now there was Jenna Tripp. Jenna Tripp could see it too.

He passed Max as he turned down the road to his school. Max threw him a look of fear blended with disgust. Freddie totally blanked him. As he followed behind him through the school gates he pictured himself with a pair of giant rusty scissors hacking off his stupid long hair and shoving it down his throat.

He handed his phone in to the school receptionist sitting in her big mahogany panelled booth; then he headed to his locker. Here he unloaded his rucksack and his coat before heading to the toilets. That was another shit thing about these old-fashioned private schools housed in Victorian mansions: terrible, cold, echoey toilets. He examined his face for a while in the mirror, the face that Jenna Tripp had just engaged with during their conversation this morning. He stared at himself, trying to see what she might have seen. He looked like his mum. That's what everyone always said. It hadn't meant much to him when he was younger – who cared which one of his parents he looked like? He didn't want to look like his mum; he didn't want to look like his dad either. He ran his hands over his hair. He had very straight, very shiny hair, like his mum. She wore hers in a short bob. It looked nice on her. But did he, with his shiny, poker-straight fringe, maybe look a little monk-like? Or a bit like a girl? He pushed his smooth hair off his forehead and examined the planes of his face. He thought of Max and his infuriating girl's haircut. He pulled hard at his hair until it was all bunched inside his hand and he could barely see it. He grimaced. He snarled. And then he smiled.

That night he walked home via the Greek barber's on the corner and paid them ten pounds to shave it all off into what the barber referred to as a number three. Afterwards, as they swept his hair away and unpinned his cape and brushed the snippets from his shoulders he stared hard at the boy in the mirror who had suddenly transformed into a man. All the weakness and passivity had been expunged from him with the removal of his hair. He was no longer one of Max's *guys like us*. He no longer looked like his mum. Neither did he look like his dad. He looked hard-baked. He looked fierce and fresh and feral. He looked, he thought, running his hand over the suede of his scalp, totally fucking amazing.

He walked home past Romola's school and then past Romola's house and then, just for old times' sake and to test out the feeling of walking about with a shaved head, he walked past Whackadoo. He saw neither Romola nor Joey, but it didn't matter. Just the very act of allowing himself to be seen in this new and somewhat alarming guise was exciting and made his blood pump. People might think he was a yob, he thought, they might think he was about to mug them, or start a fight with them. He passed a group of older teens, swaggering in cheap, baggy sports gear, rangy, swinging limbs, roll-ups pinched between fingers, greasy hair, gimlet eyes. Usually he would shy away, move inside a shadow or to the other side of the street. Often there would be something like cat calls or dangerous looks. Today he strode past them, bristling with fake attitude. He held his breath, waiting for it but it didn't come. They had not registered him. He no longer looked like a kickable private-school freak. He was not on their radar.

His mother was on the sofa when he got home. As much as Freddie found his mum's hyperactivity exhausting to live with, he found these slumps of hers even harder. He propelled himself into the room, to a point directly in front of her, hoping to shock her into some kind of reaction with his new haircut.

'Tada!' he said, striking a pose. 'Whaddya think?'

She glanced up at him. For a moment he saw only the foggy blankness behind her eyes that had been there since Saturday morning. But it quickly lifted and was replaced by a look of sheer horror.

'Oh my God. Freddie. What on *earth* have you done?'

'Got my hair cut off,' he said. 'It was getting in my eyes.'

'But, but . . . you have such lovely hair.'

'No,' he said. 'I don't. I have stupid long shiny hair that made me look like a freak. And anyway, it will grow back.'

He sat alongside his mother on the sofa and smiled at her. 'Stop looking at me like that,' he said teasingly.

'But you don't look like you any more.'

'I know. It's great. I feel great.'

'Oh God, I hope it grows back before we see Grandma next month. She'll probably have a heart attack.'

'It's just hair,' Freddie said, thinking that actually it was much more than just hair. It was his very essence. He looked at his mum and saw that she was crying. 'Oh, God, Mum,' he said. 'God. Please don't cry. I'm sorry. It's just something I needed to do, for me. It's not about you. I swear. Please don't cry.'

But his mum kept crying and he moved across the sofa so that he was closer to her and he put his arms around her and he tried to hug her but she shouted out in pain and pushed him away. 'What?' he said. 'What's the matter?'

'It's nothing. Just a bit of back pain.'

He remembered the dark shadows on her throat yesterday, the raised voices in his parents' room on Friday night. He backed away from her and looked her in the eye and he said, 'Mum. What happened with you and Dad on Friday night?'

She wiped away her tears, sniffed and said, 'What do you mean?'

'I mean, Dad went out in the middle of the night and came back with cornflakes and then you were both shouting at each other and ever since then you've been really depressed. And this . . .' He gently pulled down the fabric of her polo neck. She flinched away from him and pulled it back up. 'What is that?'

'It's nothing,' she said. 'Some kind of friction burn.'

'A friction burn? On your neck?'

'I don't know what it is, OK? I just woke up in the morning and it was there. It doesn't even hurt.'

He stared at her and sighed. And as he stared into her eyes he had a sudden overwhelming sense of her being a stranger to him. *Who are you,* he wanted to ask her, *who are you?*

'What happened', he found himself asking, 'that day in the Lake District? Who was that woman?'

'What woman?'

'Oh, come on, Mum. You know what I'm talking about. I heard you and Dad talking about it in the kitchen the other day.'

He felt emboldened and brazen. He was sick of living like a gimp in his room at the top of the house, letting his life happen to him passively. He was sick of being *the kid*. He wanted more autonomy, more power, more say in how things happened. And buried somewhere in the dark, tangled roots of the incident at the Lake District back when he was nine years old was the key that could unlock the strange darkness at the heart of his family.

'It was nothing,' she replied. 'You know that. We've talked about it enough times.'

'I don't think it was nothing,' he continued firmly. 'I think that woman did know Dad. And I think she was cross with him because he'd done something bad. And I think you're both lying to me.'

'Don't be silly, darling.'

'I'm not being *silly*. I'm being deadly serious. What did Dad do to that woman? I need you to tell me. I need to know.'

'Oh, it was probably just something to do with his job. You know. Maybe he had to expel her daughter or maybe she wasn't pleased with her last report. You know how over-sensitive parents can be.'

'Daughter?' he said. 'How do you know it was a daughter?'

'I don't!' she shouted.

He looked at her in surprise.

She continued, more softly: 'Son, daughter, whatever. Her *child*.'

Freddie nodded. He'd pushed her as far as he felt comfortable. And there it was. *Her daughter*. A slip of the tongue. A giveaway. There was a story behind that moment. Not just a case of mistaken identity. But a woman with a daughter. A daughter who had had some kind of interaction with his father that had made that woman incredibly, terrifyingly angry.

43

17 March

On Friday Alfie came back from Tom and Nicola's house with an envelope of cash.

'All done,' he said. 'Paid in full. I'm taking you down to the Melville for champagne!'

'Or,' she said, thinking of her sore feet and her dirty hair, 'we could buy a bottle of champagne and drink it in bed with pizza and sex?'

He eyed her curiously. 'Pizza and sex, you say?' He smiled and began stripping off his overalls. 'Here.' He passed her the envelope of cash. 'You go and get the champagne and I'll have a shower and order the pizza.'

She peered inside the envelope, her fingers touched the edges of the notes. *Tom's money*, she thought. She caught her breath.

'OK,' she said, grabbing her trainers off the floor. 'It's a deal.'

The village was buzzy. The early spring weather had brought people out of hibernation. Some of the restaurants had even put their pavement tables out and for a moment she wished she'd taken Alfie up on his offer of a night out in the village.

The chilled cabinet was at the back of the shop. Alfie had told her to spend up to thirty pounds. She found a bottle of something vintage for £29.99 and took it to the till, only to turn a corner and find herself standing right behind Tom Fitzwilliam in the queue. She almost put the bottle down and left, but before she'd had time to make a move, Tom turned and saw her standing there. His face opened up into a smile of genuine pleasure and he said, 'Josephine! Hello!'

'Tom,' she said, 'hi!'

She moved ahead of him to put her bottle on the counter. Tom eyed it. 'Are we celebrating happy news?'

She shook her head. 'No,' she said, her voice coming

out far too loud and far too intense. 'Just celebrating pay day. With *your* money, I believe.'

'Aah,' he said, looking at the notes in her hand. 'Alfie's last day. Of course.'

She turned back to the guy behind the till and handed him the notes. He passed her her penny change and began rolling the bottle in tissue paper.

'How are you, anyway?' she heard Tom ask from behind her.

'Absolutely fine,' she said, without turning around. 'How are you?'

'I am also absolutely fine.'

'Good,' said Joey, her heart racing, 'good.'

The man put the bottle in a bag and passed it to her and she said good evening and thank you and turned to find Tom Fitzwilliam waiting for her. He had a small smile playing on his mouth and he was so handsome that she could barely look at him.

'Are you walking back up the hill?' he said.

She nodded.

'Good,' he said, 'me too. I'll walk you up.'

She managed a smile. 'OK.'

'It was lovely to see you the other night,' he said as they stepped out of the wine shop.

'Likewise,' she said.

'Freddie was most perturbed.'

She threw him a look.

'Boring old Dad talking to a mysterious, beautiful young woman.'

'Oh!' she said. 'Right. Although I refute any suggestion that I am beautiful or even young.'

'Don't be disingenuous.'

'I'm not! I'm going to be thirty in three years. And I am cute, at a push, but I am definitely not beautiful.'

'Thirty is shockingly young when you're fifty-one. And yes, you're very cute. *And* very beautiful.'

Joey swallowed. There was nothing ambiguous about this. Tom was flirting with her. A situation that had lived inside her head for weeks was now happening in reality. She needed to cut it off right now. But instead she found herself saying, 'Well, thank you, I am very flattered.'

He stopped for a moment, and she stopped alongside him. His mouth half opened as though he wanted to say something, but then it closed again and he smiled at her. 'You know,' he said, 'what happened outside the pub that night—'

'Please,' she said. 'Please don't. I can't even bear to think about it.'

'But that's the thing,' he said. 'I can't *stop* thinking about it. When I'm alone, in the car or in the shower, I replay it in my head, over and over again.'

Blood rushed to Joey's face. 'Oh.'

'I'm not expecting you to say anything. I'm not expecting you to do anything. I just wanted you to know.
That I liked it. That it was nice. That I didn't think
badly of you for it.'

'Thank you,' she said. 'I appreciate that.'

They'd crossed the pedestrian crossing opposite the
Melville and were at the bottom of the escarpment. Here
there was a narrow pavement, overhung with foliage,
muted street lights buried deep inside heavy spring blossom. There were no houses down here, just an old red
telephone box and a tiny Victorian letterbox built into the
wall. They were, to all intents and purposes, invisible.

It occurred to Joey that they could, right now, and
with very little risk of being caught, have sex. It could
happen. Easily. But then she thought of Alfie in their
bedroom, shower-fresh, waiting for her.

She was about to pick up her pace, break into the
awkward ripeness of the mood with a brisk comment
along the lines of how the champagne would be getting warm when Tom suddenly stopped, leaned right
into towards her and said, 'Could you do it?' His breath
was as warm as a summer heatwave in her ear. 'Could
you do it to me now?'

'What?'

'What you did. Before. Outside the pub. Just . . .' He

took her hand gently and she closed her eyes and knew what was about to happen and wanted to stop it but didn't want to stop it and then her hand was there, right there, her fingers cupped around him. She heard his groan of satisfaction soft in her hair, felt his hand upon her hip, pulling her towards him, his mouth falling into the soft place in the crook of her neck that made her tense and liquid all at the same time. She let the bag of champagne drop on to the earthy under-growth and she ran her other hand around the back of his neck and pulled the smell of him deep down inside herself. For a moment they stood like that, like two people melded together into one, a gently writhing mass of urgency and need and breath and lust.

But then an arc of car lights swung across them and Joey and Tom broke apart. Joey reached down for the bag with the bottle in it and they turned as one, con-tinuing on their way up the hill in complete silence until they got to Joey's door, when Tom turned, nodded courteously and said, 'Well, enjoy your champagne.'

Joey nodded, once, and let herself into the house.

Joey awoke at seven the next morning and, unable to find her way back to sleep, she pulled on a cardigan and Rebecca's rubber gardening shoes and took her morning coffee to the bottom of Jack and Rebecca's garden. Here she stood for a while, staring through the gauzy twilight towards the back of Tom's house, hoping to find him staring back.

There was a little gate at the bottom of the garden. She'd never noticed it before. She pushed it open and found herself on a gravelled footpath. On the other side of the footpath was a wooded area. The trees overhead shivered and stirred with small birds. From here she could see that all the houses in Melville Heights had access to the same pathway. Leaving her coffee on the wall, she walked quietly along the path and stopped for just a moment at the back of Tom's house.

She peered through the gaps in the wooden fencing, watching the vague outlines of Tom and Nicola moving about their kitchen, her stomach churning with guilt, with lust – with jealousy.

There was a fresh bunch of 50p daffodils on her mum's grave.

She rested her own flowers next to her father's flowers and then stood. 'Hi, Mum,' she said. 'I see Dad's been again. He's a sneaky one, isn't he?'

She breathed in sharply against the tears that came at the thought of her estranged father – the loss of both of her parents in under a year – and then out again, her breath emerging as a cloud of icy smoke.

'So, Mum, I'm fucking everything up. I mean really, really fucking it up. Worse than anything I've done before. Worse than the vodka incident. Worse than the running-away thing when I was sixteen. Worse than Robbie Miller. Worse than the thing with the moped. Just so, so bad. It's that man again, Tom Fitzwilliam. We had another . . . encounter.' Her voice caught on the words and she gulped back her tears. 'Last night. While Alfie was sitting in our bedroom waiting for me to help him celebrate something really important . . .' She checked over her shoulder, then whispered, '. . . he asked me to touch him. Again. And I did. And then we sort of . . . we clinched. Is that even a word? I don't know. But we didn't kiss. So I don't know what you'd call it. But it was amazing and bizarre and one of the most intense things that has ever happened to me. And now, I don't know – I don't know who I am any more. I've been trying to forget about it, but I can't. It's all I can think about. *He's* all I can think about. I feel a bit mad, Mum, I feel like I'm getting obsessed. Like . . .' She paused and turned her eyes to the ice-blue sky. 'Like I might be about to do something really, really stupid. And knowing I'm going to do it isn't going to stop it happening. I feel like I'm one step away from the abyss and just I wish so much that you were here, Mum, I wish you were here to pull me back.'

III

44

20 March

Bess didn't come into school on Monday.

Jenna felt a growing sense of alarm as the day wore on. She approached Ruby awkwardly in the home room at lunchtime. 'Where's Bess?' she asked. 'Is she sick?'

Ruby shook her head. 'No,' she said, 'don't think so.'

'Do you think she's OK?'

'Yeah. I'm sure she's OK. She's probably just bunking off.'

Jenna said, 'Yeah. Maybe.'

'What's going on with you two, anyway?'

'Hasn't she said?'

'No,' Ruby replied. 'Just said it was something personal. Between you and her.'

Jenna was surprised. She'd assumed Bess would have told everyone everything. Discretion was not one of her key attributes.

'Are you going to sort it out?' Ruby asked. 'Because it's really doing our heads in.'

Jenna shrugged. 'I hope so,' she said.

Bess did come in the next day. She looked tired and unapproachable. Jenna watched her across the sports field during triple PE that afternoon. She was fidgety and edgy, looking like she had somewhere else she needed to be. She saw her go up to the assistant coach after a few minutes and say something to her. She saw the teacher look at her intently for a moment before nodding tersely and gesturing with her head towards the school. Bess grabbed her hoodie and her water bottle and walked quickly into the building.

Jenna jogged over to the assistant coach. 'Miss, my tampon's leaking. I need to change it really badly.'

The teacher grimaced at her. 'Isn't that something you should have dealt with *before* triple PE?'

'Yes, miss. I know. But I only changed it an hour ago. I thought it would be OK?'

'Go on then,' the teacher muttered. 'And be quick.'

She ran as fast as she could towards the doors and flung them open. She peered into the girls' changing rooms but they were empty. Then she tried the girls' toilets located a few metres up the corridor towards the main hallway. They appeared at first to be empty, and she was about to leave, but then she heard a shuffling sound from one of the cubicles and peered down to spy a pair of child-sized feet in pink Adidas trainers.

'Bess,' she hissed. 'Are you OK?'

The shuffling sound stopped and there was a beat of silence before Bess called out, 'Who is that?'

'It's me, you twat. What are you doing?'

'What do you think I'm doing?

'I don't know. That's why I'm asking. You looked all weird out there. Thought you might be ill.'

'Yes,' Bess replied, after another beat of silence. 'I'm not feeling good. Feeling a bit sick.'

'Do you want me to get someone? Shall I get the nurse?'

'Are you literally stupid?'

Jenna sighed. 'Can you come out then? So I can see you?'

'No.'

'Oh, FFS, Bess. Just come out. This is daft.'

There was a protracted silence and then she heard the lock slide back and Bess stood before her looking extra small and very wan.

'What's going on?' she asked.

'Nothing,' said Bess.

'What's the matter with you?'

'Nothing.' She paused. Then, 'I think I might be pregnant.'

The room spun around Jenna's head for a moment. Her eyes closed and when she opened them Bess was still standing in front of her and still, she assumed, possibly pregnant. 'What do you mean?' she asked, ridiculously.

Bess was a virgin. They were both virgins. Neither of them had the slightest interest in sex, in being penetrated by boys, in doing *that*. Both of them thought they would lose their virginity when they were eighteen. It was what they'd said. For years. Jenna felt something slipping away from her, a sad sense of loss, of having been in the wrong place all along. She felt like an idiot.

'I don't know what I mean,' said Bess. 'Just that I'm two weeks late. I feel bloated. My boobs.' She cupped them tenderly and peered down at them. 'They're so sore.'

'But . . .' Jenna started. 'I don't get it. You haven't even got a boyfriend.'

'A *boyfriend*?'

Jenna stared at her, desperately. 'Bess,' she said. 'Who have you had sex with?'

'No one,' she said. 'I didn't have sex with anyone. It's an immaculate conception. OK?'

'Bess! For fuck's sake! Talk to me!'

'I can't. OK? I just can't. And anyway, I'm probably not pregnant. It's probably just PMT. My period will start tomorrow. Probably.'

'Meet me after school,' said Jenna. 'We'll go to Boots. Get you a test. Yes?'

Bess nodded. Then shook her head. 'No,' she said. 'I can't. I'm busy.'

'Busy doing what?'

'Nothing, all right?'

Jenna sighed. 'OK, then, I'll buy you one and bring it in tomorrow. We'll do the test at breaktime. Yes?'

'Yeah,' said Bess. 'OK.' There was a brief silence and then she said, 'I'm sorry. For what I said about your mum. You're not like your mum.'

Jenna smiled and pulled her friend towards her for a hug. She felt Bess wince and pull away.

'Are you OK?'

'Yes,' said Bess. 'I'm fine.'

'Are you hurt?'

'No,' she said. 'I told you. I'm fine.'

'Shall we go back to class?'

'Yeah. OK.'

They left the toilets together, hand in hand.

45

21 March

The previous Saturday had proved to be one of the worst Joey could remember at Whackadoo. They'd had thirteen separate birthday parties booked in and then it had started to rain at about ten o'clock and of course by lunchtime the place had been filled to capacity and everyone seemed to be in a bad mood; two separate fights had broken out, one between a group of ten-year-old boys, the other between two fathers in their forties. The police had been called to deal with the latter and then there had been a blockage in the boys' toilets that remained unreported for over an hour by which time the floor was swimming in wet toilet paper and faeces.

And then a young girl on her first day in the job had accidentally knocked over a table in a party room, laying to waste a birthday cake that looked like it had cost around a hundred pounds and upturning thirty cups of blackcurrant squash. The whole day had been a fire-fighting exercise: every time one situation had been dealt with, another flared up. Yet still her encounter with Tom the night before had played on a loop in Joey's thoughts and each and every time she felt a jolt of shock, of horror, of guilt, of shame – and of bone-grinding desire.

The day had passed and she'd emerged, soiled and shabby, into the damp evening air half expecting to see him standing there with that terrible look of desperate longing on his face. But, of course, he was not there. He was not there as she sat on the bus back to Melville. He was not there when she got off the bus. Neither was he there as she walked past the very spot where it happened the night before. He wasn't there when she stood at her front door for an inordinate amount of time looking for her keys, pretending to read a text message. She went through an entire Saturday night, Sunday morning, Sunday night and Monday without a glimmer of his presence.

On Tuesday morning Alfie had said, 'Are you OK, babe?' and rubbed her feet. And she'd wanted to cry because she was so far from OK and really, when she thought about it, she'd never been OK. Not ever. But she'd said, 'I'm fine. Just tired.' And he'd said, 'You know you can talk to me, don't you? About anything?' And she'd nodded and sucked back her tears and stroked his hair and thought about all the lovely girls she passed in the street every day who would be better for Alfie than she was.

And then later that day Alfie got a call from a woman in the village. She'd heard from Nicola that she'd just had her place done up by a really good decorator and would he be able to come to her house and quote on a job for her. 'Can I borrow your phone?' he'd said. 'I want to take some new photos of the work at Nicola's to show her and the camera on my phone's shit.'

She'd said yes absent-mindedly. And then, as she put the phone down, a thought came to her. She'd called him straight back and said, 'I'll take the photos. I'm much better at taking photos than you. Leave it with me. I'll go after work.'

The boy opened the door. He'd had all his hair shaved off and looked strangely raw and animal. There was a tiny frisson of embarrassment in the moment. He blushed and almost tripped over his own feet as he moved backwards to let Joey in.

'Door!' he shouted crossly over his shoulder down the hallway. 'The door!'

Then Nicola appeared. Joey had not seen Nicola for quite some time. Last time she'd seen her she'd been in her usual costume of shiny Lycra and fleece and baseball cap, rosy-cheeked and smiling, light on her feet as though she could just take off spontaneously. Now she was in jeans and a jumper and worn-out socks, her hair tied back in a bunch, her skin dull and blotchy. She looked equally as alarmed as her son to see her standing there.

'Hi!' she said. 'I'm Joey. Alfie's wife. I live a couple of doors down? With Jack and Rebecca?'

Nicola managed a smile. 'Oh!' she said. 'Yes. I've heard lots about you from Alfie. What can I do for you?'

Joey brought her phone out of her pocket. 'Alfie's going to quote on another job tomorrow. He wanted to show the new client some pictures of his previous work. He's a bit crap with a camera so I offered to take them for him.' She passed the phone from one hand to the other, her smile still stapled in place. 'Is that OK?'

Nicola closed her eyes and opened them slowly. Then she shook her head and smiled again and said, 'Yes, sure. Of course! You'll have to excuse some of the mess. We're not exactly minimal around here. But sure, yes, come in.'

Freddie moved aside and let her through. She felt sure he sniffed the air as she passed.

'Where should I start?' Joey asked brightly.

'Well,' said Nicola, smoothing down her jumper with her hands. 'He did all this' – she gestured around the hallway – 'and the kitchen and the front room and the stairway. All the way up to the landing.'

Joey's gaze followed Nicola's hand as it gestured upwards. She felt breathless suddenly with the audacity of what she was doing. She had crossed the breach into Tom's house. Made it beyond the hallowed portal into a world that Joey had only been able to imagine, a world that contained Tom's things and Tom's child and Tom's wife and Tom's breath and dander and shed hairs and dried sweat. The trousers she'd gripped inside her hand were in here somewhere, buried in a laundry basket or clipped to a wooden hanger in a cupboard full of Tom's clothes and jumpers and big, serious shoes. The swinging lanyard was pooled on a tabletop, the wayward ties tamed in a drawer. He dreamed in here and drank in here and ate in here and grew older in here.

'Would you mind', she asked Nicola, 'if I turned on a light or two?'

The Fitzwilliams' house wasn't as Joey had pictured it. Alfie had told her it was a shithole, but she hadn't envisaged it to be quite so much of a shithole. Even with

Alfie's perfect, immaculate paintwork, it felt unloved, unwelcoming. There were no paintings hanging on the walls, no colour, most of the lights were switched off. It was also cold.

'Gosh, no. Please do. And can I get you anything? A cup of tea or something?'

Nicola was not what she'd imagined either. She'd pictured her as a proper Melville housewife, whipping up a kitchen supper with ingredients from the deli in the village, chopping the stalks off expensive flowers to arrange in heavy glass vases, chatting with a friend over a dewy bottle of half-drunk wine around a kitchen island, an open laptop glowing blue with a half-completed Ocado order. She'd imagined Nicola as a proper grown-up woman, but she seemed more like a young nanny not sure how to deal with a visitor in her employer's absence, too scared to switch on lights or open cupboards or turn up the heating; not properly formed, not quite right.

'No,' she replied, 'no, thank you. I'm fine. I won't be long.'

Nicola disappeared for a moment and left Joey to it. She switched on an overhead light that gave out a cruel yellow glare and took a few photos. But without the softening effects of flowers or gentle lightbulbs or table lamps her pictures looked institutional, uninspiring, bleak.

She popped her head into the kitchen. Nicola jumped slightly. 'Please,' she said, getting to her feet, 'come in. Please. He did the walls in here, obviously, and he also repainted the dressers and all the shelving in here.'

She moved out of Joey's way to allow her to take the photos.

'So,' she said, 'Alfie tells me you met at a tacky all-inclusive resort on Ibiza?'

'Yes,' Joey replied, somewhat surprised. She hadn't imagined Alfie and Nicola chatting much. 'Although I wouldn't say it was tacky. It was four-star. It was quite nice actually.'

'Oh,' said Nicola vaguely. 'Well. It *sounded* tacky, the way he described it. And I suppose I can't quite picture it. I've never holidayed abroad.'

Joey started at this pronouncement. 'Really?'

Nicola nodded. 'It's Tom's job, you see. It's all-consuming. It's everything. It always has been.'

Joey nodded, as if that was an acceptable explanation for a thirty-something-year-old woman not to have been on holiday abroad.

'If we do go away, we tend to stick close to home. So that Tom can get back easily if there's an emergency.'

'Did you not go abroad on your holidays when you were younger? Before you met Tom?'

'Ha, well, there wasn't really much *being younger*

before I met Tom. So no, I've never been abroad on holiday. Not properly.'

Joey nodded. She was desperate to ask Nicola how old she was but couldn't think of a discreet opening.

'He's madly in love with you, you know.'

Joey stopped, statue-still, and caught her breath. A blast of adrenaline shot through her. She turned and looked at Nicola. 'I'm sorry?'

'Alfie,' said Nicola. 'He adores you.'

'Ah.' Joey's insides turned liquid and her head fizzed with relief. 'Yes,' she said. 'Alfie. Yes. I know. He's a sweetheart.'

'He really is,' she said. 'And ever so good-looking. You're a very lucky girl.'

Joey blanched and crossed the kitchen to take some photos of the French doors on to the back garden. There was a bench here with a pile of old newspapers hanging off it; washing drying on a radiator: underpants scrunched into small stiff twists of fabric, a tired drooping bra, a pair of jeans that looked as though they could stand up by themselves. A cold breeze whistled through an open window.

'Here. Let me get out of your way,' said Nicola.

Joey noticed a grimace as Nicola got off her chair and walked to the other side of the room, a slight limp. 'Are you OK?' she asked.

'Yes,' said Nicola. 'I'm just taking a break from running and my body doesn't like it. My muscles get all, you know, *gnarly*.'

'You should do some stretches.'

'I do try to remember, but it's all or nothing for me when it comes to exercise. Once I get out of the routine, it all goes to pot.'

'What made you stop running?'

Nicola stood leaning against the hob of a five-ring burner. It was covered with pans, piled into one another, then layered over with baking trays. The sink was full of old washing up. The dishwasher stood with its door open, half empty. A school timetable two terms out of date was pinned to a small cork board by the door.

'Oh. I just go through phases. You know.'

'Can I?' Joey gestured towards the front room.

'Yes,' said Nicola. 'Sure.'

Nicola followed Joey and stood in the doorway watching her as she photographed another load of magnolia walls and shiny white woodwork. There was a faded blue sofa in here, an old piano against the wall, a chrome floor lamp, a small gilt-framed mirror above a fake stone fireplace, a high-backed chair in the window that looked as though it should be in an old people's home.

'So, the landlord didn't mind you having the place redecorated then?' Joey asked.

'No. She was delighted. We went halves on it. But I just couldn't live with it another second; it was yellow in here. Yellow walls! Can you imagine?'

Joey shrugged and smiled. She wasn't a fan of yellow walls but at least they might have injected some warmth and sunshine into this drab room.

'And I'm so glad that Alfie's getting some more work. It's hard to get anyone decent, in cities. Much easier in the sticks.'

'So you used to live in the countryside?'

'We've lived virtually everywhere. Even east London for a while. Now that was hair-raising.'

'Was it?'

'God, yes. Ninety per cent Bengali intake at Tom's school. Luckily, we lived a bit further out, in a more gentrified area. But really, it was like Calcutta!'

'Wow,' said Joey. She turned so that Nicola couldn't see her face. '*Wow*,' she said under her breath. So, she thought, Tom's wife is an ignorant, small-town racist. Yet married to a man who dedicates his life to underprivileged children, to improving their prospects, a benevolent man with charisma to spare. How did that work?

'Do you think you'll stay here?' she asked. 'In Bristol?'

'I doubt it,' said Nicola. 'Tom likes to conquer, triumph, consolidate and move on. Shame. I like it here.'

317

'Where are you from originally?'

'Originally from Derby. Grew up mainly in Burton-on-Trent.'

'And where is Tom from?'

'Tunbridge Wells. He's a fancy southerner. Went to boarding school. Mother was an honourable something. Way posher than me. Anyway,' she said. 'Are you done?' Her mood had turned. She seemed keen to get rid of Joey now. And Joey was happy to leave. She didn't like this house. And she didn't like Nicola.

'Yes!' she said brightly. 'I am pretty much done. There's just the landing to do. If I can? I'll be really super quick.'

'Sure,' said Nicola, turning out the lights before Joey was even out of the room.

The stairs were carpeted in baggy grey carpet that looked like a health-and-safety hazard and she watched her step carefully as she ascended. There were three doors on the landing: one to a bathroom, one to what looked like a small bedroom and another to what looked like a bigger bedroom. She heard floorboards creaking above with careful footsteps and realised that the son was lurking about, eavesdropping.

She took the photos as fast as she could, but halfway down the stairs she stopped on the half-turn and peered through the long window that looked out over the back gardens and the 'secret' woodland beyond. From here she could clearly see the gate at the foot of Tom's garden where she'd peered through the gaps in the fence on Saturday morning. She touched the glass briefly with her fingertip, before completing her descent.

'Well,' said Nicola, waiting for her by the front door. 'It's been lovely to meet you. Please do send Alfie my love.'

'Yes. Yes I will. And send mine to Tom.' Her voice caught on the last consonant of his name. She had no idea if Tom had mentioned their neighbourly encounters or not.

But Nicola looked unfazed and smiled and said, 'Yes. I certainly will. If he ever gets home, of course. The hours he works are extraordinary.'

'Yes,' said Joey. 'I can imagine.'

She looked upwards at the attic bedroom window as she left Tom's house and saw the shadow of his son move quickly out of sight.

46

22 March

Bess did not come into school on Wednesday, nor did she reply to any messages on her phone. After school, Jenna headed directly to Bess's house.

Bess, like her, lived alone with her mother. Unlike Jenna she didn't have a brother or a father living elsewhere. Her father was not known to Bess or to her mother, but was probably called Patrick. Her mother was only eighteen when she had her and she and Bess were a very tight little unit. Very bonded. Jenna had envied their bond over the years as her relationship with her mother had slid slowly downhill alongside her mum's mental health.

Bess's mother was a beautician and worked at a big salon in the city. Their flat was owned by a charitable co-op, and they paid hardly anything to live there. It was small but beautiful: gilt mirrors and fluffy cushions, fairy lights and scented candles. Her mum had even painted their kitchen units baby pink. It wasn't the sort of flat where a girl who got pregnant by her head teacher at fifteen would live; Bess's mother wasn't the sort of mother whose daughter would get pregnant by her head teacher at fifteen; and Bess wasn't the sort of fifteen-year-old girl who would get pregnant by anyone, let alone her head teacher.

Her mum's little car was where it always was, parked in the tiny car park behind the block, but the lights were off in their flat on the first floor. Jenna rang the intercom and waited a moment before ringing it again. Her mum was probably still at work. She pulled out her phone and called Bess. It went straight through to voicemail. She opened Snap Maps but Bess wasn't logged into it. She messaged Ruby: *Any idea where Bess is?*

Ruby said, *No, ask Tiana.*

Tiana didn't know.

Jenna looked at the time; it was nearly five.

She opened Snap Maps again. This time she noticed

that Ruby was at the same place she'd been last week, the house in Lissenden. *Jed's house.*

She turned and headed for the bus stop.

Jed's house was a grey, pebble-dashed post-war box on an estate of similar houses. There was a blue van parked out the front and an old green Mazda MX5. She could hear, even from down here, the sound of youthful hilarity coming from a room upstairs. She rang on the doorbell and a woman with long, hennaed hair and a nose ring answered.

'Hi,' Jenna said. 'Is Bess here?'

'Bess? Is she the little blonde one?'

'Yes. That's right.'

She shook her head. 'She was here a while back. But she left about half an hour ago.'

'Any idea where she went?'

'I have no clue.'

'Did she – did she look OK?'

The woman shrugged. 'I suppose. She called out goodbye. I came to the door and let her out. She seemed OK. Are you one of Ruby's friends? From the Academy?'

'Yeah,' said Jenna.

'Ruby's here.' She tipped her chin to indicate the stairs behind her. 'Why don't you go up and ask her?'

She thought of Ruby's assertion that she hadn't seen Bess. She heard another blast of adolescent mirth coming from upstairs. She smiled and shook her head. 'No,' she said. 'No. Don't worry. It's fine. I'm sure I'll find her.'

'I think her dad picked her up,' said the woman.

'She hasn't got a dad,' Jenna said, startled.

'Well, someone picked her up. Looked like a man but I wasn't really paying attention. Maybe it was a taxi.'

'What sort of car was it?'

'A big one,' she said. 'Black.'

'Was it a BMW?'

'I don't know,' she said. 'It might have been. That kind of thing anyway.' She paused and looked at Jenna, maternal concern blooming over her features. 'Is everything OK?' she said. 'Is Bess in trouble?'

Jenna shook her head. 'No,' she said. 'No. I just needed to talk to her. That's all.'

RECORDED INTERVIEW

Date: 25/03/2017
Location: Trinity Road Police Station, Bristol BS2 0NW
Conducted by: Officers from Somerset & Avon Police

POLICE: This interview is being tape-recorded. I am Detective Inspector Rose Pelham and I am based at Trinity Road Police Station. I work with the serious crime team. If you could just give us your full name?

FT: Frances Ann Tripp. My professional name is Frankie Miller.

POLICE: Professional?

FT: I used to do some modelling and, more recently, some small acting roles.

POLICE: I see. And can you tell us your address please?

FT: Yes. Number 8, Bellevue Lane, Lower Melville, Bristol BS12 6YH.

POLICE: Thank you, Mrs Tripp. And can you tell us where you were between the hours of 7 p.m. and 9 p.m. last night?

FT: Yes. I was outside Tom Fitzwilliam's house.

POLICE: Outside?

FT: Yes. There's a small wooded area opposite the houses. I had a fold-up chair and a camera.

POLICE: Right. And could you explain exactly why you were sitting in the woods outside the victim's house with a fold-up chair and a camera?

FT: Yes. Happily. It's a relief to finally be taken seriously about all of this. Do you have any idea how long I've been trying to get you lot to take my concerns about this man seriously? And I've just been ignored and ridiculed.

POLICE: Mrs Tripp, if you could just return to the original question. What were you doing outside the Fitzwilliams' house?

FT: I had a tip-off. On one of my chat rooms.

POLICE: Your chat rooms?

FT: Yes. I'm being gang-stalked. Thousands of us are. And no one will talk about it. It's a global disgrace.

POLICE: Mrs Tripp? The chat rooms?

FT: Yes. Someone on one of my local chat rooms, a woman from Mold, I don't know her name. Tom was the head at her local school a couple of years ago. She knows what I'm dealing with. Anyway, she sent me a message at about 6 p.m. last night saying that she had it on good authority that there was going to be a big meeting at Tom's house that evening, of all the members of his stalking cooperative. That I should go and watch and take photos so I'd have proof of what's going on. The full extent of it. So I did.

POLICE: And could you please describe to us exactly what you saw, Mrs Tripp, starting from the time you arrived.

FT: It would be my pleasure.

47

22 March

Freddie had got back from school an hour ago to find his mother sitting at the kitchen table, her hair pushed back into a bunch, wearing a hoodie and pyjama bottoms, knitting the never-ending baby blanket.

'Why aren't you wearing proper clothes?' he'd asked.

'I've been in bed all day,' she'd said, putting the knitting down on the table and yawning. 'I just got up.'

'What's the matter? Are you sick?'

'Yes,' she'd said, staring wanly at him. 'I think I have the flu.'

He'd looked at her. 'Does Dad know?'

She shook her head. 'No. It came on after he left.'

'Do you want some pills?'

'I've taken some.'

Freddie had felt irrationally cross. His mum did not have flu. She was lying. It was impossible to concentrate on something like knitting when you had the flu. Freddie had had flu when he was eleven and he hadn't even been able to sit up, let alone knit. She just wanted a proper reason to stay at home all day being miserable and weird. She wanted everyone to feel sorry for her. Which was stupid because he'd feel much sorrier for her if she told him the truth about the marks on her neck. He took a pile of buttered crumpets and a mug of camomile tea to his room and closed the door behind him.

Now, changed down to his underwear and wearing a fleecy dressing gown he'd been given by his grandmother for Christmas, he ate his crumpets and drank his tea while flicking through pictures of Romola on his phone.

Behind him, his new suit hung from the top of his wardrobe, still in its plastic packaging. His mum had got it for him at the weekend from Debenhams. Beneath it sat a pair of shiny black shoes, also from Debenhams, the arrangement looking somewhat like a hanging man. He hadn't asked Romola to be his date yet. He kept getting close to it each time he followed behind her, then losing his nerve at the very last moment and slowing down, cursing to himself under his breath. The ball was two days away. It was now or never.

He went to his window and focused his binoculars on to Jenna Tripp's road. She would know, he thought. Jenna Tripp would know how he should ask a girl to a ball. She must get asked to balls literally all the time. He decided that the next morning he would ensure that his path crossed with hers on the walk to school and he would ask Jenna Tripp what to do.

As he thought this, his eye was taken by two women talking animatedly at the bus stop. One was Jenna Tripp's mum. She was wearing an oversized parka with a purple fur trim and smoking an e-cigarette. He could see the huge cloud of vapour clearly from here. And when the cloud cleared he zoomed in on to the face of the woman talking to her. Youngish. Brown hair. A big black coat. A bit fat. He saw her take a piece of paper from her coat pocket and he saw her writing things down on it, things that Jenna's mum seemed to be telling her to write down. Then they said goodbye, Jenna's mum turning towards her road, the fat lady turning in the other direction. Freddie instinctively snapped a photo of the encounter and for a moment he thought of logging it in *The Melville Papers*.

But then he thought, *No, I am no longer interested in what the boring old people in this village are doing. I am only interested in Romola Brook.*

48

That morning as Joey sat at the bus stop, she heard a car horn hooting and there was Tom, on the other side of the street, his window wound down, indicating that she should approach.

Her stomach turned into a clenched fist.

She rose slowly to her feet and crossed the street. Staring down through the open window she waited for Tom to talk.

'Jump in,' he said. 'I'll drive you to work.'

'Are you sure?' she asked. 'Won't you be late for school?'

'I may well be late for school,' he said, 'but I'm the boss, so who's going to be asking me questions?'

She slid into the passenger seat. Her breath was caught halfway to her mouth. She couldn't speak. She could barely breathe. For a moment they drove in silence. Joey tried to think of some arrangement of words to puncture the silence that wouldn't make things more awkward than they already were, but failed.

And then Tom turned off the radio and said, 'We should probably talk. About this thing.'

Joey nodded, exhaled, felt relief wash through her. 'The you-and-me-on-Friday-night thing?'

'Yes. The you-and-me-on-Friday-night thing. I have to say that I am completely and utterly flummoxed. I mean, this has never happened to me before . . .'

She nodded again.

'I'm just not the sort of man . . . really, I'm not. I need you to know that. It's very, very important to me that you don't think I make a habit of sexual impropriety.'

She shook her head, encouragingly.

'But, I don't know, there's something about you. Or more to the point, ever since that night at the pub when you . . .'

'Assaulted you?'

He laughed, softening the edges of the conversation. 'Well, that's not how I saw it. But yes, since *that*, I just haven't been able to stop thinking about you. And

I want to apologise for Friday night. I allowed my instincts to take me over. I saw you in the wine shop and all I could think was *wow, wow, wow*. But I never for one moment intended for what happened next to happen. That was primal, that was base. And I can only apologise. Profoundly. I'm so sorry.'

'Tom,' she said. 'I don't need an apology. I really—'

'You know,' Tom interjected, 'I have spent days frantically trying to avoid you, hoping that this feeling would go away, and then I saw you this morning, from my bedroom window, saw you leaving and it was clear that not seeing you hadn't made any difference at all. In fact, it had made it even worse. So, the question is, what shall we do?'

There was a beat of silence. 'Do?' she said.

He looked at her intensely. 'I think we need to . . . we need to stop this.' He paused, briefly. 'But in order to do so I think we need to get it out of our systems. And I've taken the liberty of booking a room. At a hotel. And I thought, maybe, we could meet there, after work. On Friday night.'

Joey inhaled sharply. 'Friday?' she said.

'Yes. If you think that's a good idea. I mean, God, I don't know. Maybe it's a dreadful idea. But I just can't . . . I can't get past this. I can't get past you.'

'And then, afterwards, we . . . ?'

'We stop. Yes.'

'But what if we don't want to?'

'We have to.'

'But . . .' Joey paused. Her head told her that this was an appalling idea. Her gut, the deep ache that she'd carried around inside her for weeks told her that if she didn't go she might die. 'I can't promise, Tom. I can't promise I'll want to stop.'

'I'm not asking you to promise. I'm just asking you to try.'

She nodded.

'So, you'll do it?' he asked. 'You'll meet me? About seven p.m.? Friday?'

Joey tried to listen to the voice inside her head that was screaming at her to say no, *say no*. But the ache symphonised inside her; it grew layers and notes.

'Yes,' she found herself saying. 'Friday. Yes.'

RECORDED INTERVIEW

Date: 25/03/2017
Location: Trinity Road Police Station, Bristol BS2 0NW
Conducted by: Officers from Somerset & Avon Police

POLICE: Ms Mullen, going back to last night. Friday 24 March. You say that in room 121 at the Bristol Harbour Hotel you and Mr Fitzwilliam sat and talked. Could you tell me exactly what you talked about?

JM: Not really.

POLICE: Not really?

JM: I mean, no, we chatted. About lots of things.

POLICE: What sort of things?

JM: I can't remember.

POLICE: And so he, Mr Fitzwilliam, asked you to meet him in a hotel room on Friday night? In order to . . . ?

JM: He said it was to . . . he said we needed to get it out of our systems.

POLICE: 'It' being . . . ?

JM: Our mutual sexual attraction.

POLICE: So he intended for you to have sex that night?

JM: That's what I took it to mean, yes.

POLICE: And you intended to have sex that night?

JM: I wasn't sure. I hadn't made up my mind.

POLICE: And did you? Did you and Mr Fitzwilliam have sex that night?

JM: I would prefer not to answer the question.

49

22 March

'You know,' said Freddie's dad, later that evening, 'I'm starting to really like your hair. Genuinely. It suits you. You'll be fighting the girls off now, I reckon.'

Freddie threw his dad a withering look. 'That is the single most hopelessly inept dad thing that you have ever said. And you have said *a lot* of hopelessly inept dad things.'

His dad laughed. 'Just trying to be, you know . . .'

Freddie put his hand in front of his father's face. 'No,' he said. 'Just no. You're not cut out for this kind of repartee, so it's best you don't try.'

'OK,' said his dad. 'OK. I'll back off. But you do look very handsome.'

Freddie nodded the compliment away. This conversation was unnerving him. When he wasn't with his dad, when he was *thinking* about his dad, or looking at the marks on his mum's neck or talking about his dad with Jenna Tripp, the man loomed in his consciousness like an angry bear: dark and lethal, capable of anything. But here, in the soft evening light, the radio murmuring in the background, his dad sitting with him, cool and calm in a baby blue lambswool sweater, being the sweet to Freddie's sour, the concept of his dad being a predator or a wife-beater – it all seemed mildly ridiculous.

'There's a girl that I like,' he found himself saying. 'Her name's Romola.'

'Oh!' His dad glanced up from his laptop, his eyes wide. 'I see. And who is this girl?'

'She's from St Mildred's. She's in year ten. She's new.'

'And?' said his dad. 'What's the deal? Have you asked her out?'

'No,' Freddie said. 'Not yet. I want to ask her to a dance.'

'How very old-fashioned.'

'No it's not,' said Freddie. 'What's old-fashioned

about asking a girl to a dance? It's timeless, isn't it? What about you?' he began, sensing a space in the conversation to dig a little. 'How did you ask Mum out for your first date?'

'Well, I would say there was never really a first-date scenario. We just got chatting on a bus. She recognised me from her school days.'

'You mean she was at your school?'

He watched his father closely for signs of bristling. 'At my school? You mean, where I taught?'

'Yes.'

Freddie saw definite signs of bristling.

'No. Well, not exactly. There may have been a brief overlap, between me starting and her leaving. But I didn't know her then. And then we bumped into each other on the bus, and the rest is history.'

'When she was nineteen?'

'Yes. When she was nineteen.'

'And you were thirty-five?'

'Yes, or thereabouts.'

'Did anyone mind?'

'Mind?'

'Yes. Like her family? Did they mind that she was dating her old teacher? Didn't they think it was a bit weird?'

'No,' his dad said, too fast, too firm. 'It wasn't like

338

that. I wasn't your mum's teacher. I never taught her. She just happened to be at the school where I worked. That's all there was to it.' He banged down the lid of his laptop and got to his feet.

'Have you ever had an affair, Dad?'

'What!'

'I mean, have you ever been unfaithful to Mum?'

'What on earth . . . ? I mean, why on earth would you even ask a question like that?'

'Because women seem to like you. And Mum is a bit annoying. And maybe sometimes you regret choosing her and wish you could be with someone else.'

His father shook his head slowly. 'Freddie Fitzwilliam, you do say the strangest things.'

'Why is that strange? I think it's perfectly rational. Loads of men have affairs. Even really ugly men with crap jobs have affairs. And you're . . . well, you're not ugly and you don't have a crap job.'

'Gosh, thank you, Freddie. I'm flattered.'

'It wasn't supposed to be a compliment.'

'No, Freddie. I know it wasn't.' His father paused and closed his laptop. He slid it into its padded case and looked at Freddie. 'No,' he said. 'I have never been unfaithful to your mother. And neither have I ever wanted to be.'

'Not even with Viva?' he said, speculatively.

'Viva?'

'Yes. The girl from the school where you taught whose mum was hitting you in the Lake District. It would explain why she was so angry with you.'

He stared at his father unflinchingly. It was possibly the worst thing of all the bad things that he had ever said to his father. He saw a muscle twitch in the corner of his mouth. The soft shawl of geniality was slipping. There was the angry bear. Right there.

'I have no idea what you're talking about. And I have no idea who Viva is. Or was. But I have never had an affair with a student and I most certainly would never dream of such a thing.'

50

23 March

Jenna hadn't recognised him at first. He'd had all his hair shaved off and he looked slightly alarming, like the sort of person who might snatch your phone out of your hand and run. For a moment she thought about pretending she hadn't seen him. He was such an awkward boy and his awkwardness made her feel uncomfortable. But she allowed him to catch up with her and he arrived a moment later at her side, breathlessly.

'Jenna,' he said. 'Jenna Tripp.'

'Yes,' she said. 'That's me.'

'I need your advice.'

She looked from left to right to see if anyone else

was witness to this strange exchange. 'Right,' she responded cagily.

'I want to ask a girl to a ball. It's not you, so don't panic. Although you are pretty. But you're too old for me. And too tall.'

'Right . . .' she said again.

'I wanted to ask you, in your experience of being an attractive girl, how would you like someone to invite you to a ball?'

She narrowed her eyes at him, gauging if she was perhaps being pranked in some way. But he looked back at her guilelessly and so she sighed and considered his question. 'That depends if you know if she likes you or not.'

'She doesn't know I exist.'

'Right. So she won't be expecting it?'

'No. She won't be expecting it.'

'In that case,' she said, 'I wouldn't ask her face-to-face. I'd text her. Or message her. Give her a chance to find a nice way to say no. If she wants to say no.'

He nodded, frantically, his eyes wide and unblinking. 'Great,' he said, 'that's absolutely great. You've been . . . great.'

'No problem,' she said.

He turned away from her and then back again. 'I'm going to school now. I'll see you around.'

She watched him for a while as he walked double pace up the hill towards the city. She smiled.

Jenna wondered if the rest of their friendship group knew about Bess's 'pregnancy'. She wondered if they even knew about her having sex in the first place. Maybe it wasn't Mr Fitzwilliam after all? Maybe it was just a boy? A boy from this school or maybe a boy from another school, a posh school, maybe, like Freddie's? Maybe it was Jed? But no, Bess had said she thought Jed was an idiot. But still, if it was just a boy and she'd had sex with him and now she was potentially pregnant, why had she chosen to shut Jenna out at this point of her life, the point, surely, where your best friend was the person you wanted to keep closest?

Maybe Bess thought that Jenna was a prude; maybe she was worried that she'd be judgemental, that she would disapprove somehow of the choices she was making?

Maybe Bess had outgrown her?

But the idea was preposterous. Jenna had always been the 'grown-up' one in their friendship. She'd always kept Bess afloat, stopped her from getting into trouble, explained things to her about the world and how it worked. And Bess, with no siblings and a mother who was more like a fun-loving big sister than a mum, had needed that in her life. There was no way that Bess was emotionally ready to step outside of Jenna's influence. There was no way that she could make good decisions without Jenna's guidance. Surely.

Jenna saw Tiana and Ruby coming out of the girls' toilets after lunch on Thursday.

'Is Bess with you?' she asked.

'No,' said Tiana, 'haven't seen her since food tech.'

'Did you not have lunch with her?'

'No.'

'What's going on with you, Jen?' Ruby laughed. 'Why are you stalking her?'

'I'm not stalking her. It's just, you do know there's stuff going on with her, don't you?'

Jenna watched their reactions for a glimmer of understanding or subterfuge in their facial expressions or body language. But they both stared at her blankly and Tiana said, 'Like what?'

'Nothing,' Jenna said. 'Just personal stuff. I thought she might have told you. Don't worry about it.'

Ruby's eyes widened. 'Tell us! What? What's going on with her?'

But Jenna headed away from them, leaving Ruby

and Tiana standing staring after her, eyes wide and hungry for scraps.

It was almost worse, Jenna thought, that the people Bess had been hanging out with for the past few weeks didn't know what was going on with her. It meant, she theorised, that things were clearly at the worse end of the theoretical scale. If it *was* just a boy, and Bess was simply too embarrassed to tell Jenna that she'd had her sexual awakening two years earlier than planned, she would have told her other friends. The fact that she hadn't set alarm bells jangling in Jenna's mind.

She went to her locker to collect her books for double geography and then she headed towards room 138. She passed the offices on her way there and peered surreptitiously, as she always did, towards Mr Fitzwilliam's door at the far end. As she did so the door opened and there was Bess leaving his office, smiling brightly, Mr Fitzwilliam's hand upon her arm.

'I will,' she heard her saying. 'You know I will.'

'That's my girl,' she heard him reply, 'that's my girl.'

51

Freddie wrapped the dress from Urban Outfitters in some tissue and slid it into his rucksack.

He'd ironed his school shirt the night before even though it was a non-iron shirt, and he was wearing his best trousers, the ones that didn't need the hem letting down or have encrusted acrylic paint from art class splattered all over them. As a nod to his new sense of vague rebellion, he wore black trainers instead of his crappy, ugly lace-up things that were so worn out they slipped off his heels when he ran in them. If a teacher picked him up on the breach of uniform policy he would simply say that the other ones were broken, which wasn't too far from the truth. He touched his fingertip against the rim of his dad's aftershave bottle and pressed the scent into the dips of his throat. He flossed his teeth. He sprayed on extra deodorant. He used a dab of his mum's foundation on a spot, realised it drew more attention to the spot than the spot on its own, and wiped it off again.

And then he headed to school, his jaw set with determination, ready to crawl through the eight hours between now and home-time.

It was four fifteen and he was standing outside St Mildred's School, watching the girls oozing through the gates, a river of royal blue and grey, idly tossed hair and Fjällräven rucksacks, laddered tights, Skinnydip phone cases and loud, loud voices.

Jenna Tripp had told him to write to Romola Brook. She'd told him that that would make it easier for Romola Brook to say no. Which was the exact and precise reason why Freddie was standing outside Romola's school about to ask her to come to the ball with him, face-to-face.

He straightened up at the sight of one of the bitchy-looking girls he remembered from the night he'd stood outside her house, the one who'd modelled the Urban Outfitters dress on Instagram. Her name was Louisa. And sure enough, following behind was Romola. For a worrying moment he thought maybe they were all going somewhere together and that he'd have to spend an hour standing outside Caffè Nero waiting for them to finish. But to his relief he heard Romola say, 'See you tomorrow,' and watched as she peeled off from the bitchy girl and he followed her as far as the end of the road before falling into step with her.

He'd practised this all night lying in bed. He'd run through it a hundred, two hundred times, finessed the timings and the nuances and the precise wording of the thing. And he was feeling cool and he was feeling fine. The very worst thing that could happen would be that she would say no. Rejection was a fact of life. It wasn't a nice fact of life. But it was a fact. And Freddie was bright enough to know he had to accept that if he ever wanted to get anywhere.

'Excuse me,' he opened.

She turned at his approach and he saw her do a double take, probably assessing whether or not she should be scared, then seeing the emblem on his blazer and wondering if maybe she should know him.

'I'm sorry to bother you,' he said, 'my name's Freddie. Freddie Fitzwilliam.' He offered her his hand to shake and she stared at it uncertainly for a moment before turning to see who might be watching, then gave him hers. It was limp and icy cold, bones as thin as kindling. 'I'm at Poleash Hall,' he said then, with a flourish, pointing at his blazer, 'which is clearly totally obvious.'

'Do I know you?' she asked.

'You've probably seen me around,' he said, boldly going off script. 'But no. You don't know me. Or at least *not yet.*'

He smiled and she looked at him pensively as though scared of what he might say next.

'Listen,' he said, 'and I have no idea if this is a good idea or a bad idea but I've got a ticket for the spring ball tomorrow night and I was going to try and be really cool and just show up by myself like an independent dude. But then I lost my nerve. And I just wondered, I've seen you around, and I think you're remarkably beautiful and I wondered if you might like to come with me?'

'You mean, as your date?'

'Yes,' he said, firmly. 'As my date.'

He saw her face fall by just a tiny degree and he knew, he just knew she was already mentally flipping through her stock of polite let-downs. 'Or not,' he said, quickly. 'Doesn't have to be a date. I could just be, you know, your *chaperone.*'

She smiled at this and he mentally fist-bumped himself for hauling it back so smoothly.

'That's a very old-fashioned idea.'

'Yes,' he said. 'It's retro. A kind of vintage thing. You know.'

She smiled again and he could feel the weight of the thing tipping back in his favour.

'Freddie?' she said.

'Yes. Freddie. And you are?'

'Romola,' she said.

'Romola,' he repeated, as though he'd never before heard the name. 'What a great name.'

'Thank you,' she said. 'I was named after an actress.'

'Called Romola?'

She laughed. 'Yes!' she said 'Called Romola!'

God, he felt ten feet tall, this was going so well. He'd known it would.

'So,' he said, letting his hand drop into his pocket and leaning into his heels, 'what do you think? Would you allow me to chaperone you to the spring ball?'

'But not a date?'

'Well, we could play that by ear. Maybe. See how I do. We could always upgrade it to a date? Halfway through.'

He was knocking this one out of the ballpark. Completely.

But then he saw that look pass over her face again, the look that said *I am not 100 per cent sure about you.*

'I don't know,' she was saying, 'I'm not really looking for a date. Or a chaperone. I was just going to hang with my friends.' She looked scared when she said this, as though she thought he might punch her in the face for rejecting him.

He played his last and his best hand. 'Look,' he said. 'No pressure. And I totally understand what you're saying. I myself have only very recently got into the idea of dating. But, whatever you decide to do, this . . .' He unzipped his bag and pulled out the tissue-wrapped dress. 'Is for you.'

'Oh my God,' she said, looking at it with wide eyes. 'Oh my God. What is it?'

'It's a gift. Something I saw and thought of you. Take it.' He held it out closer to her. 'If you don't like it, you could give it to a friend.'

'I can't,' she said. 'I can't take a gift from you. I don't even know you.'

'Please. I insist.'

'No,' she said. 'I can't.'

'Are you worried that if you accept the gift then you'll feel like you owe me something?'

She nodded.

'Well, you have my word, Romola Brook, that you can take this gift and walk away and never acknowledge my existence again.'

Her mood changed again. He bridled. 'How do you know my surname?'

'Ah,' he said. 'Yes. Fatal error.'

'What do you mean?'

'I mean, I was trying to be cool and make out like I didn't know who you were. But I totally know who you are.'

'You do?'

'Yes. I suppose that was obvious though, as I'd bought you a present.'

'Yes,' she said. 'That makes sense.'

'So,' he said. 'Will you accept it?'

She nodded, awkwardly, and said, 'Yes. OK.' Then she looked up at him and fixed him with her grey-blue eyes and said, 'Did you send me the brown skirt?'

'Yes,' he said.

'So you know where I live?'

'Yes,' he said again.

'Oh,' she said. 'Right.'

'I've liked you for quite some time,' he said by way of explanation.

'That seems clear,' she replied. And then she softened again, and she looked more gently at him and she said, 'Freddie, are you an Aspie?'

'What?'

'Have you got Asperger's? Are you on the spectrum?'

'What? No. No of course I'm not.'

'I am,' she said. 'That's why I asked you. Because some of the things you say and the way you say them and the way you stand and the way you look and lots of things about you seems like an Aspie.'

'You've got Asperger's?' he said.

'Yes. Mild. But . . .'

He looked at her in awe and wonder as something rushed up through his core, something buried deep under years of denial. The little prep school in Manchester where they'd taken him out of class one day and he'd been observed by a woman with a clipboard and some weird toys and his parents had been called in and he'd sat in the office outside with the lady who worked at the front desk and he'd eaten an apple and they'd come out and they'd looked worried and they'd taken him out for tea and the atmosphere had been wrong and strange and then his mum had said, *Your teacher thinks maybe you have a special brain.* And his dad had said, *No, Nicola, that's not what she said. She said your brain works in a special way.* And his mum said, *That's the same thing, surely.* And he'd said, *No, not quite. But here's the thing. They want to give a name to the special way your brain works. They want to call it something. They want to call it Asperger's, which is the name of an Austrian doctor who noticed lots of children with the same special way of dealing with the world. But Mummy and I, well, we don't think you need a name for the way your brain works because your brain is just the most remarkable thing. All brains are remarkable, but yours is more remarkable than most and I think you should just focus on what that brain of yours is capable of and not get hung up on labels and names. So, you may hear people bandying words about over the years. You may see things on the TV about people with Asperger's and think they're talking about you and get worried. But you mustn't worry. Because Mummy and I are not worried. We just love you and think you're brilliant. And you will always be so much more than a label. OK?*

He remembered his dad stroking his hair and his cheek and under his chin and he remembered thinking that clearly names for things were to be avoided when you were clever, as he was. And he'd barely thought of it again. Until now. And now there was a beautiful girl standing in front of him who'd been given a name for the way she was and she was proud to use it.

'I think I do,' he found himself saying. 'I'm fairly sure in fact that I do have Asperger's. But I don't really talk about it because it is probably the least interesting thing about me.'

Romola laughed. 'That's funny,' she said, 'because it's the most interesting thing about me.'

'Is it?'

'Yes. Definitely.'

'I'd love to find out more about your Asperger's.'

'Would you?'

'Yes.'

They both fell silent for a moment and then Romola put out her hands for the gift. 'I'll take this,' she said. 'And I'll think about the dance. Think about if I want a date or a chaperone. And thank you for the skirt. It really suits me.'

She didn't wait for him to reply and she didn't say goodbye. She simply turned and walked away.

52

Jenna saw Freddie Fitzwilliam about to turn up the hill to Melville Heights. Even from here she could see there was something different about him, something beyond the haircut. She crossed the road at the zebra and called out to him.

He turned and put his hand up to her in some kind of greeting.

'Are you busy?' she asked.

'No,' he said. 'I don't think I am.' He looked at her and she saw for the first time in his eyes a glimmer of something commanding; something of his father.

She said, 'Can we talk somewhere?'

'Now?'

'Yes. Now.'

'Well, you can come to my house.' He glanced up at the painted houses in the distance. 'If you like?'

'Will your dad be there?'

'No.' He shook his head. 'He never gets home till eight. At the earliest.'

'Will your mum mind?'

'No. She'll be pleased that I know someone well enough to ask them to our house. You know what mothers are like.'

She looked up towards the houses, the pale, gold eyes of them in the afternoon gloom. She'd never been inside a Melville Heights house before. Her mother had; she'd had a best friend at primary school – the family had long since moved away – who'd lived in the pink house. Her mother had spent dozens of after-noons up there, she said, kneeling on a window seat and staring down into the village, making up stories about the people they saw below, small as dolls' house figures.

'If you're sure?' she said.

'I'm sure,' he replied.

Freddie's house was cold. She pulled her padded coat closer around her as she followed Freddie down a wide, tiled hallway towards a kitchen at the back.

'Where's your mum?'

He shrugged and dropped his school bag and coat on to a settle. 'Maybe in bed. She says she has flu.'

'Oh,' she replied. 'Poor thing.'

'She's putting it on,' he said, somewhat harshly. 'Attention-seeking.'

'Oh,' she said again.

'Do you want to take off your coat? I'll make us some tea. If you like tea?'

'I like tea.'

'Cool.'

She left her coat and bag next to his and followed him into the kitchen.

'English Breakfast. Camomile. Peppermint. Earl Grey. Rooibos.'

She had no idea what the last word he'd said was but nodded and said, 'Just normal tea. Please.'

He pulled an English Breakfast teabag from a box and dropped it in a mug. He asked her if she wanted milk. She said yes. Divested of her coat, she was even colder. She noticed a window in the glass extension at the back of the kitchen, held closed with string. She could see the tail of the string wagging from side to side in the draught.

'You should get that window fixed,' she said. 'It's freezing in here.'

He glanced at her. 'My father likes cold houses. He says it keeps the mind focused.'

'Just keeps the mind focused on how cold it is,' she said, tucking her hands into her jumper sleeves and shivering.

She watched him make her tea. His movements were very measured, almost robotic. He took the brewed teabags from the mugs without squeezing them dry, leaving a trail of tea splashes in their wake as he transferred them to a bin.

'Did you ask the girl?' she started. 'To the ball?'

'I did ask her. Yes. I asked her just now. About thirty-five minutes ago. She didn't say yes. But she didn't say no. She has Asperger's.'

Jenna nodded politely and took the mug of tea from him. More tea splashed on to the table and she mopped it up with the cuffs of her jumper. She didn't know what to say about the Asperger's so she didn't say anything. She wondered if Freddie had Asperger's too, but decided it would be rude to ask.

'So,' he said, sitting alongside her, one thin leg crossed high upon the other. 'What was it you wanted to talk to me about? Did you want to ask me something about boys?'

She laughed, gently. 'Er, no. Not exactly. No. It was . . .' She paused. How could she broach this? In his house? With his mother upstairs, ill in bed? She sipped her tea and then put it down. In a very quiet voice she said, 'I wanted to talk about your father.'

His whole demeanour changed in a flash. He un-crossed his legs and leaned in towards her, his eyes wide with concern. 'What about my father?'

She shouldn't do this. She should thank Freddie for the tea, collect her bag and coat from the hallway and go. But then she thought of what she'd seen earlier: Mr Fitzwilliam's hand on Bess's arm, calling her *his girl*. She thought of the man in the black BMW who'd collected Bess from Jed's house last week. She thought of Bess and Mr Fitzwilliam in the village, chatting in the dark of night, in the hotel in Seville, sitting on the landing. She thought of the love hearts Bess used to draw on Mr Fitzwilliam's face, Bess crying in the toilets because she thought she was pregnant. She thought about the way that Mr Fitzwilliam sometimes looked at her, Jenna, the intensity of his gaze, the velvet of his voice, the softness of his jumpers, the well-placed box of tissues, the uninvited intimacy of their encounters. And then she thought, yet again, of the woman in the Lake District who had hated him so much and a voice screamed out somewhere deep inside her saying this is all *wrong, wrong, wrong!* And she looked straight into

Freddie Fitzwilliam's eyes and she said, 'Do you think he likes young girls?'

She watched for his reaction, her bottom lip pinched between her teeth. She prepared herself for anger, or hurt. But instead she saw his face open into an expression of intrigue and he said, 'No. Do you?'

'I don't know,' she whispered.

Freddie got up then, walked across the kitchen and closed the door. Then he returned and sat next to her again. 'Has he done something to you?' he asked.

'Me? No.'

'Then who?'

'My friend. Bess Ridley.' And then she told him everything, right from the beginning. He nodded as she talked and looked oddly unsurprised, almost as though he knew what she was going to say before she said it. 'I suspected', he said, when she told him about the hotel-landing incident in Seville, 'that there was an ulterior motive for him going on that trip.'

When she'd finished talking he leaned back against the table and breathed out into his cheeks. 'God,' he said.

'I'm sorry,' she said. 'This must be really hard for you. I can see that. This is your dad we're talking about.'

'I love my father,' said Freddie. 'In many ways he's one of the greatest men I know. But in many others . . .'

Jenna waited for his next words, alarmed by the thought of what they might imply.

'I have no idea if he likes young girls. But I think maybe he hurts my mother,' he said.

Jenna flinched.

'Sometimes,' he began slowly, very carefully, 'I hear things at night. From their room. Really weird, like thumps, and hard whispering, and it suddenly goes really quiet and then sometimes I'll hear something that sounds like someone throwing up and then the next day, quite often, my mum wears a polo neck or a scarf or has bruises on her wrists and looks really ill and then she stops running and stops smiling and this happened a few days ago and she has a huge bruise on her neck which she will not talk about. And so, although I think my father is a great man I also, at the exact same time, think he may be one of the worst men I know. And I want to know, in a way; I want to know a truth-based bad fact about him so that I can properly decide what I think. Because it's hard having two opinions, two types of feeling, both at the same time. I would prefer just to have one.'

Jenna thought suddenly of Bess wincing when she went to hug her in the toilets the other day.

'Have you ever asked your mother?' she asked. 'Have you ever asked her about your dad? About the bruises?'

'Yes,' said Freddie. 'But my mum thinks my dad's perfect. He's all she cares about. She loves me – but she cares more about him. All the food in our house is for him. It's all just food that he likes. The heating is off for him, because he doesn't like being warm. Even though I really like being warm. We never go on holiday, because he doesn't like holidays. Even though I really do. But that doesn't matter. He is the only person in our house that matters. My mum would never say anything bad about my dad. Ever.'

Jenna suddenly wanted to hold his hand, put an arm across his shoulder. But she had no idea how he would react. She wondered if maybe he was going to cry, but instead he looked up at her and said, 'So don't worry about saying bad things about my dad. I can take it. I really can.'

They fell silent for a moment and Jenna stared out towards the garden.

'You know,' Freddie said, 'my mum was a student at my dad's school. He was an English teacher there. He says they didn't meet until my mum was nineteen, but it makes you wonder, doesn't it?'

'Do you think maybe there was something going on between them, then? When she was still a student?'

'I don't know,' he replied. 'It's possible. I sometimes think . . .' He paused and rubbed his fingertips over his lips. 'I sometimes think I don't know either of them at all. And there's another thing.' He lowered his voice again. 'My mum, the other day she said something interesting. I was asking her about the angry woman at the lake and she said . . .' and then he broke into an incredibly convincing impersonation of what she assumed was his mother's voice: '*Maybe he had to expel her daughter or maybe she wasn't pleased with her last report. You know how over-sensitive some parents can be.* So obviously she knows more than she's letting on about who she was and what was happening.'

Jenna's eyes widened. 'Did she really say that?'

'Yes. I swear.'

'You know,' she said, 'I bet we could find something on the internet about it. Do you know the names of the schools your dad used to teach at?'

'Er, yes. Kind of. At least I know the names of the places he's lived and could probably remember the names of the schools if I saw them.'

'Have you got a laptop?'

'Yes,' he said. 'Yes. I'm going to get it right now. Wait there. Just wait there – and don't move.'

She smiled. 'I won't move,' she said. 'I promise.'

He was gone for a minute or two. Jenna didn't move

a muscle, paralysed somehow by the strangeness of being in her head teacher's kitchen. When he returned he plugged his laptop into the wall behind him and flipped it open.

'Right,' he said, opening his browser. 'So, the first place he taught was Burton-on-Trent. That was where he met my mum. So, let's look up schools there.'

Jenna turned to face the screen and let Freddie scroll through the results.

'There,' he said. 'That's the one. Robert Sutton High. I've heard them mention it before.'

'OK. Now search for things about that school with your dad's name in the search.'

He did this and they found a long list of newsletters about clubs and awards, local news stories about trips and plays. But nothing to suggest that Mr Fitzwilliam had done anything to make a parent angry enough to hit him.

'Add "Viva",' she said.

He glanced at her. 'Good thinking,' he said. 'Really good thinking.'

He typed the word *Viva* into his search terms and pressed find. When they saw the first line of the first search result they both inhaled audibly. They turned to look at each other.

'Oh my God,' whispered Jenna.

Freddie left the cursor blinking next to the result, his finger hovering over the trackpad.

'Go on then,' said Jenna. 'Click on it.'

'I'm scared to,' he said.

'Do you want me to?'

He nodded and she moved the laptop towards her. She clicked on the link.

53

It was a warm afternoon. Warm for March, anyway. Joey unzipped her coat and crossed to the sunny side of the street. She'd just left work and was shopping for clothes. To wear tomorrow. For her appointment to have sex with Tom Fitzwilliam in a hotel room. Which may or may not happen. She hadn't yet made up her mind. She might go to the hotel and have sex with Tom Fitzwilliam. She might go to the hotel and not have sex with Tom Fitzwilliam. Or she might not go to the hotel at all. A hundred voices shouted in her head all at the same time and all of them were saying something different.

When her mother had died, the hurricane in Joey's

head had stopped. Stopped completely. It had been there since she was a young girl. It was why she'd failed her GCSEs. It was why she'd been expelled from two schools. It was why she'd never managed monogamy, not even when she was madly in love. It was why her friendships didn't last the distance. It was why her underwear was tatty and her bank account was empty and her job was shit and her roots were nearly an inch long. Because all the elements of her existence were constantly going round and round her head like a load in a laundrette, churning and turning and presenting themselves to her in a dozen different conflicting ways. Things that felt like a good idea at ten o'clock would seem like the worst idea in the world by ten thirty. Someone once said to her that the key to a happy life was making good decisions. But making good decisions was beyond her because she could always see an infinity of outcomes and all of them seemed good for at least a moment. Yes, she might think about an invitation to a holiday with people she knew she'd hate being on holiday with, yes, why not, maybe it will be OK. And she'd say yes and then it wouldn't be OK. Because she had no idea how to pay attention to her own instincts, she was incapable of taking control of her own destiny.

She was, as her mother always used to say to her

with affection but also exhaustion, her own worst enemy.

But after watching her mother die, seeing the last rasps of life leave her broken body, everything had cleared. Her head stopped spinning and everything seemed millpond smooth. She was nearly twenty-seven and it was time to take steps towards a more grown-up existence. She'd married Alfie and handed in her notice at the resort and pictured herself coming home to Bristol to do the sorts of things that grown-up women who lived in Bristol did. She would get a proper job, a nice flat, she'd cook meals, spend time with her father and her brother, go to the gym, make some friends, proper solid friends, not a scrappy, transient stream of gap-year cuties popping pills all night. Maybe she'd join a reading group, book regular appointments at the hairdresser's, get a car, take the car to a car wash, get a pet, get two pets, buy plants, get manicures, eat salads, have a baby . . .

And then she'd come home and realised she couldn't afford a nice flat, and that without the nice flat there'd be no cooking nice meals, no fun reading group meetings with her fun friends. She'd realised that she wasn't equipped for a proper job and she wasn't ready for a baby and she couldn't afford to go to the gym and she couldn't afford a car and that making nice, fun, solid friends was harder than it looked. And slowly the hurricane inside her head had started up again. And then Tom Fitzwilliam had appeared above the maelstrom, looming tall and handsome, floodlight bright over the whirling and the wheeling of her thoughts, and it seemed that every minute she spent thinking about Tom was a minute not spent thinking about her crap job and her overgrown roots and her stultifying fear of taking the necessary steps towards a solid and fulfilling adulthood. As long as she was thinking about Tom and his hands at the back of her neck, his body hard against hers in the darkest corner of Melville Heights, as long as she was wondering what colour bra to buy for the sex appointment she may or may not attend tomorrow night, then she didn't need to think about the baby Alfie wanted to have with her and the fact that she knew, deep down and without a shadow of a doubt, that she should never have married him and that one day, probably quite soon, she was going to take his perfect heart and break it clean in two.

Blue, she thought, her hand against the unyielding lace of a £4.99 Primark push-up bra. Blue, she thought, putting the blue bra into the cloth shopping basket looped over her arm. Blue.

54

TEENAGE GIRL
SUICIDE VERDICT

Schoolteacher held for questioning

A verdict of suicide was passed yesterday after the death of local schoolgirl, Genevieve Hart, 14. Genevieve – who was known as Viva to her friends and family – was found dead last April in an abandoned chicken restaurant in Waterloo Street in the town centre. She had hanged herself using a pair of her school tights. A male teacher from Miss Hart's school, who has not been named, was questioned by police shortly after the schoolgirl's death after entries in her diary suggested that they might have been having an affair, but he was released after half an hour without charge. Sources close to the schoolgirl say that she had been the subject of a prolonged campaign of bullying at her school. They also say that Miss Hart left no note, and had cut off her hair with a pair of scissors shortly before taking her own life.

Jenna blinked slowly, trying to dislodge the image stuck in her head: a young girl, hanging from her own tights, a pool of her own hair on the floor beneath her swaying feet. Subconsciously she touched her own hair, imagining how it might feel to hold it in one hand while hacking it off with the other. She imagined the feel of it, the sound of it. It was unthinkable, barbaric, almost. She gulped and brought her fist to her mouth. 'It's so sad.'

Freddie nodded. 'It's horrible.' But then he straightened and said, 'But it wasn't my dad. Was it?'

She looked at the article and thought that people not

being charged with crimes didn't mean they hadn't committed them. It just meant that no one could find enough evidence to say that they had. But she didn't say that. She smiled instead and said, 'Doesn't look like it.'

'She was being bullied,' he continued, pointing at the relevant section. 'That's probably why she did it. That happens a lot, doesn't it? People being bullied at school and killing themselves?'

'Yes,' she said vaguely, 'yes it does.'

'So, that's probably what happened. Isn't it?'

'Yes,' she said again. But if that was the case then why was Viva's mother hitting Mr Fitzwilliam? Why was she not hitting the bullies who had hounded her daughter to her death? What was in Viva's diary that had made her mother believe that Mr Fitzwilliam was to blame for her death? There was no way of knowing. The only people who would know what was written in Viva's diary were her family. The Harts.

'Here,' she said, turning the screen towards herself again and pressing the back button. 'Let's see what else we can find.' She scanned through the search results until she found an article accompanied by a photograph. She zoomed right in on the photo and stared for a while at the image: a pretty girl with long, very dark hair, big eyes and an air about her of imminent hilarity. She looked kind, Jenna felt, and thoughtful. It was impossible to imagine this girl taking herself to a dank old chicken shop, chopping off all her beautiful hair with a pair of scissors and hanging herself with a pair of tights. It was impossible to imagine her being dead.

The mother's name was given in this article. She was called Sandra. No father was mentioned. She typed in *Sandra Hart* but it brought her full circle back to the newspaper articles about her daughter. Then she went on to Facebook and clicked on a few 'Sandra Harts', but each turned out to be too young or too old or to have no connection with anyone or anything apposite to any elements of the Genevieve Hart story. And then she clicked on a Sandra Hart who lived in Sheffield and had been born in Derby in 1957. Her page was set to private, so Jenna clicked on the only link that was available: her friends' list.

She only had twenty-two. Jenna went through them one by one until she got to the profile of a younger woman called Rebecca Louise Hart. Her page was also set to private but her personal information was available, and Jenna learned that she was born in Burton-on-Trent in 1981 and was a systems analyst for Charter Redwood Financial Management.

'Hold on,' said Freddie, leaning in towards the screen. 'I know that woman. I know her! I . . . I . . . Hold on.' He pulled his phone out of his blazer pocket and switched it on. He swiped through some photos, all of which, as far as Jenna could tell from this angle, were of the same person: a pretty girl with chestnut hair and a royal-blue school blazer. 'Look,' he said, turning the phone to face her.

It was a long-range shot of a woman in a big black coat, talking to Jenna's mum at the bus stop outside the Melville.

'Look. It's her. Isn't it? The same woman? And she's talking to your mum.'

'Wait. Wait.' Jenna reeled away from the screen and closed her eyes for a brief moment. 'This is . . . I don't understand.' She looked at the screen again and let her eyes confirm what she had seen. That was definitely her mother and that was definitely the same woman as the woman in the Facebook profile photo and they were definitely both standing outside the Melville.

'When was this?' she said.

'Yesterday,' he replied.

'And why . . .' She cupped her temples with her hands. 'Why do you have a photograph of it?'

'Because it was interesting.'

'Interesting?'

'Yes. I find your mother interesting. I find your mother talking to people interesting.'

'So you do . . .' she said, awareness flooding through her, '. . . you do take pictures of my mother? You actually do?'

'Yes,' he said. 'But not often. Hardly ever in fact.'

'She always said you were up here watching her from your window and I always told her she was imagining it.'

'Well, she wasn't imagining it. I was. But she's as bad, you know. She's always down there looking up at us. All the time. Sometimes she even sits outside our house. At least I don't do that.'

Jenna shook her head slightly from left to right. She couldn't process all this right now. She brought her thoughts back to the issue at hand.

'I wonder where she lives, that woman. She looks familiar. I'm sure I've seen her around.'

'Well, she'd be hard to miss, I reckon. She's pretty fat.'

Jenna looked at the photo and tutted at Freddie. 'She's not fat,' she said incredulously. 'Look.' She pointed at the outline of her black coat, the 'B' shape of her profile. 'She's pregnant.'

Freddie peered closer and then looked at Jenna and said, 'God. You're right. *Of course!*' He clicked his fingers together. 'Now I know exactly who she is. She lives two doors down. She's practically my next door neighbour!'

* * *

Jenna went straight from Freddie's to Bess's house. Her hands shook as she pressed the intercom button and her heart pounded. Bess's mum answered.

'Hi, Heather, it's me, Jenna. Is Bess at home?'

'Yup! Come up, sweetheart!'

Bess was sitting on her big double bed, surrounded by fake astrakhan cushions in sorbet colours and haloed by hanging fairy lights. A red scented candle glowed in a glass jar on her bedside table, making her room smell like Christmas. 'What's up?' she said, seeing Jenna's anxious expression.

'Bess. This is really, really serious. You have to listen to me. And you have got to be honest with me.'

She saw Bess swallow and then shrug. 'What?'

'It's a really, really long story. But the short version is this. There's a woman who lives up there' – she pointed – 'in Melville Heights, and when she was younger her sister killed herself. And do you know why she killed herself?'

Bess shrugged again. 'Why?'

'Because she was having an affair with Mr Fitzwilliam.'

Bess narrowed her eyes at her. 'What?'

'She and her sister were at a school up north and Mr Fitzwilliam was a teacher there and her sister was having some kind of an affair with him, and then one

377

day she was found dead. And not only that, but apparently Mr Fitzwilliam beats his wife.'

Bess gave her a look askance. 'And you're telling me this because?'

Jenna sighed. 'You know why, Bess. You know exactly why.'

'Er, no. Actually, I don't?'

'Bess. Please. Stop lying to me. You and Mr Fitzwilliam and what's been going on between you.'

Bess stared at Jenna blankly. 'God. Wow. Jen. *Nothing* has been going on between us. Are you on glue?'

'So what's with all the secret meetings?'

'There haven't been any secret meetings!'

'Yes, there have! That night, when I saw you and him outside the pharmacy at, like, eleven o'clock. And earlier today, I saw you coming out of his office and he was, like, touching your arm.'

'Oh my fucking God, Jen. We were talking about *you*.'

Jenna stiffened. 'About me?'

'Yeah. About your mum. About what would happen to you if your mum got sectioned or something. He wanted to know if me and Mum would be able to have you live with us. Here. So that you could stay on at the Academy and not have to move down to your dad's place. That is all. Literally. And I couldn't tell you because I knew you'd lose the plot over it. I told you, Jen, he's such a caring man! And I don't know who this woman is in Melville Heights and I'm sorry for what happened to her sister, but, I swear, there's no way that Mr Fitzwilliam had anything to do with it. No way.'

'But what about this . . .' Jenna pointed at Bess's stomach. 'This pregnancy thing. I mean, whose baby is it then?'

'There is no baby!'

'But . . . I don't . . .'

'Look.' Bess sighed and pushed her hair behind her ears. 'I was just . . . I met a lad. Ruby's cousin. Jed. And we went quite far. Like, really quite far. And some of his, you know, his stuff, it sort of . . .'

Jenna wrinkled her nose. She really didn't want to think of Jed's *stuff.*

'It went on my belly. And then when my period didn't come I just freaked out. I thought, maybe, you know, it had somehow got all the way down there. And I knew I was being stupid. I knew I was. That's why I didn't want to talk to you about it. Because I knew you'd tell me I was an idiot.'

'I wouldn't!'

'Yeah, you would. But that's fine because you're you and I'm me and that's how we roll. And anyway. My period started this morning. So. You know. Yay.'

'So, you're still a virgin?'

'Yeah. I'm still a virgin.'

'And you're not pregnant?'

'No. I'm not pregnant.'

'And you're not having an affair with Mr Fitzwilliam?'

'No. I'm not. And I never would because I love him too much and it would spoil everything if we did something like that.'

'Has he ever, you know, tried . . . ?'

'No! Never.'

'And you and Jed. Is he your boyfriend?'

'No. I told you. He's a dick. But he's so good-looking. I just wanted to know what it would feel like to kiss someone that handsome. And then it just went a bit further than I thought it would. But it was a one-off. We're just mates now.' She stopped and smiled at Jenna.

But Jenna had one more question. 'In the toilets the other day. When I hugged you. You flinched. You pulled away. Like it hurt. Like you were injured? What was that?'

Bess shrugged. 'Probably just sore boobs. Because they were – oh, God, they were so sore. So so sore.'

Jenna gazed at her friend for a moment. Her sweet Bess. The greatest girl in the world. Suddenly the terrible distance between them seemed to ping back like an elastic band. Suddenly it was like the past weeks hadn't happened.

She put her arms out and Bess put hers out and they hugged.

'I'm sorry I made you worry,' said Bess.

'It's OK,' said Jenna. 'I like worrying about you. It gives me something to do.'

Bess laughed and then she stopped and she said, 'By the way, my mum says it's totally OK for you to come and live with us, if anything, you know, if your mum . . .'

'I know,' said Jenna. 'And thank you. I hope it doesn't happen. But if it does . . .' She hugged her again. 'I love you, Bess Ridley.'

'And I love you, Jenna Tripp.'

She held her best friend in her arms for a while, relief that she was safe flooding through her. But when she closed her eyes, all she could see was the dreadful image of Genevieve Hart hanging from a ceiling, her beautiful dark hair strewn across a dirty floor.

55

Freddie felt a bit bad about barging in to his mum's bedroom and talking to her about horrible things while she was supposedly ill. But there was too much stuff surging and lurching around in his head. It needed to go somewhere otherwise he was going to drown in it all.

He brought her an old-looking banana from the fruit bowl in the kitchen and a cup of cranberry and raspberry tea. The curtains were closed and the room smelled of thick breath and used sheets. He placed the tea carefully on her bedside table and offered her the banana. She shook her head and groaned slightly.

'I've got loads I need to talk to you about, Mum,' he

began, lowering himself on to the edge of the bed. He couldn't see any reason to pussyfoot about. It was nearly seven and his dad might be home any minute.

'Oh, love. I'm not sure I'm up for a big chat.'

He put the palm of his hand to her forehead and then to his own and then back to hers again. 'You're not hot,' he said, 'so you're probably not as ill as you think you are.'

'I just took some paracetamols,' she said. 'They've brought my temperature down. I promise you, I feel awful.'

'Well, I'm not asking you to do anything difficult. '

She groaned again. 'What?' she said. 'What is it?'

'Number one,' he began, 'do I or do I not have Asperger's?'

'What?'

'Asperger's. Do I have it? Because I met someone today who does have it and they said they thought I might too and it reminded me of something that happened when I was at infant school. That teacher, Miss Morrison or whatever her name was, who thought there might be something wrong with me. And you took me out for tea after and Dad said I mustn't ever accept a label, that I must just focus on being clever and not worry about what other people said I was or wasn't. And I'm sure he said the word Asperger's. And

I've been googling it and it makes sense and I just think that maybe you and Dad didn't think I should have a label, but that maybe it would be good if I did. Because Max at school thinks I'm like him, and I am *not* like him. Because he's not special. He's not an Aspie. And I think I probably am.'

His mother edged her way up the bed as he spoke, and then sat straight and gazed at him. He saw the fog lifting behind her eyes, the pretence at 'being ill' falling away. 'Who told you this?'

'A girl. I asked her to be my date for the dance tomorrow. I think she's going to say yes.'

'And she's got Asperger's?'

'Yes.' He nodded. 'And she's not scared of having a label.'

She sighed. 'Well, that's good for her. But for me and your father—'

He cut across her. 'Not you,' he said firmly. 'It was Dad who said I shouldn't have a label. You just went along with it. Like you go along with everything Dad says.'

'That's not true.'

'It is true. You know it's true. I mean, look at you. You're lying here in this cold room. Pretending to be ill. Because of whatever the hell it was that happened last week. Something *he* did.'

'I am n—'

'You *are*. And your whole life is all about Dad. Dad, Dad, Dad. And you act like he's the only person in the whole world who matters. Like he's the only person who hurts or the only person who gets sad. Or hungry. Or hot. Or cold. Like everyone else is just . . . peripheral. But yet – he doesn't seem to make you happy. He doesn't make you laugh. He never does anything nice for you. Or takes you out. He just leaves you here in this big, cold house, and I saw you when that Alfie guy was here and he made you laugh and he made you happy. And I never see you like that. Ever. So it's not as if you can't have fun. It's more like you wake up every morning and choose not to.'

'God, Freddie! I really have no idea what you're talking about.'

'You do, though, I know you do. Mum, you *know* – you know that Dad's not a good man. You know that he's done bad things. He hurts you.'

'Hurts me?'

'Yes. And he hurts other people. He made that girl kill herself.'

'What girl? Freddie? What girl?'

'You *know* what girl. *Viva. That* girl. I've seen the news articles about it. In black and white. And you always told me that that woman at the Lakes was just a loony. But she wasn't a loony. She was Viva's mum. And Viva was at the school where Dad taught when he was in Burton upon Trent. Where he met *you*, Mum. I mean, God. You probably even knew her! She might even have been in your class. You were probably there when it was all happening. When it was in the papers. When Dad got taken in for questioning. *Everyone* must have been talking about it. So don't say you don't know what girl I'm talking about because you totally, a million and ten per cent, know.'

His mother sighed and grimaced. 'Yes. I was at school with her. But I didn't know her. She didn't know me. And it was nothing, literally nothing whatsoever to do with your father. Because, you know, everyone knew. Everyone knew what was going on. That Viva had a huge crush on your dad. Followed him about. Stalked him virtually. But he wasn't interested. And that was probably why she killed herself. But nobody would want to admit that.' His mum drew in her breath, long and deep. She massaged her forehead with her fingertips and then she said, 'Her suicide was nothing to do with your dad. Nothing.'

'Mum,' Freddie said, feeling redness hurtling through his gut and his head and his chest. 'Why are you protecting him? Why are you so obsessed with him? Why is *everyone* so obsessed with him?'

'They are not—'

'They are, Mum! That Viva girl was; you are. And there's that woman at number fourteen. *Joey*. She's always hanging about with big moon eyes.'

'Oh, that's ridiculous.'

'No it's not! I've got photos of her, Mum, standing outside our door staring up. Dad gives her lifts in his car. She went to the pub with him once. And I've seen her sometimes standing at the end of her garden staring up at our house. I've even seen her touching Dad's car when she walks past it. And everywhere we've ever lived there's been something going on in the background. And you know, people with Asperger's find it really hard to deal with change and making friends and yet, because of Dad saying I shouldn't have a label and because of his stupid career, I've been moved around all over the country all the time and I shouldn't have been. I should have been allowed to stay in one place. But no. Because of Dad. Everything is because of fucking Dad.'

He paused for a moment. He'd already said ten times more than he'd expected to say. But his mum was still listening, and he might never feel able to talk to her like this again. He sucked in his cheeks and let them go. 'You were really young when you got together with Dad. He'd been your teacher. That's quite bad, when you think about it, even though it ended up fine. But it shows, it shows that he's prepared to do things that are quite bad, things that a responsible adult shouldn't do. And there's a girl down in the village, Mum, she's fifteen and she's in love with him too and Dad meets up with her at night sometimes, he has special meetings with her in his office at school. She's the whole reason he went on that trip to Seville! And my friend told me that this girl might even be pregnant by him!'

He saw her flinch, as though he'd just flicked water at her face. 'Please, Freddie,' she said. 'That's enough. Stop it. Just stop it.'

'I don't want to stop, though. I can't stop. It's all just coming out of me and I can't stop it.'

'Freddie. Please. Just go. I'm ill and you are being vile and I absolutely cannot take it.'

'I'm not being vile, Mum. I'm being real. And truthful. It's you and Dad who are being vile. By lying all the time. About me. About everything.'

'Get out, Freddie!'

'No! I won't.'

'Yes! You will! Now!'

'No.' He folded his arms hard across his chest. 'I won't.'

Suddenly she sat bolt upright and she leaned right

into his face and screamed, '*Get out now, you fucking little* shit! *Now!*' And then she pushed him, hard, right in his gut, so that he could feel all the air he'd just breathed in turn into a hard ball and smash into the base of his spine and he fell backwards and then he looked at his mum, waiting for her face to turn soft, for her to look shocked at what had just happened.

But she didn't; she just stared at him and then in a really calm, really hard voice, she said, '*Get off the floor and get the fuck out of my room.*'

This time he did. He scrambled to his feet, strode to the door and ran up to his bedroom, three stairs at a time.

56

Alfie got back from work at midnight. He slid into bed beside her smelling of shower gel and toothpaste, and also something else, something Joey couldn't quite define but which made her feel strangely queasy.

She crawled into the open space between his arms that he offered up to her and buried her face between the solid planes of his pectorals and she breathed in hard, a sense of release and relief, but also of sadness, that by this time tomorrow night she would have done something unbearable and irreversible, something cruel and shattering. She felt his heart beating under her cheek, a slow, hypnotic pulse, the rhythm of his life force, his innocence, his purity. She sighed and held him tighter. She didn't want to let him go. But she didn't want to let go of her feelings for Tom either.

'How was your night?' she asked, her lips grazing the sweet-smelling fuzz on his chest.

'It was . . .' He paused. She felt him tighten up, heard his heart begin to pound a little faster, a little harder. But then he loosened again, kissed her behind her ear. 'It was fine,' he said. 'Busy. But good.'

'Good,' she said, burrowing herself back into Alfie's body, her hands curled in towards her chin. She took a deep breath to calm her heart. And as she did so, it hit her, hard and clear. The smell on Alfie. It wasn't shower gel. He didn't use shower gel. It was perfume. And it wasn't hers.

57

Freddie's dad got back from work really late that night.

Freddie watched the time on his bedside, watched it drip slowly through the minutes. He was too scared to go downstairs. He'd spent all night in his room waiting to hear the soft footsteps of his mum coming up to make her peace, to apologise for calling him a *little shit*, maybe to bring him up some supper. But she hadn't. The house had stayed silent. His stomach growled and he thought of steaming bowls of Maggi chicken noodles and towers of thick buttered toast. He remembered the big box of chocolates his dad had brought home a couple of nights ago, a gift from a grateful parent. There was an espresso martini truffle in there that he would love to eat right now. And a soft hazelnut mousse.

He didn't know why he was too scared to go downstairs. It was stupid. But it felt as though there was a hungry lion in the house, something dark and unpredictable locked away behind his parents' bedroom door.

Jenna had messaged him a couple of hours ago. Her friend wasn't pregnant and she wasn't having an affair with his dad. Freddie had felt a terrible rush of guilt remembering the things he'd thought, the terrible things he'd said to his mum about his dad. He wanted to make everything right. He wanted to fix his mess.

At the sound of his dad's car door locking on the street outside, Freddie jumped out of bed and ran down the stairs. He heard the front door open and saw the light go on in the kitchen.

'Dad,' he whispered into the gloom.

His dad turned and said, 'Freddie! You're up late.'

He edged into the kitchen and leaned against the wall. 'I was hungry,' he said. 'I haven't had any supper.'

'Why not?'

'I had a row with Mum. I thought she might bring me something up as a peace offering. She didn't.'

'You had a row? What about?'

'About you. About not telling me that I have Asperger's. And some other things.'

His dad opened a cupboard and pulled out a loaf of bread. 'Toast?' he said, waving it in his direction.

'Yes,' said Freddie. 'Three slices please.'

'Well, we can only get four at a time in the toaster, so how about we start with two each?'

'OK.'

His dad stood over the toaster for a while, staring down into it. The back of his shirt was all creased from where he'd been squashed against a chair all day. Freddie held his breath through the silence, not wanting to break it with even the smallest noise.

Finally his dad turned and looked at him. 'So,' he said, 'what's all this about Asperger's?'

'Someone asked me, today, if I had it. And I remembered that teacher in Manchester who said I did. And you and Mum taking me out for tea and telling me that I shouldn't have a label. And I've been googling it and a lot of it sounds like me. Like the fact that my voice is so high-pitched, for example. And that I find it hard to look people in the eye sometimes. The fact that I am so good at languages and accents, because some people with Asperger's like collecting things and I like to collect languages and accents. And sometimes people with Asperger's are really good at chess, not that I really care about chess any more. But overall, I tick a lot of Asperger's boxes. And I actually think it would be quite great to have a label, if it was a label that made me understand myself better. And I'm cross, really, that I haven't had that.'

The toast popped up then and his dad turned back to take it out and butter it for them. It was Dad's favourite bread – of course – with a thick jacket of seeds and nuts. Usually Freddie would reject it on the grounds of the seeds and the nuts, not to mention the unfairness of them never having plain white bread. But tonight he was too hungry to care.

His dad cut the toast together in a pile and then passed Freddie his two slices. Freddie pulled the crusts carefully away from the soft centres and then rammed a piece into his mouth. His dad sat down and stared at Freddie with his tired green eyes and said, 'I'm really, really sorry.'

Freddie hadn't expected his dad to say sorry. He wasn't sure how to react.

'You know, it was such a long time ago and you were so little and it seemed far too early to be calling you things. I just wanted to wait and see. See how it went. And every time we took you to a new school I'd be waiting to see if anyone would say anything, if we'd be called in for another little meeting. But nobody ever did. Not really.'

'Not *really*?' said Freddie.

'Well, there was one teacher, in Mold, Miss Camilleri. Remember her?'

'Yes. She was Maltese. She taught me how to sing "Happy Birthday To You" in Maltese.'

'Yes. That's right. She did say something once, at a parent–teacher meeting. She asked if you'd ever had a diagnosis. And we said yes. But then we left Mold three weeks later and never followed it up. But that was the only time, in seven, eight years. And you've been doing so well. I just thought . . . I thought I was doing the right thing.'

'I find it surprising, as a professional educationalist, that you would choose to ignore a diagnosis like that.'

'I didn't ignore it, Freddie. I just wanted to wait and see. I've been watching you. All along. Watching everything you do, waiting to see if you needed us to step in and give you extra support. But you never did. Because, Freddie, you are just totally brilliant. And I am so proud of you.'

Freddie smiled, just a flicker of a smile, as much as he could muster. 'I am clever,' he said. 'But I am also quite shy and find making friends very difficult, and I think I make some really bad mistakes with people, and I misunderstand them, and it might be useful for me now, maybe, to have some extra support. I'd like my label please.'

'Here?' asked his dad, pointing at the kitchen table. 'Or out in the world?'

'Out in the world. At school. Yes.'

His dad nodded and ate some toast. 'I'll make an appointment at your school,' he said. 'For next week. We'll get it all sorted. And Freddie?'

'Yes?'

'I am really sorry. I thought I was doing it for the best.'

'That's OK, Dad.'

'So, what else did you and your mum argue about?'

Freddie looked at his dad. He was now at the opposite end of the spectrum to the angry bear that lived inside him. He looked soft and kind. A teddy bear. A nice dad. Not a bad man. Not a man who made teenagers pregnant and made them kill themselves and strangled his wife in bed at night and had affairs with blondes in red suede boots.

'Nothing,' Freddie said. 'That was it really. And she got really, really cross and pushed me over and called me a fucking little shit.'

His dad sighed. 'Your mum's in a strange mood at

the moment. A very strange mood. I'm sorry you were on the receiving end of it.'

Freddie shrugged and picked up the last half-slice of toast. 'That's OK,' he said. 'I don't mind.'

His dad smiled at him and Freddie smiled back. But inside all he could think was: *Dad, what really happened to Genevieve Hart?*

58

24 March

Joey threw Dawn a cheery goodbye and left, her heart thumping hard under the cheap lace of her brand-new bra. It was Friday night, she was on her way to meet Tom and she was so scared she wanted to throw up.

Tom had booked them into a remarkably beautiful hotel on the harbour. She hadn't been expecting the Bristol Harbour to be something so grand; she'd been imagining a Holiday Inn or a Novotel type of affair. Something modern and convenient. Something suitable for a discreet one-night stand. But this was a grand boutique hotel, high ceilings, arched windows, teal velvet and bronze light fittings, perfumed with scented candles. This was a honeymoon hotel.

'I have a reservation,' she said to the girl behind the desk. 'In the name of Mr Darwin?'

'Yes,' said the woman, staring at her computer. 'Yes. Just the one night?'

'Yes,' she said. 'Just the one night.'

Joey handed the receptionist her card. Tom had said he'd pay her back with cash, that it would keep things cleaner, and simpler.

Their room was on the first floor. It had a view over the twinkling lights of the city. It had a tall, golden, buttoned-velvet bedhead and a red velvet armchair with turquoise silk cushions. It was the nicest hotel room Joey had ever been in. She took off her boots and let her feet sink into the soft patterned rug.

Alfie texted again: *Are you on your way home?*

No, she replied, *I'm going shopping.*

Food shopping?

No. Clothes and stuff.

How long?

No idea. As long as it takes.

Text me when you're on your way back.

Will do.

Love you.

Joey couldn't quite bring herself to return the

sentiment so typed in a love-heart emoji instead and turned off her phone.

Tom had said he'd get away when he could. He'd said he'd text when he was on his way. It was twenty past seven. She looked in the minibar. Then she looked at the price list for the things in the minibar and decided not to take anything out of it. She went and put her toothbrush and toothpaste in the marble bathroom. She checked her reflection. She looked fine. The dress she'd chosen in a wild, blue shopping panic yesterday was actually quite nice. Her skin was OK. Her hair was behaving. She put on an extra coat of red lipstick and went and sat on the bed.

And then the nerves kicked in. Big, sickening waves of terror and uncertainty.

What exactly was she doing here? What on earth was her objective? Tom had said that they would do this only once and then move on. But move on to what, exactly? They would still be neighbours. She would still bump into him in the wine shop. See him in the bar at the Melville. There would be a couple – maybe more – of intensely awkward years and then Tom and his strange wife and odd son would move out and on to the next place and the next school and she would never see him again.

Joey suddenly realised that the ache inside her, the

burning flame of desire that had informed her entire existence for the last three months – it wasn't profound. It wasn't meaningful. It was simply an itch that needed to be scratched, no more profound than any other itch she'd ever had. And surely her life should be more than just a long, unfulfilling process of itch-scratching.

She checked the time. It was nearly seven thirty. She put her hand to herself, looking for the hot, urgent tautness that had been there for weeks. But it was gone; she could almost feel the dregs of it, ebbing, drizzling away.

And then there was a gentle knock at the door.

59

Freddie saw her the moment he walked in. She was wearing his dress. 'You're wearing my dress,' he said.

Romola looked at him strangely. 'No,' she said. 'This is not your dress. It's my dress. You gave it to me.'

'That's true,' he said. 'You look beautiful in it.'

'Thank you. You look incredibly cool.'

Freddie glanced down at his black suit and red tie and shiny black shoes and said, 'Thank you.' Then he said, 'You didn't tell me if you wanted me to be your date or not. I just decided I'd come anyway.'

Romola smiled. 'I'm glad you came. I couldn't decide and I couldn't decide and I kept thinking about what I should say to you because I knew you'd be waiting to find out. And then my mum said I should leave it to destiny. So that's what I did.'

'Destiny?'

'Yes. She said I should just come to the dance and that if you came too I could decide then.'

'And have you decided?'

She looked him up and down and smiled. 'Yes,' she said. 'Literally this very minute. I'd like you to be my date.'

60

Tom stood shyly in the doorway for a moment looking exhausted before collapsing on to the edge of the bed a foot or so away from Joey and saying, 'Christ. I am shattered.'

She was unsure how to respond so she jumped to her feet and grabbed the room-service menu from the desk. 'A cocktail?' she suggested. 'Some wine?'

He shook his head. 'No,' he said. 'I drove. I shouldn't . . .'

'No,' she agreed.

'But you order something. Please.'

'No,' she said, sitting down again, 'it's fine.'

And then suddenly, and without much in the way

of a preamble, he leaned across and he kissed her on the mouth.

She pulled away and looked at him. 'Tom. I—' She wasn't sure what she was going to say. Something like, *We don't have to do this if you're tired.* Or, *We could just talk.* But his mouth was back against hers before she had a chance to form a syllable. She attempted to give herself into him. She wanted so much for her body to follow her brain's train of thought: that this was what she'd wanted, that yes, maybe she'd had doubts, and yes, maybe he was having doubts too, but that maybe if they just kept kissing for long enough, somehow or other the spark would be reignited.

They kissed for a few minutes, but her body did not follow her brain and in fact she did not enjoy the kiss. It was cumbersome and slightly sour. He had come straight from work, from a day of tea and coffee and lunch at his desk. He hadn't brushed his teeth. She tried again to lull her body into wanting what was happening to it. She moved closer and pressed her breasts against him, pulled the fabric of his shirt away from his waistband and placed her hands against the bare skin of his back. She remembered that day on the bus when his jumper had lifted and she'd seen his flesh, the power of it. This stirred her for long enough to unbutton his shirt and pull it open. But then suddenly he was pulling away from her. She looked at him and his eyes were full of something she'd never seen there before.

'What?' she said. 'Are you—?' And then she stopped when she saw the marks on his body. Scratches. Bruises. Bite marks. The indents of actual teeth. 'Oh my God. Tom . . .'

He pulled his shirt closed but she pulled it open again.

'What is all this?'

'It's nothing. Just . . . breaking up a fight in the playground. You know.'

'But Tom – those are teeth marks.'

'Yes, yes they are.'

'Who bit you, Tom? Who did this?'

He sat back. His head dropped into his chest and the soft paunch of his stomach collapsed into two rings of flesh over his waistband. He looked tired; he looked broken. 'It's Nicola. She gets, I don't know, overly emotional. She gets very jealous. She carries a lot of anger inside her. And most of the time she contains it. But sometimes she can't . . . and she takes it out on me.'

'She attacks you?'

Tom nodded.

'And you let her?'

'Most of the time I let her. Yes.'

Joey paused for a moment to absorb the awfulness of what he was telling her. 'But – how? Where?'

'At home. In our room. At night. She'll say it's something I said or something I did. This' – he looked down at the marks on his body – 'this was because she saw me talking to one of my students in the village. We talked for all of thirty seconds. But Nicola was convinced there was more to it. I mean, the girl was fifteen, for crying out loud! Fifteen!'

'And coming here tonight? Was this deliberate? A cry for help? I mean, you must have known I'd see all this.' She gestured at his marked body. 'You must have known I'd ask?'

His head dropped forward again and she stared into the crown of his hair, into the place where the pink of his scalp showed through. She put out her hand and she touched it.

'Yes.' He nodded heavily. 'Yes. I guess. It's just been this *thing*, this awful dysfunction I've carried around for fifteen years. This twisted, wrong thing. It's like she hates me as much as she loves me, but that the hate is where she gets her passion. It's the hate that makes her feel, and when she feels she wants to hurt me. And when she hurts me I want to hurt her. And it's this rotten, awful cycle and I've had enough, Joey. I've had enough.'

'Do you hurt her too?'

'Sometimes . . .' He looked up at Joey with desperate eyes. 'But you have to believe me, it's never out of control. It's self-defence. I don't do this to her.' He gestured at the marks on his body. 'It's all so wrong and my poor boy, my Freddie, I know he knows something's not right. I know he does. He's nearly fifteen. He's just starting to look at the world and see what's going on. Ask questions. And now she's started being cruel to him too. She hurt him yesterday. She pushed him over and called him a little shit. My lovely boy. My amazing lovely boy. And I just . . . I don't want to do it any more. She's cruel and she's dark and you – you're the opposite! From the moment I saw you that day in the bar at the Melville, when you knocked over those leaflets, I could just tell; you were so good and so bright and so pure. Everything that Nicola isn't. And I wanted you so much, more than I ever wanted anything in my whole life.'

He'd begun to cry and Joey put her arms around his neck and pulled his head against her shoulder and stroked his hair and she felt a terrible realisation that Tom Fitzwilliam had not brought her here to scratch an itch. He'd brought her here to rescue him.

'Do you love her, Tom?'

She felt his head shake. 'No,' he murmured into the

soft jersey of her dress. 'No. I've never loved Nicola. Sometimes I think I hate her.'

'Then why . . . ?'

'I don't know. She was just always . . . she was *there*.'

'There?'

'Yes. From the moment she came up to me on the bus that day when she was nineteen years old and said, *Hello, Mr Fitzwilliam*. And then suddenly she was pregnant. Only weeks after we met. And I was thirty-five and it seemed – I don't know, the right time to be settling down, I suppose.' His face fell into a wry smile. 'You know, she told me that she fell in love with me when I was a teacher at her school. When she was four-teen years old. She told me that she decided then and there that she was going to marry me one day. And that nothing was going to stop her. And yet, I don't even remember her. She was invisible to me. If any-thing should have been a warning, it was that.'

'Tom, you can't go on like this. It's . . . it's mental!'

'I know,' he said. 'I know I can't. But how? How do I escape? If I leave her it will all come out. She'd tell the world about the sickness between us. I know she would. And then Freddie would know and the school would know and the world would know – and then what? Then what would happen? Everything would be over for me. Everything I've worked for. Everything I care about. I'm trapped, Josephine. I'm completely trapped.'

'I can't save you, Tom,' Joey whispered. 'You do know that? I cannot save you. You're going to have to save yourself.'

'You're right,' he said. 'I know you're right. And I will. I will save myself. I'll find a way. I'm sure I will.'

She held him for a little while longer and then he said, 'I should probably go home. I don't know what I was thinking. Using a beautiful young woman like you to try and fix my own stupid mess. I'm so sorry.'

'No. Tom. Please. Don't be sorry. I was using you too. To fix my own mess. Go home. We'll finish this conversation another time.'

She watched him button up his shirt, tuck it back into his trousers.

'Please don't think badly of me.'

'I don't, Tom, trust me – I am not in a position to think badly of anyone.'

Joey watched him go. He looked smaller somehow, and older.

She lay for a while after he went and she closed her eyes. Immediately her head filled with images of Nicola, her teeth in Tom's flesh, her fingernails raking through his skin, her sharp little face knotted with anger. Then she thought of Tom saying, *I will save myself. I'm sure I will.*

She sat upright, her breath catching in the back of her throat. Then she quickly collected her possessions, threw them into her handbag and ran from the hotel.

61

Freddie felt like Charles in *The Rachel Papers* when he finally gets Rachel into bed. Not that he'd got Romola into bed. Not that he had any *intention* of getting Romola into bed. But he felt magnificent and triumphant. They'd danced together. Probably quite badly. And her bitchy friends had looked on in appalled disgust and made faces at each other and then Romola had said she was finding it all too stimulating, that she was experiencing sensory overload and that she wanted to be somewhere quiet. So they'd left. They'd sat for a while on a bench, Romola wearing his suit jacket slung over her shoulders. And he hadn't touched her. She seemed to be a little uncomfortable with touching. She said it was her Asperger's. He'd said he had no problem with touching, that he liked hugs and affection. She'd said, *We're all different.*

And then he'd walked her home, to the mews on the edge of the city, and the tiny dog had barked a lot, and she'd dashed in the door without saying goodbye, but that was fine because it was part of her Asperger's not because she was rude.

And he'd called his dad, hoping for a lift. But his dad hadn't answered his phone so he'd started walking and just kept walking until he'd reached the village and then he'd walked up the hill to Melville Heights and he'd let himself into his house and he'd followed the sound of movement into the kitchen and there he'd seen his dad, and his mum.

And his mum was on the floor.

And there was blood, lots of blood.

And his brain, his big, brilliant brain, had not been able to translate what he was seeing, not for quite some time.

And when it did he screamed.

RECORDED INTERVIEW

Date: 25/03/2017
Location: Trinity Road Police Station, Bristol BS2 0NW
Conducted by: Officers from Somerset & Avon Police

POLICE: So, Mrs Tripp, talk us through what happened after you arrived in Melville Heights on Friday evening.

FT: Well, for a while I sat outside Tom Fitzwilliam's house.

POLICE: Outside?

FT: Yes. There's a small shrubby area opposite the houses. I had a fold-up chair and a camera. The woman in Mold told me the meeting was starting at 7 p.m. So I got there at six forty-five. I saw the boy leaving the house at about six forty-eight.

POLICE: The 'boy' being?

FT: Their teenage son. He's one of them too. He sits up there in his room, watching me all the . . .

POLICE: Mrs Tripp. If you could just describe what you saw?

FT: Well. He was all dressed up in a suit and tie.

POLICE: And did he see you?

FT: No. It was getting dark by then and I was well hidden.

POLICE: Then what did you see?

FT: Well, nothing, for ages. Seven p.m. came and went, then seven thirty. Then at eight the blonde woman came.

POLICE: Could you identify the blonde woman?

FT: I don't know her name. But I know she lives two doors down. Number 14. With the heart surgeon and his wife.

POLICE: Is this her? For the sake of the recording we are showing Mrs Tripp a photograph of Josephine Mullen.

FT: Yes. That's the one.

POLICE: Could you tell us what she was wearing?

FT: Well, I can show you what she was wearing. I have photos.

POLICE: For the sake of the recording could you describe in your own words what Ms Mullen was wearing?

FT: Yes. She was wearing a black leather jacket, a big scarf and a tight dress. And boots. Coloured boots. With heels.

POLICE: Was there any form of decoration on the boots?

FT: Yes. There was. A kind of tassel.

POLICE: Thank you, Mrs Tripp. So, you saw Ms Mullen outside the Fitzwilliams' house at 8 p.m. Can you describe what you witnessed?

FT: Yes. She'd got out of a taxi in the village. She was breathless. She'd been walking up the hill, very fast. Almost running. She stopped outside her own house and turned, seemed to be looking for something on the other side of the road. Then she slowed down, walked towards Tom Fitzwilliam's house and stood for a minute with her hand near the bell. Then she took her phone out of her bag and looked at it. It looked as though she was thinking of calling someone but thought better of it. She looked up at Tom Fitzwilliam's windows and then she turned round and went back to her own house. I immediately realised of course that she was one of them. She'd obviously been invited to the meeting but for some reason she changed her mind about knocking on the door. Maybe she realised that Tom Fitzwilliam's car wasn't there and decided to wait.

POLICE: So, Tom Fitzwilliam's car was not there at 8 p.m.?

FT: No. It wasn't. So, I waited a few minutes for him to arrive. The blonde woman had clearly been expecting him to be there. And then I remembered: when I was a child I had a friend who lived up in Melville Heights. She lived at number 3, the pink house. I'd go over to play quite a lot and there was a kind of secret garden behind her house. A little woodland. All the houses had access to it from their back gates. And I remembered that there was a footpath to it from the bottom of the hill, just behind the phone box there. And I suddenly realised, you know, if they're all getting together they're hardly going to be walking in through the front door, bold as you like. And I thought, I'll bet you that's what the blonde girl's going to do. She's going to go through her house and round the back. So I took my camera and I walked down to the entrance to the woodland and by now it was really very dark. I couldn't see much. But I did see a figure, ahead of me, someone leaving the back of one of the houses. I ducked into the shadows so they wouldn't see me.

POLICE: And did you see which house this person came out of?

FT: It was the yellow house. It was Tom Fitzwilliam's house.

POLICE: And where did this person go after leaving Tom Fitzwilliam's house?

FT: They walked two doors down. Into the back of the blue house. The heart surgeon's house.

POLICE: Did you recognise this person at all?

FT: Well, it was the blonde woman. The one you just showed me a photo of. Who else would it have been?

POLICE: And you say you had your camera with you. Did you happen to get a photo of this person?

FT: Yes. I did. Just the one. And it's terribly blurred, I'm afraid. Would you like to see it?

POLICE: Yes, Mrs Tripp, we would.

62

24 March

The kitchen floor was covered in blood. Freddie's mum was lying on her front covered in blood. Freddie's dad was sitting in the blood, crying and rocking and moaning.

'Freddie,' he said, in a strange, thick voice. 'Your mum! She's . . .'

He got to his feet. His hands had blood all over them. His clothes were sticky with it. He had streaks of blood down his cheeks with channels where his tears had run through.

'Dad,' said Freddie softly. 'What have you done?'

'God, Freddie, it wasn't me! I didn't do this! Someone

else did this!' His dad ran the back of his hand underneath his nose, leaving yet another stripe of blood on his face.

'Is she dead? Is Mum dead?' His stomach was clenched hard. He wanted to be sick. He wanted to scream. He wanted his mum to wake up and stop being dead.

'Yes.' His dad gulped back a huge cry and sounded as though he was being strangled. 'Yes, she is. And look!' He held a sheaf of paper in his hand, large paper printouts of photographs. 'These were left on her body. I don't understand!'

Freddie stared at them for a moment or two before he realised what he was looking at. They were *his* photos. Of Jenna. And Bess. He hadn't looked at them for so long and blown up to this size they looked obscene, crude, twisted.

'They're mine,' he said, his voice small and weak.

'What do you mean?'

'I mean, I took those photos. They were on my computer.'

'On your . . . ?' His dad looked confused. 'You took them?'

He nodded. 'I'm sorry,' he said. 'It was just a log I used to keep. It was called *The Melville Papers*. About the neighbourhood. It was just something to do. It wasn't meant to be—'

'Fred,' his dad cut in. 'We have to get rid of these. I need to call the police. And I can't call the police until all of these are gone. Shredded. Do you understand?'

He nodded.

'And you'll need to do it because you don't have blood on your hands and I do. OK?'

For ten minutes Freddie fed the paper prints into the shredder, systematically, without talking.

'Good boy,' his dad said. 'Good boy.'

It was almost as if his mum wasn't there. As if she wasn't dead, on the floor, in a big kidney-shaped pool of blood. It was like his brain had just sliced that bit of reality out for him. And then, after he'd fed all the girls into the shredder, his dad looked round the kitchen again. He was sweating; his hair was stuck to his fore-head. He said, 'Right, I'm going to call the police now. And whatever happens, when they come, say nothing about the photos. OK?'

He nodded. He was making sense of things now. Someone had killed his mum. And whoever it was, was the same person who'd hacked into his files. But hadn't he thought it was Dad who'd hacked into his files? And in that case did that mean his dad *had* killed his mum? He might have. He really might. The girl who killed herself. The noises from his parents' room. The bruises.

His dad might have killed his mum.

They sat in the hallway to wait for the police. It still smelled of fresh paint. He thought of his mum, just a fortnight ago, laughing in the kitchen with Alfie Butter. Was it Alfie Butter who'd killed her? For a moment he wished more than anything that it would be Alfie Butter who'd killed his mum. Or maybe it was Joey. Red Boots. Yes, he thought. *Yes.* It must have been her. Not his dad. She was always hanging around. She'd tried to kiss his dad when she was drunk. She'd come over and taken photos of their house. She'd done it on purpose so she'd know how to get into the house. She was obsessed with his dad and she wanted Mum dead so that she could have him. Of course. It was obvious. There was no way his dad had killed his mum, just no way at all.

He ran from his dad. His dad said, 'Where are you going?'

'Nowhere,' he said. 'To wee.'

'Don't touch anything. Whatever you do. This is a crime scene. Please don't touch anything.'

He ran to his room and he pulled out the small drawer in the centre of his desk and his fingers found the soft nap of the suede tassel, the one he'd found on the landing after Red Boots had been here on Tuesday photographing the house. He gripped the tassel in his fist and then he took it back downstairs and he dropped it through a gap in the kitchen doorway.

Then he sat with his dad, his hands clutched tightly together on his lap thinking, *Now they'll know who it was. I have helped them. Now they will know that it was definitely not my dad who killed my mum. They'll know it was her.*

It was Red Boots.

RECORDED INTERVIEW

Date: 25/03/2017

Location: Trinity Road Police Station, Bristol BS2 0NW

Conducted by: Officers from Somerset & Avon Police

POLICE: Ms Mullen. Can you tell us again exactly what happened after your liaison with Mr Fitzwilliam at the Bristol Harbour Hotel? After he left?

JM: I got ready. I went downstairs. I got in a taxi. I went home. I nearly knocked at Tom's door—

POLICE: But you didn't.

JM: [Shakes head.]

POLICE: Please answer yes or no.

JM: No. I didn't.

POLICE: Why was that?

JM: I don't really know. Tom wasn't back yet and I thought maybe I might talk to Nicola.

POLICE: And what were you planning to say? To Mrs Fitzwilliam?

JM: I was going to say . . . I don't know what I was going to say. I was worried . . .

POLICE: Worried about?

JM: I was worried about both of them.

POLICE: And why were you worried about them?

JM: Because. Because of things that Tom said when we were at the hotel.

POLICE: What sorts of things?

JM: Things about their relationship. It was abusive. He was feeling trapped. He wanted an escape.

POLICE: So you were worried that – what? That Tom Fitzwilliam might harm his wife?

JM: [Silence.]

POLICE: Ms Mullen. Could you answer the question?

JM: Yes. I suppose. Or that Mrs Fitzwilliam might harm him.

POLICE: Her husband?

JM: Yes. It sounded like they had a mutually abusive relationship. It sounded a bit sado-masochistic. With Nicola being the sadist. It just seemed – I don't know. It felt like Tom had reached a point of no return. I just had this really bad feeling. I can't explain it. And I thought that maybe if I was there when Tom got home, then I could stop something bad happening. But then I thought, I *realised*, that it was none of my bloody business. So I changed my mind and went home.

POLICE: And what did you do when you got home?

JM: I've already told you all this. I went home. I went up to my room. I watched TV with my husband.

POLICE: And when you got in. Before you went upstairs. Did you go anywhere else?

JM: I went into the kitchen. I got myself some water.

POLICE: And did you see anyone there?

JM: No. There was no one there.

POLICE: Did you go outside? Into the back garden?

JM: No. No, why would I . . . ?

POLICE: Ms Mullen – for the purposes of the recording we are showing Ms Mullen photograph number 2198. This is the plughole of the sink in the utility room of 14 Melville Heights, your address. As you can see, it is holding sizeable traces of mud. And there are also some traces of wet mud on the soles of these gardening shoes, also found in the utility room.

JM: I don't see . . .

POLICE: So someone in your house went outside in these shoes on Friday night, around the time of the murder.

JM: Well, it wasn't me.

POLICE: So, in your opinion, who might it have been?

JM: Well, they're Rebecca's shoes. So I assume it must have been her.

POLICE: Rebecca Mullen?

JM: Yes. My sister-in-law.

POLICE: Mrs Mullen claims to have been in her home office all night, working. We have a witness who says they saw a figure at her window at the time she claims to have been there. And you say she wasn't downstairs when you got home?

JM: No, but—

POLICE: So, Ms Mullen. This is what we have so far. We have you, in a hotel room with the victim's husband on the night of her murder. We have photographs taken on Tuesday of this week on your phone clearly showing the assailant's probable means of entry to the Fitzwilliams' house: the broken window. We have photos from another witness of you watching the Fitzwilliams' house for many weeks leading up to last night; photos of you touching Mr Fitzwilliam's car on more than one occasion. We have a tassel from the boots you were wearing last night found at the scene of the murder; we have photographic evidence of a figure at the back of the houses at around the time of the murder. And we have fresh mud on these boots that matches mud found at the scene of the murder. Ms Mullen, I suggest very strongly at this point that you exercise your right to the representation of a lawyer.

63

25 March

'Jack!'

'God. Joey. Thank God. What's going on? Are you still there?'

'Yes! They've been questioning me for over an hour!'

'About what?'

'They think I did it, Jack! You have to get me a lawyer!'

'They think . . . ?'

'They think I killed Nicola Fitzwilliam!'

'What! But that's . . .'

'I know. It's nuts! But they have so much evidence! They found a bit from my boot. Next to the body!'

'What?'

'It doesn't make any sense. But it was there. They showed me the photo. It was in the blood.'

'Joey—'

'Just get me a lawyer, Jack. Please. The best one you can get.'

'Alfie's here—'

'I don't want to talk to Alfie. I don't want to talk to anyone. I'm just – I'm so scared, Jack. I'm so scared!'

Jack sighs. 'I'll call David Moffat. He'll be able to recommend someone. Just leave it with me. But, Joey. Listen. Don't say one more word to anyone. Not one more word. Not until the lawyer arrives. Promise?'

Joey sniffs. 'I promise. God. Of course I promise. Just get someone.'

The line falls silent for a moment and Joey listens to the rhythm of her brother's panicked breathing. Then she says, 'I have to go now, Jack. I love you so much. I love you so, so much.'

'I love you too, little sister. Take care.'

Then the call cuts off and Joey sits with the receiver limp in her hand until someone takes it away from her.

RECORDED INTERVIEW

Date: 25/03/2017
Location: Trinity Road Police Station, Bristol BS2 0NW
Conducted by: Officers from Somerset & Avon Police

POLICE: Your name please.

TF: Thomas Robert John Fitzwilliam.

POLICE: Thank you. And your full address?

TF: 16 Melville Heights, Bristol BS12 2GG

POLICE: And if you could just confirm your relationship to the victim?

TF: I'm her husband.

POLICE: Mr Fitzwilliam, could you tell us exactly where you were last night between the hours of 6 p.m. and 9 p.m.?

TF: I was at school between 6 p.m. and 7 p.m.

POLICE: And were there any witnesses to corroborate this statement?

TF: Yes, a few. I was in my office for most of that time; I also spent a short while in the staff room, socialising. And I left the building at the same time as Mr Kirk, my deputy. Our cars were parked side by side.

POLICE: And at 7 p.m. you left the Melville Academy?

TF: Yes. Or just after.

POLICE: And then?

TF: Then I drove into town.

POLICE: Where exactly did you go?

TF: I went to the harbour and I parked my car in the Nelson Street car park. Then I walked to the Bristol Harbour Hotel. I got there at about seven twenty-five.

POLICE: And did you talk to anyone when you got there?

TF: No. I took a lift straight up to a room.

POLICE: Can you remember the room number?

TF: No. No, I can't. It was on the first floor.

POLICE: And what did you do when you got to the room?

TF: I knocked on the door. Josephine Mullen answered. I went into the room.

POLICE: And then?

TF: I kissed her.

POLICE: Did she reciprocate?

TF: Yes, she did. At first. But then, very quickly, it became apparent that neither of us was feeling comfortable with the encounter. That it had been a mistake. So I left.

POLICE: And what time was this?

TF: Roughly seven forty.

POLICE: So you returned to the Nelson Street car park and drove home?

TF: That is correct.

POLICE: A journey, typically at that time of night, of around twelve minutes?

TF: Yes.

POLICE: Yet you didn't get home until eight seventeen?

TF: That sounds about right.

POLICE: Could you explain what you were doing between 7.40 and 8.17 p.m.?

TF: I was driving. Just driving around. Trying to get my head together.

POLICE: So you didn't feel quite ready to come home? To face your wife?

TF: Exactly.

POLICE: Mr Fitzwilliam. Would it be fair to say that your relationship with your wife was somewhat strained?

TF: No more so than anyone else's.

POLICE: So you wouldn't say that there was possibly a physical aspect to your relationship, that maybe, occasionally, stepped over the boundaries of normal marital discourse?

TF: No. I wouldn't say that.

POLICE: So, you didn't tell Ms Mullen that you had a sado-masochistic relationship with your wife?

TF: No. Not at all.

POLICE: Mr Fitzwilliam. As well as the multiple stab wounds to your wife's chest and back, there was also some bruising to her neck. The bruising appears to be quite old, at least a week or two. Could you explain this bruising?

TF: No. I have no explanation for that.

POLICE: So, the bruising wasn't inflicted by you?

TF: No. Not as far as I'm aware.

POLICE: As far as you're aware?

TF: No. I mean no. It wasn't.

POLICE: And do you have any idea what might have caused it?

TF: None whatsoever.

POLICE: This isn't the first time you've been brought in for police questioning, is it, Mr Fitzwilliam?

TF: [Sighs.]

POLICE: In April 1997, you were held for questioning at Burton Police Station in relation to the death by suicide of Genevieve Hart, a student at the school where you were teaching.

TF: [Sighs.] Yes. That is correct. But I don't see what it has to do with—

POLICE: Her parents believed they had evidence that you'd been having some kind of inappropriate relationship with her.

TF: They did not have evidence. They had a diary with some references to her feelings towards me, some flowery descriptions of our – entirely normal and appropriate – encounters. Nothing else.

POLICE: There was some suspicion at the time, was there not, that according to what she'd written in her diary, you had arranged to meet her at the location where she took her life. That she had been expecting you to be there.

TF: No. There was nothing in her diary to suggest an arrangement to meet with me. Nothing at all. She alluded to an
arrangement of some sort and her parents assumed it
was with me. But it was not. I had a rock-solid alibi and
the police let me go within minutes. And again, I don't see
what any of this has to do with my wife's murder.

POLICE: We're just trying to form a picture, Mr Fitzwilliam,
a fully rounded picture. Ms Mullen tells us you made a
very sudden and specific invitation to her earlier in the
week to meet at a certain place, at a certain time. In order
to have – or at least to talk about – having sex. It suggests
a pattern of behaviour, Mr Fitzwilliam. That's all.

TF: I did not arrange to meet Genevieve Hart for sex. I did
not arrange to meet her, full stop.

POLICE: Then who, in your opinion, did?

TF: [Groans.] I'm sorry, officers, I really am, but I am not
prepared to answer any more questions about Genevieve Hart. No more. OK?

POLICE: Fine. Fine. Moving back, then, to the timeline of
events last night. You returned home at 8.17 p.m. And
then what?

TF: I let myself into the house. There was no one there. I
called out for my wife. She'd been ill all week and she'd
spent the day before in bed. So when she didn't reply I
went up to our bedroom. She wasn't there. So I went

through the rest of the house, then I went back downstairs and opened the kitchen door and that was . . . [Silence.]

POLICE: That's OK, Mr Fitzwilliam. Take your time.

TF: She was there. Nicola. On the floor. She was dead.

POLICE: Did you check for any vital signs?

TF: Yes. Yes, of course I did. But it was clear to me that she was dead. Just from looking at her. The amount of blood. I mean, she must have been dead for some time.

POLICE: Well, actually, Mr Fitzwilliam, the forensics report suggests the time of death at approximately 7 p.m. to 8.30 p.m.

TF: Does it?

POLICE: Yes. It does. And now, moving on to your call to the emergency services. This came through at 8.40 p.m. Could you tell me, Mr Fitzwilliam, what you were doing between the time of your return at 8.17 p.m. and the making of the phone call at 8.40 p.m.?

TF: Well, as I said, I went upstairs. Looking for Nicola. And I . . . yes, I used the toilet. The one in our en suite. I might have spent some time in there.

POLICE: Twenty minutes?

TF: No, possibly not twenty minutes.

POLICE: So, let's say five minutes? Shall we? And then you came back downstairs and found your wife. So, fifteen minutes later you called emergency services. Please can you explain what you were doing during those fifteen minutes?

TF: I was . . . God, I don't know. I was crying. I was in a state of shock. I went back through the house, searching for the killer, searching for clues. I went into the garden . . . [Crying.] . . . It all felt like a blur. It didn't feel like fifteen minutes. It just didn't.

POLICE: And then?

TF: My son returned. At some point. I don't really know when. And then we sat in the hallway and waited for the police to come.

POLICE: Thank you, Mr Fitzwilliam. I think we'll take a break here.

64

As the 218 had pulled into Melville Village the previous evening, Jenna's heart had begun to pump at the sight of blue lights flashing. She'd burst through the doors of the bus as they slid open and peered upwards towards Melville Heights: there was a ribbon across the lane and a policewoman standing guard. 'You can't go through, I'm afraid. There's been a major incident.'

'What sort of incident?'

'I can't tell you. Do you live up there?'

'No,' she'd said. 'No, I don't.'

'In that case could I ask you to leave the vicinity. We need full access for our vehicles.'

She'd dashed back down the lane and towards her

house. Her mum sat in the living room, her e-cigarette in one hand, a mug of tea in the other.

'Mum!' Jenna had said, dropping her bag on the floor and going to her side. 'What the hell's going on up there? In Melville Heights.'

'I don't know. Why?'

'There's blue lights! And a police cordon.'

'Well,' her mum had said, 'I was up there earlier. Got back about half an hour ago. There was nothing happening when I left.'

'What were you doing up there?'

'Watching him.'

'Who?'

'Tom Fitzwilliam. He was supposed to be hosting a big meeting. All of them.'

'All of—?' She'd stopped. 'You didn't do anything, did you, Mum? Tell me you haven't done anything?'

'What? Of course not. What on earth do you think I might have done?'

'Nothing.' She'd sighed. 'Nothing. Of course not.'

The next morning it's all over the news. A murder in Melville Heights. Tom Fitzwilliam's wife. Stabbed in her kitchen, more than thirty times. The husband held for questioning. An employee of the Bristol Harbour Hotel in the city coming forward to say that

Mr Fitzwilliam had checked into a hotel room the night before, just after a blonde woman called Josephine Mullen, who was also now being held for questioning. The local neighbourhood in a state of shock.

Jenna sits cross-legged in her pyjamas watching the news. Her mum sits at the dining table watching too.

'There,' says Mum. 'You see! It's all going to come out now. All of it. He's killed his wife. Probably because she knew too much. If only they'd listened to me earlier. If only.'

Jenna's head spins. Mr Fitzwilliam. Genevieve Hart. The woman two doors down. Mr Fitzwilliam. Genevieve Hart. The woman two doors down. There's something linking them all together: she knows there is. 'Mum,' she says, 'tell me again exactly what you were doing up there last night?'

'I told you. Watching.'

'But you didn't see anything?'

'No. I didn't see anything. Just the blonde woman coming home. And then a few minutes later I saw her round the back of the houses on the secret path.'

'The blonde woman?'

'Yes. Look, I took a photo . . .' Her mother takes her camera from her handbag and switches it on. 'Here,' she says, 'it's the last one I took before I gave up and came home.'

She turns the back of the camera towards Jenna. Jenna takes the camera from her and presses the zoom button into the tangled blotchy mass of grey and green and brown and black. There at the back is a figure, shadowy and vague, eyes reddened to pinprick rubies by the distant flash. It's impossible to see what colour hair the person has, even what gender the person is. But the flash has picked up something else on the figure: a splash of white light just at the centre. Jenna zooms up close on it and then pans out again. It's a button, a single oversized button. She's seen a coat with a button like that somewhere recently; someone she knew had been wearing it. And then she remembers, in a flash. The woman in the photo Freddie had shown her, the one talking to her mum. She'd been wearing a big, black coat, held together just above her pregnant bump with one large button. Ice plunges through Jenna's heart.

'Mum,' she says, 'you know this might be the person who killed Mr Fitzwilliam's wife.'

Her mum takes the camera back from Jenna and gazes at the screen. 'But – Mr Fitzwilliam killed his wife.'

'How do you know?'

'Because – who else?'

'Mum,' says Jenna. 'We need to go to the police station. You need to tell them what you saw. And you have to show them this photograph. Right now.'

65

Joey closes her eyes and forces herself to think. There must be a rational explanation for all of this. She needs to get it straight in her head before the lawyer arrives.

Think, she hisses to herself, *think.*

Someone has brought her a cup of tea in a paper cup. It tastes of the insides of a vending machine. She drinks it so fast it scalds her mouth. She doesn't care.

Think, Joey, think.

A moment later she brings her hands down against the tabletop, hard enough to make the female police officer assigned to watch over her jump slightly.

Of course. Tom Fitzwilliam killed Nicola! Of course! He'd taken her to that hotel deliberately. It was all a set-up. He knew his son would be out and so he'd taken her there so that he could make her complicit, so he could take the tassel from her boot. Or maybe he already had it? Maybe it had fallen off in his car? Maybe that was when he'd hatched the whole plan? Then he'd made up the big woe-is-me act at the hotel and disappeared into the night and then parked somewhere, waiting for her to get home. Why else would he not have been there? He'd left the hotel five minutes before her. And then he'd sneaked through the back of the houses and gone in through the back door and . . .

She groans.

The gardening shoes.

How was she going to explain the gardening shoes to a lawyer?

Tom wouldn't have sneaked into her house and taken Rebecca's shoes. Not even as a red herring. The back door was always locked and double-locked. And besides, his feet were enormous.

Someone had worn the gardening shoes and rinsed them off. Jack had been working last night and there was no way it would have been Alfie, which just left Rebecca. But she said she'd been in her room all night. Someone had even seen her there.

And as she thought this an image flashed through her mind, bright as sunlight off water. Turning on to the first floor landing the night before, a glass in her hand, her head spinning with the events of the preceding hour, nervous about seeing Alfie, pulling herself together, calming her nerves, making herself normal, she'd paused for a moment to take a last breath before heading up the stairs and had had a brief glimpse through the small gap in the doorway to Rebecca's office and wondered for one hazy confused moment why on earth she had moved the life-size cardboard cut-out of Jack into the window.

66

DC Rose Pelham stands in front of number 14 Melville Heights. Accompanying her is DI Philip Makin, her boss. This is his first visit to Melville Heights. He'd been visiting his parents in Bangor last night when the first call came through, but rushed back at the first opportunity. Rose is secretly pleased. What looked like a simple uxoricide – the husband had been covered in the victim's blood, there was the missing twenty minutes between his arrival home and the call to the emergency services, the affair with a blonde woman half his age, the hearsay about a sado-masochistic relationship between him and his wife – had suddenly within the last few hours became much more complicated. Philip Makin is the most experienced detective on the force. He will bring her back into her depth.

Fourteen Melville Heights is an attractive blue house. It has pronounced bays on the ground and first floor and a panel of stained glass spanning the upper floors through which is visible the outline of a staircase. The house next door is carmine red and flat-fronted, empty at present, its owners seconded to San Francisco for a year. Next to that, of course, is number 16, the Fitzwilliams' house, still cordoned off with plastic ribbon, blue lights still flashing lazily from two squad cars parked outside. Rose has already visited number 14; they came early this morning to bring Josephine Mullen in for questioning and to examine the rear access at the back of the house. She'd been let in by Josephine Mullen's brother: Jack Mullen, sleep-rumpled and boyishly handsome, charming beyond words. He'd made her a cappuccino with his shiny noisy machine while they waited for Josephine to get dressed. He'd even sprinkled chocolate powder on it for her.

'You know,' he'd said, looking at her earnestly across the kitchen table with his soft, sky-blue eyes, 'there is literally no way my sister had anything to do with this. I mean, she is genuinely the sweetest, gentlest, loveliest person in the world. Genuinely.'

Oh, how she had wanted to believe him.

But now, a few hours later, the door is opened by a woman. She blinks at them. 'Hello?'

'Hello, good afternoon. Mrs Rebecca Mullen? I'm DC Rose Pelham and this is my colleague DI Philip Makin. Could we come in for a minute?'

'Sure,' she says. Her fingers are hooked tightly around the edge of the door. She slowly releases them. 'Please come in.'

'Great.' They wipe their feet and follow the woman into the house. The staircase sweeps dramatically to the left and light from the stained glass falls in coloured puddles on to the pale seagrass stair runner. To the left is an antique coat-hook panel, bronze and ivory. Rose scans it quickly as they pass. She finds what she's looking for and stores it away. Ahead is the kitchen where she sat early this morning drinking Mr Mullen's cappuccino and to the left is a large living room. Mrs Mullen calls into the kitchen, 'Jack, the police are here again.'

Jack Mullen appears, less rumpled now, in a grey T-shirt and dark jeans. He smiles anxiously. 'Is my sister OK?' he says. 'Is the lawyer there? Are you letting her go?'

'Not quite yet, Mr Mullen. Her lawyer arrived about an hour ago; we've had a quick chat with them both and things are starting to sort themselves out. Shouldn't be too long now.'

'Good,' he says. 'Thank God. She sounded so scared when I spoke to her on the phone.'

'Shall we sit in here, Jack?' says Mrs Mullen, gesturing at the living room.

'No,' says Jack, quite firmly. 'Let's sit in the kitchen. It's cosier.'

Cosy, thinks Rose. Not a word you hear very often in the middle of a murder investigation.

Jack offers them coffee but it's too late in the day now for coffee so Rose asks for a glass of water instead. Jack and Rebecca sit on one side of the table on a long bench. Rose and Philip sit on pale linen upholstered chairs on the other.

Rose studies Rebecca Mullen's face. She is not what she might have expected in the context of Jack Mullen. Where Jack is solid and warm and jolly, Rebecca is chilly and wan and tense. She wears a navy shirt dress over her pregnant belly, with a fabric belt that ties just above the bump. Her dark hair is parted on one side and tied back with a plain brown elastic band. She wears a wedding band and a locket around her neck. Her pale hands sit folded together on the table but Rose can hear the *tap tap* of her ballet pump against the table leg.

447

'So,' she begins, first looking at Philip for affirmation that she should begin the interview. 'Could you tell us again, Mr Mullen, for DI Makin's benefit, what you told me this morning about the visit from Mrs Fitzwilliam yesterday lunchtime?'

'Yes,' he says brightly. 'Of course. Well, it was around two o'clock. I was about to leave for work. And the door went. I answered it and it was Mrs Fitzwilliam. She looked a bit . . . I don't know. A bit scruffy? Not her usual self. She said she'd had the flu, but she was trying to get herself out of the house. She'd brought us a gift.'

'And could you show the gift to DI Makin?'

'Yes, sure. Hold on, it should be . . . here. Yes.' He reaches for a package on a shelf by the back door and passes it to her. 'This is it.'

It's a cream knitted blanket with yellow and blue blobs on both ends that are apparently supposed to be bunny rabbits, though without Jack Mullen explaining this to her earlier she might not have known.

'She said it was a gift for the baby. That she'd knitted it herself. She said it was the first thing she'd ever knitted and she apologised for it being a bit amateur.'

'And Mrs Mullen – were you present during this encounter?'

'Yes.' She nodded. 'Yes I was. Jack called me down from my office.'

'And you were in the hallway?'

'Yes,' says Jack. 'We were all in the hallway.'

'You didn't invite Mrs Fitzwilliam in?'

'No,' says Jack, shaking his head heavily, a sob catching at the back of his throat. 'And now I feel so bad that we didn't invite her in. It was just . . . she'd been ill and she looked terrible and Rebecca's pregnant and I thought . . . *we* thought . . . Anyway, we didn't invite her in. No.' He sniffs and Rose sees tears in his eyes.

'So she hands over the package. Then what?'

'We thanked her profusely. I told her I hoped she was going to get lots of TLC from her family tonight. She said that was unlikely, her husband was staying late at work and her son was going to his first school dance. We talked about that for a while. How he was taking a girl and how thrilled she was about that. She said they must have us over for supper some time. And then she sort of shuffled off.'

'And then?'

'I went to work.'

'And Mrs Mullen? What did you do?'

'I went back up to my office. Carried on with my work.'

'And your work is?'

'I'm a systems analyst, for an accountancy firm.'

'Ah, so you're tech savvy?'

'No more so than most people of my generation.'

'And Mr Butter, your brother-in-law. He says he got home from visiting his mother at about seven o'clock. Did you see him or hear him return?'

'No.'

'And your sister-in-law, Josephine Mullen. She says she returned at about eight o'clock. Did you see or hear her return?'

'Again, no. I was in my office until nine o'clock or so, when I heard the sirens coming up the hill.'

Rose pulls in her breath, ready to take the questioning around a sharp bend in the road. She consults her notebook, smiles, looks down again and clears her throat. 'Mrs Mullen, your sister-in-law, she says when she came upstairs last night, at roughly ten past eight, she noticed that you had moved a life-size cardboard cut-out of your husband into the bay window of your office.'

There's a shard of silence.

'What?'

'As she walked past your office door last night, she noticed that a cardboard cut-out of your husband had been moved from a corner of your office to the bay window.'

'No,' says Rebecca. 'No. That's wrong.'

Rose inhales and smiles. 'Would you mind?' she says. 'Could we have a quick look?'

'Of course,' says Rebecca. 'Please do.'

She moves lightly up the stairs for a woman so far into her pregnancy. 'Here.' She pushes open the door of her home office. Her desk faces the wall, there's a small sofa against the other wall, lots of shelving. Rose casts her gaze across the room, taking in the things she hoped to find in here. There, on the desk, a photograph of a smiling teenage girl with long dark hair, her arm around a Border collie. Tucked in the corner is the cut-out of Jack Mullen. Rose moves to the bay window. From here she can see virtually the whole of Lower Melville Village. She can also see into the mirror bay of the Fitzwilliams' house. She looks down at the spot below where Mrs Tripp sat last night in the undergrowth watching the houses of Melville Heights and then glances back at Rebecca's desk, her chair tucked neatly beneath it.

'Thank you, Mrs Mullen, that's great.'

At the bottom of the stairs, Rose pauses. 'Is this your coat, Mrs Mullen?' she says, pointing at a long black woollen coat with a dark red scarf still threaded through its collar.

'Yes,' she says, her breath catching almost, but not quite, inaudibly on the syllable.

'Would you mind,' she asks, 'just trying it on for us?'

Jack steps forward. 'Er, excuse me?'

'Just something we need to do, to eliminate a line of inquiry.'

'A line of inquiry? Into my wife's coat?'

'I'm sure it's nothing, Mr Mullen. Just something that a witness mentioned. We just need to see the coat and then we can move on with the inquiry. If you wouldn't mind?'

Jack and Rebecca exchange a look. Jack shrugs and Rebecca plucks the coat from the hook and Philip helps her to put it on. Rose makes a mental note of the single large button that holds it together over her bump. She exchanges a brief glance with Philip and then smiles. 'Great,' she says brightly. 'Thank you! And now, just a few more questions, if that's OK with you both.'

They head back into the kitchen and retake their seats.

'Moving away from last night for just a moment, and going back quite some time, Mrs Mullen, could you tell us a little bit about the events of 1997? Back when you were living in Burton upon Trent?'

Mr Mullen bridles again. 'Erm, right, OK. I don't like this. I don't like this at all. First my sister, now—'

'Mr Mullen. I appreciate that this is unsettling, but

in an inquiry like this we really can't afford to ignore any avenue of investigation, even the unlikely ones. We could take Mrs Mullen into the station for questioning but in her condition we'd rather not. So if you wouldn't mind letting us get on with it?'

She finishes with a broad smile which he returns, being the kind of man hard-wired to return smiles.

'Thank you.' She turns back to Rebecca. 'Mrs Mullen, I know this is probably hard for you to talk about, but it would be really helpful if you could tell us about what happened to your sister, back in 1997. Please.'

'How do you . . . ?'

'We just do.'

'But what's it got to do with . . . ?'

'Probably nothing. But we do need to discuss it. Thank you so much.'

Rebecca looks at Jack, who clasps his hand over hers. 'Well, my sister killed herself.'

'And your sister was called?'

'Genevieve. Viva. Viva Hart.'

'And why did she kill herself?'

'We don't know. She didn't leave a note. But she'd been bullied at school.'

'I believe you found her diary, after she killed herself?'

'Yes.'

'The contents of which led your parents to report one of her schoolteachers to the police?'

'Yes.'

'And the name of that teacher was Tom Fitzwilliam?'

Jack Mullen turns sharply to glance at his wife. His jaw is slightly ajar and he makes an odd, breathless noise.

Rebecca drops her head. 'I don't know what his name was. I just know it was her English teacher.'

'Well, we have seen copies of the salient pages of your sister's diary that were brought to Burton Station by your parents and they clearly state the name of the teacher in question. Tom Fitzwilliam. He was brought in for questioning.'

Rebecca shrugs.

'And released thirty-five minutes later without charge. And now, twenty years later, you and Tom Fitzwilliam are close neighbours!'

Rebecca folds her arms over her bump, her body language becoming increasingly defensive.

'Which is a bizarre coincidence whichever way you look at it. Don't you think?'

Jack peers at Rebecca, trying to get her attention, but her gaze is fixed on a spot on the tabletop, just to the right of Rose's notepad.

'It is a coincidence,' says Rebecca. 'Very much so.'

'You must have been quite horrified, in fact, to move into your dream home and find that you were two doors down from the man your family believed was responsible for the death of your little sister.'

'I didn't think that about him,' she says, her fingers plucking at the fabric of her dress around her elbows. 'I was only a kid. I didn't know what to think.'

Rose pauses. 'And your parents? Where are they . . . ?'

'My mother is dead. She died in 2012. Of cancer. My father . . . I don't know where he is. He's gone off radar. He has a chronic drink problem. He tries to keep away.'

'So, it's just you?'

'Yes. Just me. And now Jack, of course.'

'And one on the way?'

Rebecca glances at her bump and forces a smile. 'Yes,' she says. 'One on the way.'

'When are you due?'

'May the first.'

Rose smiles tightly and thinks, *Please, for the sake of this unborn child, let this all be wrong, please let this all be the ramblings of a delusional woman and her over-imaginative teenage daughter. Let this just be nonsense.*

'I'd like to show you a photograph, if I may.' She pulls an envelope from her bag, eases the print out of it and slides it across the table towards Rebecca. Rebecca touches it with the tip of her right index finger.

'This was taken at the back of your house, last night, at eight eighteen, around the same time that Tom Fitzwilliam got back to his house. It shows someone walking away from the Fitzwilliams' and turning into the gate at the back of your house. Just here.' She gestures at the back door.

Rebecca pulls it closer towards her, studies it for a second and then pushes it away again. 'Who is it?'

'Well, yes, it's hard to tell isn't it? It's not a great shot. But if you take a close look just here' – she points at the bright flash point in the centre of the figure – 'you can just make out a circular shape. Like a large button. They're enhancing the image right now so we should have a better idea of who this person might be within the next few minutes. But looking at it now, Mrs Mullen, do you have any ideas?'

'None,' she said. 'None whatsoever.'

'No,' says Rose, leaving the photograph in the centre of the table. 'No, that's fair enough. Right.' She grips the table and turns to Philip. 'I think that's about it for now? Unless there's anything you wanted to ask, Philip?'

Philip breathes in and runs his fingers down the

length of his navy tie. 'Well, there is just one thing, Mrs Mullen, just quickly before we go.' He puts on his reading glasses and consults his notebook, slightly vaguely, just as they'd discussed in the car on the way here. 'Erm, do you happen to know a Mrs Frances Tripp?'

'Never heard of her.'

'She lives over there in the village. I believe you've had an encounter or two with her. She's the lady who thinks she's being persecuted.'

'No. I don't know who you mean.'

'Here, this lady.' He slides a photo of Mrs Tripp towards her.

'Oh, yes,' she says, 'yes. I think I've seen her around. She's a bit . . .'

'Delusional. Yes. Mr Fitzwilliam's son has a photo, in fact, of the two of you chatting on the street, just a few days ago.'

'Yes. Yes, I do recall that.'

'What were you talking about?'

'She was just talking about all her crazy stuff, you know. All the people who were stalking her. That kind of thing. I was kind of trapped. Couldn't get away.'

'So,' says Philip, removing his glasses and then spreading his fingertips out across the tabletop, 'here's a thing. Mrs Tripp received a message from someone on her chat room at about six o'clock yesterday informing her that Tom Fitzwilliam would be having a big meeting of all her stalkers at his house tonight, telling her to come along and take some photos. The woman claimed to be living in Mold, but we've traced the IP address and in fact the message was sent from the Melville area.'

Rose sensed a muscle in Rebecca's jaw clench slightly.

'And it was convenient, I suppose, that Mrs Tripp was there last night as she was able to clarify that you were in your office all night. She claims to have seen you there. Sitting in your bay window. Except of course your desk isn't in your bay window, is it? It's against the wall? And didn't your sister-in-law claim to have seen a cardboard cut-out in your bay when she passed by your office at around eight o'clock?

'And this.' He taps the photograph of the figure on the back path. 'This could well be you, if you hadn't in fact been sitting at your desk in your office as you claimed to be. The button on the coat sits quite high up when you wear it over your bump. As does this button on this coat.' He taps it again; then he breathes out and leans back into his chair. 'Mrs Mullen, is there anything you'd like to tell us about your movements last night? Anything you haven't already told us? Anything that might be helpful?'

The following moment is entirely silent.

Jack looks at Rebecca. 'Bex,' he urges gently. 'Bex?'

Rebecca stares pointedly to the right.

'Mrs Mullen?' says Philip.

Finally she turns to face Rose and Philip. Her gaze is black and determined. 'Why on earth', she says slowly, crisply, 'would I want to kill Nicola Fitzwilliam?'

Rose inhales sharply. There it is. The crux of it. Why would a heavily pregnant woman go into a neighbour's kitchen in the dark of night and stab her to death? With or without a twenty-year-long grudge against her husband? It was the question that had been perplexing her ever since Jenna and Frances Tripp had walked into the station this morning with their big bag of curveballs. She'd spent two hours going through everything she had at her disposal, trying to find the thing that would answer the conundrum. And then about an hour ago it had hit her, hard.

Jenna Tripp had told them that Nicola Fitzwilliam had also been a student at Tom Fitzwilliam's school back in the nineties, although they'd not got together until a few years later. So Rose had read and reread the pages from Genevieve Hart's diary, and again and again in the sections outlining the terrible bullying campaign she'd been subjected to, the same name kept coming up.

Nikki Lee had been the ringleader and also the puppet master; she stood to one side and let her minions administer the worst of the abuse. Nikki Lee smelled of cigarettes and boys' aftershave. She bleached her hair and wore it tight off her face revealing cheekbones like razor blades, plucked eyebrows that never moved, eyes like chips of dirty blue ice. She kept her hands in her pockets even when she was kicking Genevieve in the back. She told Genevieve she smelled of teachers' cum. She spat in her hair and rubbed it in with the ball of her foot. She spread a rumour that Genevieve had chlamydia. She spread another rumour that Genevieve's cold sore had been caught from a teacher's cock. She got her acolytes to tear up Genevieve's art homework – on one occasion a watercolour of her mother's hair that she'd been working on for a month. She sat on the wall opposite Genevieve's house at night with her hands in her pockets watching and smoking, her presence sometimes only described by the small burning circle of red growing bigger and smaller. She told Genevieve that if she told anyone about what was happening to her she would kill her pet dog by pushing a piece of scaffolding up its arse until it came out if its mouth. Genevieve described how Nikki Lee watched her what felt like every minute of every day; wherever Viva went, there she was.

Waiting, watching, insulting, pinching, spitting, hitting, following, hating, lying, kicking, hurting. For a whole terrible, painful, unthinkable year.

Rose had called the school, asked them to email over the yearbook for Genevieve's year. They'd obliged within minutes. Rose had sat breathlessly waiting for the attachment to download. And there it was. In her hands. She and Philip had set off for the Mullens' house thirty seconds later.

Now Rose looks at Rebecca, her heart aching with the awfulness of it all, and she sighs and puts her hand into her bag, one last time, and pulls out one last photo.

'Here,' she says. 'Look at this photo for me, will you?' She watches Rebecca's face, waiting for her reaction. 'Can you tell me who this is?'

'Yes,' whispers Rebecca, 'it's Nikki Lee.'

'That's right. Nikki Lee. Your sister's bully. The girl who drove her to kill herself. And you know who else this is, don't you?'

Rebecca's eyes have filled with tears. She makes a loud noise in the back of her throat trying to pull them back into herself. She nods.

Rose hears Jack murmuring 'Oh my God' in the background.

'It's Nicola Fitzwilliam,' says Rebecca.

'Oh Christ,' says Jack Mullen. 'Oh Jesus.'

'That's right,' says Rose gently. 'That's right. And now, would you like to tell us, Rebecca? Tell us exactly what happened last night?'

Rebecca Mullen nods. 'Yes,' she says. 'I'll tell you everything.'

IV

67

26 August

Dear Mr Fitzwilliam,

I got my GCSE results yesterday and I just wanted you to know that I got eight GCSEs! Level 7 in English Lit and Language and a level 6 in Maths. And a B in Spanish! And I just wanted to say thank you, for everything. For looking out for me. Even when I probably didn't deserve to have you looking out for me. For sorting it all out with the social services. For sorting it out with Bess and her mum. It was a bit squashed living there those few months but I've moved back with Dad for the summer and I've got my own big room down here so it's been really nice. Mum's doing OK. She's in a hospital in Weston-super-Mare and me and Dad and Ethan go and visit her every other day. I don't know what will happen after the summer. I've got the grades for the sixth-form place I wanted but I'm not sure now if I'll go back to Melville. I'm going to think about it.

Anyway, I hope you're OK. It's terrible what happened to you and Freddie. I think about you both a lot. If you're ever down in Weston-super-Mare, come and say hello. It would be great to see you.

Lots of love,
Jenna Tripp

68

The baby kicks her feet. Joey picks them up, brings them to her mouth and blows on to them. This delights the baby, who kicks her feet even harder and beams at Joey in stupefaction.

Joey slides the nappy under the baby's bottom and pulls the fasteners together across her distended belly. Then she pulls the baby's arms and legs into a soft yellow babygro and expertly pops together all the popper buttons. The balled-up nappy she tucks into a scented plastic bag.

'There,' she says to the baby. 'All done.'

The baby smiles at her again and she scoops her off the changing mat and carries her downstairs.

The baby is called Eloise. She is Jack's daughter, Joey's niece. She arrived ten days early and is now four months and six days old. She has dark hair like her mum and green eyes like Joey. She is perfect.

Jack gets home from work an hour later. She sees his face change, as it does every day when he returns and his eyes find his daughter, from haunted awe to tired joy.

'There she is,' says Joey, passing the soft body to her brother. 'There's your girl.'

Jack had brought the baby back from the hospital when she was two days old. There was no space on the nearest mother-and-baby unit and Rebecca had let the baby go without shedding a tear. 'I want Joey to take care of her,' she'd said, folding babygros and nappies into a bag. 'Not a nanny. Joey.'

Those first weeks had been a huge shock. Alfie had moved out shortly after Rebecca's arrest. After being held for questioning by the police for the best part of a day, Joey had had no choice but to tell him about her ridiculous infatuation with Tom Fitzwilliam and he in turn had told her about all the girls he'd kissed at work since he'd realised that she didn't really love him. Alfie had cried; Joey had breathed a sigh of relief.

And so she finds herself alone now for long, quiet days. Just her and Eloise in this big house that had

468

once felt like a slightly unwelcoming hotel and now feels simply like the place where she lives with Jack and Eloise. Some days she feels lonely, some days she feels numb, some days she feels like escaping to an Ibizan beach bar and drinking herself into oblivion. But no longer does she feel useless. She had not wanted a baby of her own; even less had she wanted another person's baby. But now that baby is here and she loves her with a primal ache.

Rebecca asked them not to bring the baby to visit. She's on remand at Easthill Park. She hasn't been granted bail and is due to be sentenced on 3 September. She will never be coming home to raise her baby. Joey had never told Jack what Rebecca had once said to her about not wanting a baby, about getting pregnant to make him happy. She didn't want anything else to cast darkness across what should have been the happiest moments of his life.

She'd asked him, a couple of weeks ago, when they were both drinking whisky at the kitchen table at three in the morning; she'd said, 'Why her, Jack? Why Rebecca? Even without the murder thing, I always wondered why you chose her?'

And he'd smiled sadly and said, 'I didn't choose her. She chose me.'

She'd started at that. So similar to what Tom had

said about Nicola. She wondered if that was how it worked, that while most women spent their lives searching for the perfect man, men sat around waiting to be chosen and then made the best of it.

'But you loved her, right?'

'Of course. And I still do. But it's terrifying to think that I never knew her at all. Not even a tiny bit.'

Joey had seen Tom in town the week before. He'd been dressed down in jeans and a short-sleeved shirt. He was wearing sunglasses and carrying a shopping bag from Russell & Bromley. She'd watched him from the bus stop where she sat with Eloise by her side in her pram. He still had presence, she'd observed detachedly, he still occupied space with a certain swagger, a certain élan. For a brief moment she'd remembered herself in the dark shadows of Melville Heights, his hands pulling her body towards his, everything so hard and desperate and frantic. A brief flicker of something passed through her. Something bright and urgent.

But then she pictured his sad, heavy face in the Bristol Harbour Hotel, the slump of his shoulders, the defeated rolls of his stomach, the pale sheen of his scalp through the thinning spot on the crown of his head. She remembered the terrible marks on his body, as though he'd lain down and allowed himself to be savaged by an animal. The thickness of his breath. The smallness of him as he headed from the hotel room.

She had no idea what she'd been thinking. None at all.

The next day Joey takes Eloise to visit her mother. Or Nana Sarah as she and Jack have decided that Eloise should refer to her once she is old enough to refer to things. The sky is heavy with summer storm clouds and she doesn't have an umbrella and should be heading home, but something brought her here today. Some sense of life moving on. Babies did that to you: they pinned you down in the moment at precisely the same time as hurtling you into the future and hitching you back to the past.

There's a small bunch of tulips on Mum's grave, growing gnarled and papery in the August heat. She lays her dust-pink summer roses next to them and sits on her bottom, one hand on the frame of the buggy, jiggling it gently to keep Eloise asleep.

'Hi, Mum,' she says. 'It's me. I've brought Eloise to see you. But she's sleeping so you won't get much out of her today. Things are settling down at home. But Jack is so, so sad. It kills me to see him like this. I'm so used to him being the one jollying everything along, jollying *me* along. It's weird how we've swapped roles.

471

But it's good. I needed to stop playing the helpless child and having a brother like Jack made that so easy to do. I know I keep coming here and telling you that I'm growing up, but before I used to think that being grown-up meant doing grown-up things. Now I know that's not true, that being a grown-up is not about getting married, about smart flats and reading groups, it's about taking responsibility for your own actions and the consequences of those actions. So yes, I'm getting there, Mum. I'm definitely getting there, I—'

She stops then at the sound of a presence behind her. She catches her breath and turns. It's a man, a middle-aged man in a Stone Roses T-shirt and combat shorts, grey hair cut shaggy around a craggy face, a bunch of red 99p Asda tulips in his hand. 'Hi, babe,' he says.

'Dad,' says Joey.

'Brought Mum some flowers,' he says, tapping them against his other hand.

'Yes,' she says. 'Me too.'

His eyes go to the buggy. She sees them fill with tears. 'Is this . . . ?'

'Yes. It's Eloise.'

He nods and suck the tears back. 'Wow,' he says. 'Wow.'

'She's sleeping.'

He nods again. 'Don't wake her.'

They fall silent for a moment.

A raindrop lands between them, fat and heavy. Then another. They both look upwards and then at each other.

'Shall we?' says Joey.

'A drink, maybe?' says her dad.

'Yes,' says Joey. 'That would be nice.'

69

20 April 2018

Dearest Eloise,

Happy birthday to you! You are one year old today which means that it has been 363 days since I last saw you.

Your daddy tells me everything about you, your daddy and your aunty Joey of course. They show me photos and films of you and tell me what you're learning to do. But I have asked them not to bring you here. I don't want you to think of me as That Strange Woman in the Scary Place Where I Have To Go When I'd Rather Be Doing Fun Stuff at Home.

I don't want you to think of me at all. I just want you to enjoy being a child, enjoy having the loveliest daddy in the world, enjoy spending time with your aunt Joey who is about a hundred times more fun than I am. And then hopefully, one day, they'll let me come home and then I can be a cool new person in your life. Or not. Whatever you want. You're in charge of you and me. You get to decide all that.

But before that day comes, I thought it would be really important for you to understand why I did this to us, why I hurt someone so much that it meant that I would be taken away from you and from Daddy. So I'm writing this to you now and will let Daddy decide when you're old enough to read it. And I'd love to be able to tell you it was an accident, that I didn't mean it to happen. I'd love to say it wasn't my fault, that it was somebody else's fault, that I'd never have done something like that knowing the price I might have to pay. But that's not true, and I'm sure, by the time you're old enough to read this letter, you'll know it's not true too.

I went to that woman's house with the intention of hurting her. And I went there knowing that there was a chance – a slim chance, I thought – but a chance that I would be caught and then I would have to go away for years and years and miss out on all the good things I should have been sharing with you and Daddy. I hoped I wouldn't be caught. I hoped the police would think it was her husband and that he would go to prison – but that didn't happen. And now I'm in here and you're out there and I have to accept that it is entirely my fault, mine and nobody else's.

Daddy will have told you about my little sister Viva and what happened to her. But I really want you to hear it from me, because the answers to all your questions are contained in the way I felt about her, and that's not something anyone but me can really express.

I was two when Viva was born. I was furious about it. Absolutely furious. I was cross for years that my mum and dad hadn't thought I was enough for them. I was livid that I had to share them with someone else, and not just anyone else, but with this little butterball girl with dimples and shining eyes, this child who beguiled every adult who came across her. She was always in a good mood, always ready to play, always hugging everyone and kissing everyone. When she started school, everyone wanted to be friends with her. She was so different to me; it took me years to make friends at school, and even then I kept them at arms' length. I never wanted them to come home after school, to encroach on my space. I was an introvert. Viva was an extrovert. I adored her. I hated her. But by the time I was a teenager we'd found a way to coexist. She looked up to me because I was clever and self-contained. I admired her because she was gregarious and sweet. She was my favourite person in the world.

I never told her that. I wish I had. There isn't a day that passes when I don't regret the fact that I never told her how much she meant to me, how much I adored her. And then when she was fourteen, it all slowly seemed to fall apart. She got quieter and quieter. She lost weight. She was grumpy, monosyllabic. The light died in her eyes. It just died. And I tried to talk to her about it and she would say: I'm fine, I'm fine. But I knew she wasn't fine and I'd heard rumours about a girl at school giving her a hard time but I never saw any evidence and she refused to talk about it.

And then one day my silly, shining, bouncy, chatty, gorgeous baby sister went to school and she never came home.

A few days after she died, my mum found her diary. I expect you know about this and what was inside it. Daddy will have told you by now. Viva had a big crush on one of her teachers, and he in turn gave her a lot of attention. Way too much attention in my opinion. He led her on. He made her think she was a big part of his life. More than just another student. On the night she died she'd written in her diary that she thought he might be waiting for her somewhere in town. That she was going to go along and see if he was there. But he wasn't there. He was at the school until late. Maybe she'd thought he was going to save her from her bully? That he was her last chance? No one will ever really know why she went there, but when he didn't turn up, she felt bad enough to take her own life. And when she took her life, she took mine with it.

You don't have a brother or sister yet. But until you've experienced the incredible mix of emotions that a sibling brings to your life it's really very hard to imagine. The love and the hate, the fun and the fights, the rivalry and the kinship. No one else knows your world like a sibling does. They're there, every crap summer holiday, every day off school, every time your parents argue, every boring Christmas Day, every birthday party, they're there. And they are a part of you. And with Viva it sometimes felt like we were continuations of the same person, that I began where she ended, and vice versa.

When she left, she took with her any sense I had of myself as a worthwhile person. Without her

I was just this blank space. When she died my whole world turned black. The blackness faded over the years, but it never went away. Sometimes a good day might feel grey. But nothing ever felt white. Not ever. Not even my wedding day. All I could think was that my sister should be there.

Lots of people lose a sibling. But not everyone does what I did. And while I cannot ever excuse the choice I made last year, and the terrible actions I took, I wanted to explain to you exactly what pushed me to do the unforgivable thing I did. Because not only did Viva's diary tell us about her feelings for her English teacher but it also gave us the full and shocking picture of the bullying she'd been subjected to by a girl called Nikki Lee. I won't go into the detail. It's too upsetting. It's too vile. But I remember sitting there at sixteen years old, with my sister's diary in my hands, tears flowing down my cheeks, vowing to myself that if I ever saw Nikki Lee I would kill her. I would kill her with my own hands.

And then one day, during a visit to the Lake District with my mother in 2011, I saw her. We'd stopped for ice creams at the side of Lake Buttermere when a coach pulled up. I saw him get off, our old English teacher, and then I saw his wife and son. I pointed her out to my mum: I said, Look, isn't that Nikki Lee? It seemed unbelievable, unthinkable. But the more we looked, the clearer it became.

My mum went mad. She ran across the street and confronted Tom Fitzwilliam, screamed at him and hit him. Nikki must have seen my mum coming and was already back on the coach with her son. Tom calmed my mum down and the coach left. But after that I became obsessed. I googled them all the time, working out where they were, what they were doing. The fact that the two people who, in my opinion, had destroyed my sister were living together as married couple, had had a child, had made lives for themselves while my sister lay rotting in the ground sickened me. I became consumed by rage and hate. So when I read in the local paper that Tom Fitzwilliam had been appointed the new head at the Melville Academy I found out where they were going to be living and bought a house as close to theirs as possible.

For months I watched them. I watched Nikki Lee running around the village, pretending to be a normal person. And then on that dreadful Friday last March, she actually came to my front door. And because she was Nikki, all her attention was fixed on Daddy, not me. It was as if I didn't exist.

She gave us a blanket she said she'd knitted herself. It was so ugly. Daddy tried to pass it to me, but I couldn't bring myself to touch it. I could hardly breathe, and I threw up after she'd gone. I decided then that I would confront her, that night, while her husband and son were out. I decided then that I would tell her I knew who she was, who she *really* was, that I would tell everyone who she really was. And I knew without a doubt that there was every chance I might kill her.

When I arrived she was sitting in her kitchen. I knocked on the back door and she let me in. She was surprised to see me there, but she was friendly. I said I'd come to thank her for the blanket. Then I asked her if she recognised me. She said no. Then I asked her if she remembered a girl called Viva Hart. She said she didn't but it was clear she was lying. I saw it all flash across her face: the realisation of who I was and why I was sitting in her kitchen. The conversation became fractious. I got angrier and angrier. I showed her the photos of teenage girls I'd found on their hard drive when I hacked into their network. I told her her husband was still a pervert, that he shouldn't be allowed to work with children. She called me a mad bitch. I grabbed her. I thought she'd fight back but then I remembered my sister's diaries: Nikki Lee never did her own dirty work. She wasn't a fighter. She was a coward. And so, of course, she ran away from me. She turned her back.

And that's when it happened, Eloise. That's when I made the decision that shaped your life, my life, Daddy's life, all of our lives, forever. It didn't feel wrong at the time; in fact it felt horribly right. For days afterwards, I felt euphoric. I was glad I'd killed Nicola Fitzwilliam. I had no regrets. As far as I was concerned she deserved to die. I had honoured my sister. I had balanced the universe. I was at peace.

But now, as I sit here writing to you, I wish more than anything that I hadn't done it. I wish I could turn back time and do everything differently. I wish I'd confronted Nikki Lee at Lake Buttermere, climbed on board that coach and told her what she'd done, told her exactly what I thought of her and her seedy pathetic husband. I wish I could have exposed her in front of all those people and then walked away and got on with my life.

Instead I let the shock of seeing her sit in the pit of my stomach like a poisonous seed. I let it grow and grow and grow until it consumed me, consumed me to the point where I put my hatred for Nikki Lee before my love for you and Daddy.

Watching You

I only had you for two days before Daddy came to take you home. You slept in my bed the first night. Every time the nurse put you in your crib you cried. So eventually I asked them to leave you in my bed. I was in and out of awareness all that night. Everything felt dreamlike, hazy. But there was one moment when I awoke from a short, hard sleep and turned to face you and you were awake, eyes wide open in the dark, and you had a piece of my hair clutched tight in your fist and you were staring at me. Staring with the widest, gentlest, calmest gaze. And for a split second I thought you were Viva. I cried and my tear splashed on your cheek. I wiped it away with my fingertip and your skin was so soft it took my breath away. And you blinked at me, and it was as if you were saying, It's OK. We're all going to be OK.

And then Daddy took you the next day and I didn't cry because I knew you'd be fine. I'd seen it in your eyes. You'd shown your true self to me and I saw you. And I knew you. And I let you go.

Happy birthday, beautiful child. I don't know you. But I do love you. Always and forever. And ever after that.

Your Mummy

Epilogue

The chihuahua is called Diego. Freddie thinks it's a superb name for a dog from South America. It follows him to Romola's front door now as he goes to leave. Romola doesn't follow him. She's still at the kitchen table, being served her dinner by her mother who is called Maxine and is really nice. Romola never sees him to the door when he leaves. She never says goodbye at the end of a date or at the end of a phone call. She says it makes her feel anxious to say goodbye, she can't explain why, it just does.

Maxine had offered to cook for him too, but they're having lamb and Freddie can't eat lamb, the texture is too textural, the flavour is too dead. Plus his dad had said that maybe they could get a takeaway tonight.

So Freddie says goodbye to Diego and he closes the door of Romola's little house behind him and he walks the five minutes towards the flat where he and his dad now live.

They'd moved out of the big yellow house in Melville and now they have a nice two-bedroom flat in a Georgian house really close to Freddie's school. It had seemed a shame to have to leave the big house in Melville, especially so soon after spending all that money on having it redecorated. But it was a crime scene now and who wanted to live in a crime scene? Well, Freddie wouldn't have minded actually. After his experiences with the police last year, when he'd had to tell his dad about planting the red suede tassel from Red Boots's boots at the scene of the crime to try to incriminate her and then had to wait outside the interview room while his dad told the police what he'd done, he'd become obsessed with police procedure. He no longer wanted to work for MI5. He wanted to be a forensic detective.

The governors at the Academy had asked Dad to step down. It was too much of a distraction, they'd said. They'd kept him on in an advisory capacity to steer the year elevens through their GCSEs from the back seat. But that was almost a year ago and he is currently officially unemployed. He says he's taking a sabbatical, then deciding what he wants to do next.

Freddie's main hobbies now are seeing Romola (which he does virtually every day, even if it's just for five minutes after school), seeing his trauma therapist once a week (which is boring but interesting at the same time), and investigating his mum. Because after what happened to his mum he'd basically felt as though he'd never known her at all. Rebecca Mullen had killed her because she'd bullied her sister. Rebecca Mullen said his mum had been horrific and terrifying, that everyone at her school had lived in fear of her and her gang of cronies. Yet to Freddie, she was just Mum. She never bullied him or shouted at him or made him feel scared. Apart from that one last time, when she'd been ill in bed and screamed at him and called him a fucking little shit and pushed him over. And he'd seen it then, the possibility of this other side to her. And that is his latest project. It's called *The Information*, after another Martin Amis novel. Because that is what he needs. Information about his mum, to try to work her out.

He'd brought all his mum's stuff from the house in Melville, put it in three big cardboard boxes labelled 'The Information 1', 'The Information 2' and 'The

Information 3'. He's going through it forensically and also augmenting his research with occasional question-and-answer sessions with his father. But these are generally unhelpful as on the whole his father appears to know nothing about his former wife, about what made her tick. He says that when he met her on the bus that day, when she was nineteen and he was thirty-five, he hadn't known that she was the school bully who'd ruined Viva Hart's life. He said he hadn't known that brown-haired Nicola Lee on the bus was the same person as blond-haired Nikki Lee. He hadn't known at any point. He hadn't known until Viva Hart's mum had hit him in the Lake District. And then, he said, he'd known immediately and then, he said, everything had made total sense.

He hadn't been able to explain exactly what he'd meant by that. All he'd said was that his mum had always had a *cruel streak* and now he understood why. Freddie had written down those words – 'cruel streak' – and pondered them, wondering if maybe he had inherited a tiny bit of his mum's 'cruel streak' because of the secret things he sometimes thought or did.

And then yesterday Freddie found something really strange in one of his mum's boxes. Freddie brings it out after their takeaway. It's a DL envelope that's so old that the bit that you lick has gone bright yellow and crusty. There's nothing written on the outside of the envelope and inside the envelope is a bunch of shiny dark brown hair tied with an elastic band. It's way too long ever to have been Freddie's hair and it's too dark to have been his mum's.

'What is this?' he says, pushing it across the table to his dad.

He watches his dad peer into the envelope, sees his fingers going inside, pulling out the hank of hair.

He glances up at Freddie. 'Where did you find this?'

'In Mum's stuff.'

His dad returns his gaze to the envelope.

'Whose hair is it?' asks Freddie.

His father's face has gone grey. All the skin on his face looks like it's suddenly fallen away from his bones. He sees him gulp.

Freddie stares at his dad, waiting for him to say something.

But he doesn't.

Acknowledgements

Book number sixteen and it feels like I am always thanking the same people in the same way for doing the same things. But that is because I am a very lucky author. I have such loyal teams working on my behalf in a dozen or more different countries, I have the best readers in the world and a brilliant support network of friends and family.

So thank you, as ever, to Selina, Susan, Najma, Cassandra, Celeste and everyone else at Cornerstone.

To Richenda Todd, for impeccable copy-editing.

To Jonny, Catherine, Melissa, Alice, Luke and everyone else at Curtis Brown.

To Deborah and Penelope and everyone else at Gelfman Schneider.

To Sarah, Ariele, Daniella, Haley, Kitt and everyone else at Atria.

To Pia, Christoffer, Anna and everyone else at Printz Publishing.

To all my publishers across the world who I've yet to meet.

To all my readers, the ones I've met, the ones I've yet to meet, the new ones, and the old ones.

To all the booksellers everywhere

To all the librarians.

To my wonderful family, my lovely girls, my remarkable friends.

To the Board. You are stupendous.

To you, for reading my book. I hope you liked it.

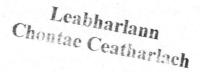